ALL PATHS TAKEN

DAVID JAMES LYNCH

Western Cahruia

For Jim and Mary Lynch,
who put me on the right path,
then taught me how to choose my own

Dedicated to the memory of John Lynch
Gentlest of souls,
Strongest of warriors

Faeries, come take me out of this dull world,
For I would ride with you upon the wind,
Run on the top of the disheveled tide,
And dance upon the mountains like a flame...

-William Butler Yeats
The Land of Heart's Desire

SYNOPSIS OF ALL THINGS BROKEN
BOOK ONE OF THE EGIMIAN CHRONICLES

Sixteen-year-old Sivino Spallic lives a peaceful life with his family in the hamlet of Egim, but his life is irrevocably changed one fateful day when a cow on the family homestead is brutally attacked. The following day, Sivino and his friends Ston, Torla and Kef discover who has done the killing when they find their friend and mentor Lomin Lailoken injured and engaged in a battle with a *Nylac* – a terrible creature that was, until now, thought to be purely myth.

The Nylacci are powerful, nightmarish beasts who kill all they encounter. Sivino and his friends manage to escape with the help of Drip, the ill-tempered *trenoc* who has lived and worked with the Spallic family all his life. With the Nylac dead, they set out with Lomin to find aid in Levebar, after being informed by Drip that Nylacci block the way home to Egim. When the reach Levebar, they find the village has been destroyed, and the lone survivor, a deaf boy named Tonnis, narrowly escapes death as his friends come to his rescue.

The Nylacci have been brought to Sivino's world by Cehron Cen Kohr, a renegade faerae who grows increasingly unstable and malicious as the years pass. After rescuing Tonnis, Sivino's group encounter Cen Kohr and a group of Nylacci outside the ruins of Levebar, and are spared death only by the arrival of the faerae Niamh, daughter of the Fae king Obaeron. Niamh has a complicated bond with the world of Cahruia, the realm of Embarria, and the citizens of Egim in particular. Her *shifting* (movement between different, adjacent worlds) is extensive and takes a physical toll, but she keeps a watchful eye on the Egimians for reasons that are hers alone. During a heated exchange, it is revealed that Cen Kohr has brought the destructive Nylacci from the world of Dreg to prove his firm belief that worlds should be kept separate, that the "reckless interaction" of different worlds should be ended. He references Niamh's relationship with "the mortal"- the long dead warrior Oisin - who was Niamh's lover. He also references the *prophecy* (a message or vision received by fae creatures from the *Faant*, the divine Creators of all worlds). The enigmatic prophecy references the blood that will be "spilt on the sword of a boy". Niamh then gives Cen Kohr a warning that the surrounding forest holds more threat than Cen Kohr may be prepared to address, and the renegade faerae leaves with the Nylacci. Niamh remains with Sivino and his friends.

While these events transpire on the outskirts of Levebar, a similar catastrophe unfolds back in Egim. The town has come under attack by a band of Nylacci, and Sivino's father Dels finds himself responsible for leading the townsfolk to safety. In the forested hills outside Egim, they mounted a defence that while admirable, is insufficient to stop the beasts. It is only through the intervention of winged faerae creatures called *hyter sprites* that the townsfolk are saved. Before the hyter sprites leave, their leader informs Dels and his son Leath that Sivino and the others are safe and heading south, but the townsfolk must travel east to Ras, the home of the foreboding Drales. After burying four fallen Egimians, the townsfolk reluctantly head east.

Back in Sivino's camp, Niamh shares a little information about herself and the fae homeland of Elysium. The group is unable to agree on how to proceed, and some – particularly Torla – are distrustful of the faerae. Sivino asserts that he will follow Niamh, and with some trepidation, the others agree to join him. For Torla, the decision is upsetting as it will lead them south, into a land that is afflicted by conflict, a land where her older brother was killed. The western realm of Rentorria is under assault from the eastern realm of Isror, and the realm of Embarria, just north of both these regions, has joined the fray to lend assistance to their Rentorrian allies. Soon afterward, Niamh leaves the group in order to visit with her father, King Obaeron, in Elysium.

Rentorria is led by their king Doran Dunarrk. For the past year, he has worked to drive back the Isrorian forces who, under the leadership of their king Idach Garron, continue to move further into the western realm. Garron asserted that, in a dream, he'd been told by the Goddess Dahnu that the lands surrounding Lake Madimest had once been Isrorian and could rightfully be reclaimed. The truth is that Isror's valuable ore resources were depleting, and great deposits had been discovered on the fringes of the realm of Rentorria. And so, the battle rages. In the days that follow, Doran learns from the trader-turned-spy Staid Dyrro that the city of Ronec has fallen, and the Isrorians move west to the city of Nahcin.

To the north, the queen of Embarria, Inlonia Talchol has been forced to make difficult decisions. While her realm was not under direct attack, it was entirely possibly that a successful campaign by the Isrorians could lead them to turn their eyes to the northern realm. Additionally, Rentorria was an ally, and should Embarria ever find itself faced with invasion, Inlonia was sure that the Rentorrians would come to their aid. And so, in recent months, Embarrian forces had been sent to help their southern neighbors. Unsatisfied to sit idle in the capital city of Levebule while her people fought in the south, Inlonia sets forth to make the journey with a small, trusted group of her Guard, including her friend and advisor Ennis Tinod'atu. It is her hope that standing with her army will lend strength and resolve to their forces, as well as those of Rentorria.

In Elysium, Niamh is reunited with her father, as well as his advisor, the faerae Tryn. While there, she is unable to escape the cascade of memories of her time with the warrior Oisin, who accompanied her to Elysium in an age long past. Having come to Elysium, Oisin had been unaware that the passage of time was different in most worlds, especially in Elysium, also known as Avalon or Tir Na N'Og. The faerae Cehron Cen Kohr, who, even in this long-ago time was beginning to venture down darker paths, was well aware of this fact. Steadfast in his belief that the populations of worlds should not mix, he tricked Oisin into returning to his homeland, where one hundred years had passed. When he discovered Cehron's motivations (which include revenge for capturing Niamh's heart), Oisin jumped from his horse to confront the faerae. The moment his feet touched the soil he aged rapidly and met his untimely death. Niamh would remain unaware of who led her lover to his demise.

Amongst the Egimians, Dels and his company question the wisdom of seeking help from the Drales. Known to dismiss other populations, these tall, pale, sharply-muscled people live in a high city carved in the face of the Cudgel Mountains. There are stories of them refusing assistance to lost and injured travelers, and the group questions their potential hospitality. Dels encourages all, including his son Leath, to maintain hope, and they set out. As they journey, Dels remembers his wife Rhenna's final days, and the words she whispered to him on her deathbed concerning Sivino. Soon thereafter, the Egimians encounter the Drales, who had just recently killed two Nylacci. After a terse introduction, the Drales agree to lead the Egimians to the safety of Ras. The Egimians learn that it was a faerae who convinced the Drales to wait for them, and see them safely to the stone city.

As Sivino and his friends continue their journey without Niamh, they encounter unexpected company - queen Inlonia Talchol and her small contingent. Though the meeting seemed by chance, the faerae Niamh had directed Inlonia toward Sivino. For two days, they journey together and get acquainted with one another. During a rest period, Sivino inadvertently insults Drip, who storms off. When Sivino goes looking for Drip, he stumbles upon an enchanted spring from which he drinks. He awakens in another world. In the mist by a lake, he is addressed by a voice that he will come to realize is that of the Goddess Dahnu. From her, he attains a sword of magnificent power, though he has no idea how he'll use it. When he questions his ability to wield the talisman, Dahnu recounts the prophecy of the blood on the sword of a boy, telling him to "do those things which much be done." She leads him to the lake, whispering *It is time* as she sets him once more on his uncertain path...

PROLOGUE

'It is time…'

These words, the words of the Goddess, float as they're spoken, sailing outward, upward, steady on an uncertain ocean of time and space and purpose that is all but impossible to comprehend. Like the handcrafted toy boats of children, they are the messages in corked bottles set adrift on steadfast belief that destinations can and will be reached.

They have waited so long.

Such words, spoken so gently, will reach unknowable distances.

The words are heard, though they extend far beyond the ear of the young boy who stands in the shallow water, awkwardly holding his newly acquired sword. They are heard by the Faant – a *consciousness* in three parts; *Perception*, *Judgment* and *Preservation*. It is a transcendent consciousness, everywhere and nowhere at the same time, distinct but interconnected, found in the tiniest form of life while also spanning the face of the world.

It is *Perception* that hears the words of the Goddess; *Perception* that hears all, sees all, feels all. As the Goddess speaks and the blade of the boy touches the water, *Perception* senses the meaning and manifests itself as a ripple - though it is in fact the entire lake, the entire countryside - composed of all the lifeforce that resides within. The Faant's *Perception*, the ripple that emanates from the sword in the lake, will convey the message of the Goddess; will share the urgency of her wishes.

The ripple spreads.

A flash of lightning illuminates a meadow.

The meadow, if it can still be called such, has been all but destroyed - a bloody stain, a ruined shadow of its former glory. Trees have been felled. The once lush field has been trampled, ripped apart by the fighting, the feet and fire that have ravaged the area for days. The bodies of men, women and beast lie strewn across the landscape where wildflowers once held sway, and the dead air vibrates with the constant buzzing of flies. Occasionally, the squawk of an angry bird punctuates the incessant drone as the fowl battle for the choicest selection of carrion. Yet, there is little need to fight.

Dead flesh is plentiful.

Dark clouds roll over the hills, and quickly cover the sun. The sky passes a grey hand over its face as if to hide the sight below, and deepens the darkness of the meadow until the lightning, brief and brilliant, reveals all.

It is time.

In that instant, the *Judgement* of the Faant is passed.

Little deliberation is required in the process. In that moment, receiving this message, the stark truth of the situation is laid bare, and the Faant, in its unknowable way, sees, senses, understands what has occurred and what must be done. In that moment, perhaps it is the tiny corpse of a fawn, torn to pieces, that might be considered the deciding factor in the Faant's judgement. Perhaps it's the way the fawn's glassy eye caught the flash of lighting, as if capturing all the light left in this darkening world.

Death is the way of things, but the Faant is aware that the way of Death, the *path* that leads to the culmination of a life stage, may or may not be just. The Faant cannot bring life back to the corpses of the meadow; *would not*, even if it could. But *Judgement* sees that a balance has been disrupted, and this altered equilibrium needs what some beings might refer to as *divine intervention*.

In another world, where lightning never strikes, that verdict is felt in the form of a breeze.

Though the distance between the elements of the Faant may, on some level, be deemed great, it is something that cannot accurately be measured. The interconnectedness nullifies ideas of the space between.

Preservation, perhaps more than its counterparts, understands how to address a disruption of balance. It understands that there is a need for some form of intervention, some form of influence that, while not dictating the order and certainty of events, may nudge them in a particular direction.

There is indeed chaos in the universe; a necessary chaos inextricably woven within and around the workings of the Faant, and it may be that their workings, their interconnectedness creates the pattern which sees the repetition and organization of events.

To correct what it deems to be an abnormality of the

pattern, *Preservation* acts to adjust. Like a child who re-thinks the move she is about to make with a piece on the gameboard, *Preservation* makes a move of its own. Through the open window of the highest room in a castle, this element of the Faant shares its whisper - a sudden, yet gentle breeze that caresses the face of a king, moving his intent and his deep red hair with the slightest touch.

It is time.

A goddess, while immortal, will not keep her true form for all eternity. Such is not the way of things. As death is but a passage to another stage of existence, so now does this stage of Dahnu's life wane. The Faant recognizes this. It appreciates this.

At some point, all pieces must be removed from the game.

It is time.

And so it is, that in the span of a moment, the sword of the boy touches the lake and the influence of the Faant touches the world. All is perceived, judged and set in motion. In that one instant, lightning flashes and the soft breeze blows, all before the second ripple has ushered from the tip of the sword.

There are, of course, so many other worlds that require attention...

1

THE CROSSROADS OF FATE

Niamh watched as a fierce sun rose over the Silver Wood.

Beside her, Obaeron leaned heavily on the thick stone sill of the window; his aged fingers rubbing the smooth, worn surface.

For countless years he had led the Fae; had stood firm and solid as other worlds changed incessantly. His rule was one of steadfast certainty. He was a being of magic, powerful beyond reckoning and filled with the knowledge of ages.

And he'd been fooled.

"Cehron." He spoke without looking up. The pain in his face was evident. For centuries, Cehron Cen Kohr had been a trusted friend of the king. There had been talk in some circles that Cehron might even have been the most obvious choice to lead the Council, and in doing so, his authority would be second only to Obaeron. The king had passed his three thousandth year, and the effects of time were increasingly evident. While the life of a faerae was long indeed, the day would come when that final path would have to be taken. It was quite likely that the dark and difficult revelation they now discussed would only further his slow decline.

"Yes, Father. Cehron." Niamh continued to watch the sunrise as she spoke.

"He's been telling me of this activity for years, Niamh. *Rogue faerae activity*, he called it. We all trusted him, everyone on the Council. For that matter, there may be none in our entire Seelie Court that would ever doubt him. You know as well as I how respected he is in Elysium. Such power, and the knowledge he gained from his constant wandering only helped to inform us better of the doings of other worlds, their progress and their failures. The things we *learned* from him." He smiled bitterly as he continued. "He was so strong, at such a young age. A prodigy, some called him, even by Fae standards. He could create a Path in the tiniest trickle of water. And the Gates, Niamh! How in the name of the Faant he was able to master the language to open the Gates with such ease, I don't know." He stood fully and walked back to the plush green throne beside his fireplace. Heavily, he sat and put a hand to his forehead. "Rogue faerae activity. And all the while, it was him."

"He knew that you and the Council would need more than sufficient reason to forbid movement on the Paths, Father. We all know that Cehron considers the Fae to be superior to all others, but none could have known the depth of the disdain he held for other races."

"The signs were there, Niamh. They were there. Cehron repeatedly raised the issue of Oisin to the Council."

At the name, Niamh stopped short. In her chest, she

felt that familiar feeling rise once more; the emptiness that engulfed her more often than she cared to admit in recent years. She laid a hand over her breast, breathing deeply, though her father failed to notice. The king was lost in thought, recalling the many conversations he'd had with the Cernunnos; conversations in which Cehron had expressed great concern for the future of the faerae world, among others.

"He was so convincing in his arguments, Niamh. I can still see the look on his face as he implored me to take action. *'How can one of our own be so reckless?'* he'd asked. *'They must be mad! Too many Paths are being used. Too many being opened, carelessly, by faerae creatures that would flood worlds, including ours, with those that don't belong. The Paths, the Gates; all will lead to further destruction and eventual chaos. Weapons are moving. Disease is spreading. The time for action has come,'* he told me. And I believed him."

"His manipulation was great," Niamh offered. "The words he spoke were truth. But the more important truth, the truth he hid so well, was that the rogue faerae activity was his own, and not that of other faeraes, be they Seelie or Unseelie. The Paths will forever exist. There is no eradicating the Fingers of the Faant. But his stability is failing, Father. You can see it in his eyes. Perhaps this is why he's not graced your presence of late."

It was true, Obaeron realized, that Cehron had visited the king's home less frequently in recent decades. When he did call upon the king, he was void of the pleasure that once filled him. It was distressing to see this in a faerae, but Obaeron had assumed that Cehron's change was the result of the worrisome affairs that he saw and experienced in his wandering.

He could not have known that Cehron had long since

begun a descent into madness, ignoring the will of the Faant, facilitating shifts that instead of maintaining balance had the opposite effect; to bring about disorder, confusion and fear.

"How," he whispered, "how could I have missed this? It is my *duty*, my responsibility to not only protect the Fae, but to control and guide those who go astray." He released his grip on the armrests of his throne, and moved again to the nearest window. As he watched a lone lipizzaner stallion wander the gardens far below the high window, he sighed and shook his head. "I have failed."

Niamh moved to him and placed her hands on his strong shoulders; shoulders that had borne the weight of great responsibility for long millennia. "No, Father, you have not failed. In the face of madness, the eyes of reason are often unable to see with clarity. That is why I could not go along with the talk of possible edicts to avoid the Fingers. The will of the Faant is too important. The Paths are essential."

He nodded, but Niamh could see that he was unable to absolve himself of this oversight. Based on Cehron's deception, he and the Council had begun discussions which could change the very nature of Elysium and the role that the Fae would play in all worlds. Obaeron sighed, and looked beyond the gardens to the dense foliage of the Silver Wood. Her return, Niamh realized, had been a bittersweet experience for Obaeron. So long he had requested her return to Elysium, only to be put off each time. He knew that Niamh's life was dedicated to the work and will of the Faant above all else. Niamh had resented the fact that Obaeron had considered such divisive action; action which would essentially put the wishes of the Fae before that of the Faant. Obaeron understood this. They

had both inwardly known that had Niamh returned to
Elysium in recent times, the result would have been an
intense confrontation that would have resolved nothing.
The daughter of Obaeron was nothing if not steadfast in
her beliefs. While she could not have changed the king's
looming edicts – they being supported by the authority
of the Council as well as most of the Court – they had
both known that she would challenge it vehemently. Both
knew as well that she'd never have followed such edicts,
and subsequently, she, the king's daughter, would have
been considered *rogue*. She'd seen the futility of such inevitable disputation. And so, she'd stayed away.

"Cehron will continue," she said simply. "I've come
to inform you of this, but more importantly, we need to
decide what can be done."

"I appreciate this, Niamh. As I appreciate your returning."

"It's a return of necessity, Father." She stopped, her
thin hands resting on the table. "There is so much in this
land that reminds me of him." Her father knew of whom
she now spoke. In the centuries since she had lost Oisin,
she'd spent virtually all of her time in worlds other than
her own. The sorrow, she'd told her father many times,
was unbearable. "Every meadow, every river holds dear
and devastating memories that invite darkness and widen
the void inside me."

"It is a void I shared, to an extent," Obaeron replied.
"With Oisin's death, I could not help but feel a part of you
had died as well. Your vitality, your energy, were so affected, I feared you'd never recover."

"I never have," she said simply. "My sole purpose
now, as I've said, is to see to the Faant's will. We must
deal with Cehron. He will continue to wreak his havoc,

he's made that clear. But if this edict is enforced, then Elysium will essentially be cut off from all other worlds. The connections between *all* worlds will end. Cehron attempts to back you into a corner. What he's done in Cahruia is a precursor to what he'll continue to do, until you act. I don't think for a moment that he'd spare Elysium." She saw the grimace on the king's face turn to anger, but continued before he could speak. "Cehron has chosen Cahruia to begin his reign of terror. He knows that this is the world I hold most dear. He likely knows that this world is where the Whispers of the Faant would be fulfilled. We've both heard the words. Seen the visions. The Egimians are important to me. He knows this. He toys with us. That is why he fuels the fires of war that continue to burn in their lands. He calls us to engage him."

War. The very thought of this brought an ache to Niamh's heart. Cahruia was, as Cehron had said, a relatively simple world. It was a younger world, where technological advances and scientific progress were in their earliest stages. It was a world where, despite the current conflict, the potential for growth and peace was great. This potential would never be realized, of course, so long as Cehron used the land to flaunt his disdain for the Faant, and shifted those that would do nothing but facilitate ruin.

"*Nylacci.*" The king shook his head, still unable to believe what he'd been told. "Of all creatures to shift… It's unthinkable."

Niamh pulled her sleeves about her wrists. *Shifting*. So necessary, but dangerous as well. If a person was unready for such a change, or the receiving world was unsuitable for the individual, the results could be disastrous. In these instances, there were always risks that could not be avoided. The individual entering the world might be

deemed insane or delusional. Often, when a shift was facilitated, the individual was unable to adapt to the world,
to find their place, especially in such cases where the entered world was quite advanced and where curious minds
questioned the history of the shifted. Most often, however,
the greatest risk was sickness. The Darkness. Even when
Fate required such moves, the body – and, in rare cases,
the mind – of the individual was unable to cope with the
move. In these instances, the Darkness slowly consumed a
person. Such tenuous requests by the Faant were rare but,
as with all the requested shifts, they were necessary. *How,*
Niamh thought, *could her father even have considered forbid-
ding movement on the paths, the crossroads of Fate itself?*

"I don't know…" Obaeron said from the window,
considering the question with which Niamh struggled but
had not voiced. He smiled bitterly. "If only I'd been able
to read the face and thoughts of Cehron as I am still able
yours, Niamh. Long did I consider what could be done.
The consultations with the Council resolved nothing; perhaps even made the situation worse."

A look from his daughter.

"I knew what your answer would be. So many of us
have been responsible for the Faant's will, but none as
steadfast and determined as you. I didn't need to ask."

"Maybe I needed to be asked, Father. Do you know
how difficult it was to receive the news of such important
decisions as a message from your servant? Tryn himself
was embarrassed to play such a role." She clasped her fingers, her lips tight. "I should have been involved much,
much earlier."

The king nodded. "Perhaps you are right. The arguments were bitter, and hard feelings exist still." He paused,
and shook his head. "Several Council members, like my-

self, were swayed by Cehron's warnings too quickly. We could not have suspected this."

"The time for suspicion is past. We now know. We must decide what is to be done. Cehron's Nylacci roam throughout Cahruia. He will continue to stain other worlds with this filth – and worse, no doubt – unless he is stopped. His wrath must end. *He* must end."

She looked at her father, the implications of her words hanging heavily in the early morning air.

"Niamh, what you suggest... it cannot be done. You know this as well as any. No faerae can bring harm to one of their own. It has always been so. It is the Law of Fae."

"What does *Law* mean, Father, when we stand on the cusp of disaster? The ruination of worlds, of the Faant's will? The loss of the balance we keep? The fate of worlds, Father, cannot be determined by one mad faerae!"

"You *know* the Law, Niamh. Any faerae who slays one of his own will find his own life forfeit. This Law was laid down in the First Days. Do you not see the paradox of our situation? You criticize the Faant's Law because it forbids the necessary action to save our relationship with those who gave us the Law."

"Then, the Laws must be changed. The will of the Faant must come before all."

"Are the Laws of the Faant not their will?"

"It's what *must* be done."

"Niamh, Laws such as these cannot be changed to facilitate such action. There is reason and logic to all decisions made by the Faant. Perhaps they allow this because it is their *will*. The movement that Cehron speaks of, the movement of destructive forces from one world to another... perhaps the Faant have long foreseen this. Perhaps *this movement* is their will."

"That is not possible."

"Who is to say what is possible, and what is not, in the eyes of the Creators?" He paused, thinking. "Perhaps they test us?"

Niamh shook her head, and moved to the window by which her father had just stood. She tried to see things from his perspective.

Obaeron began to move around the room, his hands joined behind his back.

"Let us think logically, Daughter." He stopped beside her as he spoke. "We have but few choices. Cehron cannot be reasoned with. The madness of a faerae has never been remedied. In our extensive history, we've never seen a complete descent. History tells us of Fae who were able, to an extent, to see the madness which began to grow in them. They chose to exile themselves before their fall was complete. Yet, Cehron… From what you tell me, it seems he embraces it. He is lost."

"And that is why we must act. The Whispers, the prophecy, must be fulfilled, must be given every chance to reach fulfillment, whatever that may look like." Her father listened with narrow eyes, allowing her to continue. Niamh pulled a cloak about her shoulders, signalling that their time together was nearing an end. "To do so, we must ensure that those most directly involved are given every opportunity to see these events unfold as the Faant prophesied. The solution, though it may not appear to be so, is simple.

"We need to protect the Egimian."

2

EMP'SANNI LOH

"...him back to camp..."

"...was trying to find..."

"...get that blade? Not the one he had..."

"...hear me?"

Voices. Words. Sivino tried to piece them together; tried to link them into sense and tie them to individuals. Slowly, very slowly, he opened his eyes.

Lomin's face was above him. "Sivi?"

"I'm fine." His voice was raspy, his eyelids heavy.

"We'll be the judges of that," Ennis grunted as he helped Sivino to his feet. "Come. Let's get you back to camp."

"You're fortunate that Wyncor spotted you," Inlonia said when the others had stopped fussing over him. Being gone for several long hours, they'd feared he had ended up a tender meal for a Nylac. Sivino ate and drank from the foodstuffs that the group had abandoned by the fire when they'd begun their frantic search. The queen gave a small piece of dried meat to the bird. "We would likely have spent the evening trying to track you down – to no avail I'd imagine – as your track disappeared entirely." She looked at Sivino expectantly. He nodded slowly, and sat up.

He recounted the story with surprising clarity, given the haze that surrounded both his entrance and departure from the purple-sky world. His companions listened, leaning forward to take in every word as he spoke of the foreign land. Drip sat off to the side, his muttering finally subsiding when Sivino spoke of the person he'd encountered. Seeing the incredulity of the faces before him, he decided not to share Dahnu's name, fearful that with one word, he would completely discredit the story he told. He described her appearance, and how she had disappeared into the water with his broken sword and re-emerged a short time later with the new blade. For some reason, he'd been chosen to bring this blade to the Three Realms. Sivino felt an unfamiliar sense of pride as he relayed the details of his encounter. It was a foreign feeling. He had done nothing to warrant such an honour, as he saw it, and could see no reason why any would want him to have such a weapon, but holding the blade now he felt for the first time in his life that he might be capable of something meaningful. Something important.

"Yet the strangest part of all of this," he said quietly as he concluded his story, "was the last thing she said to me." As he paused to recall Dahnu's words, he was struck by the weight of the silence, as if the entire forest listened. "She said the shepherd would fade when his blood is spilt on my sword…"

The silence was absolute, the confusion obvious. Sivino pushed himself to his feet, standing a little taller than he'd have previously stood. This was a story that was in no small way unbelievable. He was grateful that he had the talisman beside him, a tangible piece of evidence that showed the others there was truth in what he said. Yet, he was changed in more ways than the weaponry he possessed. As he stood, he held the eyes of any who looked his way, daring them to challenge his claims. None did.

With sure hands, he sheathed his blade in the scabbard that Ennis had provided for him. It was not a perfect fit for the sword, Sivino thought, but then, neither was he. He glanced toward the trenoc, who looked away quickly. From Drip, his gaze moved to Ston, and again he felt the weight of scrutinizing eyes.

It's those who are closest to me, Sivino thought, *who doubt my capability the most.*

He'd been told by his parents from an early age that there was no need to prove himself to anyone. *Your best is always enough*, they'd said. *There's no need to rise to a standard set by others. You set that standard.* This talk usually came following an encounter with Leath, and a desperate attempt by Sivino to gain the respect of his brother. He'd always known that Dels and Rhenna had accepted him without condition, just as he'd known that the conditions of Leath's acceptance would be many.

What would Leath say if he could see him now, preparing to mount a golden mare, wearing a blade forged by the Gods? The very thought made Sivino's head feel light. In his most far-fetched dreams, he could never have imagined occupying his current position. *But would I have wished for this?* he thought. While there was an immense feeling of purpose in him now, he longed for the simple life of Egim; the smell of the fields, the feel of the river. His family. As it had so often since he'd left his home, a terrible unease filled him. He knew this feeling would continue to plague him until he'd received news of his family's fate.

As his eyes studied the etching of his sword hilt, the faerae emerged from the trees.

None had seen her approach, and several of the company jumped as she walked into their midst. Gilsanna spun, knife in hand, poised and ready to throw. Niamh barely glanced in her direction.

The faerae moved closer, and noticed the blade that hung at Sivino's side. She looked from the blade to Sivino.

"Someone's been wandering," she said.

Sivino began to speak, but Niamh raised her hand slightly, silencing him with the gesture. "I'll hear your story in due time. Right now, we must continue our journey." She looked to the trail before them, her face dark. "Have a keen eye. The forest feels unsettled."

Through the following day they continued their journey south, and while the damp air created some discomfort, the trek was uneventful.

On several occasions, Sivino felt the weight of Drip's gaze. He knew that the trenoc was questioning how he, a scrap of a lad, could be entrusted with such a weapon. Sivino sat tall on his mare, giving the impression of a confidence he'd never demonstrated while on horseback. No, there was no need to prove himself, he knew, but today he felt like showing the trenoc that maybe, in some small way, things had changed. When Drip's eyes met his own, Sivino held them. From the time Sivino had been of toddling age, Drip had been able to stare him down in a moment.

This was no longer the case.

Physically, he was essentially the same, lacking any great strength, speed or agility, but there were other ways to grow, Sivino knew. He wondered how long it might take Drip to shift a mindset that had been set in place for the entirety of Sivino's life.

He was pondering this still when Ennis raised a hand at the front of the group, drawing them all to a halt.

The queen's guard moved quickly to his side. Gilsanna remained close to Inlonia as Sivino and the others moved forward.

"Droppings," Ennis said, leaning forward. "Left by a creature that we would do well to avoid."

"Nylacci?" Kef asked.

The corner of Ennis' mouth curled, though it didn't remove the concern from his face. "No, my young friend. I can assure you that while I'm quite unfamiliar with the waste of those monsters, what I *do* know well are the droppings of a brudog." He moved up the trail, his face growing graver with each step. "There's more," he called over his shoulder. "And based on the tracks, quite a few came through together. Recently. Both the tracks and the droppings are fresh."

"Do we change course?" Gilsanna asked Ennis.

"Even doing so will not guarantee we don't walk directly into their midst." The big man looked at the queen, and then the faerae. "I assume you would both agree that we continue on?"

"We continue on this path." Niamh was looking south.

"Right then. Tregg. You and Hargen take the higher ground for a bit. Don't stray too far now, but find a vantage point. See what you can see."

Both men nodded and moved out. Lomin approached

Ennis.

"This is not brudog territory," the ragged man remarked. "I fear that something has spooked them, got them on the run."

Ennis nodded. "Possibly. I'm guessing a dozen at least in this pack." He lowered his voice, so that only Lomin could hear. "What concerns me is that they were here so recently. They'll not have gotten far, and those brutes have noses that can pick up a scent from leagues away. We'd best get moving." He turned to the others. "Have your weapons ready, folks." He offered an unconvincing smile. "Just in case."

For the next hour, they travelled in relative silence. The entire group was on edge. Drip had taken to the treetops immediately after the departure of Tregg and Hargen. When he finally did descend, he moved with purpose. At the same time, Tregg and Hargen came around a bend in the trail. All bore the same news.

"They've got our scent," said Tregg. "Headed our way."

"Damnation!" Ennis looked around, seeking a location from which they could make their best defence. Drip saw what he was doing.

"A little to the east," the trenoc offered. "A small clearing on the slope that will give us room, allow us to form a rough circle. Defend against all sides… Defend the queen." He hesitated, then moved off in a rush as if embarrassed by his words. He slowed as he passed Niamh, and glanced up. "I'll need your help with the young ones."

They moved with their weapons already drawn, urging their horses forward. The animals were, as Ennis had discussed upon their first day of travel, masterfully trained by the best in the realm. Though they might outrun the brudogs for a short time, it would only delay the inevitable confrontation. In the thick of the forest, the brudogs could move with much greater agility than the horses. And the company had no interest in fleeing north, knowing that they'd only have to turn and come back south once more. Sivino felt the taut muscles of his mare, and wondered what he'd be able to do if the animal bolted. He prayed he wouldn't find out.

Niamh, it appeared, had considered the same possibility. As they reached the clearing, she moved from one horse to another, gently stroking the head of each, whispering quiet words that had an immediate effect. The anxious neighing and beating of hooves subsided. The animals shook their manes, huffed, but did not move from their place in the clearing.

Sivino hefted the sword in his hand. A thousand thoughts ran through his mind. Was he ready for this? Did the sword change anything? Would the others be looking to him to protect and fight valiantly, or would they continue to expect little of him? He looked around fearfully, and chastised himself for the pride he'd allowed himself to feel upon gaining the sword. He was, he realized, a boy with a blade almost as long as himself, and no idea how to use it.

In moments, the savage growling of the beasts reached the ears of the company. Beside him, Ston, Torla, Kef and Tonnis stood ready. Though Torla was equipped with her bow, the others possessed longknives and swords that were pitifully short. In the distance, glimpses of the dogs could now be seen through the trees to the right as they sped along the path. Then, the lead dog made a quick, deep bark and half the pack veered right, entering the trees. As Ennis cursed, Sivino stepped forward and raised his sword higher.

The brudogs racing through the forest were only slightly slower than those upon the path; their huge legs tearing the earth as they wove between the trunks with terrible speed. Torla fired her first arrow, and missed her mark. Beside her, Raid and Hargen unleashed arrows of their own. One struck a brudog in the shoulder, and it went down in a spray of dirt and leaves.

From the corner of his eye, Sivino saw Lomin pull the willow stick from his pocket. Pointing it at one of the brudogs, he hissed strange, foreign words at the snarling creature and then gave a small flick of his wrist. An instant later the dog jerked to the side as if pulled, and collided with a massive oak, shattering its neck. Holding the new sword firm, Sivino spun, trying to see if there was an exposed or otherwise vulnerable part of their group. From her boot, he saw Torla retrieve a knife.

Niamh moved to the center of their circle. She moved with no particular haste, though she glanced back and forth as if taking account of the remaining dogs that grew ever closer. *We only have moments*, Sivino thought. Then, the faerae stopped and pulled a handful of dirt from the inner pockets of her thin cloak.

"Hellfire! What is she doing?" Drip hissed.

Ennis brought down two of the dogs with his arrows, and Gilsanna planted one of her knives into the shoulder of another, but it was not enough. Seeing that Torla had no arrows remaining – and had thrown her only knife at a dog – Sivino rushed forward and pulled her behind him, stepping between her and the advancing animals. Behind him, the voice of Niamh rose, barely perceptible above the shouts and barking. It was, as far as Sivino could tell, a language he'd never heard.

And then, she was in front of him.

Staring down these ravenous beasts, she raised a handful of dirt in her left hand, and with a sweeping arc to the right, threw it in front of herself and the young ones, hissing strange words the entire time. The dirt hit the ground just before the lead dog reached them, its mouth snapping as it skidded to a halt.

Niamh took a few steps backwards, and did the same on the other side of the small clearing, which spanned perhaps twenty paces. Two sides were effectively cut off from the beasts while two were left exposed. On one side, Lomin and Ennis held the beasts back, while on the other side, Inlonia's remaining guards did the same. Screams sounded as one dog took Raid Smillo from his feet, tearing at his pant leg. Hargen was upon it immediately, attacking its throat. Niamh reached into her cloak, extracting another handful of the rust-coloured earth, and turned toward Lomin. Though she did not run, she crossed the small distance in an instant, as though a mighty wind had sucked her from the spot she'd stood and deposited her next to her old friend. Again, the clay was thrown before the dogs; a protective barrier, somehow empowered by her words and touch. She did the same next to Inlonia's guards, appearing at their side quicker than Sivino could follow. He watched as the last of the dirt was thrown to the ground. He noticed as well how Niamh's empty hand went slowly to her chest.

The brudogs howled their fury. Sivino spun around, watching as the creatures encircled them. There was nowhere to run. Every member of the group held what weapons they had before them, fully expecting that at any moment whatever form of enchantment Niamh had created would be broken.

The dogs walked in slow circles. Several looked past the people directly in front of them, trying instead to find the creature who'd cut off their access. They sniffed at the ground, snarling when they got too close to the barrier of dirt. While the others appeared doubtful of the protection, Sivino trusted fully in its power, and lowering his sword he moved to Niamh.

"I've never seen so many together," Lomin said. "Or so aggressive."

"As you said, they're spooked," Ennis replied, his voice low. "They can usually be driven off with a quick assault. I think the forest conceals predators they've not known before. Look at their eyes."

Indeed, the beasts seemed as uneasy as they were enraged. They stood low, growling more lowly, but the quick jerks of their heads and wide, darting eyes were uncharacteristic of these lean, confident hunters. Occasionally, one of the pack would turn and face the direction from which they'd come, sniffing the air warily.

The faerae removed her hand from her chest, and silently walked forward. She stopped so close to the edge of her enchantment that Sivino feared the animal before her might suddenly rip a piece from her slender body. The faerae lifted her slight dress a little in both hands, and lowered herself to her knees. Sivino held his breath as the massive dog, obviously the alpha, now towered over her. She traced a tiny finger through the dirt, her hand inches from the brudog's paw. "Go now," she said. The dogs quieted to hear her voice.

"Go," she repeated. Slowly, a couple of the brudogs stepped back from the circle. These were followed by several more until, after a few moments, all but the alpha before Niamh had retreated.

"Emp'sanni loh," the faerae whispered.

As the words were uttered, Sivino was certain that for the smallest moment, the dog's back had shuddered, the fur that covered it raised ever so slightly. It tilted its head southward, looked past the faerae and emitted a low growl. Looking back at Niamh, the beast growled again but not so deeply, and then, the smallest whimper escaped its throat. Niamh nodded.

The brudog turned and followed its brethren.

Niamh remained on her knees. As she watched the brudogs depart, she put out a hand, attempting to steady herself. Lomin rushed to her side, and caught her just before she fell.

"Niamh? Niamh! Ston! Get some water."

The faerae looked at Lomin, and then to the others. Her eyes rested on Sivino. "Tired," she said softly. "I just… need a moment." She offered a smile, a small effort to reassure them. "The brudogs are gone. They will not return."

"What did it say?" Sivino asked quietly.

Everyone stopped and looked at him.

"Say?" Ston, pulling a waterskin from the nearest horse, stopped suddenly. "What in *Creation* are you talking about, Siv? *Say?*"

Niamh lowered herself to a grassy patch of earth beside the path. "You hear much, Sivino Spallic."

With those words the faerae fell unconscious.

3

HOW QUICKLY DREAMS FADE

The morning sun of Elysium continued the slow grace of its arc as King Obaeron watched from his highest window.

In the palace yards, the stallion had been joined by a filly. Upon seeing the young horse approach, the stallion tossed his head toward the higher field and the filly moved in that direction. To the casual observer, it would have looked as though the stallion gestured to be rid of the young intruder. But such was not the case, Obaeron knew. The stallion had directed the filly to the lushest area of the field, and then followed her as she headed toward the tall grasses and arrowleaf clover.

He let her go ahead as he led her where she needed to go.

"She is dying."

It pained him to speak of his daughter so, but Obaeron knew it to be true. He turned to the faerae Tryn, who sat in a dim corner with arms folded, listening. His head was lowered, and Tryn noted how Obaeron's thick red hair had begun to show traces of grey in the last century. The king rubbed his brow with one hand, his other on the back of the chair nearest him. "How quickly she fades. There is darkness that has come over her. It seems to steal the very air from her lungs, like a sickness."

"It *is* a sickness."

The king sighed. He walked past an array of exotic fruits that had been laid out by his servants, taking only his golden wine goblet. He walked towards the window, raising his wine slightly to indicate to Tryn that he might partake if he so chose. The faerae remained seated, then reconsidered and moved to pour himself a small amount of the honey-rich drink. He sipped slowly, and sighed through his nose.

"That amount of shifting – it will… *reduce* a faerae, given enough time," Tryn said bluntly. Obaeron's shoulders sank. Several quiet moments passed.

"How long has it been, Tryn? Since the last faerae passed?"

Tryn thought for a moment. "Three hundred years."

Obaeron shook his head. As Tryn moved to stand beside his king he saw that along with fear and sadness, anger shone upon his face. The eerie song of a beautiful falsetto wafting from the lower levels of the castle lent sound to the look that now hung upon the king's visage.

"Three hundred years." He laid his goblet on the table with an unsteady hand, knocking it on its side. Its contents ran the length of the mahogany board, slowly and certainly, before spilling over the edge. From the window sill Tryn raised an open hand and with a grimace snapped his hand shut in a tight fist.

The wine stopped – suspended in the air – a moment before it hit the floor.

"I should have prevented it, Tryn." Obaeron tilted his head upwards. Ancient paintings of long-forgotten tales faded upon the ceiling far overhead. His eyes rested on one in particular: a man, his clothing torn, a fire burning before him. Within the flames, a sad young woman stood. In her hand, she held a well-used timbrel, though it would be played no more; the small metal rings had fallen from the edges and burnt at her feet.

"I should have stopped it," Obaeron finished.

Quietly, Tryn retrieved the goblet and walked the length of the table. He stooped low, and placed the goblet beneath the unmoving stream. Then, he passed a thin finger through the wine, and it continued to flow, filling the cup once more.

"You know as well as I that Niamh was... *is* aware of the risks," Tryn said as he placed the goblet beside Obaeron. "It was her decision – her charge, she would say – to shift as frequently as she did in order to do the work of the Faant. You know as well that once her mind has been set, the persuasion of eons will not alter it. I've spent a century or two testing that theory."

"The Faant, the Fae, and the Goddess in between." The king rubbed his goblet absently. "Has there ever been a Trinity so enigmatic?"

"I know of one or two," Tryn replied. "Some have spent millennia trying to understand such divine mysteries."

"But can we *ever* fully understand? Niamh has spent centuries shifting between worlds; worlds into which, in many cases, she should never have ventured. Why should her service have been requested so often, Tryn? Because she was so *effective* in executing their orders? Or because she was so *eager* to move between worlds?"

"I know not, Sire."

"Either way, I should have stopped her. Her love of those worlds and their little villages; her heart seems drawn to such tiny places. She always maintained that even the smallest hamlet could raise a child able to change the world. She's done such work, more than she ever should have, and I let her. She is my daughter, Tryn. I knew this could happen." He stopped, and closed his eyes. When he spoke again, his voice was low. "I knew this could happen.

"The sickness that comes with excessive shifting is unpredictable. Niamh has shifted so extensively that her body has begun to falter. It is breaking down, and cannot repair itself. The Paths, they take something from us each time they are used – a minuscule amount of our energy and magic, but over time, over thousands of shifts, it takes a toll. Couple this with the energy that she expended through the use of magic. That energy is finite. There's no replacing it. It creates a void that nothing can ever fill, leaving the faerae a husk of their former self."

The king brought his clasped hands to his face, the tips of his index fingers resting on his bottom lip. His eyes focused straight ahead, to the lush hills and beyond. He remained this way for long moments until a gentle breeze floated through the window, barely moving his long red locks. He nodded, almost imperceptibly. Missing nothing, Tryn tilted his head, waiting for the king to speak.

"Tryn, do you know how long it has been since your king has ventured from Elysium?"

Tryn's eyes narrowed. "I do," he replied. "The Uprising of the Underworld. The revolt of the Unseelie. Many felt certain that you'd be defeated by Arawn. Myself, I knew you'd emerge victorious, but you can't blame those who doubted you." He pursed his lips, shaking his head at the madness of the memory. "Arawn was a foe like no other."

"Arawn." Obaeron spoke the word reverentially. "It took the Lord of the Dead to draw me from my homeland the last time. I didn't even *have* a child in those days. Only a kingdom and an incomprehensible dream of pleasure and glory."

Looking into his goblet, into the absolute stillness of the wine within, he saw a reflection of his daughter.

"How quickly dreams fade," he whispered.

4

NAHCIN

Doran Dunarrk stood on a parapet on the eastern edge of Nahcin.

Its seven thousand residents made it the second largest city in Rentorria. For the merchants and traders of the capital, Nahcin was a preferred destination for their goods, and the roadways between the two cities were heavily worn.

Nahcin was the third major city to develop in the realm, having sprouted up centuries past when settlers had laid roots in a quiet lakeside region removed from the activity of Orshos and Ronec. Ronec had, until recently, benefited from its proximity to Isror and for this reason had matured quickly on the eastern fringe of Rentorria. Located between these two cities, Nahcin had divided its commerce between both Ronec and the capital, though on the far-reaching shores of Lake Madimest and beyond, a scattering of towns had sprouted up that had relied upon Nahcin as the regional hub.

The parapet, under more favourable circumstances, would have provided a magnificent view. The sweeping grasslands to the east were slowly beginning to sway with the evening breeze, and beyond them, the vast plains that stretched to Ronec. Doran and Kellert Sentero had arrived only an hour prior, taking with them just over two thousand soldiers who would help reinforce the high walls of the city.

The walls, he thought, were a blessing. Though the city continued to grow, much of this growth was upward, as opposed to outward. Nahcinian architects and builders prided themselves on their ability to reach toward the sky, crafting structures unlike those seen anywhere in the realm. In recent decades, they'd begun creating large buildings that served as homes to a number of families – each family dwelling set apart from the others. It was a great feat. For the first time in Rentorrian history, one could have a neighbour above or below oneself, instead of just to the side.

Doran looked beyond these buildings to the wood and steel monstrosity that surrounded the capital city. In Nahcin's early days, the barrier had been a simple palisade; the wooden stakes barely ten feet tall. With Nahcin's growth, Rentorrian leaders saw fit to significantly reinforce this enclosure, and in the past fifty years had erected a fortification that, while not as high and long as the walls of Orshos, should repel any attack the city might face. Though Doran was relatively satisfied with the number of soldiers that were posted around the city's perimeter, it was good that they would not have to be spread as thin as would be the case in Orshos, if the capital came under attack.

If, Doran thought. It was one of the most commonly used and vehemently detested words in the language of war, to his mind. There were too many ifs, too many maybes, and unlesses and perhaps. *If* Nahcin could resist the force of the Isrorians that marched west, *perhaps* the great coastal city would be spared such an assault. *Maybe* Orshos would remain unscathed. *Unless*, he thought solemnly. Unless that massive cloud of dust rising in the east was indicative of the size of the host that marched on Nahcin at present.

He descended the stone steps of the parapet, and stormed through the building that was currently being used as a headquarters for the military commanders. When he arrived in the war room, Kellert and several other men stood around a table, debating the possible location of the initial assault.

Kellert had pleaded with Doran to remain in the capital, to oversee the preparation of the defences. Both knew full well that the battle at Nahcin had the potential to be a long, drawn-out affair. That being the case, it would be important for the king to be in the capital, able to strategize and make decisions, free of distraction and ultimately, the risk of death.

Doran had scoffed at the idea. A king, he'd maintained, should stand with his people. A king should fight – not stand back and watch his subjects fall before him. The ruin of Ronec still smouldered in the king's mind.

Doran moved to the middle of the table. One of the commanders, a bald, surly man named Crowlt whose long black beard reached his chest, was tapping his knife on the map before them. "We can easily position four hundred archers at present," said Crowlt. "The Madimest sits south of Nahcin, and I don't anticipate Idach employing watercraft of any kind. Nor can I see him splitting his force to attack both the east and west sides, though it's possible. North or east, I believe, will receive the initial assault."

"Unless he assumes we'll think this way as well," Doran noted as he leaned over the table, his thick fingers tapping locations on the map before him. "North and east would be the obvious targets. Perhaps for this reason, he'll attack the west side, hoping that defences are weaker there. How many catapults on the west wall, Commander Crowlt?"

"Five," the bald man replied. He didn't sound happy about this fact. "And five on the east. Six on the north."

Doran nodded. "They'll arrive during the night. Likely attack at sunrise. It's also likely that the army will consist of more than Isrorians."

He'd informed the Nahcinian commanders of the information he'd received from Staid Dyrro. While the news was ill received, it was not entirely surprising as word of some unfamiliar form of beast had spread from various corners of the realm. Crowlt had refused to believe in such a creature, maintaining that he was certain Dyrro had seen a contingent of the fur-wearing Kourg that had come across the mountains to join forces with Idach Garron. Doran did not see the use in an extended debate regarding the nature of the beast. Either way, Idach was adding a high degree of savagery to his ranks.

Doran chewed the corner of his lip. He turned to Crowlt. "Have the citizens on the outskirts of Nahcin all been accounted for? And those around the lake?"

The commander nodded, his face a constant grimace. "A good number have entered the city walls. A few of the more foolhardy have chosen to hide in their homes; most of these are some distance from Nahcin, so they may fare well." He emitted a low grunt. "Most, however, have fled for Orshos."

Doran nodded. "The capital will take them in and protect them."

"For the time being," Crowlt muttered.

The king let the comment slide. Crowlt was nothing if

not cynical. Indeed, the portly old warrior admitted this outright, and credited his cynicism for keeping him alive on numerous occasions. *Show me an optimist who's not a fool and I'll eat my scabbard*, he'd often said.

Doran took comfort in the fact that the general populace of Nahcin had not fallen to despair. This was, he knew, one of the proudest cities in the Three Realms, alongside the capital cities of Orshos, Levebule, and Iskall. Yet, in Nahcin, it was a pride that did not border on arrogance. These people were content, and they celebrated their lives and accomplishments with a deep sense of satisfaction. Though they worked as hard as any in the realm, the citizens of Nahcin strove to more effectively develop the creative arts, and the city likely had more musicians, thespians, painters and writers per capita than any other. In his brief walk through Nahcin, Doran had been greeted by a number of citizens. They were kind and welcoming, and though the city prepared for an assault like none they'd ever seen, the citizens presented a strong exterior. On one corner Doran had seen a young woman in a storefront window, carefully removing the paintings as staff behind her secured them in boxes. She smiled proudly at the king, and nodded. The final piece that she was removing depicted a little boy, walking with a woman that Doran assumed to be the mother. The pair were walking past a Rentorrian soldier. Only the back of the uniformed man was visible as he splayed the fingers on a slightly raised hand in greeting of the pair. The little boy's face beamed as he pointed a chubby little finger at the soldier. The mother's hand rested on the boy's shoulder. She smiled as well, but Doran could easily see the pain and fear that resided in her emerald eyes. He recalled the last portrait for which he'd had to pose. The artist – the brilliant but nononsense Lady Bonita – had respectfully asked him which king he'd like painted. When he'd expressed his confusion, she'd explained, mixing small amounts of black with the burgundy on her palette. *I can paint you as the public sees you. I can paint you as you see yourself. I can paint you as I see you. I can paint you as you wish to be seen, or… I can paint who you are.*

You can do all that? he'd replied.

She'd smiled wryly. *My palette is extensive, and I trust the paint to reveal the subject.*

Trust, Doran now thought with a sigh. The people of Nahcin had placed their trust in the commanders and in their king. The city would stand, they felt, and would repel the black stain that moved across the fields toward them. Most faces presented this certainty as surely as if it had been painted there.

Doran was not so certain. If the enemy's numbers were as big as Dyrro had suggested, Nahcin would easily be surrounded and, like Ronec, it could be effectively cut off from the outside world. Doran had recognized this, and he and Kellert had left orders with Solstia and the commanders in Orshos to prepare for this and other possibilities. If the Isrorians utilized attrition warfare, additional bodies would be sent to Nahcin from the capital. He'd also instructed them to continue preparations for the defence of Orshos. *The grounds outside the city walls must be prepared for battle,* he'd implored Solstia and the others, *and word must be sent to the fisherfolk to return home and make ready.* He'd stopped then, and considered the words he was about to speak.

Send word to Inlonia Talchol as well. Tell her we are falling.

Doran pushed these thoughts aside. There was a time for reflection, and that time wasn't now. Quietly, he rolled up his sleeves and stared at the map; the map of a city that had no idea what it would face with the rising sun.

5

CITY OF STONE

The trees thinned on the eastern fringe of the Nucono, as if the forest itself was reluctant to encroach upon the city of the Drales.

Ras.

Long years had passed since Dels had been so close to the place. The city was carved into the very face of the sandstone cliffs, rising from the ground and taking its shape from the contour of the mountainside. The awe felt by the Egimians was audible as they drew near. Dels could not help but slow himself to take in the sight, and those around him did likewise.

Rising three hundred feet above the ground, and easily twice this length in width, the Drale city was as foreboding as it was formidable. All across the face of the city, stone pillars supported the upper echelons. Yet, they were not the pillars of marble that one might find in Levebule or the fabled city of Corapall. These were solely practical in nature, carved in strategic locations to support that which lay above.

Staircases rose all over the city. Even from a distance, Dels could see that the slope, width and depth of the steps varied tremendously. When the first builders had set out to hew a city from the stone, it was the stone that had dictated its creation. In some places, the steps were wide and inclined gently. In others, they were so steep and small that they resembled a ladder more so than a staircase. Yet, the Drales that were visible high in the city moved about with a deftness that was remarkable. Quickly and smoothly the inhabitants traversed the staircases that were perilously narrow, hundreds of feet up, with no rail or rope to protect against falls. Their long, lean legs carried them about almost gracefully, and they paid very little heed to the height of the walkways that, to an Egimian, would be frightful beyond measure.

What the Drales of Ras *were* heeding now was the group of Egimians that Daurr was leading toward their reclusive home.

From the heights above, the rhythmic sound of chisel against stone slowly ceased. The low murmur of conversation subsided. One by one, the Drales moved to the precipice of the city, looking down at the strange sight below.

Humanfolk. It was apparent to the Egimians from the cold stares and the sideways stance of these creatures that mats of welcome would likely not be unrolled. Dels noted that Daurr did not even bother to look up. Whether he didn't care what his kin thought, or didn't care to see their looks of disapproval, the Egimian did not know.

As they approached the massive gates of Ras, the sun slipped further behind the horizon. Shadows continued to slide across the city wall, and the entrance to the Cudgel Mountains darkened, resembling a great mouth that would feed the city within.

"Goddess protect us," Kitt Rallo whispered from the back of the cart.

When they'd just about reached the gateway, Dels noticed a pair of Drales approaching from the left, having come from another corner of the Nucono. Between them, they carried one of the biggest stags Dels had ever seen. Surely, he thought, the beast must weigh five hundred pounds. He noted the eighteen points of the stag's antlers; rare but not unheard of in the Realms. But what was most awe-inspiring, to Dels and all those around him, was the fact that the Drales carried the beast almost effortlessly. The front and back legs were tied firmly and secured around a wooden pole. The Drales – one male and one female, in Dels' estimation – each carried an end, and they strode as if hefting a mere sack of potatoes. Upon seeing the group, the pair stopped suddenly, and lowered the animal until its antlers dug into the soft earth.

As Daurr passed by the pair, he glanced at the animal they carried. "Your hunt was fortunate. Give thanks to the Good Mother."

The male looked from Daurr to the Egimians that accompanied him and the other Drales. "More fortunate than some. What is the meaning of this, Daurr?" he rumbled.

The big Drale stopped then for the first time in hours. His face, if possible, grew more severe as he spoke to the hunter. "They will rest in Ras for a time. They needed to be protected," he said pointedly.

"Protected?" The female spoke now. "Did the Good Mother tell you?"

Daurr hesitated for the slightest moment before shaking his head. "She did not. I spoke with one of the First Children."

The female glanced at her counterpart, shock apparent on her face. Dels recalled the anger that had surged in Daurr when he had let his disbelief show upon hearing the big creature speak of the faerae race. Yet, from Daurr's own kind, there was no thought given to questioning the validity of his statement, for the Drale race did not believe in speaking falsely. They spoke the simple truth, and had little interest in embellishment or pretense. From his childhood, Dels recalled the faerae tales that explained how lies were impossible for the Fae. While this was likely not so for the Drales, they uttered falsehoods with equal scarcity.

"Come," Daurr said as he resumed walking. "The animal needs to be cleaned."

Quickly, he led them through the gaping archway, thirty feet high and almost as wide. Dels felt an instant chill as they stepped into the shadow of Ras, and he suddenly missed the warmth of the sunlight. He had to remind himself that they'd come here for protection, that Daurr had led them here to keep them safe. He could see the terror on the faces of his friends, but there was little he could do to assuage their anxiety aside from not letting his own show. He quickened his pace, until he came to the side of Daurr.

"Your city is quite impressive," he said to the Drale as they passed under the archway.

Daurr stopped then, and slowly craned his neck to see the upper levels of Ras. "Our city is rock," he stated. "It is the Drales that are impressive."

Dels hesitated for a moment, and then nodded. He looked back at his people, joining his hands behind his back as he smiled, hoping that his casual stance might help relax the tension that gripped each and every one of the townsfolk.

It did not.

"Come," Daurr rumbled as he turned and strode across the threshold and into the city beyond.

As the Egimians passed beneath the archway, the enormity of the city overwhelmed them. Walking with cautious steps and a skyward gaze, Dels and his companions were transfixed by the slowly spiralling tiers of the city. There was a sense of vertigo experienced if one walked too long while looking at the structures above.

Beyond the archway, a vast courtyard spread in a semi-circular fashion. All along its edges were archways similar to the one through which they'd just entered, though significantly smaller. Through these, wide tunnels and staircases that would take one deeper and higher into the city could be seen. Though deep, the light of the sun was not absent in these tunnels, which reminded Dels of the alleyways of East Rovil, though the alleys of Ras were smaller and devoid of the malicious scoundrels that lingered in Rovil's underbelly.

The ground was a lightly coloured dirt, so smooth and well-kept that Dels wondered if it was groomed on a regular basis. He recalled the stories he'd heard, and indeed passed on, regarding the Drales. A rough race, content to scrape a living from the harsh surroundings of their damp, dark caves. He'd always considered the Drales to be a crude race, uncivilized and base. Yet the sights that now lay before him dispelled all of his preconceived notions. The architecture, the precision and order of the city suggested that these were a people capable of creating beauty and wonder beyond what most could ever have dreamed. To confirm this, one need look no further than the fountain at the center of the courtyard.

At the base of the fountain, sharp, angular rocks jutted from the earth to create a circular formation that was perhaps fifteen feet from one side to the other. Though the huge rocks were not straight or placed uniformly, there was a symmetry to their arrangement which reminded Dels of the flames of a fire. Indeed, he wondered if this had been the intention of its architects. Whoever had created this work, they were skilled beyond measure. In the midst of the rock circle, two massive figures had been hewn from stone. Dels moved closer to get a better look. Beside him, many of the townsfolk did likewise. He heard Sianah exclaim softly as she took Leath's hand and pulled him toward the structure. One of the stone figures, a brutally muscular male, was standing. His eyes looked directly through the main gateway of Ras, as though scrutinizing all that entered his city. In his left hand, he held a club. His right rested upon the shoulder of a woman, her robe of flowing rock billowed behind her. Her hands cupped a stone water pitcher, which overflowed with the water of the spring below. As the Egimians neared, the light gurgle of the water could be heard.

Dahlah appeared by Dels' side. Behind her, the Egimians continued to observe the city as low voices began to initiate the first conversations since entering Ras. "I don't know that I've ever seen anything more beautiful," Dahlah whispered, as though afraid the stone figures might hear her comment.

Dels nodded. In Levebule, he'd seen works created by the great Embarrian artists – Helonia Gamcel, an emaciated woman who worked only at night, out of doors by the light of torches so that her hands could sculpt the shadows she saw, and Nidor, the recluse who'd emerge from his ramshackle cottage only when struck by inspiration from

the Goddess. In many instances, years would pass between his creations, and the only people with whom he'd
interact were his servants who, apparently, had changed
as frequently as the tide. *An eccentric lot, those creatives*,
Dels thought. He turned to question Daurr on the origin
of the fountain, and found himself facing the female that
they'd seen as they'd approached the city. Dels stood his
ground, fearing that to back up suddenly might cause offence to the woman who towered above him.

"Daurr will speak with the Wise Ones," the Drale
noted in a deep voice that was just a hint softer than that
of Daurr. Dels looked beyond the Drale before him. Sure
enough, he saw Daurr disappear through an archway and
down a staircase with two of his kind. *So, Ras goes down as
well as up*, Dels thought as the Drale began to speak again.
"He said that I may show the leader the heights of Ras, at
the request of the First Child with whom he spoke. *Only
the leader*." She did not wait for a response; she simply
started walking. "Come," she said over her shoulder.

Dels glanced toward Dahlah, and then to Leath. He
could hardly refuse the offer, and there was little doubt
that he was in fact the leader of these people. Stellen Tros
moved through a small group of people, and put a hand
on Dels' shoulder.

"She has quite a stride," he said with a forced smile.
"You'd best stop wasting time." He gave Dels a gentle
shove to get him moving. Dels returned the smile weakly
and nodded.

It was, he thought as he hurried to catch up with the
Drale, quite an opportunity, all things considered. Just being able to enter the gates of Ras was a monumental feat.
Whenever there was trade to be done with *outsiders*, the
business of the Drales was conducted a considerable distance from the city. And now, not only were Dels and his

people inside the renowned walls, but he was about to be given a personal tour of this magnificent, albeit foreboding place. He hurried to catch the Drale who lumbered on toward a narrow archway. She'd not looked back since beckoning him to follow.

"I'm grateful for this opportunity, uh–" Dels' words trailed off as he realized he didn't know the Drale's name.

"Saroon," she said, picking up on his hesitation.

"The fountain back there, Saroon. It's magnificent."

The Drale nodded.

"May I ask who made it?"

"A Drale of old," she replied.

Dels saw that Saroon, true to her kind, was a creature of few words. Yet, his curiosity was piqued, and he could not help but continue his questioning.

"The figures in the fountain, who are they?"

Saroon slowed, and turned to look at him. Dels waited through several awkward seconds of silence. He could feel the eyes of his people on him as they undoubtedly watched the exchange. Saroon cast a look at the Egimians, her face serious. "Do all of your kind ask so many questions?"

"Actually, I'm one of the more reserved of our folk," he replied, glancing at his people. "Others would ask considerably more questions than I."

The Drale looked at him for another long moment, as though trying to decide whether he was making a joke. Though she didn't smile, Dels could have sworn that for just a moment, her frown was less deep. She turned on her heel and began walking again.

"They are the Good Mother and the Just Father. The Protectors." She ducked slightly as they walked through an archway and entered a short passage at the eastern fringe of the city. Walls of white lent a subtle radiance to the space, which inclined slightly before turning into a staircase. The pair began to climb.

"I heard Daurr mention the Good Mother outside the gate," Dels said.

"She is the provider. The one who ensures that our needs are met; that we do not go without. We work hard for what we have. The Good Mother rewards hard work."

"And the Just Father?" Dels asked.

"The Just Father rewards as well. If you work hard, waste nothing, respect the land, and give thanks for all that is provided by the Mother, he'll spare you his wrath."

Dels tilted his head, though Saroon did not see the gesture. She continued up the stairs with a steady, quick gait. *Wasting nothing,* thought Dels, *must also apply to time.* He tried not to let his shortened breath become apparent as he struggled to not fall too far behind.

"His wrath?" Dels asked. "Can I ask what that involves?"

"Unpleasantness," Saroon answered. "In most cases, the offending individual will bear the brunt of the Father's ire. They will fall sick…" She trailed off momentarily, looking to the towering walls above her. "Or sometimes, they simply fall. They may be cursed with misfortune and fail in the hunt, unable to provide for their people. The Good Mother is also aware of all that happens, and supports the Father's judgement. She will not provide to those that the Father has judged unfit."

Dels could not help but be drawn into the belief system of the creatures. "So, they support one another?"

"Of course. No one, *nothing*, exists of itself. They are

like the amilliat of the forest, standing side by side as they oversee all. At times, their branches may interlock with each other, but it is what happens beneath the surface that shows the true support. The roots. They are intertwined. One will not fall while the other holds firm. The Mother supports the Father, and the Father supports the Mother. Such is life."

And I thought these creatures lacked depth, thought Dels. He was now pushing himself hard to keep up with Saroon. She navigated the staircase with incredible ease, her muscular legs showing no fatigue. Dels noted the bloody scratches that covered her pale legs – likely from the earlier hunt – and the older scars that ran beneath. He had little doubt that Drales such as Saroon were held in high favour by the Just Father.

The staircase twisted erratically, and at times grew narrow enough to give Dels pause. Occasionally, Saroon paused as she tried to determine the best route to their destination. Dels could only assume – and hope – that she did so in consideration of his limitations in navigating the more treacherous stairways of the cliff's edge.

A few moments later, as they walked a mercifully level alleyway, Dels stopped short. Upon the flat wall, a scene that extended for dozens of feet had been engraved. "Goddess," Dels whispered, and Saroon stopped.

"The Father's Call," she replied.

Dels stepped closer. Within the rock, hundreds of Drales had been carved. They stood on what appeared to be a cliff, or the precipice of a plateau. A short, cylindrical item was held to the mouth of the apparent leader, and Dels could not be sure if it was an instrument or a weapon.

"In the Old Times, when great battles were waged, the Drales would not engage without the consent of the Just

Father. It is he who would decide if the battle was just. This instrument," she indicated the mouthpiece of the Drale carving, "is the Father's Call. It would be sounded before the Drales engaged. If the battle was justified, the Father would answer the call. If it was not... he would not."

Dels gaped at the creation. Above the etched Drales, heavy storm clouds had been moulded from the sandstone. The late sunrays that penetrated the alley struck the clouds and cast shadows beyond the chiselled precipice.

"Come," said Saroon. She was walking again.

After a seeming eternity of ascension, Saroon stopped. She did so suddenly, causing Dels, who'd scarcely been able to raise his head, to almost bump into her. They'd reached the top of Ras. Dels' laboured breath caught in his throat as he beheld the wonder of the sight. The land stretched for leagues, drenched in the deep orange hue of the sinking sun.

The Nucono swayed as if breathing, its limbs and leaves rising and falling in the evening breeze. The vantage point allowed them to look over the entire city and all that surrounded it. Dels had never seen so much of his realm in a single glance. He turned in a slow circle, taking in the landscape and the feeling of weightlessness that he felt.

"We live within and upon the rock," Saroon began, "but it is the Nucono that supports us. Under that vast green blanket are the animals and the soils that the Good Mother has given us. We treat the lands with respect, and in turn are given that which we need." She moved a few steps away, and Dels instinctively followed. "Over there," she continued, pointing, "are the gardens." Dels stepped around her to see the area she indicated, careful not to get too close to the open precipice. It was a space that one could not have seen upon approaching the city, as it would be entirely obstructed by the forest. Large rectangular sections of the Nucono had been cleared and fenced, and within these spaces, the gardens of Ras were tended. Even in the dying light, Dels could see the big creatures moving about the troughs. Row upon row of tilled earth spewed forth a variety of growth, from which the Drales pulled vegetables and filled the hemp bags they carried over their shoulders. In an adjacent field, several Drales led a group of horses, each of which were harnessed to a plow that loosened the earth. Saroon watched as they completed the day's work.

"The Just Father and Good Mother have been pleased this year. They've given us a plentiful yield."

Dels could not help but think of the gardens of his village. *Would the time ever come that his people would once again harvest a crop from the fields of Egim?* As he watched the Drales work, he thought about the way things had once been. On many evenings such as this, his family had pulled vegetables from their gardens in preparation for the supper meal. Leath had always yelled at Sivino for picking the vegetables that were not fully grown, while Rhenna would wink and whisper to Sivino that the smallest carrots were the tastier of the lot. Dels' face must have reflected his thoughts, as Saroon folded her hands behind her back and studied him carefully.

"You've lost much," she said quietly.

"More than you can realize."

The Drale was quiet for a moment. "It is never as much as you think."

Dels' eyes narrowed, and he turned to deliver a sharp response to Saroon, but the look of sympathy in the Drale's eyes stayed his tongue. He'd not seen such a look from one of the creatures.

He stood motionless as Saroon held his gaze. It was a situation that should have felt awkward – this silent, elongated exchange – but it continued for a time that seemed to stretch with the dying rays of sunlight.

"The Good Mother will provide for your people once more, Egimian. In time, you will see this."

Dels sat on an outcropping of sandstone, and rubbed his eyes with the heels of his hands. He thought of his people, torn from their land like a crop that was never ready to be reaped.

"I'm afraid we don't believe in the Good Mother," Dels replied. "In our land we have a Goddess, and at the moment, I have no faith in her ability to provide us anything."

Saroon exhaled slowly. She tilted her head, gesturing toward the realm. "No *outside man* has ever stood atop the city of Ras. Daurr always says that standing at this pinnacle, one cannot help but feel so small and so great at the same moment. It is a contraction that makes sense, if you are able to acknowledge that you are both. You now stand at this precipice, Dels Spallic. That which your people need *will* be provided."

Dels was struck by the depth of Saroon's words, which were so incongruous with his previously held notion of this race.

"Perhaps," he said, "life would be simpler if we shared your belief in the Good Mother."

Saroon reached out a hand, and helped the Egimian to his feet. "Our Good Mother. Your Goddess." Though Dels was now standing, she continued to grip his hand firmly as she leaned closer. *"Who is to say they are not one and the same?"*

Releasing his hand, she turned quickly and began the descent through the city of stone.

6

SMOKE AND FIRE

The sound of screams brought Doran Dunarrk to his feet.

There'd been little hope of sleep on the eve of the enemy's arrival, but Kellert had insisted that the king try and find a few hours of rest before dawn. *Tomorrow will be a trying day*, the advisor had asserted. *Not a day that you want to be burdened by fatigue.* He'd assured Doran that the enemy was not yet in the vicinity, and that he'd be sent for immediately when they arrived. Doran had conceded, and had let himself be led to comfortable accommodations on the southeastern side of the city. But even the most comfortable chamber could not allay his troubled mind, and desperate thoughts kept his weary body from finding rest.

He'd just begun to drift off when the shouting began.

Doran was halfway to the door when Kellert burst into his chamber, breathless. "They attack from the north."

"Damnation," Doran cursed. He grabbed his sword and chased Kellert down the stone staircase that led to the street below. "What's happened so far?"

"Arrows," Kellert replied. "They're raining fire on the northern region of the city."

"Anything from the other walls?"

"Nothing, far as I know. The commanders will send a portion of their forces, as we planned, and maintain their own gates."

As they ran toward the northern wall of the city, they were joined by dozens of soldiers who'd been posted in other parts of Nahcin. Among them, Kellert and the king immediately noticed a familiar face.

"Dyrro?" Doran yelled as they ran.

Staid Dyrro turned and, seeing the king, ran to his side. "Highness!"

"You'd jump from the frying pan to the fire, no?" Doran asked.

"I have a need for retribution," he yelled back over the din around them. To the north, the screams rose into the broken night.

Doran could see the smoke and flame. He cursed. A strong wind was blowing from the west, which could only worsen the situation. The sky glowed orange over the city; a fiery dawn that preceded the natural one by a couple of hours. The attack was much earlier than expected, and while watches had been set along the city walls, none had anticipated an actual assault before sunrise. A fresh chorus of screams sounded as hellish trails of orange filled the dark sky, sailing over the walls of Nahcin to land directly in her heart.

While the flaming arrows were not as explosive as the larger fireballs that some military forces employed, the resulting damage could still be devastating. Hundreds of arrows were flying into the city. If only one in ten found a target that could be set ablaze, these fires – coupled with the increasing winds – would have the fair city burning in short time.

Doran inwardly chastised himself for not assessing the emergency water supplies more thoroughly. Yet, from his experience he'd come to see that in war there were possibilities, inevitabilities, and enough variables in between to drive one completely mad. There were so many times, in so many ways, and from so many directions that an enemy could attack. East in the day. North in the night. Fire or hurled stone; it didn't matter. The result was the same.

The battle had begun.

"There's as much stone as wood in this city, my king," said Kellert. "There'll be initial panic, fires that will be dealt with, and then the sun will rise. We'll regroup, and those cowards will see that our mettle is solid."

Doran nodded as they sped toward the north side of the city. Staid Dyrro now ran just ahead of them, looking for danger in every direction, including the sky. He held his shield ready, and Doran felt with a degree of certainty that he was positioning himself to protect the king from potential threat.

The people of Nahcin, especially those in the neighbourhoods affected by fire, were by this time pouring out into the streets of the glowing city. As the fires grew, the citizens did what they could to put out the flames. In some of the more desperate cases, soldiers stopped to lend assistance. All around them, people screamed. *Damnation!* Doran thought. *Why hadn't these citizens left days ago?* Women ran past carrying babies, the elderly hobbled from the fires as quickly as they were able, while others simply threw their hands to the sky, pleading for the Goddess to intervene. The initial panic that Kellert had mentioned was raging in full.

The king was reassured, however, to see that many of those not caught up in the firefighting had fallen in with the soldiers, running with them to the north. The city knew that this battle would be fought by every citizen that remained, whether they wore a uniform or not.

By the time they reached the wall, the assault seemed to have ended. The fields to the north were covered in a heavy silence that mocked the madness that raged within the walls of Nahcin. As Doran and Kellert reached the top of the ramparts they saw Crowlt running from the left, the wind whipping his long beard around his chin as he raged.

"Damn cowards, the lot of them!" he spat. "To come in the darkness, send a shower of arrows, and then turn on their heels and run away! Gutless!" He stopped by the king. "When they lit the last arrows, we were able to see some of them retreating back to the northeast."

"How many were there, Commander?"

"In the first group? Sixty or seventy. They sent about a dozen volleys. We fired back, with little success I fear."

Doran grunted. He stepped around Crowlt and leaned upon the stone wall, straining to see the field in the early hour, though he knew it was futile. The sun continued its slumber in the far east, oblivious to the screams and the smoke that rose on the horizon.

"My lord," Crowlt said as he placed a hand on the king's elbow and ushered him away from the parapet. "I'd prefer you didn't stand so exposed. We still don't kn–" Crowlt didn't finish. The arrow struck him in the back. Before Doran could process what was happening, he felt himself grabbed and thrown to the floor, covered by a heavy body with heavier armour. An instant later, he heard the sharp clang of an arrow striking that armour, and felt the man tense as tight as stone, before rolling over and pulling the king into the relative shelter of the rampart.

Everyone was shouting. Beside them, Crowlt collapsed. Lying on the boards, the commander's left foot twitched as though he meant to regain his feet. He made a couple of weak gurgling sounds before he lay his head on the boards and went still. From both sides soldiers appeared, forming a protective barrier around the king.

"Send a volley!" Doran roared from behind a half dozen men.

Staid turned and screamed in both directions of the wall. "Volley!" Along the wall, dozens of men notched their bows and fired into the darkness.

"Set arrows alight!" shouted Kellert. "We need to see how many are out there!"

Torches were pulled from the wall, and long boxes of fire arrows were brought forth. The defenders of Nahcin had planned to use these arrows at a later time, hoping to set the oil dampened fields alight when they were filled with the enemy. Some of the hemp tips still dripped mutton fat as they were lit and sent flying into the vast black field. In short time, small pockets of flame pin-pricked the grounds outside the wall. The light was not intense, but it served its purpose as it grew.

"There!" Kellert shouted. Doran was on his feet once more, pushing through his protectors to reach the wall. His sharp eyes picked up the movement to the northwest, and as a volley was sent in that direction, it was clear that perhaps two dozen archers had advanced after the initial assault, likely awaiting just such an occasion as Crowlt's exposed back had provided in the firelight of the city.

"Fire on them!" Doran yelled, thick veins standing out on his neck. "Flame, no flame; I don't care! Just fire!"

As the arrows of fifty archers were released, the night

sky lit up. It was, thought Doran, a sight that was as beautiful as it was deadly. He'd seen the fireshows of the alchemists in Levebule several years ago, but it did not affect him half as much as the rainbow of flame that now shot from the city. In a long sweeping arc, the arrows sailed through the stars and descended on the retreating soldiers. The silence of the field was finally broken. Cries of pain rang out as several of the Isrorians fell. Those that continued to run tripped over the bodies of their fallen comrades and the panic that tangled their heels.

"Another!" Doran ordered. "They're still in range. Another volley!" Fire burned in his eyes, and his face glowed red against the night.

This time, the light from grass fires lent the arrows accuracy, and the volley landed directly upon them. The cries of agony continued, the loudest coming from the two unfortunate archers whose clothing had been set aflame. Doran watched unmoving as the enemy burned. Behind him two soldiers were pulling Crowlt away. Kellert stepped around the soldiers and stood beside his king.

"The fire spreads," he said. "The land is dry, and the wind will fan the flames."

All upon the wall watched as the fire continued to grow, spreading out to the north and east, where presumably, the rest of the army were gathering. The grasses, while not as tall as they'd be in a month, were sufficient to maintain the flames. Doran leaned a hand on the nearest parapet and scanned the far edges of the field. As the fire spread, more of the land came to light. Like a glowing monster it crept through the grass. As it reached the height of its strength, its light was cast hundreds of feet.

It was then that Doran first saw the army.

They were so insubstantial that he questioned if he was seeing accurately, but a moment later he heard a man shout from further up the wall, followed immediately by another. Soon, a dozen men were pointing in the same direction.

"What in hell's fire is that?" a soldier to Doran's left whispered.

Doran's hand slid slowly down the parapet, and he leaned forward, his eyes straining. Silently, he urged the fire on; he needed to see what awaited him on the other side of the flames. He waited impatiently, unwilling to blink. And then, as the blaze reached the front lines and the enemy was fully illuminated, he felt the air go out of his lungs. His face contorted as his mind sought to understand what he was seeing.

Kellert moved to Doran's side, and stood, mesmerized at the sight before them.

"My lord," he whispered to his king and closest friend. "That army... it's not human."

Doran didn't turn. He stood facing the army, as though hoping it was some trick of the smoke. But while the smoke and fire shifted and moved to the east, the army did not.

The Nylacci would not.

Finally, Doran Dunarrk exhaled. Kellert knew the king well enough to hear the fear that laced his breath, causing it to tremble ever so slightly. He heard the same fear in the voice of Staid Dyrro as the trader-turned-soldier moved to the king's side and placed a hand on his forearm.

"Highness," he said. Doran felt Staid's hand grow tight, as if to prevent its shaking. "We must sound the alarms."

There would be no need. He'd no sooner spoken the words than the roar of the army tore the night sky apart. The city of Nahcin stopped and listened as an army of nightmarish creatures screamed of the doom that awaited the Rentorrians just outside their walls.

7

PROPHECY

Sivino sat silently in the moonlight, and watched as silver beams reflected upon the metal of his blade.

On the side of a steep hill, Lomin had found a location where they might wait out the night in relative shelter. Yet, they all realized that danger could lurk behind any tree or rock. Security was a thing of the past.

The trenoc dropped from a tree, and informed them that there appeared to be no danger in the immediate area. "That is not to say it doesn't exist," he continued. "The stealth of a brudog is disturbing, especially when they move at night. They blend too well with the forest."

The brudog attack was still fresh in the mind of all. In some small way, Sivino actually regretted the fact that he'd not been able to test the sword – or more rightly, to test himself. He felt that events were drawing closer to an end; at least, he hoped that was the case. It was an end he could not yet imagine, but he desired to prove himself before things came to a head. His mind raced with possible outcomes, many of them gruesome, as Lomin came to his side and seated himself beside the young man.

"How are you?" he asked in his low, rough voice.

Sivino looked toward Niamh, whose unconscious form had been made comfortable by the queen and her people. "Confused."

He nodded. "It's to be expected."

"Expected," Sivino scoffed. "Those brudogs weren't expected. This..." He held up the sword, turning it over in his hands. "This wasn't expected. It seems uncertainty is the only thing that *can* be expected these days."

Lomin leaned forward, and picked up a stick that lay at his feet. "You're right," he said as he studied the gnarled twig. "Completely right. I'd be a fool to sit here and give you a 'There there, it'll all be well' talk. In truth, I don't know that it will be." The brutal honesty, while tightening the knot in Sivino's stomach, was something of a relief. He didn't need false promises and cheery optimism right now. What he needed was someone to look him in the eye, and agree that the situation was crazy.

"But you know what?" Lomin continued as he scratched absently at the ground with the stick. "There's no one in the world I'd rather face this mess with than you folks."   Sivino snorted a little laugh as the old wolf turned to him. "Niamh, through her mysterious ways, has seen that you have a part to play here, Sivino. Of *that*, we can be certain. I've seen strength in you for as long as I've known you. And I've seen it grow. It does not, in any way, surprise me that you would fulfill this role. And fulfill it you will, I have no doubt." He patted his young friend on the leg, and rose. "Try to get some sleep. We have a long day tomorrow."

Sivino nodded as Lomin moved away to check on Niamh.

"Lomin?"

The old wolf turned.

"Thank you."

He nodded, and made his way to the faerae.

Sivino looked around the camp as his companions slowly, apprehensively settled in for the night. He began to sheath his sword, thought better of it, and lay it beneath his cloak, the intricate carved hilt held firm in his hand.

It was still dark when Niamh awakened.

She did so slowly, but was able to gain her feet unassisted. She scanned the camp, and noticing Drip's absence, spotted him atop the trees above. He sat unmoving, watching her as she steadied herself. She gave a slight nod in his direction. After a moment, the trenoc returned the gesture. Niamh drank from a nearby waterskin, and then disappeared quietly into the forest. Hours passed before she finally returned and sat in the silent company of the trenoc as they waited for the sun to rise.

There was great relief when the group saw the faerae up and about. Sivino watched as Lomin quickly made his way to her side, and the pair shared quiet words. They spoke for several minutes, but try as he might, he was unable to hear any of what they said. A couple of times, Sivino saw Lomin shrug his shoulders, and a distressed look was apparent on his face. Before the conversation ended though, he nodded sadly, and his shoulders sunk.

The faerae approached Sivino who, having finished breaking camp with the others, waited anxiously to hear what the faerae had to say.

"We'll set out shortly," she said to the group. "But before we do, Sivino, I wonder if you'd take a walk with me."

She walked ahead of, rather than beside, the young man as she led him through the forest.

He knew better than to press her with questions. She would speak when she was ready. After a few minutes, she stopped in a clearing. Without turning around, she spoke.

"The path is difficult, is it not?"

He knew that she was not talking about the mossy trail they'd just traversed.

"It is."

The sun glittered on the dew of the leaves, adding a small magic to the clearing and the faerae that stood at its center. She turned to face him.

"You spoke with Dahnu." It wasn't a question.

He was about to ask how she knew, but realized how foolish the question would sound. He nodded. "She gave me this," he said, indicating the sword.

Niamh reached out and took the sword. She didn't study it. She simply looked at it with a casual interest.

"She told you what you were to do with it." Again, a statement.

"She spoke in riddles. I didn't share with the others all of what she said. Nor did I say that it was Dahnu that I met." He shook his head. "Niamh, it was the *Goddess*. How in Creation does a simple Egimian come to speak with a Goddess?"

The faerae's smile was so small that none but the most observant would have noticed. Sivino, however, also noticed that it was a smile tainted by sadness. "You, Sivino Spallic, are not a simple Egimian."

"Perhaps the time has come for you to elaborate a little." He paused. "If it pleases you." He was keenly aware that this was as direct as he'd ever been with Niamh, and the faerae seemed to appreciate it.

"Yes," she said. "The time has come. Did Dahnu speak of the Shepherd?"

His eyes widened momentarily, before narrowing. "She did."

Niamh did not speak. He realized that she simply waited for him to continue.

"She told me, essentially, that this wasn't going to end until his blood was on my blade. Niamh, who is he?"

The silence of the clearing hung so long that Sivino wondered if she'd heard. Finally, she spoke.

"You are special, Sivino. More special than you know. There is a connection between your kin and the race of faerae that has existed for generations. It is, indeed, the reason that you find me in your midst. What Dahnu shared with you is the prophecy that brought me here. I would see it fulfilled – would see you fulfill it. In doing so, I protect you to the extent that I can." She paused, studying his features. "Just as I protected your mother."

"My mother?" Sivino took a step forward. "What does my mother have to do with this?"

"I protected her, just as I protect you. I knew that the child she'd bear would be important." She folded her hands before her. "The prophecy."

"Yes, the prophecy. You've mentioned it, Niamh. *Creation*, the Goddess mentioned it." The frustration crept into his voice, which he raised as he spoke. "I still have no bloody idea what it is I'm supposed to do."

The faerae was undaunted by his anger, her face unchanging.

"You are destined to use your blade when you encounter the Shepherd, as the Goddess told you. As the prophecy foretells."

"Damnation, Niamh! I don't even know who the Shepherd is. How am I supposed to find him?"

Niamh turned to the south. "We'll follow the smoke."

"Smoke?"

"While you slept this morning, I ventured out to see what I could. I travelled quite a distance in fact; far enough to see the smoke. It rises over Nahcin." She turned back to him. "That is where we are headed. That is where we'll find the Shepherd."

Sivino fully realized how sharp he was being with the faerae, but he didn't care. He was sick of the riddles. He was sick of the confusion that surrounded his role in this drama. Sick of the unanswered questions. He inhaled deeply through his nose, trying to relax as he let it out.

"Niamh. Who is the Shepherd?"

The trace of sadness he'd noticed earlier was now fully apparent. He could tell that she was reluctant to share what she was about to tell him. But the time, as he'd told her, had come, and she knew it well.

"Sivino. The Shepherd is the leader of the Nylacci."

8

NEVER ENOUGH

We do what we must.

The words echoed faintly in Doran's head. It had been years since he'd heard them spoken, lifetimes since he'd held the strong hand of the man who'd uttered them.

His father had died at the enviable age of seventy-five. Wilkren Dunarrk had lived a life of wonderful health, which was fortunate, as he'd needed every advantage to see his realm through many difficult years. Wilkren's father, Jorg, had been broken at the age of forty in the Battle of the Cliff. It was the only time in Rentorrian history that saw the Kourg – the great savages who resided east of the Cudgels – leave Central Cahruia and venture into the Three Realms with large numbers and hostile motivations. Why they'd bypassed Isror remained a mystery, though theories were whispered for many years afterward. It was on his deathbed, months after the battle, that Jorg had told his eleven-year-old son, the soon to be king of Rentorria, that a wall was to be built around the capital city of Orshos and every major city in the realm. *Never again*, he'd said, shall an enemy walk unimpeded to the very heart of our home. When the good king passed, it fell upon his son, Wilkren, to see that his father's final wish was realized.

There is nothing more important than protecting that which you love, Wilkren had told a young Doran as they stood atop the wall, years later. It was on the wall that Wilkren imparted what wisdom he had to the lad, preparing him for a role few are ever ready to face. *When you're the protector of many, as you'll one day be, you will be faced with difficult choices. My father Jorg burnt an entire fleet of our vessels in the Battle of the Cliff after the Kourg overtook the docks. Imagine, a Rentorrian king ordering the boats – the lifeline of our people – to be set aflame! I'm sure the fact that the women and children of Orshos stood vulnerable on the little island of Solla loomed large in his reasoning, but the decision must have been difficult nonetheless. It's what being a king is all about, Son; making choices that you don't want to make. Making the choices that must be made.*

The young boy had looked at his father. *But how will I know what decisions are right? How can anyone know?*

King Wilkren had leaned heavily on the wall at the comment, and watched as distant seagulls streaked over the city toward the boats that preceded the setting sun to the shore. The ocean shone the colour of blood as he entwined his fingers, looking at scars whose sources were long forgotten.

It's not necessarily about knowing what is right in every circumstance, Doran. He'd turned to the boy. *When the time comes, we do what we must.*

Doran Dunarrk knew that Nahcin would fall. It was inevitable. The army that awaited the sun outside the walls of the city was more massive than any that had ever marred the earth of Western Cahruia. The Kourg, those great brutes that had pillaged and burned their way across the realm so many years ago could not even compare to this sea of fury.

To the south, the Nahcinians heeded the king's order and raced to get the remaining women and children into the boats on the Madimest and down the River Eridanos, or at least onto the relative safety of the far shore. How safe the shore would prove to be was unknown.

We do what we must.

Hundreds of creatures had been illuminated in the light of the hungry flames, but the rising sun had exposed a sight that froze the blood of Nahcin's defenders. A host of thousands covered the northern fields that had been blackened by the fire. They stood waiting, these beasts – waiting for the order to march forth and eat this city alive. *Who*, Doran thought, *could hold authority over such a force? Surely not Idach. That coward, however imposing he may seem to his own people, could not control the seething rage that was evident in the roars of these creatures.* They yearned for release, beating the ground with greataxes and black swords, working themselves into a frenzy as they leaned forward, fists clenched and teeth bared. The sun had barely crested the hill and exposed the enemy before the evacuation was begun.

Three main battalions were set in strategic locations. The largest of these stood ready on the northern wall, waiting with dread anticipation for the beasts to move. Two slightly smaller contingents would defend the eastern and western corners of the city where it met the river. The dark army, Doran thought, was sure to try and force its way through the north wall to gain access to the city. Yet, there was also the possibility that the enemy could skirt Nahcin's edges and gain access to the city at the points where it met the river. Their access would be devastating enough. What would make it doubly so was that the evacuation of Nahcin's vulnerable would be cut short in a most gruesome manner.

Doran looked to his side, and watched as Kellert's narrow eyes surveyed the enemy. Occasionally the advisor shook his head, but for the most part, he just watched the beasts with equal parts confusion and worry. He knew, as all did, that the city would fall. The walls of Nahcin were significantly shorter than those that surrounded Orshos, and the number of armed defenders was but a fraction of the host that paced in the distance. He knew there'd be more fleeing than fighting on this day.

Beside Kellert, Staid stood motionless. Doran could only imagine what was going through the young man's mind. To see what he had seen, and be fortunate enough to escape that fate, only to find himself back in the creatures' midst days later. The spy was possibly the only man to see their savagery up close and live to tell the tale. Staid had seen the blood that dripped from their blade-like teeth; had smelt their repulsive stench. The fact that the soldier had thrown himself back onto the frontlines, Doran thought, was nothing short of admirable.

Doran turned his back to the army, and leaned against a catapult that had been hastily erected in the days prior. Like the wall, the weapons were not of a quality to match those in the capital. Though they were certain to inflict death on the enemy, the king now knew it would likely not be enough to stay the advance in any significant way.

To the south, he could see the water and the boats that carried the residents away from the doomed city. Many of the boats, loaded beyond capacity, floated low in the water. He glanced to his west. How long, he thought, before the enemy noticed the fleeing Nahcinians? Would they rush the lake, or would they maintain focus on those still remaining in the city? He prayed it was the latter as he watched Nahcin's people quietly put their oars to the water. Doran leaned forward, muttering a curse. Several individuals were in the water, clinging desperately to the boats that could not hold them. People would drown today, he was certain. In the frantic effort to escape death at the hands of these unknown creatures, many of Nahcin's people would sink to a different demise. Old Grim did not care by what means people came to Him, Doran thought with disgust, for His arms were long and his embrace ever widening.

"Damnation," he muttered.

Kellert glanced in his direction. After the plan had been put in place and orders executed, the advisor had grown quieter than Doran had ever seen. Good men surrounded him, Doran realized, but even the best men, the most courageous, did not know what to think of this threat. Kellert had had the presence of mind before the evacuation had begun in full to send a small group of riders out the western gate to ride to Orshos and warn them of the force that would soon march upon the capital. Now, there was little left to do but empty the city of as many citizens as possible and wait for the battle to begin. The sun had passed behind a mass of growing clouds, casting a shadow on the land. The chill that accompanied its absence was deepened by the despair that was felt by every man, woman and child that wondered if this day would be their last. Doran pushed aside the hair that blew before his face, and was about to inspect the counterweight arm of the catapult when he heard Kellert speak beside him.

"There."

He moved to Kellert's side, his eyes following the pointing finger. In the distance, on the eastern fringes of the army, a rider made his way through the mass of lumbering bodies. So tall were the surrounding beasts that this newcomer was not immediately noticed. However, when the army parted to create a path for the rider who rode leisurely through their ranks, he could not be missed. He appeared to be a man of average build and height, though the stallion he rode was one that would dwarf the majority of those in the Rentorrian cavalry. The rider was hooded and cloaked in black. As he made his way through the army that he presumably commanded, a great roar rose from the beasts. Soon they were howling, screaming as they beat their swords against shield and helm. The rider instilled bedlam as he rode in their midst. Looking neither left nor right, he sat motionless, his hidden gaze bent on the city that rose before him.

"That's him," Staid whispered, loud enough for only Doran and Kellert to hear.

On the wall, no one else spoke as the rider made his way to the front of the enemy line. From somewhere behind him, Doran heard the whimper of a young man – likely one of the strapping lads that had been recruited in recent days to load the catapult, but had never seen a day of actual combat. It was a sound that could only be made by one who'd lost all hope. He turned briefly, and looked at the faces along the northern wall. There were seasoned men and women, to be sure, but there were also a number of people – some of them boys – who were here simply because there was a need for every able-bodied person in the city to help hold the wall. While the vulnerable had been ushered to the lake, those remaining were delegated soldier responsibilities they never dreamed they'd have to fulfill; readying the pitch and fat, shaping the throwing spears, and preparing the projectiles for the catapults. Others moved to the southern end of the city, helping to send the citizens across the Madimest where at least a slim hope of survival remained. In this waking nightmare, the people of Nahcin simply did what they were told.

They did what they had to do.

"He leads them," Doran said to Kellert.

"An unlikely leader," the advisor replied.

"An unlikely army. Still no sign of the Isrorians?"

"None."

Doran rubbed his neck. "Can these creatures truly be allied with Idach?" He spoke up to be heard over the din rising from the beasts. "How in hell's fire could anyone form an allegiance with a savagery as unspeakable as this?"

Kellert shook his head. "In wartime, what constitutes 'savagery' is a matter of opinion."

Doran let the words hang in the air, and continued to watch the lone rider. He'd stopped before the host, unmoving as he looked to Nahcin. Just when it seemed the madness of the creatures had reached its pinnacle, the rider slowly took his right hand from the reins and held it to his side. The roar that came from the beasts shook the earth on which they stood.

His hand fell, and the dam burst. The Nylacci crashed forward, surging around the rider as raging river water around a solid, enduring stone.

"Make ready!" Doran screamed. Yet he knew that the walls were not built to repel such a force. What they must do, he now realized, was slow the tide enough that the majority of his people could escape. Death rushed toward them, and he shook his head.

Not enough, he thought. *It's never enough.*

The fair city of Nahcin was about to be flooded.

9

LITTLE CHOICE

"We will go to Orshos."

Daurr stood before the fountains of the Drale deities, watching the water flow. Dels turned. He'd been watching Patua Cor apply a poultice to young Karm Naphor's arm after being given some needed herbs and supplies by one of the Drales. Looking now at Daurr, he could not help but feel dwarfed by the enormity of the creature before him. His stoic, deathly white face was unmoving. At his sides, his massive fists were clenched.

"We will go to Orshos," he repeated. "The force that has allied itself with the treachery of Isror is great, and will sweep across all the lands if not stopped." He gave a look to several of the Drales that stood in the shadows of the city. They were as tall as the others of their kind, though a little thinner and slightly stooped. "The Wise Ones speak truly. Unjustified destruction is unacceptable. It is an insult to the Good Mother and the Just Father. Wasteful slaughter. It is needless. And we can be certain that the hunger of this threat will not be sated." He inclined his head, looking over the walls of his city. "They will come to Ras. Sooner. Later. They will come. And they will come in numbers that will be difficult to repel. The First Child said it would be so." With the memory of Dels' earlier reaction, Daurr looked in the direction of the Egimian. "Do *you* believe it is so, small man?"

Dels, with Leath and Dahlah by his side, opened his mouth to speak. However, he was cut off by a voice that arose from behind them all. A voice that, though lithe, was strong and confident.

"I'm certain he does."

They turned as one to see the creature. He sat on the ground by the edge of the fountain, his back resting against the haphazard rock base that rose around him. He was small, perhaps a head smaller than the average man; several smaller than the average Drale. One leg stretched out on the ground, the other was pulled up to his chest. His thin fingers were joined loosely about his knee. Even in the pale light, the streak of green hair upon his head was unmistakable. The subtle point of his ears was barely visible beneath the waves of blond that fell to his shoulders.

"In fact, I'd wager there are few who believe as strongly as this fellow."

The faerae stood up, and made his way toward Dels. Hushed whispers arose, but evaporated as the creature approached.

"My name is Tryn," the faerae said. "I'm an infrequent visitor to Cahruia, though some of my kin have spent a fair amount of time here, relatively speaking."

Dels put forth his hand. "Dels Spallic," he said with a nod. He realized then that his nod was almost reverential. He gestured over his shoulder. "These are my people."

"I'm aware," Tryn replied. "I'm also aware that you have had encounters with the Nylacci, and managed to survive nonetheless."

A short pause. "Loved ones fell," Dels said, his face growing a little harder.

"Yes, they did," Tryn replied. He inclined his head, and his eyes narrowed as if he were studying the sunset. He took a short breath, and exhaled slowly. "Let us hope their sacrifice will help serve the greater purpose." He turned to Daurr, and then glanced in the direction of the elder Drales. "You've come to a consensus?"

"We have little choice," Daurr replied, his voice kinder by several degrees as he addressed the faerae. "We believe the Just Father will see that things are set right."

"The Just Father, among others." Tryn joined his hands behind his back, and walked amongst the people. The Egimians pulled back instinctively, allowing the faerae space to move about. "There are things at work here that are more complicated than armies and falling cities. Yet, you all play a role, and I would ask your help. It pains me to say that a faerae is responsible for this madness." His lips tightened slightly at this point, and a hint of disgust crossed his face. "Cehron Cen Kohr, once highly respected in the world of Elysium, is now afflicted with an insanity that none could have predicted. It would appear that he is the one behind all of this; bringing the Nylacci into your world, and allying them with the forces of Isror. It's likely that he's been whispering in King Idach's ear for some time now." He noted the surprise on the face of the Egimians, and nodded. "It is my business to know things," he said. He moved back toward Dels, and spoke to him directly. "The Drales will move toward Orshos. Nahcin will fall. A massive army of Nylacci marches now on the city, and it will be razed to the ground. Tomorrow. The day after, perhaps. I can't say for certain, but fall it will, and horribly. The army will then head to the capital. They will likely be joined by a host of Isrorians." The faerae looked up at Daurr, who stood close by. "Your assistance will be welcomed, you can be sure."

"And what of us?" Leath spoke up. "We can't stand idly by while this happens."

"Nor should you," Tryn replied. "I've been tasked with asking for your assistance as well. A friend of mine requested that I come here; to enlist the Drales–" He gave a respectful nod to Daurr, which was promptly returned. "–but to also send a small group of your people south." He paused. "It is my understanding that there are young ones you wish back in your fold."

And then, everyone was shouting. Gasps of shock and cries of joy rose into the evening air. From the group, Stellen and Fallette Tros rushed forward, as did Lumb Velto, laughing as he raised his hands above his head. Sianah threw her arms around Leath, as Dels turned to Dahlah. Unable to control her emotion, she began to sob, shaking as Dels wrapped an arm around her.

"Where are they?" Fallette cried. She released Stellen's arm, and moved toward the faerae. A moment later, Tryn found himself within a tight circle of Egimians.

"Please," Dahlah pleaded, struggling to find her voice. "Please, where are they?"

Tryn hesitated. It was a hesitation that, to Dels' mind, was not done for effect, or out of confusion. The faerae, it seemed, kept the answer from them because it was one they'd not want to hear.

"That, my friends, is the issue." Even the Drales moved closer to hear the faerae speak to the group surrounding him. "Nahcin," Tryn said quietly. "They're heading to Nahcin."

10

SO MUCH BLOOD

"Nahcin?" Torla's voice was a hiss.

She immediately stopped poking the cookfire she tended, and stood to full height. A small burst of embers rose from the flames, mixing with the heady scent of tea that hung on the air.

"Why," she said quietly, turning to look directly at the faerae, "would we want to go to Nahcin?"

Sivino looked from Torla to Niamh. Inlonia Talchol moved past Torla, resting her hand on the girl's shoulder for a brief moment as she approached the faerae. In the short time that the queen had been in their midst, Sivino and the others had grown comfortable in her presence. Though there was still an air of reverence in the way they addressed their liege, the sense of awe had lessened somewhat.

"Niamh," Inlonia spoke calmly. Through all the tension, Sivino noticed, the queen composed herself with quiet dignity and repose. "I would hope you know how deeply I trust your instinct, and the knowledge you possess." The faerae nodded as the queen continued. "But I must echo Torla's question. My mission since leaving Levebule has been to reach the capital city of Orshos, to work with King Dunarrk and offer my support to the Embarrian soldiers we've sent south. I need to be with my people, to the bitter end."

Niamh moved a few steps to her left, and half sat, half leaned on a large rock. Her arms were wrapped around herself in a manner that suggested she was cold. Sivino watched her, wondering if the Fae experienced temperature as most people did. It was evident to him that she was suffering. To what extent, he couldn't be certain.

"I am aware of your plans, Queen Talchol, and I'd not interfere with them." Niamh adjusted her weight on the rock as she spoke. "I agree that there's no more appropriate place for you right now than Orshos. It's the young ones that I would have accompany me."

Torla could hold her frustration no longer. "What makes you think, Niamh, that we'd accompany you without question?"

"Torla, please." Lomin stepped up beside the girl, and put a hand on her arm. Torla shrugged it off roughly, unwilling to be silenced.

"No, Lomin. *No*. I'm sick of being led down the winding path, no idea where we're going, what we're doing, or why. *Why*, Lomin? Tell me. Why are we doing this?"

"The prophecy," said Niamh.

Torla turned on the faerae. "The prophecy." She looked about to spit. "This prophecy which we know so little about? You may be privy to divine messages, Niamh, but we are sheep; innocent, ignorant sheep being led to a Shepherd that has no intention of doing us well. Lambs to the slaughter are what we are. Does the prophecy see us all dead?" She shook her head, rubbing her forehead as she scoffed a bitter laugh.

Niamh looked eastward, as though her attention was caught by the wind rising over the plains. She looked at none as she spoke.

"I received messages; visions from the Faant. I've seen you all, standing in the ruins of the fallen city. I've seen the Shepherd, his eyes shining with malice. And I've seen hope on the horizon."

"Hope on the horizon," Torla muttered. "Were you a poet in your long-forgotten youth?"

"Torla!" Sivino spoke with an authority that surprised all gathered. This was not the boy who had set out from the village days ago. This was not the boy who had accepted ill-treatment from his older brother, nor the boy who second-guessed his ability to face a challenge, or avoided confrontation. He moved toward Torla, his hand on the hilt of his sword – not in a threatening manner, but more as though to draw confidence from the blade at his side. "Torla, we've been down this road. I wish, as I'm sure you do, that we could retrace our steps, and head back the way we came. But I can't do that. Our future, whatever it will be, does not lie in the past." He looked at his friends. Drip watched him, unmoving beside Lomin. "I'm not certain of what will happen. I'm not certain of anything, really, except that what's happened, what's been given to me, was given for a reason. This sword, these companions–" He swept his eyes over all around him. "And our guide. There is reason in all of this. I can't see it, but I can feel it. I'll take the path before me, and trust where it leads."

"You sound like Kolle," said Torla.

It was then that Sivino saw the truth. Torla felt that they were slowly heading toward the same fate as her older brother, who'd fallen victim to the war, wounding his sister in a way that none could see or fully appreciate.

Kef moved to his sister's side. For a moment, it looked as though she was going to push him away. Knowing Torla as he did, Sivino knew that she feared falling apart if she was touched, as she sometimes did in those rare instances of vulnerability. Yet, she let Kef approach her and kept herself together as he put an arm around her. Tears welled in her eyes, but she kept her lips in a tight line and narrowed her eyes in an effort to stay the flood of emotion that longed to break through.

"You don't have to go, Tor," said Sivino. "You know that I wouldn't ask this of–"

"You know that you wouldn't *have* to ask," she interjected. "And you know the answer already. Damn it all, Sivino. You know that we do this together. All of us. It's just…" She paused, searching for the words.

"It's just bloody hard," said the queen. She walked over and placed a hand on each of Torla's cheeks. A softness crossed Torla's face. The queen, with a simple touch, gave the girl the maternal support she so desperately needed at that moment. "Our realm has never faced a challenge such as this, and it is my hope that it never will again. I wish I could offer you all the reassurance in the world, Torla. But I can't." She smiled, and wiped Torla's tears from her cheeks. "When all this began, I wrote to King Dunarrk and asked if the forces of Rentorria could repel the invasion of Isror. *What*, I asked him, *was he doing to fortify the cities? What was he doing to protect the people?* He, of course, read between the lines, and saw what I was really asking – *Do I need to send the forces of Embarria to fight a war in the south?* His response was brief, and to the point – *We do what we must.* Sometimes, my dear Torla, that's all we can do."

"I know," Torla whispered. "I just wish there was another way."

"Your desire to protect those you love is admirable," said Inlonia. "I know too well that your hesitance to go south is not born of a fear for your own wellbeing." She looked at the people around them. "It is good company you keep, Torla Rallo. They may be tired, confused, and in desperate need of bathing, but so are we all." She smiled at this, and was relieved to see Torla do the same. "And you have a wonderful guide," she added. Niamh's expression did not change in the least as she listened to the queen. There was an emptiness to her face that caused Sivino concern. "Trust Niamh," Inlonia said. "More than anyone in this world, she knows what needs to be done."

Torla sighed, and quickly wiped the last remnants of tears from her face. She looked at her brother and friends. These boys – though they could hardly be called boys anymore – were her whole life. She knew that Sivino would follow Niamh, and she knew as well that she and the others would follow him into the flames of Hell itself if need be.

"I guess this is goodbye then," Torla said to the queen.

Inlonia shook her head with a smile, and drew Torla into a quick embrace. "Not at all," she said. "I'll see you in Orshos…"

With the farewells bade and the camp packed once more, the group stood and watched the queen and her company ride west. On horseback, they would likely reach Orshos within two days. For a force on foot, it would take several days to journey from Nahcin to Orshos, so the queen should have plenty of time. The unasked question, the one that was on the mind of everyone, was how many Rentorrians had actually been able to escape the besieged city and flee to the capital. When Niamh and Sivino had returned from their walk, Niamh had shared with the group what she'd seen. Smoke rose in thick black plumes from the lakeside city. A dark mass surrounded the area. Niamh did not get close enough to determine numbers or the nature of the force, though she knew well that the city not would stand against such evil.

Yet, it was an evil into which she knew they must venture. The indefinite, complex visions shared by the Faant did not lay out a clear picture of future events, and were by no means an assurance of how things would turn out. They were, Niamh knew, a glimpse of what would be required for events to reach their culmination.

She watched as Ston reached to help Drip secure a saddle. The trenoc smacked his hand away with a curse. As the young man turned from the trenoc, a wicked smile flickered on his face, and he gave Kef a quick nod and wink. Kef returned the gesture.

In the midst of all this, Niamh thought, they did not lose their true selves. They did not lose their playful innocence, or, in spite of the odds stacked against them, their hope. It was this resilience, and this enduring spirit, that slowed the ever-widening void that Niamh felt growing within herself.

But the *visions*. Those prophetic whispers. She couldn't get them out of her head. She'd carried them with her for some time now, ever present in the forefront of her mind. When she slept, as infrequent as that was, her dreams morphed the visions into nightmares that tore her from her slumber, leaving her cold and unsteady.

Lomin and Sivino leaned close to one another, the older man speaking quietly to the boy, a thin hand resting on Sivino's shoulder. Niamh wondered if she could have done this without Lomin. Indeed, they all played their role. They were distinct parts of a cohesive body. Lomin, the head. Ston and Torla, the legs that moved them forward. Kef and Tonnis, the hands that gave a reassuring pat on the shoulder to those that needed such. Drip, the instinctual gut. And Sivino. Sivino was the heart. It was this realization that concerned Niamh most. Hearts, she knew, were all too easily broken.

Having readied themselves and mounted their horses, the group moved to Niamh's side. She sat upon a mare, grey with flecks of white, and gently pulled the reins in, causing the animal to back up slowly. Raising one hand, she indicated the path ahead. "I'll take up the rear this time," she said quietly. "Go ahead."

Inwardly, she breathed a sigh of relief as Sivino moved forward. He didn't hesitate. Though Niamh had addressed them all, it was Sivino that had taken the initiative to lead them. She couldn't help but feel some satisfaction for the fact that the others seemed to have waited for him to step to the forefront.

This boy, Niamh thought. What would become of him? And again, the visions that haunted her so came rushing back.

This boy. Standing in the shadow of a dead city. Bodies lay all around him, strewn across the cobbled stones, floating in the lake. Smoke continues to rise all around him. He stands, horror and uncertainty plain on his face.

In his hand, the brilliant sword hangs limp.

On the street around him, his loved ones lay fallen.

Before him stand those they've dreaded most; malicious smiles twisting their evil faces.

Niamh shudders, as she knows this will come to pass. This will happen. Must happen. Yet, it's what will happen *after* this that terrifies her most. It is an aftermath that not even she has glimpsed.

The boy in the vision looks to the ground beneath him. Blood. So much blood.

11

BREACH

The ground shook as the beasts raced toward Nahcin.

Within the city, descriptions of the approaching army had spread like wildfire, and the flames of terror had been fanned to the point that Nahcin fell into utter chaos. The evacuation degenerated into madness as the Nahcinians rushed toward what now appeared to be the only option for survival. The screams that rose from the lake echoed those that came from within the city walls. From their posts atop these walls, the soldiers were helpless to do anything for the dying citizens. They watched, agonizing, as their families and friends sank in the deep waters of the Madimest. Within the city, a similar disorder permeated every alley and side street as Nahcinians fled the northern gate. Narrow streets to the south saw residents trampled as the surge of bodies bottlenecked in several locations. This city, known for its grace and civility, its ingenuity and order, now descended into disarray the likes of which had never been seen within its proud stone walls.

Though Doran Dunarrk did not take his eyes from the

charging army, his ears heard the city falling apart.

Over a thousand beasts now rushed toward Nahcin. Within their midst, the hooded rider stood still on the field as the Nylacci rushed past him. His black robes flapped with their passage. Though his face was covered, Doran knew that he was not one of their kind. He was human, and if these beasts were able to ally themselves with humans, the king knew also that there was but one population in the Three Realms that would lower themselves to create such a partnership.

Yet, there was no sign of the Isrorians. It would not surprise Doran to learn that Idach had formed this alliance, and then devised a scheme that would see these monsters do the dirty work. He looked away momentarily, and jumped onto a wooden barrel that stood nearby. To his side, Kellert twisted toward him, ever ready to protect his king. Doran gave a quick nod to his friend, and stood upon the parapet, looking down the length of the wall. Fear masked the face of nearly every man and woman that stood on the city's edge. It was well founded, Doran knew, because this was not a force that his people would resist. But what they could do, he realized, was fight with a savagery that rivalled that of the beasts, and in doing so, allow as many of the city's people to escape across the lake. He turned, allowing himself a glance toward Lake Madimest, and the Eridanos beyond. Though the distance was great, he believed he could see the bodies that now floated upon the current. The king cursed and turned back to the enemy.

"They are almost within range," he shouted to his soldiers. "We will hold them back, and allow our own to escape. For the love of our realm and its people, let us show these creatures that our walls will not crumble easily, and those that guard them stand just as solid!"

The arrows of the defenders were nocked, and though some hands were steadier than others, each and every one of them was eager to begin the assault. In short moments, the opportunity arrived.

"Now!" Doran roared.

The air hummed with the missiles, and those upon the wall felt no small sense of satisfaction when the first group of beasts began to fall.

"Catapults!" Doran cried as he fired his own arrow. The beasts' numbers were so great that they stormed the wall as a single, massive body, making virtually every shot a successful one. However, he noted with horror that many of the creatures that were struck by the arrows continued to run as if stung by a simple bumbled bee. *Creation!* he thought. *Where in hell's depths did these beasts come from?* There was little doubt that the monsters had allied themselves with Idach, and from the report he'd received from Dyrro, this allegiance and subsequent attack was likely planned for some time. While Doran considered himself an intelligent man, he knew that his knowledge of the world outside the Realms was limited. But never, never had he heard of such vile creatures. The Kourg were bad enough. These beasts were unnatural, plain and simple.

The sharp snap of a catapult caused him to jerk instinctively, as the bucket of the structure sent its payload into the midst of the attackers. Each bucket held several rocks, each about the size of a man's head. He watched with satisfaction as the stones flew through the air, separating slightly as they did. All were lethal, bringing down a number of the filthy creatures in bloody heaps. Yet the damage, Doran realized, was not great enough.

"The pitch," he shouted to those behind him. "We need the pitch!"

"It's ready!" Kellert shouted as he rushed past his king. While the archers on the wall had made ready to attack, Kellert had been busy ensuring that pots of pitch were being boiled to scalding temperatures. On platforms below each of the six catapults, huge pots had been brought to a bubbling frenzy.

Along the wall, soldiers echoed his command, calling for the pitch. Specially constructed pots had been carefully filled and sealed with wooden lids, which had been tapped into place with mallets. Soldiers quickly slid poles though the handles and hoisted them into the catapult buckets. As Doran rushed to the nearest catapult to lend his assistance, the first Nylacci arrows fell among them.

Screams could be heard all along the wall, and beyond. The range of the bows was staggering, as the long black missiles flew over the crouching soldiers and into the city behind them. While most of the citizens had fled the northern section of Nahcin for the lake, a number remained. The arrows rained down on the residents, drawing forth screams of terror and pain.

"The pitch!" Doran cried again.

On the structure next to him the tension rope was released and the long arm shot forth, sending the pot soaring into the masses below. He instantly heard Kellert screaming for the fire arrows. In seconds, soldiers were rushing the wall's edge, their arrows aflame, seeking the locations that the pitch had landed. As they fired, an overwhelming deluge of black arrows landed among them, and several defenders were struck. Along the length of the wall, soldiers fell. Dull thuds could be heard as the arrows embedded themselves in the wooden catapults and platforms below. Crouched by a murder hole in the wall, Doran could see that the creatures were almost upon them. The pitch, and the arrows of his people, were entirely inadequate. The numbers and the strength of the enemy were just too great. In the distance, he suddenly noticed the hooded rider. It appeared that the man on the horse had not stirred an inch since the attack had begun. He watched, unmoving, as the horror unfolded, his gaze seeming to be directed toward the western plains, or possibly, the distant city of Orshos. Though Doran could not see his face, he could feel the cold indifference of the rider, and suppressed a shudder.

And then, the beasts were at the wall. Their roar was deafening. The massive structure shook with their impact. "Creation!" Doran screamed as Kellert scrambled to his side. "They must be crushing each other against the base!"

Before Doran could stop him, Kellert sprang to his feet and took a quick look at what was happening. He fell beside Doran an instant later, terror evident on his face.

"They're doing just that!" he yelled. "Falling in heaps at the base of the wall, climbing upon each other to reach the top!" He stood in a crouch, and grabbed the king, pulling him to his feet. "They will breach! We must get to the lake!"

The king looked around him, saw the terror and devastation of his people, and knew that there was no other option.

"To the lake!" he screamed. "Throw the pitch over the wall and flee!"

He bounded down the steps, urged from behind by Kellert. Glancing to his side, he saw that the soldiers remained upon the wall. Pride and horror rose in him simultaneously. He knew for certain that these men were sacrificing their lives to give him, and their countrymen, time to escape. He knew as well that they would die in the effort.

Immediately behind Kellert, Doran saw Staid emerge from the crowd and rush toward the king. Since he'd first encountered the fellow on the street that morning, it seemed the trader was going out of his way to stay near the king; to protect him. He ran with his shield held ready, as he had before, and the morning sun shone madly upon its metal, as if the very light would fend off the black arrows.

When they'd descended the two flights of stairs, he saw fully the bedlam that was now Nahcin. In every direction, smoke rose from buildings, filling the air as heavily as the screams that enshrouded the lakeside city. Most had vacated the northern part of the city, but a sizeable number of soldiers and a few residents determined to help could still be seen. He could see in their faces that most knew that running was futile. The people ran past the bodies of their countrymen and women, folk who'd been trampled or impaled by black arrows. Terror. Desperation. He heard the sobbing of a soldier somewhere nearby, a sound heavy with a pain he couldn't imagine.

"Go!" Kellert urged.

They ran, soldiers and common folk flanking both sides. Doran was amazed to see these people form a protective horseshoe around him. Even in this devastation, his people still put his wellbeing above their own.

Atop the eastern wall, he could see soldiers running past the parapets, firing out on the creatures that must be making their way to the waterfront. Well over a hundred people now ran beside their king, bows and swords still held firm in their hands. They'd passed down several streets and side alleys, alternating their route whenever fire obstructed their path, when the shout made its way to his ears.

"They've breached the wall!"

Instantly, he stopped and spun as the soldiers did the same. They could hear the roar of the beasts pursuing them, a dreadful sound that echoed through the buildings and along the cobbled streets.

"We'll hold them, Sire!" shouted a young man as he shouldered past the king. "The streets will narrow their advance!" He withdrew his sword and looked back over his shoulder, though the look was directed at Kellert rather than Doran. "Go," he said simply, and then turned and ran.

Kellert was not going to have any argument. With rough hands he grabbed the king and shoved him in the direction of the lake.

"Damn it all!" Doran screamed. Behind him, the roars grew louder.

The minutes seemed to pass like hours as they ran through the city. Nahcinians ran around them still, as did soldiers who were determined to see their king safely to the river. Doran felt his heart sink as he saw several people dart inside nearby homes, slamming doors, hoping to bar out the evil that had entered the city.

When they finally arrived at the waterfront, the scene was one of pure chaos. People spilled into the river. The water frothed with desperation. No vessels could be seen. It was only a matter of time, Doran knew, before the beasts arrived at the water, and the slaughter would be complete. He'd hoped that he'd be able to help with the evacuation, but realized immediately that there would be no order here. Nahcin poured itself into the lake, and let itself be carried away to its fate.

"This way," Kellert shouted over the din.

He took Doran's wrist and pulled him through the crowd, making for the far eastern corner of the waterfront. Some of the people made way when they saw who he was, but most were lost to even themselves, unable to see through their own tears and terror.

"There!" Kellert pointed to a small shack at the very edge of the quay. In front of the flaking red door stood two men. In spite of all that was transpiring around them, the men did not move. They were, Doran realized, watching him approach. Waiting.

"The commanders secured an escape for you, in the event that things went to hell," Kellert said. As they neared the shack, one of the men nodded in their direction and pulled the door open. The other went to the side facing the water, where a larger door was unlatched. It was quickly pulled open as well, and a dory was pushed out by three large men and deposited in the water. Two of the men then jumped into the boat, while two others moved to intercept any that tried to seize the vessel for themselves.

"We need to go. Now!" Kellert, for reasons Doran couldn't surmise, wouldn't look his king in the eye. He put a strong hand on Doran's shoulder, and moved him toward the dory.

"Kellert." The king was shaking his head. "I will not leave my people to die while I save myself. I'll stay. I will stand!"

"You must," his friend replied. "The realm needs a leader. If you die in this city today, then the enemy has decapitated us." He pushed Doran again toward the boat.

"You must get to Orshos, and prepare the capital for the attack that will come. Would you leave Orshos without its liege? Without direction? You are needed, Doran! You must go."

"I can't do it, Kellert. I–"

"Goddess damn you, Doran! You must!"

The outburst was so sudden, so severe that it took Doran back a step. He opened his mouth, but had no words for the man before him. Kellert's cheeks, he now saw, were streaming silent tears. It was a sight he'd never beheld. He couldn't process his friend's reaction. He just stood, trying to understand what was happening, waiting for his friend to speak.

Kellert Sentero shook his head as his stoic face crumbled. "I couldn't tell you, Doran. I wanted to. I needed to, but for the good of all, I couldn't. I'm sorry! The messenger arrived shortly before the attack, but I–" Kellert began to weep.

"Tell me what, Kellert?" Doran moved forward and grabbed Kellert by the shoulders. "Tell me what?"

Kellert raised his eyes to look at his king, and Doran saw a pain there that no man should ever have to possess.

"Solstia," Kellert managed. Doran's hands went limp on Kellert's shoulders, and the entire world began to fade as Kellert spoke again.

"Doran. The queen has fallen."

12

SOLSTIA'S DEMISE

She stands in a window high above her gardens, and looks out across a city and a realm.

The moon shines so brightly that it seems every blade of grass on the fortress property is illuminated. To her right, the sea is as calm as she's ever seen it, reflecting the light of Silvenna to her sill.

Her thoughts reach across the eastern fields to the man who fights now for the future of their great land. In the days since Doran left her side, she's scarcely slept or eaten. Her dark eyes reflect the fatigue of her heart and mind. She knows he had to do this. He'll stand with his men; he'll fight as the kings of old fought in years gone by.

He'll fall if he must.

She hates him and loves him for his courage. She knows that there are few rulers who would fight as he does, and at times she wishes he was not one of these. But then, he'd not be the man she'd fallen in love with if he wasn't. She pulls one of his cloaks tightly around her shoulders, and leaves their chamber to walk the hallways, as she has done for the last several nights.

The torches on the wall are all but unnecessary. Through the open windows, separated by ten paces at most, the brilliance of the night spills through. She walks silently, her feet bare and her breath nearly nonexistent. She walks to the westernmost part of the Keep, where the stone sills of the large windows are wide enough to sit comfortably and watch the stars above the ocean. She sits, and rests her head back against the ancient stone frame of the window and closes her eyes.

Moments later, her eyes open. Slowly. She sits straight, and strains to listen. She is sure she's just heard singing. She looks around, up and down the empty hallways, but soon realizes that the voice comes from outside her home. She stands, and leans forward to scan the perimeter of the property. Nothing. Below the window the grounds are bare. There is no tree, no structure or even flower bed nearby behind which a trespasser might hide. The western lawn of the royal grounds, which ends abruptly upon the cliff's edge, is empty.

She shakes her head, wondering if her stressful state has led to an overly active imagination. She stops and sits again, and realizes that she's almost aching to hear the voice again. She whispers thanks that the night is calm, and the voice will not be washed away by the usual noise of the rough coastline.

She is about to despair when she hears it again.

"Tis the last rose of summer, left blooming alone;
All her lovely companions are faded and gone;
No flower of her kindred, no rose-bud is nigh,
To reflect back her blushes, or give sigh for sigh…

She feels her heart skip a beat, and realizes that she's not taken a breath since the song slipped through her window upon the night air. She slowly gets to her feet, and almost smiles as she realizes that she is a little unsteady. The voice, that beautiful, enchanting voice has most assuredly come from outside, and she rushes to the end of the hallway, to the winding stairs that descend to the western door.

She moves outside, and for a moment there is a sense of dread, a panic that she has lost the song, and the voice which gave it life. Her head swings from left to right, searching out the one who touched her with his melody. *Was that a light on the far side of the lawn? A lantern?* For an instant, she sees Doran's face, and hears an indistinct warning. She shakes her head, trying to dismiss her husband's words, and smiles blissfully as thoughts of him are replaced by the euphoric sound that rises once more.

> *I'll not leave thee, thou lone one, to pine on the stem;*
> *Since the lovely are sleeping, go, sleep thou with them;*
> *Thus kindly I scatter thy leaves o'er the bed,*
> *Where thy mates of the garden lie scentless and dead.*

The garden, she whispers. And she feels, strangely, as if she is one amongst the flowers. Ah, to sleep in a garden, in the company of such beauty.

Her bare feet walk lightly in the cool grass, and she feels an excitement build as she approaches the cliff. She sees the light once more, floating at the cliff's edge before fading to nothing. The song, she knows, comes from here. Or from below. She needs to see the singer, this one who can expose his soul with a few simple words of a song.

For she feels sure that she's never heard a more heartfelt melody, each word sung with an aching that she somehow understands. She needs to tell the singer this. Needs to *touch* his song somehow. *So beautiful,* she whispers as she reaches the cliff's edge and peers down. *So beautiful.*

He stands upon the shore, or rather, on an outcropping of rock just off the shore. The rock's surface rises several feet above the eerily still waters, and though he is far below, she believes she can sense the smile upon his face, the gleam in his eye that rivals the moon upon the water. Slowly, he raises his hands into the air, a white rose held in each, and the night is filled with the magic of his voice.

> *So soon may I follow when friendships decay,*
> *And from love's shining circle, the gems drop away,*
> *When true hearts lie withered and fond ones are flown,*
> *Oh! Who would inhabit this bleak world alone?*

The smile on her face does not fade as she steps from the edge of the cliff. The cloak of her husband slips from her shoulders, and her thin robe whips upon her body as she plummets toward the faerae below. Her smile, Cehron Cen Kohr notes with pleasure, remains firmly on her face, right up to the moment that she lands upon the jagged rocks of the shore.

13

AN UNKNOWN RIVER

Dels Spallic locked eyes with the faerae as the people around them engaged in a heated conversation about what, Goddess help them, was to be done.

The faerae's revelation of the young ones' survival had brought about jubilation that had not been felt by the Egimians for some time. The young ones were alive and intact, and the faerae knew where they were headed. Great news, on the surface, until he'd disclosed their destination – a city that was under siege and expected to be destroyed in the coming days.

Nahcin.

This news, upsetting as it might be, would not be enough to quell the joy and hope that had arisen in Dels. One could clap a heavy lid on a boiling cookpot, but if that roiling water filled the pot, there was no lid that would entirely suppress such energy. And no one anywhere in the Three Realms held more hope than Dels Spallic.

And Dels wasn't the only one. He broke the gaze of the faerae Tryn and looked around at his people. And listened. It seemed the whole of Egim was ready to march south. This ragtag group of tired, hungry men, women and trenocs wanted nothing more than to bring the lost sheep back to the flock. Dels saw the faerae's eyes grow wide as Kitt Rallo, shaking her bone-thin fist in the air, bellowed that a search party should set out this very night. Tryn rubbed the side of his neck, his lips pursed as he looked at Dels in confusion.

"You folk did hear me say Nahcin is falling, did you not?" the faerae asked.

Dels Spallic took a deep breath and patted the faerae on the shoulder. There was a slight cringe that curled Tryn's lip ever so slightly. It was apparent that the faerae was not accustomed to physical contact, especially that of a human, but Dels cared little.

"What we heard, my friend," the big man said, "is that our loved ones are alive. And that is all we needed to hear."

As the shouting of plans continued to grow louder, the faerae sought to speak once more. He raised both hands high above his head. Some noticed the gesture and began to quiet, but others carried on the excited talk. Dels raised a hand to assist the faerae, but it was Kitt Rallo who got their full attention.

"Silence!" she barked.

Everyone turned to look at the old lady. She gave a quick nod of gratitude and turned back to Tryn. "Now, what more have you to say, little one?"

Little one? Dels shook his head and repressed a small smile. The faerae, appearing somewhat put off by the moniker, gave a tilt of his head but let the matter go. Lowering his hands, he stepped up on the fountain's jutting rocks to be better seen.

"While your valour is admirable, and your love of the young ones evident, I did not come to evoke a mass exodus." He looked at Dels. "I came to ask that a small group of you make the journey. Believe me when I say that the road will be difficult and the destination horrific. To have all of you go is to have all of you die." He spoke with no emotion. The facts, it seemed, were all that was required. "Further, you've not all been asked." At this, many began to speak at once, and the faerae raised his hands once more. "I intend no offence. I merely relay a message. I've been sent by Niamh, daughter of Obaeron, king of the Fae." A hum from the crowd. "She sees things more *clearly* than most, you might say. For as we see things as they are, she sees things as they might be. Glimpses into a future that hurtles toward us like an unpredictable northwestern wind. She has seen this future, and she knows the ones who must navigate this wind, for strong it will be, and not without its perils."

Leath moved to the forefront, beside Dels. "Are you saying that you already know who will go?"

The faerae shook his head. "I know who *should* go," he replied. "But what should happen, and what actually happens are seldom the same."

"Who will… *should* go?" Dahlah asked.

"One from each of the respective families," Tryn said. "The smallest number is required. More than that and you increase the risk to all."

Dels glanced around at his friends. During a journey such as this, difficult decisions were required at every juncture, it seemed. However, the faerae's counsel in this matter would limit the options of who would venture south, making this decision easier for all. The fewer Egimians that set out on this path, the more would be kept safe, and Dels knew that the city of Ras would protect those that remained. "That would be wise," Dels said to Tryn as he moved forward.

Dels gave a nod to Stellen, and Fallette put a hand over her face. Stellen did his best to comfort her as she sobbed quietly, though his assurances did little to alleviate her anguish.

Dahlah simply took a deep breath and nodded. No matter what any said, Dels knew, the mother of Torla and Kef was going to make that journey south.

Leath shook his head, tightening the belt about his waist. "I can assure you that there will be *two* of this family making the journey." As he secured his buckle, Dels saw Sianah's firm hand lock over his wrist.

"*One* from each family, Leath." Sianah's grip tightened, as did the frown on her pretty face. "One. Your father will do everything in his power to see that Sivino is safe. He's more than capable, Leath. There's no need for you to go."

"Sianah–" Leath began, but he seemed suddenly unsure of what to say. "I must," was the best he could do.

"You mustn't," Sianah replied. "The faerae said so himself, didn't he?"

For his part, Tryn stayed out of the conversation entirely. Hands behind his back, he directed his attention to the fountain deities before him.

"She's right," Dels interjected quietly as he stepped closer to the pair. He gestured toward Stellen and Dahlah. "The three of us will go. You should stay, Son. Oversee the protection of–"

"Our people are protected, Father. You know this. I cannot sit here, idle and useless while you walk into unknown danger. There's too much I can offer. I'm strong, and fast. There's too much–" The boy's voice cracked then, but only those closest to the lad heard it; heard the emotion that he had kept hidden under that tough exterior for many years. "There's too much I need to say to him."

Sianah's grip on his wrist lessened, and her hand slowly slid down to take hold of his fingers.

Dels sighed. He'd spent enough years dealing with the determination of his son to know that the lad would not relent. He looked around, and his eyes fell on young Karm, standing off to the side with his mother. A bandage was still wrapped around the youngster's arm where he'd been struck on the day this had all begun. He recalled Karm's words that day – *If you send me away, I'll only hide in the trees and fire on them anyway. Not that I don't respect you, Sir. It's just that I need to do this. I need to help protect our people.* Dels bit his lip. It seemed to him that there were very few in Egim who were not in possession of a strong will. He looked back at his son. In truth, he would feel better if Leath were with them on this journey. He hoped this feeling was not entirely selfish. And Leath's need... what he needed to do, what he needed to say, was likely as great as the need of any of the family members gathered. He nodded at Leath, who nodded back in gratitude.

A silent moment passed, before Sianah spoke quietly.

"Do you know what you are?" she asked Leath. "You mock Sivino as a merrow, when you yourself... you're a *finny*." She reached up and placed a gentle hand on each of his cheeks. "Elusive. Slippery. Damn near impossible to catch without the luck of the Goddess. Long before you realized, Leath, I was trying to catch you. I was trying to be caught myself. And now, when I've finally got you in my grasp, you're slipping through my fingers again to head down an unknown river." She wiped tears from her cheeks. "Where's the *justice* in that?"

Leath pulled Sianah into a close embrace. Daurr, the

last one Dels would expect to join the conversation, moved forward slowly.

"When the Just Father sees a fight that is worth fighting," the Drale rumbled, "he rewards the righteous. I see strength in you." He looked around slowly, and his eyes rested on Dels. "Many of you. There will be danger, but there will be rewards. There is justice in that. The Just Father will see to it."

The Egimians turned and looked at the Drale, who moved to Tryn's side silently.

Leath took Sianah's face in his hands, in the same manner she'd just done to him.

"I'm not a finny," he said with a reassuring smile. "I'm a wild salmon. Do you know what wild salmon do, Sianah?"

She returned his smile, though it seemed to break her heart to do so. "They come back upriver."

Leath nodded. "They come back upriver. Always."

When Dels looked away from the pair, Daurr stood alone by the fountain. The faerae was nowhere to be seen.

Overhead, the first star flickered to life.

They rose before dawn on the following day. It was a sunless morning, and a heavy grey cloud overcast the breaking of light.

Most of the townsfolk had risen to see the Egimians off. Leath stood with Sianah and her parents just inside the main gates; Sental Pella whispering the words of a traditional blessing that was believed to protect those embarking upon dangerous journeys. Stellen Tros held Fallette; her continual nodding suggested that he was assuring her that all would turn out well. Dels shared a few quick words with Lumb Velto and a couple of the smith's neighbours. They shook Dels' hand tightly, patting his shoulder as he nodded and turned to face the path ahead.

Dahlah Rallo stood alone, a heavy shawl wrapped around her shoulders as she looked south. Though she said nothing, Dels knew that she was anxious for the others to finish their goodbyes so that they could begin their journey. She'd bid farewell to Kitt before going to bed the previous night. Daurr had led the Egimians down a narrow staircase which ended in what appeared to be a common room – an area large enough to fit the visitors in relative comfort. Small fires were maintained in circular pits throughout the room, their smoke wafting out through similarly shaped vents carved in the stone ceiling. As Dahlah had helped Kitt settle into one of the blankets that the Drales had offered Egim's most vulnerable, the old woman had reiterated her wishes to be awoken before the group left on the following morning. Dahlah had told her that she'd do no such thing.

"You were always a stubborn girl," Kitt had muttered as Dahlah tucked the blanket about her bony shoulders. She brushed a wisp of thin white hair from Kitt's face, tucking it behind her ear.

"I love you too," Dahlah had replied, kissing the woman's wrinkled cheek.

Dels was fairly certain that Dahlah had not slept at all. While they were all tired, Dahlah's face exhibited a dark fatigue that could only be brought about by terrible worry. She was heartsick to find her children, Dels knew. For her sake, and for his own, he hoped that this journey ended well.

As he approached Dahlah to offer some words of support, the Drales began to file into the courtyard, led by Daurr. Dels stopped in his tracks, and turned to take in the sight. Hundreds of the big creatures began to pour from the city, clad in battle gear of rough leather. While many carried satchels, presumably holding supplies, most carried nothing but their weapons. Huge cudgels were held casually in their great hands, hanging by their sides or strapped to their backs. Dels could not help but feel a small sense of hope as the Drales congregated. Whatever force awaited them in the war-torn south, they would surely be tested when the Drales arrived.

There were no heartfelt goodbyes among the Drale folk; or if there had been, it had not been done in the public eye. The creatures moved toward the gate as one now, the ranks falling in behind each other as they marched toward their fate. When he reached Dels, Daurr stopped. Behind him, all did likewise.

Dels craned his neck to look the Drale in the eye. He waited for Daurr to speak, but after several awkward moments, the Drale still remained silent. He considered Dels, as if still trying to form an opinion of the man. Uncomfortable, Dels initiated the conversation.

"Please accept my thanks, and my wishes for a successful journey. Your people have done us a service that we can never repay." He extended his hand, but Daurr had turned his head, seeming to be looking for something near the forest's edge.

"My thanks as well for the opportunity to see the heights of your city," Dels continued as he slowly lowered his hand. He glanced around, but there was no sign of Saroon. "Under more favourable circumstances, I'd enjoy another visit."

"You will return," Daurr rumbled, "so that my gift may be returned."

"Gift?" Dels asked.

Daurr squinted as he looked beyond the crowd. And then Dels saw what he'd meant. Saroon made her way through the Drales, leading four of the most magnificent horses Dels had ever seen.

"Your legs are short and weak, and your steeds are tired and lacking. You need to travel with haste." Daurr folded his arms as the animals approached them. "You need help, little man."

Saroon made her way to their side. The horses were indeed great specimens, and nods of approval were seen among several of the townsfolk.

"A gift," said Saroon. Then, echoing Daurr's words, "A gift that we would see returned."

"They will be," Dels said with a nod. "I promise."

The Egimians sat high on their horses, lifted both physically and emotionally. Dels looked over the mountains. Though the sun seemed to be making the greatest effort to break through the curtain of dark cloud, it just wasn't able. He rubbed his steed's thick neck, and the horse snorted in return, shaking its black mane. Leath, Dahlah and Stellen waited close beside him, shadowed by the dim morning light.

The city of Nahcin lay about two days to the south if they rode hard. This was undoubtedly their intention. With luck, they would reach their destination sometime during the following evening.

"Are we ready?" Dels asked.

"More than ready," Dahlah replied. She offered Dels a weak smile, and began to move her horse forward. Stellen fell in behind Dahlah, followed by Leath.

As the others moved forward, Dels watched the Drales prepare to set out as well. They would journey by a different route, likely much faster than the Egimians. Dels hoped that the journey of both groups would be swift and uneventful – until, of course, they reached their respective destinations. The Drales were an impressive sight; seven hundred massive creatures brimming with muscle and resolve. *Glad they're on our side*, Dels thought.

As they began to move away toward the distant city of Orshos, Dels called to their leader suddenly. Daurr slowed, as did several of his kin. There was a look of irritation on the Drale's face, which was easily read. *He'd given enough, been delayed enough. What further did this outsider require?*

Dels opened his mouth to speak, and was suddenly aware that hundreds of Drales' eyes, and those of his own people, were now upon him.

"May the Good Mother reward you," Dels said. "And may the Just Father see our cause to its rightful end."

Daurr stopped, and with him, all the Drales of Ras.

"Damnation," Stellen muttered. "You've gone and offended the lot of them."

Daurr strode through his people, and stopped alongside Dels. His face was severe and, not for the first time since their arrival, Dels felt truly intimidated. A moment later Saroon began to make her way toward the pair, but stopped when Daurr lifted his hand and extended it to the Egimian.

"May your Goddess watch your back, little man." Daurr said. Dels hand was swallowed in the massive fingers of the Drale as he accepted the handshake. "I pray that she does," the Drale continued. "I'll want those horses back."

Without a trace of a smile or a backward glance, Daurr moved back into the stream of warriors, his eyes set on the distant coastal city.

Dels pulled at his horse's reins, and moved to catch up with his people.

It was time to find his son.

14

BLOOD AND TEARS

"I've failed." A whisper in a silent room.

"In ways too numerous to count, I've failed."

Doran Dunarrk turned his crown loosely in his hands, studying the ancient circlet that had rested on so many heads before his own. It was a simple crown, befitting the practical nature of his people. Wrought of iron, it was devoid of gems or decoration. Ten points, each a couple of inches tall, rose around the circumference. He rubbed the top of one of these points with his finger. As a child, his father had told him that the points were once sharp as knives, and a careless hand would quickly find itself bloodied. Through the years though, it had been through many battles, against enemies and time, and the points had been rendered dull and harmless.

"We all wear down," Doran said quietly, though there was no one there to hear him speak. "Time gets the better of us all." Sitting on the stone floor, his back against a thick pillar, he turned to his left and looked at the dead body of his wife. Since his return to the capital city in the early morning hours, he'd not left her side. He'd stood beside her for three hours, barely moving, his big hand resting upon hers. The *Preparers* – those men and women who saw that the body was made ready for its journey to the Land of Ever – had done tremendous work. The damage done to the queen was great, Doran knew. Upon his arrival, he'd been met by Tomar Valli, one of the commanders who'd been left to watch over Orshos. Tomar fell in beside the king's horse as he'd made his way to the Keep.

"My lord," Tomar had begun, his voice shaking. "I'm–"

"Every detail, Commander," the king interjected quietly. His voice, Kellert had noted with no small amount of concern, sounded like that of a wraith, void of all feeling. The death in his voice slipped quietly into his eyes as he listened to Tomar, and learned of how his queen had fallen.

How she'd been discovered.

Doran had been warned by the Preparers to leave the veil in place. With soft words, they suggested that his final memories of her face be those of several days past, when she'd stood at the gates of the city, bidding him farewell through the bravest smile he'd ever known. He knew too well that she'd been terrified, for she'd twirled her silver silk kerchief in her hands to hide her trembling; an old habit that she'd never been able to put aside. Standing over her body, Doran had taken his own kerchief from his pocket and placed it gently within her cold, clasped fingers. "Have no fear," he'd whispered to her as he released her hands and pulled back the thick white veil.

He'd leaned in and softly kissed the ruined face of his queen before he'd collapsed on the floor and wept.

The cold, hollow sound of approaching boots did not draw Doran's gaze from Solstia's body. He rested still against the pillar, a silent war raging within him. In one moment, the heavy forces of grief seemed to be overwhelming. In the next, the sharp blades of fury would slice through the sadness, demanding vengeance and wrath. As this conflict raged within him, the city outside prepared for a battle of its own.

Kellert Sentero stopped beside the king. He too looked at the body of the queen, covered entirely save for her hands, garbed in a dress of the whitest linen, resting on pale blue pillows that covered the marble block where she'd been laid. Before Kellert arrived, Doran had replaced the veil and whispered a prayer for her peaceful sleep. It had been decided that, for the time being, she'd not be placed in the common room where the public were historically granted the opportunity to pay their respect. With the coming of the dark forces of the east, such a ceremony would need to be put on hold. When the battle was done, either they would give the queen the burial she deserved, or they would all be no more. It was, Doran thought, the latter possibility that had brought Kellert to him at present. He put his head back against the pillar, tapping his crown against his knee.

"I do not believe them," he said, turning finally to his friend.

Kellert nodded. It was, to be certain, a difficult thing to imagine. Solstia Dunarrk, the sunray on the cliff, queen of the people, the cornerstone on which the Orshos Keep rested, was the last person anyone would suspect of committing suicide. Yet, the reports were consistent, and came from reliable sources. Two watchmen, each on different corners of the property, each trusted and loyal members of the Guard, had seen with their own eyes – the queen of Rentorria leaving the Keep, Doran's robe wrapped about her as she made her way to the precipice above the sea. And from there–

"She would not," Doran whispered. He laid the crown to his side, and wrapped his arms about himself. "She would not."

"She was a beacon," Kellert said. "She still is. The legacy of the queen will undoubtedly shine in this great city for years to come."

Masterful, thought Doran. Kellert offered beautiful sentiments regarding the queen while at the same time, subtly drawing Doran's attention to the future of Orshos, and by default, to its present situation.

"She would want me to fight," said the king.

"She would want us all to fight. She *herself* would fight, I'm certain."

"Does the enemy draw near?"

"We have reports that they are making progress. They do not seem to be rushing, which bodes well for us, for the time being. Perhaps. When they get here, they will be relatively rested. They will be eager to engage us."

"The city must be ready," said Doran.

"The city needs her king," Kellert replied. He extended a hand to his friend who, after the slightest hesitation, took it in his own and let himself be helped up. He gained his feet slowly, and moved to his wife's body. Kellert, keenly aware that this could indeed be the last moment the two would spend together in this world, moved quietly to the doorway, giving the pair their privacy.

Doran took Solstia's hands once more, and leaned in to kiss her fingers. Tears fell onto the kerchief he'd given her, blending with his blood that stained the thin cloth.

"Blood and tears," he whispered. "So much of our lives, so much of ourselves, spills from our bodies, Solstia. Dripping our souls into the earth, never to be retrieved." He sniffed back the emotion, trying to steel himself against another breakdown. He set his jaw, and stood taller. "You found a way to retrieve it, Sol. Every day, you poured life back into me. I feel like I am dead at my core, as though my soul died with you. But the life you poured back into me, that part – our part – will fight on. I'll fight with your strength, Sol, and in the Land of Ever I'll hold you again, and I'll thank you for the strength you've given me." He leaned in one final time, and kissed her lips through the white cloth. "I'll see you soon, Flower."

When Kellert heard the footsteps, he turned and watched the king approach. Doran's eyes were afire; not from the tears he'd shed, but from the determination and fury that raged within him. He didn't look at Kellert as he spoke.

"My father once told me that this world is the land of the dying; that every day, we are each of us closer to that death that awaits us, to Old Grim's cold, tight embrace." He stooped and swept up his crown, placing it on his head. "Grim will find himself with much company before long." He moved past his friend, his hand on the pommel of his sword. "But that company will not be ours. Not yet.

"Not until we've done what we must…"

15

YOUR MOVE

The stench of death filled the air before the group ever sighted the city of Nahcin.

It wafted through the trees and fields through which the company had travelled for the last day. When at last they crested a hill that held the last vestiges of the forest, they stood and beheld the smouldering ruin that was their destination.

Several leagues off, over grassy plains that were devoid of life, Nahcin lay still. The black plumes that Niamh had described had faded to light gray, slowly lifting the lost souls of the city into the overcast sky as they rose from the ashes.

"Damnation," Lomin muttered. He dismounted, and took a few steps from his steed. He rested his chin upon his hands, which gently gripped the top of his walking staff. "It makes the heart ache."

"Have you ever been to Nahcin, Lomin?" Sivino asked quietly.

"I have. It was a beautiful city. The people. The music.

The *theatre*." He closed his eyes, and was instantly transported to the past. "Ah, you could sit before those great Nahcinian performers with a world of worry heavy on your shoulders, and an hour later, forget the very cause of your strife. I once saw the players perform an entire scene from *An Uncatchable Current* on the waters of the Madimest, where it becomes the Eridanos." The others were watching Lomin now as he recalled the long-ago day. "Men and women, singing as they lithely moved from river ferry to raft. Their voices carried all the way down the shoreline, which was covered in spectators. And when the young girl portraying the princess saw that her love had fallen for another and let herself slip slowly into the dark waters, no one breathed. No one. The entire city fell silent." As he spoke the last word, his eyes opened and he was torn from the pleasure of his reminiscence.

"Time is an immeasurable thing," Niamh said. "The city may one day rise again." She moved past the others, signalling that it was time to move on. There was a threat of rain in the clouds, and they were now without shelter.

They walked on through the afternoon, wasting no time, but in no hurry to reach the city's remains. Conversations were quick and hushed; eyes darted in every direction for hidden threats, though there would be scarce places to hide in such an open terrain.

They rode single file, Niamh remaining at the forefront. There was a gentle decline to the topography, and the grasses through which they rode were short and yellowed. Every so often, a footpath would cross their own. Without fail, each of the riders found their eyes following the paths, silently wondering when the well-trodden trails would be traversed again. Sivino traced the nearest to a grassy knoll, where the remnants of an old fence ran in a wide, lazy circle. It was the kind of fence that he and his friends would have walked atop back in Egim. On the far side of the fence, a ramshackle little hut lay silent. Obviously abandoned for some years, the roof sagged into a smile that contradicted its sorry state of disrepair.

When Sivino looked back to the group, he saw that Niamh had stopped. One by one, the company moved forward until all were abreast of her. They waited for her to speak.

"The city will not be empty," she said. Tonnis moved forward a little to watch her lips.

"The other one?" Kef asked. "Cehron Cen Kohr. Will he be with the Shepherd?"

Sivino noted how Niamh almost imperceptibly tightened her grip on the reins. She took a breath, her slender chest rising and falling.

"He will be there."

"And who should we fear most," Ston asked. "Which one is the bigger threat?"

For the first time in several long minutes, Niamh looked away from the city, and found Ston's eyes.

"Fear neither," she said. She saw Torla move to speak, but raised a gentle finger to silence her. As Torla closed her mouth, Niamh repeated, "Fear neither." She turned her horse a little, facing the group fully. "I know this may sound absurd, but hear me. Do not give them your fear. Do not let them have it. Do not let them revel in it. You may pity their states. Abhor their actions. But we'll not give them the satisfaction of cowering to them. I have no intention."

"Will you be able to protect us, Niamh?" Lomin's tone suggested that he knew the answer already.

"I will do all in my power," she said. Instantly, a vision of the blood at Sivino's feet flashed in her mind. She blinked it away. "I know much, but I do not know what type of creature this Shepherd is. He appears to be human, but what power he possesses is unknown to me." She pulled the reins of her horse, turning the animal back to the fallen city. "Cehron has hidden him well."

Sivino moved to Niamh's side. She looked over, watching as his severe face focused on the smoke ahead. "The time for hiding is over," he said. He turned to the faerae, and nodded toward the city. "Come. Let us be done with this."

The first body was a shock.

There were no arms. No legs. Only a torso and a head that possessed a terrified face. It was a grotesque sight, as it seemed the limbless body was still struggling to escape the horror that had dismembered it. Niamh quickly ushered the group away.

As they rode forward and the looming city grew, so too did the number of dead. The riders were as silent as the corpses through which they walked. It was only when the first young victims were spotted that Torla gave a stifled sob. A woman, and two little children.

All looked away. There were no words for such a thing.

They hurried on, and were soon before the northern gate of Nahcin. Its massive doors hung open; solid wood, reinforced with steel. The wood was blackened now, as was the steel, and the doors were held open by the dead that piled at their base. Niamh deftly navigated her horse through in the least obstructive manner, never lowering her gaze. The others followed. Though the day was dull, the shadow of the wall fell over them as they passed into the city.

Inside, the devastation was just as horrendous. Corpses lay scattered all about the cobbled streets. Arrows protruded from some. Swords and spears from others. Many however, were simply mangled by means that Sivino had no desire to discover.

"Goddess give them peace," Lomin whispered.

It was only when Lomin spoke that Sivino realized how deathly silent the city lay. The clopping of the horses' feet was the only sound that could be heard. The day was still, and no breeze moved the air. They'd seen the Eridanos in the distance, but were still unable to hear its flow.

Sivino's eyes darted to the windows of the buildings that surrounded them. Despite what Niamh had said, he felt a terror growing inside him. For inside these shadowed structures, who was to say that a hundred beasts did not lurk, eager for fresh blood and renewed screams. Yet, judging from the ruin around him, he doubted such creatures could lie in silent wait.

Through blood-stained streets and unseeing eyes, they moved toward the southern end of Nahcin. Sivino could now faintly hear the river, and its effect surprised him. His mind was drawn to the Andel, and the comfort that he found upon her banks. In some small way, his spirit was lifted by the sound, and he sat a little straighter in his saddle. Beside him, Lomin suddenly stopped his horse.

To their left, the grand Nahcinian theatre stage lay silent. Sivino looked past the bodies strewn around the semi-circular, dirt-covered viewing grounds where perhaps three hundred people could gather for the spectacle. Twice that number would have been able to view the performance from the two-story amphitheatre that formed a crescent around the stage. It was the stage to which

Sivino's eyes were drawn. This stage, capable of supporting a hundred players, now played out its final macabre presentation. Frozen in time, two dozen men and women were scattered about. And if this wasn't terrible enough, the villains of the performance, half a dozen Nylacci, lay with them.

It was a play of monsters. Merciless and motionless. Damsels in distress that would never be rescued, their pale white faces streaked with blood and dirt. Heroes that had felled dark beasts before falling themselves, to lie with sword in hand; their final curtain falling before their lifeless eyes.

Sivino turned away, only to discover his friends, surrounding him, staring at the same sight.

"Keep moving," he said, and his company followed.

Through the streets of Nahcin, they saw more of the same. They were each painfully aware that the city could not go on forever; that at some point, they would have to stop, or be stopped, and face those which they'd come to encounter.

When Cehron Cen Kohr came into view, he did so without drama or any element of surprise. The group had rounded a street corner that opened onto the dockside courtyard and saw him, facing the water, his back to the city. Had he watched as the citizens of Nahcin had run, fighting for their lives as they tried to flee the city, Sivino wondered. Had he engaged in the battle at all? Likely not. It was more likely, Sivino guessed, that the creature had watched the entire spectacle unfold, perhaps from a window high above as he sipped his tepid tea. As the group moved closer, the Cernunnos still didn't turn, though there was no doubt he'd heard the steps of the horses.

When the group got within twenty feet of the faerae,

Niamh raised a hand, halting them. They sat, unmoving. For several long moments, no one moved. Sivino saw his friends look at each other, no doubt wondering what was supposed to happen. *But that was the thing*, thought Sivino. *It was impossible to know what was supposed to happen.* Events, he realized, would unfold as they would, and none could change that. Slowly, he dismounted his horse, and the others did likewise. He continued to wait, his face calm, though his heart pounded in his chest.

Finally, the Cernunnos turned. He did so slowly, picking at a loose cobblestone with the toe of his leather shoe. When he lifted his gaze to the group, his smile vanished. His eyes, Sivino thought, were significantly darker than he remembered. He surveyed the riders, joining his hands behind his back.

"The magnificent seven," he said, his voice a quiet rasp. Then, he tilted his head, as if struggling to see. "And the furry little beast, of course." Drip bared his teeth at the insult, but made no further move. "Your company remains intact, Niamh."

"We are about the only thing intact within these foul walls," Niamh replied.

Cehron lifted his head, as if to sniff the air which hung over the scattered bodies. A look of discomfort crossed his face.

"Yes," he said. "The air within these walls has become a bit… close." He indicated the far stone wall, and a gate, similar to the northern one, that hung ajar. "Please," he said, extending his hand in a courteous gesture. "Let us step outside, and rid ourselves of hideous sights." His eyes bore into Niamh. "Let us discuss other *visions*."

"And what hideous sights await us through that gate?" Sivino asked.

The faerae, though he masked it well, still seemed to find it unsettling to be addressed directly by a human, especially when the voice was one of challenge.

"Hideous, I suppose, is a relative term. If you worry over Nylacci, I assure you, the only ones you'll find beyond this gate are rotten and buzzing with flies." He stopped, and turned with a rough laugh. "Well, *more* rotten, and *more* flies than usual."

None shared the faerae's sense of humour.

Behind Niamh, the group left their horses and followed the faerae through the gate and into the grounds beyond. Though the sun still did not shine, Sivino thought, it was a relief to be away from the dark horrors that filled the once brilliant city. He steeled himself for what lay ahead, though nothing could have prepared him for what awaited him as they stepped outside the gate.

For a moment, it was hard to process. It seemed so long since he'd seen Dels, and so improbable that he'd see him again, that Sivino had trouble registering the sight of the man.

Their families, held at sword point by three armed Isrorians; their faces bloodied; eyes swollen.

The young ones burst forth with a cry as the battered Egimians did likewise, oblivious to the inept guards beside them, and the two groups met in a collision of tears and relief. Dahlah fell to her knees, arms opened, as Kef and Torla slid into her embrace. Stellen grabbed Ston in a hug that would surely have cracked the ribs of a more slender young man, pulling his head tightly to his chest. And Dels, fast as he ran, was passed by Leath, who grabbed his young brother in the first embrace that their father could recall since Sivino was a toddling child. As Dels caught them, the three Spallics held each other for the first time since the passing of Rhenna.

As the embraces finally loosened, the group began to study each other. Dahlah quietly fussed over Kef's leg as Torla tilted her mother's face to get a better look at the purple bruise that formed around her eye. Stellen held Ston's face in both his hands, his hushed questions unheard by the others. Dels and Leath formed a protective barrier between Sivino and the enemy. Yet, they could see from the hard look in his eye and the confident way he stood, his hand laid lightly on the pommel of his sword, that this was not the boy who'd left Egim days ago. He'd been changed, as had they all, but it seemed that his transformation far surpassed what might have been expected.

Dels looked beyond Sivino. Lomin stood to one side of the faeraes, his arm around Tonnis' slender shoulder. Dels nodded to the old wolf, certain that he was in no small way responsible for helping to keep his son safe. Lomin returned the gesture. And then Dels looked at Drip, who stood looking hunched and despondent. The trenoc was unable to hold Dels' eyes until the big man spoke his name.

"Drip. You said you'd bring them back to me." He raised a hand, and gestured for the trenoc to approach. Slowly, Drip came forward, certain that he was about to be dismissed from the Spallic fold for his monumental failure. When he reached Dels, he steeled himself and looked up, ready for the worst.

In the same moment, Dels fell to one knee and threw an arm around the trenoc, pulling him in close. Being the nature of the trenoc race, Drip's hands instinctively jerked upward, ready to ward off the attack. Yet, it took him only a moment to realize what was happening. With a slightly awkward motion, he tapped Dels lightly on the sides, the closest his kind might ever come to reciprocating a hug. Dels pulled him tighter, and Drip could hear the emotion when he spoke. "I never doubted you for a second, my friend."

Sivino looked from his father to Niamh. She now stood but a few paces from Cehron Cen Kohr who was, to Sivino's dismay, staring directly at him with no small amount of malice. Sivino looked away. The group quietly cried with the joy they felt, but for every tear that hit the ground, it was outnumbered a hundredfold by the blood that stained the dirt. Sivino looked around, his mind trying to come to grips with how much life had been lost to create so much blood. And all this blood, he knew, was on the hands of one creature, the one whose eyes now bore into him. Sivino suddenly recalled the day that this had all begun, the day he'd returned from daydreaming by the Andel, and the shame he'd felt. He recalled the words his father had said to him. *Hold up your head, Sivino. There is no one who can cause you to look at the dirt.*

Sivino's eyes hardened, and he looked up. So severe was his gaze that, for just an instant, he saw a look of shock on the Cernunnos' face. It disappeared as quickly as it had come.

Cehron Cen Kohr gave a nod, then turned to the Isrorian guards. He gestured to the men – a spinning of his index finger – and they ushered the company together at sword point. Sivino watched as the Cernunnos stepped around the corpse of a dead Nylacci and, with hands still clasped behind his back, regarded Niamh. He moved toward her, stopping only when their toes almost touched. He leaned in, his face mere inches from hers.

"Your move," he whispered.

16

ORSHOS

The city of Orshos, Doran Dunarrk realized, had been transformed entirely.

Gone were the smiles, the banter upon the street, and the everyday activity that filled the lives of these industrious people. The smiles were replaced with tight-lipped terror, the banter replaced by warnings, orders, and cries of sadness. All activity now focused on fortifying the walls, preparing the weaponry, and organizing those who would set sail before the great shadow to the east fell upon the coast.

"How many boats do we have?" Doran asked Kellert Sentero sharply.

The advisor thought for a second before he spoke. "Less than a hundred. The swifter among them may reach Solla in time to come back for a second load. Some of the larger fishing vessels are currently too far at sea, unaware of what's transpired these past few days. We can hope that some may return before the attack comes fully."

Hope, Doran thought. Too often had he allowed himself to hope, and been sorely disappointed. He looked around, the flurry of movement and the clamour of preparation encouraged and disheartened him at once. The city did not doubt the warnings, for Doran Dunarrk had brought them himself. The people of Orshos, and Rentorria entire, trusted their king. When an edict was sent forth, or a warning sounded, there were few who doubted the validity or necessity. If Doran Dunarrk felt that a particular action must be taken, the realm trusted his reasoning. Few leaders were able to command such trust and support, and few deserved it. It was the great fortune of Rentorria that their ruler saw this support as an honour, and not something of which he could take advantage.

Doran nodded. Kellert had delegated the work of loading and evacuating the citizens to trusted commanders, and he and the king watched as families separated, the strong urging the vulnerable to get onto the boats with tear-filled eyes. "These boats..." Doran said, his eyes on the water. "They carry the life of our city. Let us hope they have a city to which they can return."

For the remainder of the day, Orshos prepared for the arrival of the enemy. The number and description of the beasts changed depending on the street on which one walked. Everywhere there were hushed whispers of the coming horror, and no amount of preparation or reassurance could diminish the feeling of doom that hung over it like a black cloud.

Doran and Kellert rode through Lower Orshos with severe faces, the King's Guard surrounding them every step of the way. In the distance, the king spotted Staid Dyrro at the walls, lending a hand to the men and women who reinforced weak areas and solidified the strength of the huge wooden gate. Holes were dug in the earth to brace the ends of large trees, which were tilted so that their upper ends could be nailed to the high walls to repel the force that would surely shake them in the coming days. Once the walls were buttressed, sheltered areas for the archers were hastily constructed, for time allowed little care to be taken. The wall stretched for more than half a league around the city of Orshos, from the rugged shoreline of the south, curving to the thick forest to the north, and the cliff edges beyond. The location of the Rentorrian capital could be advantageous in defensive efforts, but Doran was far from comfortable. His city was about to face a foe unlike any that his forefathers had ever encountered.

As the two men approached, Staid moved to them, and asked about the progress of the evacuation.

"Slow, but many of the boats have left already, and more will come to assist," Kellert replied. He turned to Doran. "I told the officers to cut short any drawn-out goodbyes that impede the process. It's difficult, but I'd suffer seeing extra tears if it means saving more lives."

"It is heart-wrenching to watch," Doran added, looking at the reinforcement efforts upon the wall. He couldn't say if he felt more pain for those that had to say goodbye, or those that would have to remain and fight.

In the end, he guessed, it didn't really matter.

Late that afternoon, a scout returned and updated the king on the enemy's progress.

"They do not seem to be in any particular hurry, my lord," the man said as he tethered his weary steed beside a water trough. "I got as close as I could, mindful that they may have sent their own scouts ahead to uncover a potential ambush. From my vantage point, I could see that they do not race westward, though they waste little time. My

guess is they'll arrive late tomorrow, or early the following day."

Doran turned to Kellert. "We have little time. Let's
make the most of it." He nodded his thanks to the messenger, and began to make his way back through the city,
up the hill to his home. Kellert moved his horse to the
side of the king, his eyes ever watchful. He knew well that
Doran Dunarrk would not remain in his fortress while
there was so much to be done, so much to oversee. Yet, he
wished that the king would be a little more cautious as he
moved through the city. There was no way to be certain
that the minions of Idach Garron did not roam the streets
unnoticed. The guards who continually followed Doran
were skilled and reliable, but Kellert still found himself
ill at ease.

He looked at his king, and noted the lines that had
grown so swiftly across his face since the war had begun.
In recent times, the king's smile – that genuine smile that
had won hearts and lit rooms so often when they were
young men – had scarcely been seen. With the passing of
Solstia, and the wave of horror that slowly rolled in from
the east, Kellert wondered if he would ever see it again.

He mentally checked himself. Now was not the time
for wistfulness. There was much to be done, and reminiscence, to be sure, was at the bottom of that list.

They ascended the winding streets of Orshos in silence. Far to the west, a thick bank of fog hung upon the
water. It was toward this fog, and the island of Solla that
was hidden within, that dozens of boats could now be
seen to sail. It was a desperate attempt to save a city; a city
that felt itself pulled apart like a clam by hands which it
would never understand.

17

ELEMENTAL

"My move?" Niamh's lips pursed as her eyes narrowed with disgust. "My *move*? Is that what this is to you? A game?"

"All of life is a game, Niamh," Cehron replied. "You should know this. The problem is, too few know the rules. And even if they think they do, no one really plays by them." The Cernunnos walked slowly around the Egimians, whose eyes never left him.

"It's difficult when those such as yourself keep changing them." She jerked her head in the direction of the fallen Nylacci, who lay to the side in a pool of dried blood.

Cehron Cen Kohr shook his head. "And how is *my* shifting any different than yours, Niamh?"

"You shift monsters."

"Define monsters."

"Bloodthirsty creatures, who revel in death and destruction."

He turned, joining his hands behind his back as he nodded slowly. "An apt definition, I agree. Yet, the Nylacci are but game pieces that I've added to keep things interesting. I tend to bore rather easily, as you may know." He gave her a smile then. "You may come to find I've added even more unique *pieces* to our little contest, should you live long enough to see." Niamh's eyes narrowed, and Cehron continued. "Tell me, Niamh, have you ever witnessed the graceful skittering of a *takahtar*?"

"Cehron! You cann–"

"Spare me, child! Don't lecture me on what constitutes a monster. Open your blasted eyes! Who better fits this definition than the *human* race?"

"Not all humans revel in death!" Niamh replied.

"Not all Nylacci revel in death," Cehron shot back just as quickly, toeing the lower horns of the nearest Nylac with his leather shoe. "Have you ever beheld the touching sight of a mother Nylac suckling a hairy little newborn at her bosom?" He looked up in a sideways glance at Niamh, and his lips parted in a menacing smile. After a short pause, he chuckled. "Alright, neither have I. Faant knows, the creatures are just as likely as not to *eat* half their offspring. But I digress. We are indeed participants in a grand game, my dear Niamh. And you are losing."

"And why is that?" Niamh asked.

"Because you have so much *more* to lose," Cehron Cen Kohr snarled. He looked to the Egimians, his gaze meeting each of theirs in turn. "I can watch a thousand Nylacci die a most gruesome death, and it means nothing to me. Nothing. Can you say the same if even one of your loyal companions was to find themselves on the wrong end of a Nylacci arrow?"

"We've seen enough death."

"Perhaps you have." Sivino could hear the indifference in Cehron's voice as the faerae picked at a button on his cloak sleeve. "I know that your little group here holds a very special place in your ever-weakening heart." He walked behind her as he spoke, whispering in her ear. "Could it be love? Possibly. More likely it's the possibility that you feel this motley bunch will actually fulfill the prophecy of the Faant. Or, at least one of them. I must say–" He glanced over her shoulder to look squarely at Sivino. "–the child with the sword does *intrigue* me."

At this, Niamh spun and raised a finger, pointing it at Cehron's face. Her lips peeled back slowly, and she bared her teeth. "I brought them here because I knew that this is what I must do. There has never been a choice in the matter. But I did not bring them here to die, mark these words. I would find a way to set things right without more bloodshed."

"Aah." Cehron nodded, as if in agreement. "That makes complete sense. And that being the case, I'm sure your friends will have no trouble parting with their weapons. Especially you, young Master Spallic."

Sivino's hand went instinctively to the hilt of his sword, his face defiant. The faerae snorted a laugh. "It seems your little dagger has grown since last we met, my boy." His voice took on a darker tone then, and in it, Sivino somehow heard the age of this centuries-old creature. "Perhaps a bit of *friendly persuasion* is in order." At this, the Isrorians moved toward Sivino and his companions, but Cehron stopped them short. "Get back, fools. I didn't mean you." The Isrorians lowered their weapons and slowly stepped back from the group, looking at each other in confusion.

Niamh moved forward. "Cehron, I–" But she got no further. The Cernunnos spun and thrust an open palm at her chest. Though he made no contact with her, it was as though the air was sucked from the sky and, in one intense burst, flew along his arm to crash into the slender faerae. Niamh flew backward, hitting the ground hard before rolling twice, and coming to rest in a motionless heap. Drip was at her side immediately, followed a moment later by Lomin.

Torla's arrow was out of its quiver and pointed at the back of the faerae. Yet, as she took aim, the Cernunnos pulled back his extended hand and raised it beside his head, fingers splayed in a gesture that commanded one to stop. As Torla sought to release the arrow, she realized that it had been more than a gesture. Her fingers held the string taut, but could not release it. Her eyes fell shut and she whispered a curse.

"A faerae's magic is elemental, child." Cehron turned to look at Torla. "Far from the puffs of smoke and disappearing acts I've seen used by foolish illusionists throughout the worlds, ours is the one magic that is real. The one that is true." He stepped closer to her. "You see, that arrow that you point at me, that you wish to release upon me, has life within it yet. Cut from its source, it retains the life force of its tree, and this force is what I command. I could send you reeling with my command of the air, as I did her." He jerked his head toward Niamh without looking back at her. "Or, I could… *push* the life force in the arrow's wood backward. Like so…"

Torla felt the strain on the arrow grow. She released the bow, thinking to simply drop the weapon in defeat. Yet, the faerae's demonstration was not complete. The bow fell but the arrow remained. Slowly, Cehron inclined his head, and though his arm hung limp, his fingers moved in a slow, revolving circle. The arrow that Torla had pointed at him revolved likewise, floating in the air until it was pointed at her petrified face. The hardened tip hovered before her as her friends screamed at Cehron, pleading for mercy.

"Please," sobbed Dahlah. She stepped forward and raised both hands in surrender. "Please, don't."

"Not another step, Mistress." Cehron did not look at her, yet the tone of his voice froze Dahlah in place. She looked to her daughter and covered her mouth with both hands. Dels moved slowly to her side, a hand on her shoulder. Sivino considered what, if anything, he could say or do to stop this cruel display. The faerae smiled at Torla, obviously enjoying the fear he instilled. "It is known that faeraes are not permitted to use direct force to kill a human. We can persuade and influence your kind to *misstep*, as I did that beautiful Rentorrian queen, but direct murder? It's not possible." Sivino shook his head. *Did the faerae just say he killed Queen Dunarrk? Has Orshos fallen already?* His thoughts were interrupted as Cehron continued. "Now, *maiming*, on the other hand; I'm a bit… *fuzzy* on this law." He brought both hands together, palms facing outward, and the arrow's tip lined itself with Torla's left eye. "I simply wish to make a *point*," he smiled. "And a half-blind girl should suffice." He raised his right hand in a quick motion, but as he did so, Lomin pulled his willow stick from his cloak, and with a desperate shout, pointed it at the arrow. The wood exploded before Torla's face, throwing her backward. Screams rang out as her companions ran to her.

Cehron turned toward Lomin, who now directed the wand at the faerae. But before Lomin could open his mouth, Cehron splayed the fingers of his raised hand, and the wand flew from the old wolf to be caught in the faerae's white knuckle grip.

"So, you do have some control of the magic." He studied the wand, his mouth curling in disgust. "I thought it was so, but felt a little test was in order. It is rare indeed that I have the opportunity to meet a descendant of Myrddin Wyllt." He smiled. "It's been long centuries since I shared a jug of ale with that old curmudgeon. I wonder, my dear fool–" His eyes narrowed. "–how many of you remain?"

"Few," Lomin whispered.

"Few indeed," the faerae replied as he moved toward Torla and the others. "And those that do... well, perhaps hiding *is* best. Has there ever been a family that's been more shifted than yours?" Lomin was silent, visibly uncomfortable. "Yet, Niamh has never given *you* the opportunity, has she? Why does she bother to keep you here?" Sivino looked up from where he knelt beside Torla with the others, and saw the anger and sadness that flashed simultaneously in Lomin's eyes. "You must know, *Master Lailoken*, it really is best that the practice of magic be left to the true creatures of faerae." He leaned in toward Torla, seeming to Sivino to take great pleasure in how the others recoiled. Dahlah and Dels, however, paid him no heed as they attended to the girl. "Tut tut," the faerae mumbled as he looked at the girl. Torla's face was streaked with blood; several pieces of the splintered arrow having scratched her deeply. Dahlah worked on these wounds, using the hem of her dress to clean the blood. None, as fortune would have it, had injured her eyes, Sivino noted with some relief.

Cehron turned back to Lomin. "*You* know that as well as any... though you find it difficult to resist, don't you? Even when death and devastation come at the hands of its use, your family always maintained that they'd get it under control. *Fools*." He looked over at the Isrorians. "Take their weapons," he said softly. Several of the company shifted uncomfortably, and Leath stood to his full height. Cehron looked from Leath to Torla, and held the girl's eyes as he spoke to his soldiers. "If any resist, splinters will be the least of their worries."

He turned and walked to the lake as the weapons were seized and placed in a nearby shack. Beside the dock, he stopped. Behind him, Niamh began to stir, and with Drip's gentle support she sat up, favouring her left shoulder.

With his back to the group, Cehron studied the wand he still held, turning it slowly in his hands. Then, to the surprise of all, he twisted his body slightly and threw the wand high in the air. Lomin made a small pitiful sound as the stick soared through the air, landing in the lake with barely a splash. Before them, the faerae moved to an overturned fish barrel and sat with an exaggerated sigh. He leaned forward, rested his forearms on his knees. His long, lank hair fell before his face. Sivino watched with growing dread as the faerae let his right hand hang, and once again twirled his index finger, slowly, round and round. In response, the wand began to rotate in small, concentric circles. As it did, the waters upon which it rested did likewise.

"Oh, Cehron," Niamh whispered, almost too faint to hear.

Cehron looked up, surveying those before him. When the faerae grinned, Sivino felt the world go dark, as if the sun shied away from the malice of his smile. Soon, his shoulders twitched with a silent laugh.

"It is time," Cehron whispered. He picked a small wildflower that swayed between his feet in the cool breeze. And then, like wax running from a finely moulded candle, the smile melted from his face. He looked at the soldiers. "You're no longer needed. Leave the city." The men, though confused, knew better than to argue. With quick nods, they obeyed. As they began to walk away, the faerae gave them one last order.

"Before you go... fetch me the king."

18

LOYAL TO THE DEATH

The Nylacci arrived just after dawn.

For several exhausting days, the citizens of Orshos had struggled to prepare for the attack, but nothing could have prepared them for the sight of the beasts, a dark line which stretched from north to south and stained the land for leagues.

Doran Dunarrk knew that what this dark line actually represented was the border of Isror. He knew also that, for the first time in his life or that of his forefathers, he could see the potential eastern limits of his realm from the capital of his proud land. And with each step the monsters took, the realm would become smaller, until it simply ceased to exist. Pushing it back to where it belonged was the unimaginable yet necessary task that lay before him.

Doran's lip curled into a snarl. There was no curse sufficient for the hate he felt; a hate that filled his face so deeply he would be almost unrecognizable to those he loved. His thoughts, at that moment viler and baser than any he'd ever experienced, were upon the damage he longed to inflict on Idach Garron.

And yet, it seemed that the Isrorians would not be marching on Orshos, at least not right away. The reports that came to the king spoke only of the Nylacci. The last of the messengers and scouts had re-entered the city. The gates, heavily guarded since news of the impending attack had come, had finally been closed and barred the day prior.

Usually a flurry of activity, the harbour was unnaturally still. The remaining boats were tied up at the wharves, swaying on the water that gently lapped at the docks, now quiet and bare. Those who were unable to fight had all been removed from the city. When the assault finally came, a group would be set by the sea to hold the southeastern limit of the wall. If the attackers attempted to go around the wall via the water, defenders both in the city and on the water would be ready to keep them out.

In the northern region of the city, where the other end of the wall reached the cliffs beside the Nucono, the trees had been cut to allow the defenders to see and deal with an attack that might come from the shelter of the forest.

And still, their efforts didn't feel to be nearly enough. Kellert Sentero and the senior commanders realized this as well. What was important, Doran thought as he left the parapet and moved down the smooth stone staircase, was that the citizens and soldiers still believed in the possibility of success, however slim the chances. His heart would never heal following the death of Solstia, and in some strange way this comforted him; a heart as damaged as his could hardly be broken any further.

Doran Dunarrk scoffed at this thought the instant it crossed his mind. He knew better. He knew the strength of a heart, and he knew that there was nothing in this world that could sustain more hardship, more injury or more suffering.

Yet, it gave him little comfort.

Kellert Sentero waited for the king in the atrium of the fortress. With him stood Staid Dyrro and several of Doran's personal guards. Doran had personally asked that the former trader be allowed into his inner circle. There was something about the man that lent him courage. Or perhaps, even hope.

"What news?" the king asked.

"They haven't moved yet," Kellert replied. "They appear to be waiting, though for what we cannot say. Perhaps they wait for the Isrorians to join their ranks, or perhaps to let the sun rise more fully. We do not know. We cannot pretend to understand their... kind."

"Are we ready?"

"As ready as we can be, Sire." He looked toward the distant field as Doran clapped him gently on the back.

"As much as I love this land, my friend, I should like to see it stained red by the time the sun sets."

Kellert nodded, his shaking hands tightening the buckle of his sword belt. "Nothing would please me more."

Doran nodded to the door. "Come, my friend." He made the sign of the waterdrop on his heart, something he'd not done in recent memory. "In all our years, we've never faced such a terrible challenge..." He patted Kellert on the shoulder, and smiled weakly. "But then, perhaps they have not either."

At the king's signal, the huge doors of the Keep were slowly pushed open. Yet, before he could step out into the mist, the shrill shriek of a peregrine falcon split the morning air. All stopped as the sleek bird streaked through the entrance and made two wide circles before swooping down to rest on the outstretched hand of the statue that stood near a large window in the atrium. The statue was that of a Rentorrian soldier, his stone gauntlet pointing a single finger to the north. It had been a gift from Intraal Talchol to Wilkren Dunarrk many years prior. The following year, Wilkren had commissioned the building of a similar statue, that of a Ryndarran warrior, likewise pointing to the distance. The Rentorrian king had sent a message to Intraal with his gift, requesting that he position the statue to have the warrior point to the distant city of Orshos. For his part, Wilkren had written, he had had his statue positioned to acknowledge the grand city of Levebule, capital of Embarria. The gesture, he stated, would demonstrate the solid support that each realm would extend to each other for all time.

On the soldier's hand, the falcon shrieked once more as it ruffled its wing feathers, its head bobbing up and down. The early morning light glinted on a small metal ring on the bird's right leg.

"Kellert..."

"I see it." He turned to Doran. "She must be near."

Staid looked from one man to the other, his confusion evident. "*Who* must be near?" He moved closer to the bird, his eyes narrowed on the creature's leg. "What's this on its leg, some sort of tag?"

The falcon shrieked, as if insulted.

"The silver ring of Embarria," Kellert said reverently. "This is Inlonia Talchol's falcon." The king's advisor moved toward the bird, which turned its graceful head upon his approach. "The falcons of the kings and queens of Embarria–" Kellert said in a low voice, "–are loyal to the death; their *own* death, as well as those they serve. If Inlonia had fallen, this falcon would have rested by her side until he too perished. The fact that he lives and comes to us in the absence of the queen can mean but one thing. He was sent for help."

Doran rushed past the men, and out through the open doors with his guards mere steps behind. Kellert and Staid, having given the falcon one last look, followed close behind. The king ran across the stone walkway that led to the Keep bailey, and raced toward the northern wall. He took the steps two at a time as he climbed the battlements and moved along the parapet walk. Breathless, the others arrived at his side.

He scanned the distant field. The morning mist made it all but impossible to see anything beyond the hazy tree-line as it covered the land and the recently felled trees like smoke above a smouldering fire. This day, Doran knew, would see its share of smoke and flame.

"She could be anywhere, Sire," Kellert offered. "She may be leagues deep in the forest. It's not poss–" But before he finished his thought, the shrieking falcon shot between them, and sped toward the forest's edge. All eyes followed the bird, which flew straight toward the fringe of the Nucono. Narrow eyes struggled to follow the falcon as he sank low to the ground half a league away, but the increasing fog coupled with the distance obscured the bird's path. Though the men could no longer see the bird, their gaze had followed the whip-straight line which it had flown, and they scanned the trees and rocks where it had been headed. Moments later, two vague shapes, barely discernible, emerged from the trees.

"Dahnu save us. It's her! It has to be." Doran grabbed the lip of the stone wall. He jerked his head toward the distant enemy, then back toward the queen of Embarria. Leaning over the parapet, he assessed the northern gate which – now secured and locked – sat just below them. "Kellert! The gate." He pushed off the wall and began to run down the narrow stone staircase. "We have to get her in!"

Steeling himself against doubt, Doran ran, his mind furiously trying to come up with the best plan. *So much had gone wrong in recent times*, he thought. *So much suffering.* He would not allow another such loss if he could avoid it. While he considered every life as valuable as the next, he realized that if they could get the queen into the safety of the city, significant strength would be lent to the hope and morale of Embarrians and Rentorrians alike.

"Fast riders, on two horses from the northern gate!" Kellert yelled at Doran as they descended a dark stairwell which opened into the courtyard. Doran nodded; the gesture imperceptible as they raced down the winding streets of stone. Heads turned as the people of Orshos watched their king race past them. Some began to shout, fearing that there'd been an attack. As much as Doran wanted to stop and reassure, he hadn't a moment to spare. Kellert, his keen mind likely seeing the need to preclude a panic amongst the citizens, shouted at one of the king's guards to stop and tell the people that there was no imminent threat – the king wished to rescue a friend caught outside the wall.

In short time they approached the northern gate, where the soldiers anxiously watched their approach. Several horses stood nearby, their saddles empty. "Open the gate!" Doran screamed as they came into hearing range. Confused faces looked around, though none moved toward the great wooden structure. Doran shouted the command once more, pointing a threatening finger at the soldier closest to the doorway. When the man saw who had issued the order, he instantly yelled at his men to raise the huge wooden latches that had been set in place. Others worked to remove the great buttresses that had been jammed and nailed to the wood, pulling them out of their bases in the ground. Moments later, as the massive gate hinges groaned against the opening, Doran glanced at the nearest soldiers. Breathless, he turned to Kellert. "Do you know any of these men?" he rasped. "Who has the speed that would bri–"

His words were cut off by an urgent cry directly behind them. He turned to find Staid Dyrro atop a horse, pulling the animal's left rein to bring him around to face the gate.

"Dyrro?" The king took a step forward as all the others stepped back to clear a path to the doorway.

"I've seen where she is, and I'm as swift as any. There's no time, Highness. No time!"

Doran saw the truth in this. Staid had seen where the queen was located, and time would only be wasted explaining her whereabouts to another. Further, Doran trusted this man. Staid Dyrro had walked into the heart of Isror and came out unscathed. His mettle was tested and unparalleled, and such grit was exactly what the situation required.

Doran nodded. He took a quick glance at the other riders, and saw one nearby that was atop an impressive steed. "You! With him! Go!" The soldier, being well trained, did not question the directive.

Almost in unison, Dyrro and the other rider gripped the reins, gave a quick kick to the horses' hindquarters and took off through the gate, shouting at the animals to let them know the situation was dire.

For just a moment, Doran was able to look through the opening in the wall. Glimpsing the terrible black mass that lay in the distance, he closed his eyes and whispered a hurried prayer to Dahnu before the gate thudded back into place, locking out both friend and foe.

19

REVELATIONS

"For the love of the elements, Niamh. How long do you intend to hang on?"

With great effort, Niamh stood. Refusing to look at Cehron, she limped amongst the Egimians, knelt beside Torla and gently touched her face. Sivino could see that of the two, Niamh's condition was undoubtedly graver. The thin hands that touched Torla now shook, and the faerae's face, always pale, blanched even further.

"No, Cehron, I'll remain a little while yet. A true creature of faerae stays true until the greater work has been done."

"Greater?" Cehron asked quietly, as if to himself. He looked at the flower he twirled slowly in his hands. "Yes, I suppose your work is greater than most." He looked at her as he stood. "It is a wonderful thing, to wield magic that can do so much good. Your influence in many worlds will be sorely missed. And who will continue your work when you are no more?"

Niamh's eyes hardened, but still she would not look

at him.

"Perhaps Master Lailoken will take up your cause," Cehron continued. "Have you told the Wanderer the secrets of the Paths? The Mist Gates? *The Stone Circles?* No? Well, I guess his skills are just wasted then, wouldn't you say?"

"Nothing is wasted that has the potential to do good, Cehron. You knew that once."

"Do *good?* Why, this fool and his tragic ancestors have hurt more than they have helped with their clumsy use of magic. How *you* can condone, and even encourage such mortals to practice magic is beyond my reckoning." His voice grew more urgent as their discussion deepened. "Believe me, Niamh. I was right when I told Obaeron that we should cut ties with other worlds. Let them fend for themselves without our interference."

"Our *help*, you mean."

"No, Niamh. It helps nothing. The mixing of different worlds invariably leads to a clash of philosophies, beliefs and technologies, with catastrophic results. Have I not made that abundantly clear with the Nylacci?"

"Cehron, differences in beliefs exist everywhere. *Within* individual worlds, it happens constantly."

"And look at the result, Niamh. Insignificant little countries make war over differing opinions, and would tear their lands and each other apart over their squabbles. If inhabitants of the same *world* can't settle their differences, how can different worlds be expected to interact with any sense of civility? It's not right, Niamh. You know it. Even this so-called war that these peasants fight is but a morbid little microcosm of the potential havoc that will be unleashed by further mixing. I brought the creatures of Dreg here to make this point abundantly clear."

"The shifting of Nylacci to Cahruia serves no purpose but your own, Cehron!"

"The shifting of *fools* serves no purpose but yours!" he yelled, pointing a menacing finger in her direction.

"It is the will of the Faant!" she shot back. "It has alw–" But her words were lost as her breath failed. Her arms wrapped around her midsection, and she began to sway. One hand moved up to her chest, but Sivino saw that the troubling feeling that arose there did not entirely remove the frustration from her face. Torla stood behind the faerae, and held her by the shoulders.

Cehron sighed, turning away slightly. "I'll not waste my breath arguing the absurdity of your words, Niamh. It was the interference of the Faant that first allowed magic to slip into the soul of a half-mortal eons ago. And it was the stupidity of a faerae foolish enough to love a mortal that served as the conduit!" The words cut deep into Niamh, for while she knew that Cehron was referring to the lovers from whom Man's magical abilities were born, she knew also that the faerae was undermining the relationship she'd shared with Oisin.

Niamh strode toward Cehron, steadying herself, pointing a finger. "Perhaps," she hissed, "perhaps it was your selfishness, *your* recklessness that prevented you from finding love as I did!"

He spun on her, screaming. *"And perhaps it was your blindness, Niamh, that prevented you from seeing how I loved you!"*

Niamh staggered slightly to the side, and stopped dead in her approach. None moved. None breathed. All eyes were on the face of Cehron Cen Kohr, whose chiselled features and bared teeth showed raw emotion for the first time in many, many years. His face teemed with anger. *Anger that his love had never been returned*, Sivino assumed. *Anger that Niamh had accepted the love of a mortal. But likely*, Sivino knew, *it was anger that, after so many years of keeping such anguish in check, it had burst forth like a ruptured dam.*

"Cehron?" she whispered.

Sivino saw the pity that for just an instant flashed in her eyes, and it undid something in Cehron Cen Kohr. His face darkened, and he seemed to cross a threshold into a region from which he might never return. Despite all he'd seen in recent days, Sivino could not recall seeing anything as unsettling as the look of malice that now filled the eyes of the faerae.

"Why do you think I did this, Niamh?" His voice was different now. It was low, steady and spoken with a tone that chilled all. "Why do you think I brought forth the Nylacci? Why do you think I brought them to the world that you cherished so much?"

"Cehron, you're mad… you're comple–"

"Why do you think I wish to utterly *destroy* this cursed world?" He smiled, and Sivino shivered. "Because, Niamh, I would prove to you that it is wrong to bring together that which must be kept separate. I would prove that some beings are best left *exactly where they are. That* is why I unleashed the fury of the Nylacci on this pathetic world." His smile faded, and his voice lowered to a horrible whisper.

"That is why I killed Oisin…"

She staggered again, and her knees buckled like wet parchment. As her head struck the ground of the courtyard, the world, which was never really her own, faded to black.

She awakens to the sound of morning birds, and rolls over in her soft bed to smell the scent of the man who just recently lay beside her. Of late, Oisin has taken to strolling the surrounding fields at dawn. She has spoken to him of the possible danger that accompanies beauty, and he has always heeded her words.

She moves from the bed, pulls on a thin white robe, and steps out of the humble cottage which they have filled with love since his arrival in Elysium. With bare feet, she walks across the meadows, beneath the massive trees of the Silver Wood, alongside the gentle rivers that meander across the land.

But she does not find him.

She tells herself that there is no need for great concern, but at the same time, she knows that it is unwise for a man not of this world to venture into unfamiliar regions.

After a short time, her worry begins to mount, and she moves through the land with greater speed. Moving in ever-widening circles, she covers an area larger than he could possibly have traversed in the time he's been gone. But still, she does not find him.

With great effort, she steadies her mind and tries to think rationally. He must still be within the Silver Wood. He must be. He cannot have shifted by himself. Only the Paths would provide him a means of leaving Elysium, and it's impossible that he could create such a passage.

But not impossible that he might happen upon one, still open from the travel of another.

She thinks of his fondness for bathing in the river, slipping into the waters and letting them carry him along, a helpless and willing passenger of the current. Could he have slipped onto a Path?

The thought unnerves her, and she feels the cold fingers of panic reach toward her. She has seen no strangers in the area recently, though this is not to say that the Fae of other realms have not wandered through. More faeraes venture within and throughout the extensive world of Elysium than shift to other worlds. Is it possible that Oisin encountered a faerae of the Unseelie Court? Surely, no such encounter could happen so close to her home, their home, without her knowing. She pulls the robe tighter around her now, though there is no chill in the warm air of the morning. She closes her eyes to steady herself. After several deep breaths, she feels she has calmed sufficiently; though if need be, she'll uproot every tree of the Silver Wood to find him.

She opens her eyes, and sees the fox.

The reddish-gold animal bounds behind a tree as though something in the faerae's eye has startled him. However, as he rounds the tree, Niamh is standing there, and grasps him by the neck with a firm hand.

"What have you seen?"

Though the animal cannot speak, the faerae can easily interpret its thoughts.

No. Hurt.

"I will not hurt you," she whispers. "You know the man I search for, do you not? You've seen something…"

No. Hurt. Vulpes.

"Listen! I will not hurt you… unless you keep your information from me. You have seen him?"

She pulls the animal so close their faces nearly touch. "Where is he?"

Water. *Moving.* Water.

"The River Faer?"

River.

"What happened?"

Man. Talk. Home. Want. Home.

"How?"

Man. Ask. Fae. Help. Want. Home.

She releases the fox and races toward the river with a speed that tears leaves from bush and tree. Shifted! she thinks, and she curses herself for her lack of caution.

She is still ten paces from the river when she dives, hitting the water with barely a splash.

The Path is still disturbed; small currents and temperature variations tell her they have been through recently. She follows this Path, letting it pull her toward her love, and the unfortunate faerae who was foolish enough to shift him. She thinks of the various Fae that inhabit her world. So many Unseelie that live for mischief. So many that crave the opportunity to trick and deceive. So many whose heartless souls would not think twice about granting a mortal man's wishes, though they know full well the devastating consequences.

It takes but a few moments, and she bursts from the water. Her eyes adjust instantly to the foreign sky and light, and she quickly recognizes the world she's entered.

"No," she whispers. She turns and looks along the narrow shore. Twenty paces from her, the body lies face-down in the water. She shakes her head. "No."

She doesn't need to turn him over. She recognizes his clothing. The wet, white hair upon his head brings a tear to her eye, for she understands the pain this metamorphosis must have caused. Her lips tremble, and she squeezes them together so tightly they are but a thin white line on her face. She pulls him from the water and lays him on the dry sand, kneeling slowly beside his once-powerful body.

Her right hand brushes his face, her fingers resting upon his unseeing eyes.

Her left hand rests upon her belly, and the new life that slowly grows within.

She takes his hand, and holds it in her own; holds it to the child who'll never know his father, but will see the world through his piercing blue eyes.

She collapses on his chest, and weeps bitterly.

20

THE SHEPHERD

From a storehouse window just up the street, the Shepherd watched the arrow explode in front of the girl's face.

A corner of his mouth turned upward, the closest he'd come to a smile in recent memory. As he watched the group below scurry to the girl's aid, he looked at Cehron, willing the faerae to finally call for him. The pain, he'd been promised, was to be his alone to inflict. The faerae pulled a wand from the ragged man on the ground, and spoke words he couldn't hear from such a distance. He pulled his hood further about his face as the sun broke from behind a cloud, and continued to watch in silence. Behind him, a gruff voice spoke up.

"Is he yet done with this foolishness?"

The Shepherd did not turn, nor did he respond.

"It's ridiculous," the voice continued. "I should never have agreed to this." The king of Isror lifted himself from a creaking wooden chair in the corner. "I have an army in the west, marching on Orshos without its leader." He moved to an adjacent window – loath to stand too near the hooded man – and looked at the group in the distance. Leaning on the sill, he stretched his neck excessively, his implication being that he'd been cooped up in this room far too long. "I am a king," he said. "*The* king. My place is not atop a dried fish warehouse. It is with my men. The conquest is mine. The victory must be mine. I should not be stuck here."

"Who forced your hand?"

Idach Garron was caught off-guard. He'd never heard the man beside him speak, though it was true they'd only shared company on very rare occasions. Indeed, the sandpaper quality of the man's voice suggested that it was not oft used. Idach felt his mouth begin to pull into a snarl despite his wariness of the cloaked man.

"No one forces a king," he replied. He leaned back from the sill and pointed a gloved finger at the man. "I do what I will, of my own accord." He took a step toward the Shepherd, despite his reservations. "I do what I will, for the good of my realm and my people. I was given the word of the Cernunnos that I'd be given an opportunity to rule a *world*, not just a realm. It's simply a matter of… seeing out the plan. I likely could have taken Rentorria without those beasts, but kings do not take chances. They seize opportunity." He moved back to the window, but his eyes stayed on the Shepherd. "And what of *you*?" he asked in a low voice, jerking his chin toward the other. "What exactly is *your* motivation in all of this?"

The Shepherd was not given to introspection, despite the great amount of time he'd spent alone. In part this was due to the confusion he felt when such efforts were made. Never had he walked the plains of Rentorria, or seen the rugged beauty of her shores. Never had he walked the northern forests of Embarria, or met a single citizen who resided in that wide, wondrous land. And yet, the hatred which he bore for these realms and its people was overwhelming.

Below, he watched as the faerae tossed a wand into the lake that sat beside the city; a city he himself – along with the Cernunnos and the Nylacci – had helped destroy. He'd come to the region only recently, having spent the last several years in the realm of Cantavaria on the eastern side of the Cudgel Mountains. *Things were tougher there,* he thought. *Much tougher than the early years, when he got by rather easily in the Valley of Elis to the northeast of Jhora, or in Hingstenn, which was further east still. And there were other homes too,* he recalled. Then, he corrected himself. *No. They were never* homes. *Not by half.*

How long had it been since he'd met the faerae? Ten years surely. Perhaps fifteen. The enigmatic creature had a way of providing exactly what the man needed. He'd ensured that the Shepherd was never in want, and helped him to live a life of relative comfort. Wanting little more than to be left alone, his needs were few indeed. As long as the Shepherd followed the simple and usually infrequent requests of Cehron Cen Kohr, the faerae assured him his comfort would continue for many years.

And always, there was the sweet promise of revenge.

He remembered little of his past life. In the years he'd spent in the faerae's friendship, that former life faded with the slow consistency of a wilting flower. The petals of his past were gone now. All that remained was the memory of a woman; a love that had been stolen from him on a fateful day when he'd very nearly lost his own life. Left beaten and bloodied in the forest, he'd been found by the Cernunnos. Rescued, as it were, and taken to a place of safety and convalescence on the eastern side of the mountains in a strange new world.

He remembered little of those early days of healing. He could not even remember what the cottage had looked like. The only memories he had of that time were the smell of the straw bed, the taste of warm goat's milk, and snippets of songs that the faerae sang before a slowly dying fire.

The abhorrence of the lands to the west had grown in the Shepherd, consuming him slowly. The faerae checked in on him from time to time, and each time he did, he shared stories of the atrocities of the westerners, and the greed, immorality and selfishness which, in his informed opinion, defined the lot.

It was they, the faerae informed the Shepherd, *that left you broken; that destroyed your life, and took from you all that you held dear… And it was I who saved you.*

Indeed, the Shepherd felt indebted to the faerae for his rescue. Yet, while the physical recovery was swift, the Shepherd found that the mental effects of the attack remained. He could remember so little of his past life, his memory allowing him only brief flashes of days gone by, faces he'd known and places he'd been. Each time he tried to recollect important details, they would fade away in a shimmering haze, to be replaced with images of pretty maids or vile westerners which Cehron sang of in equal measure. Initially, the Shepherd was quite frustrated and oftentimes depressed by this limitation, but as time passed, the frustration turned into anger, and anger into rage. He felt that his life had been stolen from him, and came to realize that it could never be returned. He'd voiced these thoughts to the faerae initially, but found that the words of the faerae, while soft and certain, did little to console.

If anything, he found that the words fed the flames that raged in him, and over time his thoughts became menacing to the point that he feared he'd become a different person. Cehron assured him that all would be well once his love was found. He informed him as well that those who'd destroyed his former life would be brought to justice.

All in due time, the faerae would say, his eyes smiling. *If there's one thing we have, my friend, it's time.*

He'd lived a reclusive life. In the realms he travelled, he associated with the populace as little as possible. For the most part, he hunted and scavenged his own food, growing what he could depending on the soil and climate of whatever region he found himself living.

The only constant in his life was the faerae, and through the years, it was the faerae who promised that he'd have his revenge on those who'd wronged him. That promise was honoured in the most unexpected manner. Visiting with him one stormy night, the faerae had sat before a fire in the man's cottage and stared beyond the flames. *I've just returned from a fascinating land,* the faerae had told him. *The land of Dreg.* Shadows grew around his eyes. *There, I have found the means by which you may have your revenge... and I may have a piece of mine as well.* The faerae continued to look into the flames as he informed the Shepherd of the plan, and the role that he was to play alongside the faerae. *An army; an army of great and terrible beasts, that will storm across the western lands, destroying evildoers as they go. An army that* cannot *fail.* He turned and looked the Shepherd squarely in the eye, smiling a genuine smile. *And because you wield a power that even these creatures cannot stand against... you will lead them. I have spoken to the lead beast. I've told him of your power, and I've promised him that should he and his kind follow us in this great battle,*

I will see that they have the opportunity to spread their wrath very, very widely.

And so, once the mass had been assembled, the Shepherd had led them; led the most horrifying army these lands had ever seen, leaving a trail of destruction in its wake. Yes, there were some that had been unable to restrain themselves and had left the assembly, striking out on their own to satisfy their uncontrollable bloodlust. But for the most part, he was able to keep them together as one massive, horrifying body.

He was, after all, a shepherd.

He breathed deeply with the satisfaction that the realm of Rentorria now lay essentially in ruins, its people scattered with the four winds with only one city standing between it and total devastation.

He knew that he had the faerae to thank for this, but some unknowable part of his mind resented the creature as well. In a mind filled almost entirely with anger and thoughts of violence, it was futile to try and parse the reasons.

All he was interested in was release.

21

CASUALTIES OF WAR

Staid Dyrro and the soldier rode hard to the forest. The mist that crept over the land was not heavy enough to mask their flight, and he was certain that they would soon be spotted. Staid tried not to think of this as he rode. *Focus on the queen,* he told himself. *Focus on the straightest path to her, and return with her safely.* They sped north along the Sea Road, which inclined steadily for a league from the Center Gate, before it veered northeast and slipped into the depths of the Nucono.

They departed the road as it turned, and made their way due north, pushing the horses to their limit as they ran through the vegetable fields that had been left dormant for this season. *Dahnu above,* Staid thought, *let there not be a neglected plow blade left beneath this undergrowth.* He glanced over at the vaguely familiar rider, slightly behind him and to his right. *What was his name?* Staid thought. *Ven? Von? Something like that.* Staid figured him to be a good man. He must be. He'd not hesitated a moment at Doran's request, though he must have known, like Staid, that they were very likely riding to their deaths. Staid pushed his horse all the harder, slowing only slightly as they entered the area that had once been the Nucono's fringe. The trees had been cut for needed material within the city, but also to prevent the enemy from getting too close to the city unseen. The stumps stood like ominous grave markers of the forest. Looking beyond this, Staid focused on the distant boulders, an easy landmark despite the increasing mist.

As they reached their destination the two figures quickened their pace, making their way toward the riders. The larger of the two, a tall bearded man, struggled to assist the woman at his side. The man's dark skin was streaked with blood. Both were injured, though how badly was difficult to tell. Their clothing was ripped, and scratches and bruises covered their bodies. Staid could discern no grievous wound on either, though the woman's limp and the way she cringed with each step assured him that she was in no small amount of pain. As Staid and his companion pulled up beside the pair, the man drew his sword with an effort that Staid found pitiful. Despite the wretched state of the bearded man, he was still a protector, and Staid was instantly on his guard.

"From your uniform, I must presume that you are friends," the dark man rasped. "Though it is easy enough for wolves to don sheep's clo–" A screech from the falcon, which stood on a nearby stump.

"Ennis, please–" The woman's voice was even more dry and worn than her friend. She seemed about to speak again, when the air was filled with a bestial cry that filled both sky and soul with foulness. Its power could not be denied. And its message was clear. Four thousand Nylacci began to march on Orshos.

"No time for this," Staid urged. "We've been sent by Doran Dunarrk, and I'll be damned if I fail him because of time spent chattering." He dismounted quickly, giving the queen's protector a look that while urgent, was also pleading. "The queen shall ride with me. And you...*Ennis* is it?" He gave a jerk of his head in the direction of the man who might be Von. "You're with him."

"Dear Ennis," the queen rasped as Staid helped her onto the horse. "Ever my protector." She glanced back at the forest. A sound of pain escaped her, and Staid could tell the pain was not merely physical.

"Are there others?" Staid asked as he mounted.

"Gone," she whispered. "May Dahnu find and keep them. Now please, take me to my countrymen."

The falcon cried once more, and took flight.

The noise of the field was deafening. Staid cursed as they raced the horses toward Orshos, pulled down the hill by the gravity of adrenaline and the weight of responsibility. The horses, he knew, were horrified by what they saw but they were well trained and would demonstrate as much discipline as any soldier in the realm.

Staid surveyed the land. They were about halfway back to the gates of the city. From their elevated vantage point, they'd seen the magnitude of the dark army. It was overwhelming; a growling mass of black and brown. Like a bear skin, thought Staid – a discarded bear skin on a forest floor that writhed and was shifted by maggots and other small creatures that sought the rank comfort it provided. The first section of Nylacci, perhaps a third of their overall force, was slightly less than a league from the city walls. *We'll make it,* Staid assured himself. *It can be done.* The horses they rode were fast, despite the extra rider on each, and had navigated the field of stumps masterfully.

The front line of monsters did not run. They set a steady pace, conserving their energy for the work ahead. *Work, or pleasure*, thought Staid. These words were likely interchangeable to the beasts when it came to a good slaughter.

A few last strides through the entangled gardens, and they were once more on the Sea Road. Swift riders on this thoroughfare could usually be seen for leagues in dry conditions; the dust of the road rising in plumes as if the pathway was afire. On this day, nothing rose from the horse's hooves but the dull, even thud of their gallop. They were close now. Faces would soon be discernible on the parapets. Shouts of encouragement would soon reach their ears. Staid gave a shout, and pushed the horse to its limit as Von did the same.

Suddenly to the east a shift began to occur in the blanket of horror that moved toward the city. The northernmost battalion – perhaps a full third of those Nylacci that were advancing – slowly broke away from the rest of the group. Staid's eyes slanted in this direction as the horses rode on. Surely, he thought, they did not intend to send a thousand of these creatures to deal with a few riders. Perhaps it was their intent to separate the section into thirds; each group attacking the city walls from different angles, splitting and subsequently weakening the defence. But the separation of the Nylacci, Staid soon saw, was not done to divide the attacking force.

It was done to create a path.

Oh, Goddess defend me! he thought. *What in creation is* that?

From the opening raced creatures unlike anything Staid had ever seen. *No. No, that wasn't true*, he realized as he watched them, his mouth hanging open in terror. He'd seen something like these nightmares before, many times.

They were like cockroaches.

They were the size of horses, though perhaps twice as wide. They ran – *skittered*, Staid thought was a better word – on six legs of equal length. Each creature's body, though still too distant to tell, appeared to be plated – a brownish green exterior that was covered in coarse hair.

There were three of them. They set a line straight toward the northern limit of the city, intent on intercepting the riders as they made for safety. Staid screamed to the others to inform them of what was happening. Mere steps behind him, he heard Von roar at his horse and the breakneck pace of the steeds moved from urgency to terrified desperation.

No help would come from the city; at least not until the creatures were within firing range. By then, Staid feared, the massive roaches would be upon them. He shook his head. *The wall. Focus on the bleeding wall!* The northern gates, he knew, would not open, but rope ladders would be dropped in an attempt to pull the riders from the fate that awaited them. They were close enough now to see the people atop the walls preparing just such a rescue. Glancing toward the horrible loping creatures, he saw that his company actually had a slight lead. They would make the wall first, but with little time to spare. He forced his thoughts from the fate that awaited the magnificent steeds that had made this rescue possible. *I have a mission*, he reminded himself. *The queen.* He could not help what tragic end the animals would meet. *Casualties of war*, he thought bitterly.

"When we reach the city," he shouted to the queen,

"you'll grab the nearest rope ladder. Hold it firm. They'll be pulling it up as you climb!"

"What of you?" Inlonia shouted back.

"There'll be several ladders! My mission was to bring you to safety. Don't jeopardize this with noble heroics!"

"Is it the custom of all Rentorrians to give orders to foreign royalty!?"

In any other situation, Staid would have smiled.

"You get on that ladder," he yelled, "and you'll hear no more orders from me!"

He watched as the ladders dropped beside the gate. They were close now; close enough to make out the texture of the wall. The aged wood, reinforced with steel, was about to feel its first assault in many years. To his left, he saw the roaches closing in. But not just closing in. Separating. The creatures ran in three separate ways, a strategy Staid had previously expected of the army. *They're trying to surround us*, Staid thought. *Likely unaware of our means of escape.*

A moment later the horses skidded to a stop, teeth bared as reins were pulled tight. The queen did as asked, and gripped the ladder that Staid pulled into her hands. Within seconds, she was ascending the wall as a group of soldiers lifted her into the last free city of Rentorria. Staid stole a glance behind himself. *Thirty seconds? Twenty?* The beasts were fast. He could see now the many jointed segments of their thick legs. Worse, he could see the jagged rows of teeth that worked within those mouths. He felt his heart hammering in his chest. Beside him, Von helped the man named Ennis onto a ladder of his own. Only now did Staid notice the extent to which Ennis' arm had been injured; a nasty gash ran from his shoulder to the elbow on his left arm. With his right, he gripped the rope and followed his queen to Orshos.

Staid could hear the hiss of the arrows that were now being loosed on the charging beasts, and while several found their mark, it was not yet enough to bring these savage creatures down.

"Dyrro! Get on those ropes now!" A scream from atop the wall. Staid didn't need to look to recognize the voice of Kellert Sentero. He stole another glance over his left shoulder. They had to go now. The roaches shrieked behind them, enraged that their prey seemed to be escaping. The horses answered with a shrill cry of their own. Staid shook his head, disgusted at the sacrifice they had to make, and standing in his stirrups he grabbed the nearest rope.

"Sorry boy," he muttered as he took hold of the lower rung.

A shrill cry beside him tensed every muscle in his body, it being so similar to the scream of the monsters. Von's horse, having held itself together for so long, finally gave into the terror. Its rider, having only the slightest grip on the ladder, was thrown as the horse reared. Von fell hard in a clatter of armour as soldiers screamed from the walltop.

In that moment, Staid acted purely on instinct. He let go of the hemp rungs that would have ensured his safety, fell back into the saddle and grabbed the reins once more. Seeing this brought forth another roar from above, but Staid focused on nothing but his fallen comrade. He spun toward Von, only to find the roaches upon them. Von was on his feet, incredulity in his eyes. He'd seen the sacrifice Staid had made and would not let such an act be wasted. His terrified horse bolted toward the forest, drawing one of the three monsters close behind. The two that remained had slowed. Their leathery legs dug at the dirt as they prepared to face the soldiers; dark purple tongues lolling in their horrible mouths. Staid's horse beat its hooves upon the ground, the frenzied twisting of its neck pulling the reins that Staid struggled to hold. Gripping his sword before him, Von darted forward, stepping between the horse and the roaches. He did not turn as he spoke.

"To the harbour!" he yelled. "Do not let this be in vain."

"No!" Staid shouted. "We can—"

"NOW!" Von screamed over his shoulder. He burst forth, his sword a blur as he cut through the air, slicing at the beasts. Arrows pierced the hides of the creatures, but still they did not seem harmed. Their plated backs repelled at least half the arrows that were fired. Staid drew his sword, but the fight was over almost as soon as it had begun. Von moved in, attempting to stab at the underbelly of the closest creature, but in a swift motion, the roach swung one of its legs and struck the soldier in the knee. Von went down in a heap as the other beast jumped forward, bringing its leg down heavily on the exposed neck of the Rentorrian. With a single step, the life was crushed out of Orshos' first defender. The monster took a quick bite from Von's arm and turned to face Staid Dyrro, pieces of the soldier's flesh and uniform stuck in its serrated teeth.

Staid wasted no time. A violent pull on the reins brought his horse around, and they were racing for the sea.

The Nylacci screamed in excitement as they saw these events unfold. Though they were not yet near enough to join in the slaughter, the realization that blood had been spilled so quickly sent a wave of excitement through their ranks.

Staid leaned forward and shouted to the horse, as much to drown out the growls of the roaches as to encourage the steed. Racing along the wall, Staid refused to look behind himself. From above, soldiers continued to fire their arrows upon the creatures. The shrieks intensified, but the roaches were relentless.

Staid knew that his only hope was to reach the water with the horse and swim around the massive wall to the docks beyond. As they sped along the curved wall, it seemed his destination would never come into sight. He knew that the horse was reaching its breaking point; fatigue and fear eating away at its resolve. He could hear the beasts behind them still, and hoped with all his heart that the monsters were not swimmers.

Finally, the water was before them. Staid quickly pulled his boots from the stirrups. The horse did not hesitate. He threw himself into the sea as Staid jumped from his back. He went under; the cold water and the absence of the shrieking was, for a short time, something of a relief. But he knew that those nightmares would not give up. He surfaced, as did the horse, and looked around in panic. A moment later, he saw a great splash that rained water down upon him. He knew that there were only seconds left and he turned, thrashing in the brine, still firmly holding his sword.

The beasts had slowed. It seemed that while they could swim, they could not do so with speed. It was just the opportunity that the soldiers on the wall needed. Staid looked up and saw four soldiers carefully aiming their arrows. Beside them, two others hefted long, pointed spears.

The beast nearest Staid made one final lunge, a powerful leg coming up out of the water and reaching for the horse. But as it reached, the barrage of missiles flew from the wall, sticking into the creature with wet smacking noises. A final shriek and it slowly stopped moving. Its counterpart, taking less arrows and being far from dissuaded, doubled its efforts, pushing its brethren underwater as it scrambled over the lifeless body. Staid struggled to grip his sword as he treaded water. The creature moved in quickly, thrashing as though drowning. Its head bobbed upon the surface of the water; its ragged breath spitting sprays of sea water onto Staid. He watched the beast's rough purple tongue flicking on the water, and then, he saw its leg slowly emerge from the foam. Before it could strike, Staid thrust himself forward with a roar. He felt the blade enter the beast's face and screamed again, his eyes stinging from the salty water. He kicked his feet, willing himself forward, pushing into the monster. The creature's leg came down on his shoulder, but it held no strength. Staid smacked the leg away with one hand, shook the water from his face, and twisted his sword, which was buried deep in the roach's eye. Another flurry of well-placed arrows finished the monster.

Staid turned and swam away quickly, urging the horse ahead of him before either could be touched by the dark blood that stained the water.

22

A SAD GAME

In the distance, the Shepherd and the king approached.

Sivino, curious despite his fear, moved a few paces from his people to get a better look. The Shepherd, he surmised, was the hooded man riding the horse; the hooves clopping a steady rhythm as the pair slowly made their way along the flagstone. The man on foot, by his garb, was the king of Isror. Clad in thin, elegant robes of black, the king looked less than impressed as he walked beside, and slightly behind, the rider. In short time, Sivino could hear the muttering of the man's deep, rough voice.

Behind the group, Cehron Cen Kohr rose slowly from the barrel upon which he sat, exhaling heavily as though the events which were about to transpire were an inconvenience to his busy schedule. Sivino glanced over his shoulder at the faerae, and then looked back at the Shepherd and the king, whose eyes brimmed with resentment.

"Cehron," the king began. He didn't even spare a look at the group that stood facing him. It was evident that the Egimians concerned him as little as the dead Nylacci around which they stood. "Could not another horse be found? You promise me a world, and you cannot provide me with a blasted mare?"

Cehron smiled, though his gaze was focused on the Shepherd. "My dear Idach." He turned his head and looked squarely at the king, the tilt of his head allowing a shadow to spread gently across his face. "Have we shared a single conversation in which you've *not* reminded me of our little pact?"

"Little?" Idach snorted. "I remember your words well, faerae. You said that in exchange for the use of my lands and resources for your army, you'd lend your force to my own, and give me the opportunity to rule an entire world. Once Rentorria has fallen under my command, that is exactly what I intend to do." Smiling, Idach took a couple of steps toward the Cernunnos. "Don't say it won't be so, Cehron. I know the truth of the faerae lore." His voice was low. Malicious. "I know that faeraes cannot lie."

Sivino glanced from the king to the Shepherd, and noticed that the rider seemed entirely uninterested in the exchange, and was in fact staring directly at him. The skin on Sivino's arms crawled, and it took great effort not to shudder visibly. The Shepherd's hood precluded anyone seeing his eyes, but his hatred was evident in the set of his mouth. Watching the Egimians, he sat unmoving. The lower part of his face, darkened by a short, rough beard, held a scowl that made Sivino wonder what anyone could have done to cause such loathing. His mouth, lips barely parted, seemed ready to spit in the face of the first person to approach him.

"I wouldn't dream of lying," Cehron replied. "You've been a most gracious host, Idach. Your land was the ideal place to gather. A relatively short passage from Dreg, and my shaggy companions were almost suffced by the cattle and wildlife available. However, I do thank you for supplementing their diet. It kept them strong, you can be sure. Pork and prisoners. Beef and traitors. Even the old and infirm were adequate appetizers." He laughed softly, shaking his head. "Such delicate palates these Nylacci have."

Sivino looked at the king with renewed disgust. Treachery and greed were one thing, but these new revelations were something else altogether.

"Expendables," Idach said. Yet, Sivino could see that he said it without conviction. For just a moment, the sagging of the king's shoulders was perceptible, and his eyes left those of the faerae.

"Granted, you were a great help, Idach." Cehron turned then to the Shepherd. "But not so great as my dear friend here."

A slight twitch in the neck of the Shepherd. Rhenna's voice whispered in Sivino's ear. He recalled her words, repeated so often and so emphatically. *When you learn to read people, Sivi, there shall be no need for words.* Something about the faerae's comment hadn't sat well with the man on the horse. He wondered if all was as it appeared between the two.

"Be that as it may," Idach continued, "we need to get on with this tiresome ordeal. I should be with my men, watching as Orshos falls. Instead, you have me here, bearing witness to events that have nothing to do with me. I want what was promised, Cehron."

"And you'll have it." The faerae's voice was even, but Sivino saw the sharp annoyance that the faerae hid just beneath his smile. He turned a warm gaze back to the Shepherd. "When we began this little adventure," Cehron said, "I told the head of the Nylacci to spread the word amongst his brethren that this man was my faithful assistant – my Shepherd, as it were – and that he was to be followed and obeyed." *Again, the twitch,* Sivino noted. "There was some dissension, as one might expect. I sweetened the deal by assuring them that, if they followed, obeyed and succeeded, more Paths would be opened to them – Paths that would see their insatiable bloodlust satisfied. But the pact was finalized–" Cehron smiled at the Shepherd. "–when my friend here gave a *demonstration,* as it were. He showed the creatures that all their brawn and brutality could not compare to his power."

As the faerae finished, the Shepherd slipped his hood from about his head. His eyes bore into Cehron Cen Kohr, before looking around coldly at all gathered. To his side, Sivino heard Niamh exhale slowly, her body visibly deflating at the sight of the man. She shook her head slowly before closing her eyes. She had the look of one who has struggled for long, long years, and senses a final blow that may in some way grant peace. She turned to Cehron. "A wicked game," she said.

The Cernunnos winked at her.

Sivino took in the face of the man. Long brown hair flecked with grey fell in front of his face. His eyes appeared sunken, though not by the natural process of age. He had the look of an animal, weary from the hunt, eyes worn by the constant scanning for prey, and fatigued by the continual failure. Yet, the face held some familiarity to Sivino. He thought upon the residents of Egim, wondering who it was that triggered this feeling of recognition. Beside him, Niamh spoke again.

"Cehron? *Truly?*" Her mouth hung open in shock and pain. "All these years? *Why?*"

"As I've said, Niamh, I enjoy the game. And I'm a patient creature. In truth, sixteen years seems to go in the blink of an eye…"

More riddles, Sivino thought. *More shadows and secrets, as Lomin sometimes says.* It surprised Sivino somewhat that the fear that had recently gripped him was now being replaced by the heat of frustration. He knew that he and those he loved were pawns in Cehron's game; pawns that were threatened more and more with every move. He was tired of this game, he now realized. It was time to make his own move.

"Enough of this," he said loudly. He turned to the Shepherd "Who *are* you? Why do you hate us so?" As he asked the question, he stepped away from his loved ones to face the man more fully and to reduce the possibility that any attack directed at him would affect his family and friends by their proximity.

There was silence amongst them. Behind them, the waters of the Madimest lapped against the quay with a slow steady rhythm; the heartbeat of the lake.

"It's me he should hate." Niamh stood facing the Shepherd, but she did so with no hint of animosity. Her face was as sad as any Sivino had ever seen. "Perhaps with good reason," she added. She took a few steps toward him, and Sivino found it hard to decipher if it was sadness or pity that she most felt.

"Niamh," Lomin warned, but the faerae raised her thin hand to silence him.

"Cehron," Idach interrupted. "I seriously–"

Cehron Cen Kohr turned on the king of Isror, a long finger pointed at his face. The faerae's smile was a restrained snarl. "*Not* now."

"The time for secrets is over," Niamh whispered to the

Shepherd. "Let us end this."

"End?" the Shepherd hissed, his voice low. "My life ended long ago." Sivino heard the pain in his voice, and while it didn't negate the hatred, it took its place rightfully beside the anger. "What you see before you is a shadow of the man that was; a shadow so distorted by tricks of light and darkness and failing memory that I lack definition. I am *emptiness* embodied." His low voice had faded as he spoke, as if reinforcing the state of being he described. Sivino could see the Shepherd's chest rise and fall as he took several breaths in an attempt to gain some composure. He failed. His scream jarred all present, save Niamh and Cehron.

"You stole *everything* from me!"

"I did the will of the Faant," Niamh spoke quietly.

The man's face, still twisted in the visage of a scream, melted into a sardonic smile. "The will of the Faant." He looked at Cehron. The two had no doubt shared thoughts on the matter over many fireside cups of tea. "I guess it's the will of these fools that we've all converged here? The prophecy, is it? Whispers of the Creators?" He spit to his side. "I've never believed in such foolishness. Yet, you must put a lot of credence in these silly notions. Otherwise, you'd not have brought the whelp here."

Sivino's face hardened at the insult. He watched as Cehron Cen Kohr walked slowly around the outskirts of the group. His hands, joined behind his back, held Sivino's sword hilt loosely. The tip of the blade dragged in the dirt, forming a thin circle around Niamh and the Shepherd. It reminded him of the roughhouse game they'd played as children. A circle in the dirt, and the two combatants in the middle would struggle to push the other outside the boundary. Cehron's gaze was on the ground as he walked,

Sivino noted, and that terrible smile played on the corners of his mouth. Sivino wondered if the faerae was aware of the childhood game, and whether this was a joke he was using for his own amusement.

"It is as it must be," Niamh said simply.

"And how must it be?" The Shepherd's agitation was growing. Sivino could see that the man was moving more, shifting himself in his saddle the way bulls kicked the earth before they charged one another. "Cehron has told me of the prophecy often enough that its words fill my head on sleepless nights. How does it go? *Within the unnatural storm, a shepherd true and dark shall find his blood spilt on the sword of a boy. A lost soul shall know those bonds that dying blood reveals. In the shadow of loss, the shepherd shall fade, for the sword of a boy shall cut through a power both great and terrible.*"

He smirked, an expression which held no hint of humour. "My blood on the boy's sword? Do you not know that I could strike him down where he stands at this moment?" He looked at Niamh. "And you as well. For the shifting you continue to facilitate, for the life you've taken from me, I could snuff yours out in a heartbeat. I would show you the folly of this ridiculous prophecy, show you that my blood is not something that I intend to lose."

Leath was in front of Sivino instantly, with Dels right behind.

"You'll first go through us, if that's your intention," said Dels. "I'll not lose a son this day, not while I've a single breath to draw."

"Then perhaps your time is shorter than you think," the Shepherd said as he stepped forward.

Niamh moved between Dels and the Shepherd. She held a hand up gently as she intervened, but her eyes were on the ground. She paused, stood in place, as if looking for the words. Finally, she turned her eyes slowly to the Shepherd.

"You've not seen my face," Niamh told him, "but I knew yours when it was young and handsome. Fate can be cruel.

"I wish things could have been different, Daniel."

Sivino had known for some time now that nothing should surprise him when it came to the Fae. Despite this knowledge, the shock he felt was like some terrible belt tightening suddenly around his chest, constricting his breath as he realized how little he actually knew. He struggled with Niamh's words, trying to process what they meant. "Niamh... you *know* him?"

"*Knew* him, lad..." Cehron added, his voice feigning disapproval of the long-kept secret. "...when he knew your mother."

Sivino spun toward the Cernunnos. "My mother?" He turned back to Niamh, his eyes seeking answers. "What trickery is this?"

"I speak only the truth, my boy," said Cehron. "I enjoy a little deception from time to time, but dear Niamh plays the most wicked game of all. And all for the will of the Faant. Tearing apart young lovers, leaving a poor, heartbroken shepherd lost and alone while his love is shifted; whisked away to another world, and she, the poor girl..." He smiled, tilted his head to Sivino. "...carrying his child."

Sivino froze. He couldn't move, couldn't breathe. He turned slowly to Dels, whose eyes fell shut.

No, he thought. *It has to be a trick. Dels Spallic would not keep such a secret from his family. Would he?* And then, he saw the tear in Dels' eye. In that one tear, a sliver of light reflected and Sivino had all the answers he needed. That invisible belt around his chest tightened, and choked off any further questions he might have asked. Sivino turned to the Shepherd, and saw on his face that he was just as confused as Sivino. The man sat on his horse, unmoving.

"It's a sad game, some would say," Cehron noted matter-of-factly. "Not *me*, personally. I find the whole ordeal terribly entertaining." He smiled, and stepping up beside Sivino he placed a cold hand on the boy's shoulder. Sivino flinched, but his state of shock prevented him from pulling away.

"Every game must have a victor, boy," Cehron whispered in his ear. "Every prophecy must be fulfilled." As he spoke, he tossed Sivino's sword to the ground in front of them. "Step forward now," Cehron said. His eyes narrowed as he looked from the boy to the Shepherd.

"Step forward and face your father…"

23

A TRUE RENTORRIAN WELCOME

"Love of the Goddess, boy!"

The old man, submerged to his knees on the boat ramp, extended a shaky hand to Staid. The bushy grey eyebrows which stuck off skyward exacerbated the incredulity in his crowfoot eyes. A fisherman, Staid thought. The old fellow's hand was big and callused, and wore the telltale signs of a fisher's life. Raw, distinct slice marks upon the index finger and palm where the nets and lines dug in while being pulled. Hard hands, he thought, but hands that had rarely if ever held a sword. He accepted the man's powerful grip and let himself be pulled from the water.

"Love of the Goddess..." The fisherman shook his head as he repeated these words, and Staid noted how the man trembled almost as much as he himself.

"That thing–" the man whispered.

"Is dead, friend," Staid cut him off as he sheathed his sword. "But there are more of them." He heard cursing, and glanced up at the wall. Valdi Tomar, the commander assigned to the South Gate, moved hurriedly down a flight of wooden steps. His severe face was knotted just over the bridge of his nose.

"Damnation, Dyrro! What happened? Were there no ladders?"

"There were," Staid replied. "I went back–" He rubbed his brow roughly, as if to erase the image of Von's throat being crushed. "I went back to help Von, the soldier who rode with me. He fell. Lost his ladder. I thought I could save him."

Tomar's eyes narrowed. Staid, seeing equal measures of admiration and disbelief, turned to the task of removing his wet cloak. The chill overcast air hit him immediately, causing him to shudder. A soldier moved forward and removed his own outer coat. Staid raised a hand to refuse, but the man shook his head and pushed the coat toward him. Staid accepted it with a nod of thanks.

"The queen. She made it over the wall?" Tomar asked hesitantly.

"She did."

"The queen?" A soldier standing on the periphery of the conversation moved forward. Embarrian, Staid saw by his burgundy garb. His eyes, bright with hope, fixed on Staid. "Queen Inlonia? She's here?"

"She is," said Staid. "She and another. A man called Ennis."

"Tinod'atu." The soldier smiled. Staid watched as the young man's hands moved to his sword belt, fixing it unconsciously in a tighter notch, as if preparing for inspection. In this small action, Staid saw exactly why the Embarrian queen had made her way to the war-torn region.

"For the moment," Tomar barked, "South Gate is not a target. The army moves toward Center Gate."

"That is where the first assault will happen," said Staid. "That's where I need to go." He looked around. Several of the men nearby had helped his horse out of the water, and were moving the steed off the ramp. One who seemed familiar with animals was taking great efforts to calm the horse, holding tight to its reins as he put a firm hand on the animal's neck, giving him soft but firm orders. He turned, leading the horse away from the water, his commands restoring some small amount of normalcy to the disciplined but shaken animal.

"I'll need another horse," Staid said.

Tomar nodded and jerked his chin at the coatless soldier who ran to retrieve a suitable animal. The commander pulled at his breastplate, his eyes on the wall. "It's a mighty foe," he said to Staid. "Our numbers are greatest at Center Gate, but we've enough soldiers at the north and south to provide a solid enough defence."

Staid nodded. *Solid enough.* He hoped that the wall itself would prove solid enough in the next few hours.

The soldier returned with a lean-looking steed, white with speckles of brown, and an eager look in his eyes. *Ready to run,* Staid thought. He mounted the animal, his wet pants tight and uncomfortable in the saddle.

"Dahnu speed you," Tomar said. "And if she wills it, we'll speak again soon."

Staid nodded. He could not know the will of the Goddess, but he knew his own, and with a quick shout to the horse he raced northward; ready, he hoped, for the madness that was about to unfold.

Doran Dunarrk pushed away from the parapet and made his way to the queen. He'd watched in horror from atop the North Gate as the beast had crushed the fallen soldier's neck, allowing Staid Dyrro to turn and flee. What became of the trader, he didn't know, but he forced his mind to focus on the task at hand. Staid was a swift rider, and he'd whispered a quick prayer for the man as he banged down the wooden plankway toward the queen of Embarria.

He found her kneeling beside her companion, her face contorted with concern. His formal greeting evaporated as he looked past her to the man to whom she tended. Ennis Tinod'atu sat leaning against a barrel filled with arrows, his head tilted heavily to his side. His coat had been removed, his left sleeve torn away to expose a flesh wound that caused the king to grimace in spite of himself. A moment later, Kellert Sentero arrived at his side. The king spun, beckoning a couple of nearby soldiers. "Get this man to the healers," he ordered as he and Kellert moved in to help Inlonia to her feet, allowing the men to see to the injured man.

"I would stay–" the man began, but was cut off by the queen.

"You would, but you will not Ennis." Gingerly, she helped the soldiers get Ennis to his feet. "Go with them. Stay the bleeding. You'll do no good fainting at my feet. You've fought valiantly." She put a soft hand on his cheek. "You'll fight another day."

"Your leg–"

"Is fine, Ennis. I'm bruised, not broken. Or bleeding. Please, let them tend to you."

Ennis opened his mouth to speak, but the words were lost in a grimace of pain as he was moved along the bridge.

"I'll return," he slurred through gritted teeth. From a post a few paces away, the shrill cry of the peregrine falcon punctuated his words.

Inlonia nodded, and watched as he was taken down a staircase and led into the city. Doran moved to her side. He took the slender hand of the queen in both his own, and gripped them warmly. "The healers will see to him," Doran said as he watched Ennis disappear from sight. "They're anticipating a busy day, to say the least." He turned back to the queen. "You remember my advisor, Kellert Sentero?"

The queen nodded.

"Highness." Kellert made a slight bow and shook the queen's hand. While he was cordial enough, his darting eyes were evidence of his distraction. Doran nodded to Kellert, a gesture that dismissed him to return to the preparation of defences.

"I wish I could welcome you to my city under more favourable circumstances," said Doran, "but you are welcome nonetheless."

He took her by the elbow and led her to the parapet from which she'd just been pulled minutes prior. He saw her noticing a pair of soldiers who followed closely – his personal guard. Likely, she had lost protectors of her own on her journey. But a ruler such as Inlonia Talchol would know – much like himself – that there would be a time to grieve, and that time was not now. Her eyes darted back and forth, taking in everything.

"How do we fare?" she asked without looking at the king.

"Valdi Tomar and his men oversee the south wall. Kellert will hold this northern section. I'm going to join the commanders at Center Gate. The center will likely take the brunt of this army's rage."

"Army?" Inlonia shook her head. "More a herd of

upright animals. These things have no place in the Three Realms, Doran. Or anywhere in Cahruia, for that matter."

"They do today," he replied. "And unfortunately, it's on my doorstep." He glanced around and spoke to one of his guards. "Ready the horses," he said. "We need to get back to–"

"Doran!" A sudden shout from Kellert, who stood on the wall. The rough, urgent tone suggested unfortunate news.

Doran and the queen ran to Kellert's side. He inclined his head to the northeast, his teeth gritted. "Cowards," he muttered.

In the distance, beyond the mass of bloodthirsty Nylacci, the black-clad army of Isror marched toward the city.

"They'd have the beasts do the dirty work," said Doran.

"How in the Goddess' name does Idach join forces with such foulness?" the queen asked. "How does he *control* them?"

"We can't concern ourselves with such matters now." The king was already moving along the walkway, his keen eyes gauging the number of defenders, the placement of the catapults, the barrels of pitch and hot water. "It is unlikely," he continued, "that those leeches will join the fray until they deem it most advantageous. Right now, our concern is keeping those giant *curs* outside our wall."

Kellert nodded his agreement. "The defences are in place." He extended a hand to the king, and nodded to the queen. "We'll hold the North Gate. If the Goddess wills, I'll speak with you both again before the nightfall."

"Whether she wills it or not." The king's jawline was

solid stone, as was his handshake. "Stand strong. We know what must be done. Now, all that remains is to do it."

Kellert clapped a hand affectionately on the king's shoulder. "We do what we must."

Doran nodded. "Goddess protect us, friend." He turned to descend to the street.

"Hold a moment..." The queen spoke behind him. "What are they doing?"

They turned as Inlonia pointed to the field. As the Nylacci force marched ever closer, Doran could now see disturbances in the front ranks. There was no order to the progression, no defining lines to separate the sections; only a host of matted fur and hatred trudging forward with teeth bared. The disturbances, a jostling and knocking about of bodies, grew in intensity. Several gaps then formed as Nylacci split apart along their front line. Like a resisting earth unable to bear the pressure from within, the beasts broke apart and thirty of those gruesome, insectile monsters spewed from their ranks.

Whether they were ordered to attack, or were simply unable to resist the savage appeal of the hunt, Doran didn't know. They raced across the field with dizzying speed, seeming to have their sights set on the Center Gate. Beyond the firing range of the soldiers at North Gate, Doran watched helplessly as their long strange legs tore through the dirt, allowing them to swing from left to right with staggering quickness as they continued their approach.

"Damnation!" Doran swore as he spun. Turning once more, he looked down the length of the wall at the hundreds of men and women who stood facing the east and the greatest terror they'd ever know.

Doran could see the terror in the eyes of many of them. Shouting had begun. Shouts of rage, of determination and fear all combined to create a cacophony that shook the walls. *How many of those poor men and women had never fired an arrow prior to this past month?* Doran thought. The Rentorrian Guard, so severely depleted in the last several months of warfare, had been supplemented with common folk whose knowledge consisted mainly of harvesting the land and sea. In recent weeks, men and women – every able body, in fact – had been required to participate in archery demonstrations and basic training. *Teach them to kill,* Doran had said, *and allow them to live.*

"Come!" he shouted to Inlonia above the din. He gestured to the walkway that ran the wall. "We need to get to Center Gate with all speed. I want to be sure those creatures get a true Rentorrian welcome."

Above them, the peregrine shrieked.

24

THE SHIFTING TIDES

He enters the cottage quickly, a smile of pure happiness already on his face. For three days he's been hunting, covering many miles throughout the vast forested land that surrounds their peaceful, secluded home. He calls her name as he enters the modest abode, eager to see the face of the woman he loves.

"Rhen? Rhen, love. I'm home." *He's about to take off his hunting cloak when he stops, surprised by the silence.*

No answer comes. There was no sign of her outside, and she's not one to wander far. When he's away on a hunt, she rarely ventures further than the surrounding fields where she picks wild berries. He often teases her when she insists on staying at home while he travels to the larger cities. It's a big world out there, Rhen, *he would say with a smile.* Are you content to stay, and see so little of what this world offers?

She would smile back, but he could tell that it was not entirely genuine. I know what it offers, and it is not the peace of our fields.

"Rhen? Where are you?" *He grows a little concerned now as he looks around the house. Things seem to be in order. Her teacup is still on the table by the window. She's always main-*

tained that the only way to truly enjoy tea is to sip it while watching the ocean waves crash. He moves down the tiny hallway. As he enters the bedroom, he sees the note. He rushes to the bed, snatches up the piece of paper and reads the words written upon it:

> My beloved Daniel, forgive me.
> There are no words of explanation that would suffice,
> but please believe that I do what I must.
> If the shifting tides ever allow,
> I will find my way to your shore again.
> Forgive me.

Instantly, he is running. He snatches the rifle as he runs, fearful that she's been taken against her will, forced to write the short note he's found.

He stands in front of their home, among the beautiful gardens that they have created in the years they've lived together. He looks around. In the western field, their large flock of sheep graze contentedly. The eastern fields contain the potato beds that seem to be struggling this year. He looks beyond the wilting potato stalks. The gate at the far end of the garden has been left open to swing back and forth in the afternoon breeze that comes off the ocean.

The path to the beach.

He begins to run again, and as his feet hit the sand, he sees the footprints. There is only one set. He starts to run beside them, cursing the softness of the sand for slowing him down. As he rounds the first bend of the shoreline, he sees her.

He screams to her, but she does not seem to hear. She continues to walk, her long white dress moving gently in the breeze. He yells again, until finally she hears him. She turns around, and regards him for a moment. He laughs with relief as he begins to run to her, but the laughter quickly turns to silent con-

fusion. She begins to run.

She is running from him.

He recalls the note and again considers its meaning. He runs faster, and sees with horror that she is doing the same.

What the *hell* is going on? *he wonders.*

He races along the beach, confusion and fear ripping him apart. He has no idea what's happening. He wonders if she is in danger, and if she is, then why is she running from him? He sees her enter the forest at the stream. As she disappears from sight he screams to her again.

His heart is pounding in his chest, and his lungs burn as he struggles along the sandy shore. He's so intent on catching her that he almost misses the sandal just in front of him. He digs his feet into the sand, grinding to a halt, and picks up the sandal. Whenever Rhenna walks in the sand, she does so with feet bared, her sandals held within her hands or pocket. He looks at it for a moment, and then shoves it into his cloak as he begins to run once more.

Finally, he reaches the stream and bursts into the forest behind her. In the distance, through dense trees and fading light, he thinks that he can see the movement of branches and bushes. She seems to be following the stream. He charges onward through the foliage, yelling as he goes, splashing through the stream until its flow strengthens and forces him to run beside it.

Suddenly, he stops. Just ahead he sees a pool of water, five or six feet across, and it appears to be equally deep.

Upon the pool's surface, a sandal to match the one in his pocket floats in a slow circle. He spins around, hoping, almost expecting to see her in the trees beside him. But he does not. He is about to charge ahead once more when he receives the blow to the back of his head, and his world fades to black.

He awakens shortly thereafter, and gradually rises to his feet. He looks around, and sees nothing but the stillness of the

forest. And then he hears the voice that will alter his life forever.

"You were attacked." The voice is low, and has a richness to
it that gives Daniel pause. His head throbs, and he tries to focus
as the other continues.

"I would have thought it difficult to find enemies in such a
remote little corner of the world, but then, a good enemy is easier
to come by than a good friend. You were lucky I came along
when I did…"

Daniel rubs his head, and his hand comes away with drying
blood on his fingers.

"Is she worth it?" The voice, Daniel now realizes, comes
from above.

He looks up and jumps back with a start as he sees the creature sitting on a thick oak branch. He snatches up the rifle and
has it pointed at the creature's face before he even notices the
antlers that rise from its head. As his finger goes to the trigger, the faerae's hand flies out, and an invisible force sends the
man crashing into the tree behind him. Slowly, he opens his eyes
and shakes his vision clear. He looks at the creature in the tree,
who appears entirely indifferent to him, chewing the nail on its
smallest finger as he watches with cold eyes.

And then the realization hits him with brutal force. He's
no longer pointing the rifle at the creature. The end of the gun
is now jammed painfully into the soft flesh under his chin. His
finger is still on the trigger.

"I'd not be your enemy, young one," the faerae says quietly.
"So, I'll ask again. Is she worth it?"

Daniel Byrne does not truly understand the question, but
he answers nonetheless.

"Yes!"

"Then listen well," the faerae says as he falls from the tree
and walks toward the shaking man. "We have much to discuss."

25

STAND

Like parasitic flies, the Isrorians followed the Nylacci.

Staid Dyrro shook his head as from Center Gate he watched the Isrorians march in a slow, orderly fashion to take their place behind the beasts. Around him, dozens of men and women pointed, muttering vile curses on the Isrorian army.

Quickly, he looked around. The feeling of unease was quickly escalating into something much worse. One of the second commanders, a tall, grey-haired man named Trebb Santor, shouted down the rising panic.

"The Isrorians mean nothing!" he thundered. "Less than nothing! They come to feed on the scraps of war, to bask in the leftovers of carnage! They will find the only carrion surrounding our city will be the hairy beasts we slaughter. Prepare yourselves!"

Staid nodded as the defenders of Orshos shouted agreement. Not a rousing speech by any means, he thought, but it settled the soldiers, allowing them to focus on what was required.

Moments later, he saw the stirring in the front ranks of the beasts, and in short time, more of those hideous *roach-monsters* were spilling from the gaps in the Nylacci host. Even from this distance, the shrill squeals that the terrors emitted sent a shiver down his spine as they raced toward the gate.

"Ready archers!" screamed Santor, as the roaches raced toward the gate. He looked around, likely seeking out the king. Doran Dunarrk, Staid knew, would remain at North Gate long enough to ensure that Queen Talchol was made safe. Beside Staid, Santor shouted again. "On my word!"

A silence fell on the wall. It was unnerving; exacerbated by the screams of the six-legged monsters that approached. Every bow string was held taut; every set of eyes narrowed as the point of each arrow wavered ever so slowly, back, forth, seeking the closest target.

"Now!" Santor slammed the butt of his spear on the wooden planks beneath his feet, screaming at his charge. "Fire! *Fire!*"

Scores of arrows pierced the thin layers of fog that drifted in over the city. They rained down on the beasts, making contact with many but with little effect. Staid swore. Unlike the wispy covering of fog and mist, the beasts were layered in plates thick enough to repel most of the arrows that struck them. An occasional fortunate arrow struck a roach in the face or a fleshy region, staggering them, but the majority of the creatures surged on, unhindered by the assault.

The sound of their shrieks and pounding of their powerful legs filled the air as they darted through the volley. Scarcely a handful lay dead. The others picked up the pace, their erratic movements and high-pitched squeals suggested that their excitement mounted the closer they got to the city.

And then as one, the entire group swung to the south, racing to the watery edge of Orshos. It was, thought Staid, like the great flocks of small birds that fly together, and turn not individually, but as a solitary body. The behaviour had always amazed him. Today, he felt differently. Cries of warning flew along the wall as defenders realized what the beasts meant to do. Having seen the earlier chase, the roaches must have realized that they could leap from the harbour quay and swim around the end of the wall to gain access to the city. Trebb Santor screamed his orders, moving sections of soldiers toward the southern gate. In the distance, Staid could see the archers firing at the approaching creatures as they came into range. Valdi Tomar would no doubt have his archers and spear-throwers ready atop the southern wall, and upon the water the boats would be in position. The larger brigantines were anchored further off the shore, but at the dock, dozens of dories, skiffs and midsized seiners had been fitted with wooden shield walls to allow the Rentorrians to launch an assault from the water. Short time passed before Staid saw the stems of the boats come into view. *We've harvested so much from the sea,* he thought. *But who could have imagined a scenario such as this?*

Seeking a better vantage point, Staid ran a distance down the curving wall and climbed atop the highest parapet in order to see the dock. The beasts didn't slow as they hit the water. People screamed in defiance, and a flurry of missiles pierced the hazy sea air. Several of the creatures were felled before they reached the quay, but many hit the water with great splashes and screams. Staid squinted, trying to see everything despite the distance and increasing mist. The clustered roaches still on land proved the easier target, but those swimming toward the inner docks were the more imminent threat as they thrashed their way around the wall.

The defensive assault was now having an effect, as was evidenced by the roiling crimson water. Staid could see a few of the roaches floating lifelessly, jostled about by their brethren as they forged onward. As the monsters rounded the wall and headed for the dock ramps, Staid knew that all manner of weapons would be utilized. Fisherfolk who were less adept with a bow would hurl rocks and bricks at the creatures; others would use swords, mallets, and long, pointed fishing prongs. The thought of these six-legged atrocities setting foot on the cobbled streets of Orshos' harbourfront was unfathomable. The men and women at South Gate and on the water fought with a ferocity that made his heart beat all the faster. He'd almost allowed himself to feel a small sense of victory when he heard the shouting begin around him.

The host of Nylacci had broken into a run, making for Center Gate. The roaches, Staid realized, had served their purpose – they'd engaged the defenders of South Gate, and drawn many soldiers from Center Gate as well. While these soldiers struggled to defend the city's watery border, three thousand Nylacci tore across the field, closing in on the main entrance to the city of Orshos.

Staid jolted as the thunderous crack of catapults sounded beside him, filling the sky with rocks. The missiles fell amongst the charging group of Nylacci, striking dozens dead. *Creation!* thought Staid. *If every rock struck a beast, it might still not be enough.* The advancing army was now close enough to launch an attack of its own. As the rocks flew from the walls, they were met with the large black arrows of the Nylacci.

Screams rang out as the arrows found their first victims within the city. Soldiers on the wall scrambled, seeking shelter from the assault. The majority of arrows were directed at the catapult platforms, slowing the offensive efforts of the city's defenders. Staid jumped down from the parapet and fell to his knees behind the chest-high wall as the thud of arrows striking the wood and stone reverberated around him. The very act of kneeling brought with it a feeling of surrender. He stood up quickly, crouching just below the top of the wall. On the streets within, arrows continued to fall, bringing with them a panic which spread along the cobbled alleyways. Panic was contagious, Staid knew, and the arrows that now dotted Lower Orshos spread fear through the people like ink tainting clear water. These arrows were the first breach the proud coastal city had experienced in the seventy years since the Battle of the Cliff, and the feeling of security that resided behind the wall had been decidedly pierced. Around him, men and women scrambled to remove the panels that covered the wall's murder holes. He opened one of these slots nearest him, and looked out at the field.

The Nylacci were relentless. Staid watched in horror as the snarling creatures clambered over their fallen dead in an effort to reach Center Gate. Even those wounded and maimed crawled forward, trampled in their incessant desire to gain access to the city and the feast that would surely follow.

To either side, catapults continued to rain down stones. Staid grabbed a bow and joined the soldiers that fired on the beasts. He could not escape the sense of futility that came with his efforts. He shook his head, cursing out loud as he saw one of his arrows find its mark in the leg of a Nylac, only to be ripped out as the creature charged on. Along with the dreadful bows, he saw that many of the Nylacci carried axes and cudgels. They also carried large, limbed trees, no doubt to be used as battering rams. Center Gate would be tested greatly. He hoped the fortifications that had been put in place would hold the great doors.

Amidst the yelling of orders and cries of pain, Staid heard a commotion arise on the street just below the wall. Stealing a look over his shoulder, he saw the king approaching, and with him, Inlonia Talchol. A roar went up from the Embarrian soldiers as their queen rode into their midst. They were immediately joined by the Rentorrians, and Staid saw some of the panic that had gripped the people dissipate as the leaders of the neighbouring realms moved toward the Center Gate. As the pair dismounted, the gate shook with a jarring blow as one of the battering rams slammed into the wood.

Immediately, soldiers ran to the braces of the gate and checked their security. For the time being they would hold, but the sustained pressure of the Nylacci bodies crushing against the wall was worrying. As the king scanned the buttresses, his eyes found his commander.

"Seems we have company at our doors, Trebb," he called from the street.

"That we do, Highness." Another crash shook the gate.

The king ascended the stairs to the platform, two at a time. "I'd hate to be deemed a bad host, but I'm thinking we'll allow no access today!"

Staid knew full well that the king was terrified. However, Doran Dunarrk was doing what he did best. He was leading. He covered the terror with a brave exterior; he set aside the grief of losing his wife and replaced it with a resolve to save her people. He gained the platform – his guards guided him to a section sheltered from the barrage of arrows – with Inlonia close behind, and he turned and faced his citizens.

"What do you say, my friends?" he yelled. "Shall we turn these foul beasts away?"

A roar from the crowd.

"Shall we send them back to the depths of hell which spat them out?" The crowd screamed their agreement, swords and spears raised in defiance.

"For five hundred years, the unforgiving waves of the sea have crashed against us! Five centuries we have stood on this coast, proudly, and faced the greatest force of nature. And we've never backed down!" As the king spoke, Staid could see the fear melting from the eyes of his people. Their shouts of courage and determination seemed to be creating a frenzy outside the wall as well. The Nylacci roared in rage and disgust. The frequency of the battering ram assaults increased as the bodies of the beasts piled up outside the gate. The ram was joined by the thud of axes tearing into the thick wood where the two massive gate doors met.

Doran shouted over the din. "I don't have the words of the great kings of old, but today, I don't need them. *I have a people*–" He stopped and beckoned Inlonia Talchol to his side. "*We* have a people stronger and prouder than any in Cahruia!" Amidst the flying arrows and primal screams that filled the air, Doran shouted above it all. "We have an alliance of the two proudest realms the world has seen. *Embarrians*, who stand solid beside us, and will hold the grounds of our lands like the great roots of their amilliat!" A deafening response. "And *Rentorrians*, who will roar through this enemy like a tsunami, rising as one, like the proud, briny water of the sea that crashes through our veins! Stand, and wash this savagery from my sight!"

A madness overtook the crowd. They surged forward, eager for the wall, screaming their courage in the face of death.

Death, indeed, was everywhere. Rough ladders were thrown against the wall as the Nylacci desperately sought a way in. The arrows flew, spears loosed, and all along the wall, life was snuffed out like candle flames in a winter's wind. But none slowed. As both sides suffered losses, neither lost its fury or its resolve to eradicate those it faced.

Below Staid, he felt his feet shake as the rams continued to batter the ever-weakening gate. The defenders fought valiantly, but along the wall, scattered fortunate Nylacci, some pierced with arrows, made it to the top of the massive palisade. In places, the bodies of the beasts began to pile so high that some climbed atop the mounds of corpses in an attempt to gain the summit. Staid, firing at these creatures, realized with disgust that many of the bodies were not in fact dead. The Nylacci clawed and climbed over their own kind – dead *or* alive – hungry for the men and women whose flesh they smelled so near.

Another smell, that of burning pitch, soon reached the trader, and he turned to see fires burning along the wall. Scores of Nylacci were aflame, but even as death licked their flesh, they continued to climb and beat upon the wall of Orshos.

All along the wall, fighting ensued along the walkway. More and more Nylacci were coming over the barrier. Swords were drawn, and hand-to-hand combat turned from fierce to desperate in a matter of moments. The sheer size and brute strength of the Nylacci gave them a huge advantage, and those that found themselves engaged with a beast relied on their comrades to assist with blade or arrow if they hoped to survive.

Fighting alongside both seasoned veterans and simple farmers, Doran entered the fray with no thought for his own safety. His personal guard, loyal to the death, threw themselves between any beast that got within a few paces of him or Inlonia Talchol, as did many of the soldiers who fought near the sovereigns. Staid Dyrro stood at the forefront; he and a handful of other soldiers hacking away at the foes like crazed men trying to fell unrelenting trees. The queen held her sword ready, but like Doran, found herself swarmed by protectors who perceived every threat. Yet, the Guard were not invincible, and they fell, one by one, as the assault worsened. Inlonia moved to a nearby barrel of spears and with respectable precision began hurling the wooden lances at the Nylacci cresting the wall, as Staid fought beside her. Yet, for every Nylacci killed, another appeared in its place, and many defenders soon found themselves forced from the platform to the streets below, either in retreat or pushed from the perilous height. As the bodies of Nylacci piled against the base of the wall without, so too did the bodies of the defenders within.

The wooden platform was slick with blood both red and black. Bodies, and pieces of bodies lay all along the elevated walkway, and with every appendage that was separated from a fighter, the excitement of the Nylacci heightened.

And then, a deep drone reverberated through the air.

Staid spun from where he battled next to Inlonia, and listened more closely, barely able to hear the new sound over the chaos of the fighting. It seemed to be the sound of voices, of chanting. There was no sharpness in the sound, no guttural savage shriek to which his ringing ears had grown so accustomed. He saw confusion grow on the faces of those around him and on the faces of the enemy that looked around, seeking the source of the sound. Staid saw the Isrorians turning to the north, to the hills west of the area from which they'd just come. The powerful, eerie battle cry that covered the hills grew louder still as the Drales thundered into full sight.

"Creation!" Inlonia slowly shook her head. "They must have emptied Ras."

26

A GRIEVOUS WOUND

Father.

Sivino turned to Dels, opening his mouth to speak, but no words came. He looked to Niamh, and then Leath, desperate for answers. He knew in his heart that what the Cernunnos had told him was true, but couldn't for the life of him understand why such information needed to come from this malicious creature. *Why?* The question screamed in his mind. *Why could I have not been told earlier, told by my own fam–* His thought was cut off as a new one emerged. *His family? If the faerae spoke true, Dels and Leath were no more his blood than anyone present.* He stopped. *Anyone, save for the Shepherd.* His stomach turned on itself as he looked at the horseman. And in that moment, he saw why he'd had a moment of recognition when the man had removed his hood.

Creation.

"Sivino." Dels stepped in front of him. For a moment, Sivino was tempted to step back, away from the big man who'd raised and loved him his entire life. *No,* he thought.

The time had come to stop stepping away from the challenges that landed in his path. *But Goddess, why did the path have to be so difficult?* It seemed with every passing day, the direction changed, the conditions changed. He took a slow breath. He needed to push forward, he knew, through the branches and bramble, and suffer the discomfort if he was to find the clearing beyond.

"Is he my father?" Sivino asked simply.

Dels' answer was equally simple. He nodded.

The two stood facing each other for long moments. Neither spoke.

"Splendid," said the king of Isror, moving around the Shepherd and looking sharply at Cehron. "Family knots are neatly untied. Now, I'd be on my way to Orshos. This victory over Rentorria shall *not* happen in my absence. I would stand on the precipice of my new kingdom."

Cehron closed his eyes in annoyance. His lips were tight as he considered how best to deal with the impatient king. After a couple of moments, he emitted a soft chuckle and looked at Idach. Unable to keep Dels' eye, Sivino turned to watch the faerae move to the king. Though he smiled, the faerae's eyes were full of malice.

"My dear Idach. *Ever* interrupting, despite the fact that you've been given my promise, and as I've *told you*–" He jabbed the king's chest twice with a strong finger as he spoke the last two words. "–I always keep my promises." The faerae circled the king, and despite the Isrorian's imposing build, Sivino sensed a tinge of fear in the black-clad man. "As you seem insistent on getting about your business," Cehron placed a hand on Idach's shoulder, "and interfering with the important dealings of others, I'll set you on your path."

A smug smile from the king. He began to move forward, adjusting his garb in preparation for the journey west.

"It may not, however–" Cehron's grip tightened on the king's shoulder, holding him in place, "–be the path that you have so eagerly envisioned."

The king's head turned slowly. His brow lowered. The tone of the faerae's voice suggested something dark, and everyone gathered on the lakeside turned to listen.

The faerae moved his hand and walked ahead of the king. "I am a creature of promises and pacts." He stopped and joined his hands behind his back, his stance reflective. "I promised you the opportunity to rule an entire world, and the opportunity shall indeed be yours." Turning to face the lake, and the slow swirling whirlpool that beckoned within, Cehron continued. "I did not, however, say in *which* world this opportunity would be laid at your feet…"

The reaction was immediate. "No!" the king shouted as he moved toward the faerae, but one raised finger locked him in his place. Whether it was fear or an unseen physical force, Sivino couldn't tell.

"You see," said Cehron, "I've made pacts with countless folk, in many realms, many worlds. Our pact being one…" He looked at the king. "Another with the Kourg, though that one will have to wait a bit… and another with the Nylacci." Niamh appeared to weaken, and Lomin helped her sit on an overturned dory. Its aged yellow paint peeled from the hull, and dark rot could be seen in the wood beneath. "I felt that I owed them a *debt* of sorts," Cehron continued. "Not that I'm personally indebted to anyone, but I felt it wrong that *our kind*," he glanced at Niamh, "so unfairly interfered with their kind, many years ago. Really, who were *we* to rid this world of a creature that had rightfully and naturally evolved to dominate the lands?"

"It was the will of the—"

"Yes, yes, Niamh. Save your breath. It sounds as though you have precious little left. The Faant, of course, imposing their will; upheaval created with every blessed message. It's time, Niamh, that they stepped back; *retired* as it were, and let the inhabitants of the worlds decide their own fate. I will no longer be a minion to that unknowable faction."

He turned his attention back to Idach, whose hand moved to the scabbard of his sword. The gesture brought a small curl to the corner of the faerae's mouth.

"An eon ago, the creatures of Fae removed the Nylacci – thousands of them – from the bountiful lands of Cahruia. In my pact with the beasts of Dreg, I told them that I would bring them back to Cahruia, and gather them together so that, as a mighty army, they could sweep across the land and wreak their bloody havoc. But the pact involves more than a massive *shift*, you see. The pact, as agreed upon by those hairy monsters, requires a *trade*."

Sivino looked at Dels, and then Leath, who moved to his side and assumed a stance that was undeniably protective. His young mind was being torn apart with the new knowledge of his lineage, but he could not ignore what the faerae was saying. If he was hearing correctly, it would be highly unlikely that any of them would set foot in the realm of Embarria again.

Stellen stepped in front of Ston and the others, fists clenched.

"An eye for an eye, as the old adage goes," said Cehron as he smiled at the big man. "In this great and terrible game, I will make the next move; a population

of Nylacci for a population of humans... and a faerae."
He eyed Niamh. "It's only fitting, dear. It was those fools
obsessed with shifting that were responsible for the Nylacci's suffering in the first place. You'll no doubt be given
a welcome befitting your esteemed position." His smile
faded, and he turned to Idach. "But I'll start, dear king,
with you." Idach shook his head slowly, but the faerae
paid him no mind. "I'll keep my word, and in the days to
come you'll see even more of this despicable race moved
to Dreg. Unless of course, the whelp picks up his sword
and sheds the blood of his dear old daddy, ending the
chaos as was prophesied, and proving that the will of the
Faant is, and forever will be, *infallible*." The faerae's lips
parted, momentarily exposing his perfect teeth.

"No," said Dels. He tilted his head as he looked at
Cehron. There was no trace of fear in his face, only the
hard determination of a father who would risk death to
protect a child. "Sivino will face no one." He took a step
toward the faerae. "He will *fight* no one. He, like my other
son, will leave this ruined city and return home to Egim."
He stood now before Cehron, and Sivino realized suddenly that despite Dels' formidable size, the faerae was of
a height to match him. Cehron and Dels stood face to face,
though the antlers of the faerae lent an extra arm's length
to his stature.

Dels turned then, completely ignoring the faerae, and
spoke to Sivino.

"Sivi, your mother made me *promise* that I would keep
her secret. We never, *never* meant to hurt you. When she
came to me, she knew with near certainty that she'd never
return to the world from which she'd come. That life, those
people, were lost to her." To Dels' side, the Shepherd shifted in his saddle. Behind him, Idach Garron turned as well.

He flexed his fingers, seemingly free of the faerae's hold, as he moved away from the Egimians, to the side of the Shepherd. Dels continued. "She wanted... *needed* to start fresh. She said her past life was like a gold coin that slips from the hand of a sailor, sinking forever into the depths of the ocean. That coin, sitting in the darkness, is of no less value than any other coin of its likeness, but it is gone, inaccessible. It maintains its worth, but will forever remain beyond reach." Dels glanced in Niamh's direction. For a moment, Sivino could see a look of concern shadow his father's face. "Your mother was told that you were special, Sivi. She knew that anyway, of course, but as you grew, she told me that there was purpose in you that would one day shine through... like a gold coin in murky water. She could not explain your lineage to you without talking of things you weren't ready to know, things which were beyond your understanding." He looked at Cehron. "Beyond the understanding of most, in truth. And she knew it was wrong on some level. *A lie is a grievous wound that the giver and the recipient must forever bear*, she would say. She bore it with great difficulty, because she knew that it would one day wound the ones she loved."

Days later, when he would reflect on this moment, Sivino would tell himself that he should have seen what was about to happen. The malice in Idach Garron's eyes was obvious, as was the way the king had slowly approached the Shepherd, his hands deep in his pockets.

In one swift motion, the king of Isror swept a knife from his cloak, and stuck it in the side of the Shepherd. The roar of pain was immediate as Idach grabbed the Shepherd's cloak and attempted to pull him from his saddle. The Shepherd's foot, however, caught in the stirrup and as he hung, partially suspended, he grabbed the king by the throat. Unwavering, the king clung to the clothing of the rider, holding the man's cloak sleeves to prevent him from getting the knife. Sivino spun to Cehron, waiting for the faerae to throw his power at the Isrorian king. Cehron however, did nothing. His face held a combined look of bemusement and, to a lesser extent but certainly there, concern.

Idach reached for the knife still embedded in the Shepherd's side, and turned it roughly before pulling it out. The Shepherd screamed again, and his grip on the king's throat lessened. Idach pulled his neck away, dropping the knife as he secured his grip on his foe. It was then that Sivino saw that Idach was searching for something within the Shepherd's cloak. The Shepherd hit the king squarely with a closed fist, and blood spouted from the man's nose. Idach, however, smiled through the blood that ran down his face. There was madness in his eyes as he grappled with the Shepherd, who now seemed to be searching his own cloak as well.

The pair both held the arms of the other, aware that a free hand could tilt the balance of the struggle. Idach grunted heavily with each effort to pull the rider from his horse. The steed, for its part, showed little concern, moving only slightly when the combatant's efforts pulled it sideways. Sivino darted past the horse as it edged slowly toward his friends, sweeping up the sword as he stood in front of them protectively. Lomin stood before Niamh in a likewise manner. The Shepherd's foot finally came free, and the king hauled him from the saddle, throwing him to the ground. Idach was on top of him immediately, his knee pushing into the wounded midsection as he pulled an arm free and landed several solid punches to the Shepherd's jaw. Idach leaned forward, and with his left forearm attempted to choke the Shepherd as his right hand held the clothing, searching the pockets while the Shepherd was momentarily stunned. Sivino could see a look of elation on the king's face as he apparently found what he was looking for. The Shepherd reacted violently, growling at the king as he pushed himself up onto one elbow. There was desperation in the Shepherd's face now, a fear that Sivino had not yet seen. Idach dug a heel into the ground, struggling to keep the Shepherd down. Pushing against each other, the two were unmoving, until the Shepherd let himself be pushed back to the ground. Using the forward momentum of the king, the Shepherd jerked him to the right and brought him to the ground. Idach attempted to pull free the object he'd found, but the Shepherd fought him savagely. For a moment, their hands were visible and Sivino saw a glint of metal within their entangled hands.

As the Shepherd attempted to get the upper hand on the king, his cloak twisted and Sivino could see the substantial amount of blood that soaked into it.

Not long, thought Sivino. *His strength can't last much–*

It was then that the hands of the Shepherd and the king exploded. The blast of power was deafening. The horse bolted, running from the quay as lake birds burst from the wharves and water to escape the threat. Sivino heard the screams of his companions, a mix of surprise and terror. Several of them had fallen to the ground, himself included, arms raised protectively over their heads. Dahlah was pulling the young ones behind her. In front of them all stood Drip, his teeth bared, clenched fists pressed to the ground, ready to pounce.

The king screamed. Lying on the ground he gripped his shoulder, where a swath of his cloak had been stripped away. Traces of blood could be seen on his upper arm. Beside him the Shepherd lay panting, favouring his left side with one hand, and loosely holding the weapon with the other. Cehron stepped forward and deftly retrieved the weapon from the injured man. The Shepherd grimaced and made an attempt to resist, but Cehron wagged a finger gently as he hummed a quiet tune and pulled the weapon away.

Faint smoke rose from the tip of its barrel.

Cehron turned to Niamh, and held the weapon aloft. Niamh watched him for a moment, and then slowly shook her head.

"Oh, Cehron..." She closed her eyes, her chin sagging to her chest. "What have you done?"

"A final lesson, dear Niamh," said the Cernunnos, "on why we need to keep these worlds *apart.*"

"No!" Sivino was on his feet. Cehron turned, appearing to think that the boy spoke to him, but in a moment, Sivino was past him and falling to his knees beside his father. *"No!"*

Dels lay on the ground, facing the sky and the birds that screamed within it. His mouth was open, and he struggled to breathe. At his midsection, a small hole stood out on his tunic, and around it, an ever-widening stain of crimson slowly spread.

27

THE FATHER'S CALL

The fog thickened.

Gone were the delicate fingers of mist that reached for the shore, like the hands of an ocean striving to pull itself further inland. It grew denser as it reached the city of Orshos, as did the mass of bodies that now stood outside the walls of the capital. Yet, while the fog crept across the sea with a deathly silence, the din that arose onshore was of an intensity that might cause the boats to sway upon the sea.

The Drales did not run, but their long muscular legs brought them out of the trees and down to the northern field quickly. Upon the walls the fighting did not cease, but Staid saw that the Nylacci on the ground were now turning their attention to the new threat. Fewer of the monsters were attempting the ladders as they eyed the imposing army moving toward them. The Nylacci seemed to sense that this was not a foe to be underestimated. Doran turned as two soldiers finished off a wounded Nylac, and seeing no immediate threat to the queen or any other, he moved along the walkway in a crouch, assessing the battlefield.

The smoke that wafted from the north wall was concerning. The defenders knew well enough not to release the burning pitch too close to the massive wooden gate, but that didn't mean those assaulting the wall would not use a similar fuel in their effort to gain the city. The dark plumes seemed to grow thicker by the second, like the mist that did the same in the opposite direction. *Everything is closing in on us*, Doran thought. Behind him, Staid Dyrro and Inlonia Talchol stood with Trebb Santor. They too watched the smoke and flames rise.

"Damnation. That's near the gate," he shouted to the commander. He wiped blood from his eye. Whether it was his or that of the enemy, he couldn't say.

"Too near," Santor replied. He motioned Doran and Inlonia to the relative shelter of a nearby bulwark and assessed the activity around the central gate. As far as Doran could see, no Nylacci currently attempted to breach the wall, and the ones that had done so were all dead, though their defeat had come at a great price. Bodies lay everywhere. On the ground below, most of the Nylacci were now abandoning the central gate and moving northward. Santor called to one of his captains, and gave orders to have a unit of soldiers move northward.

"Stay low," Santor ordered, a concerned hand on Doran's shoulder.

The group moved cautiously along the walkway, as scattered arrows still flew through the air. Santor stopped frequently and assessed the field. More and more Nylacci moved northward. In the distance, the Drales continued to advance.

As they reached a vantage point that brought the gate into clear view, the gravity of the situation was even clearer. North Gate was indeed aflame. Thick plumes prevented the soldiers from assaulting the Nylacci from above, essentially clearing the top of the gate of defenders, as well as the top of the walls surrounding the gate. The smoke however did not prevent the Nylacci from proceeding. Ladders were thrown against the gate on either side of the battering ram that continued to hammer the wooden structure. The creatures were relentless, ascending the shaky ladders even as their matted fur was licked by the flames.

Over the clashing metal and screams of pain, Doran shouted to Trebb Santor. "How long will it hold?"

Santor shook his head, his face uncertain. "The wood is thick; half an armlength in most places. It will burn slowly, but it *will* burn. Right now, I'm more concerned about those rams." He cursed under his breath and glanced between the stone bulwarks. "If the Goddess is with us, the Drales may push those savages away from the gate." No sooner had he spoken the words than the Drales stopped dead in their tracks.

"What are they doing?" Staid shouted. "They're just standing there. Why do they not run to our aid?"

Several hundred feet before the Drales, the Isrorians formed tidy ranks; perfectly symmetrical sections that stood still between two hosts of giants. Doran thought he could see the Isrorians in the back ranks bracing for the Nylacci as much as the front ranks who faced the Drales.

He looked around quickly, assessing the situation. Center Gate, at least for the time being, was not the gravest concern. The number of Nylacci had been depleted through both death and the desertion of the gate to head toward the Drales. Doran knew what he had to do.

"Santor!" he called. The man rushed to his side. "I'm

going to North Gate. If the tides shift and the focus comes back to Center Gate, so shall I." The commander nodded as the king continued. "Send a couple of sections to North Gate by the city streets. I'll use the parapet walkway. Are we good, Commander?"

Santor nodded, and saluted his king.

"You'll not be going without me," Inlonia Talchol said firmly from behind him.

Staid moved closer, and put a hand on the king's shoulder. "I'll be with you as well, if you'll have me." He glanced toward the flames that rose on the north wall and nodded in that direction. "As you said, out of the frying pan, into the fire, no?"

Doran could only nod.

Staid nodded back, and traced the sign of the waterdrop over his heart. "Dahnu watch us all." Then, they were running, hunched, along the high walkway. Arrows were now scarce as the Nylacci attention had been shifted, and they ran with little heed to shelter. Doran stole quick glances to the field as he ran, and saw the Isrorian ranks grow increasingly shaky near the rear. Beyond the enemy, the Drales had formed their own rough formation, and the king heard Staid once again curse the reclusive race for not running with all the haste they could muster. From what little Doran knew of the group, haste was not the way of the Drales.

As if to reinforce this thought, the Drales, as one body, suddenly fell to their knees. Doran skidded to a halt on the walkway, horrified as the western giants lowered themselves before the approaching enemy. *What in Creation is this?* Doran looked from the Drales to the Nylacci and back again. As the Isrorians saw what was happening, they seemed to gain a confidence that was impossible moments before, and a battle horn was sounded by the black-clad commander. The archers at the rear raised their bows, while those in the front raised their spears. A second blast was issued, though it had little effect.

The call of Ras drowned out all.

The Drales rose to their feet. At their mouths, hundreds of strange instruments were blown, emitting a scream that wavered from a bone-chilling shriek to a deeper, foreboding cry of anguish and rage. Unlike the drone of the horn, the sound fluctuated and ended with an intonation that seemed to suggest a question. The Drales fell momentarily silent, and then once more raised the unsettling cry that seemed to cause the mists above to shimmer. The entire field, Doran noticed, appeared to falter, if only slightly. The Nylacci twitched as dogs before a piercing whistle and quickened their pace, incensed by the sound. The Isrorians charged, spears held aloft as the archers loosed a volley. The Drales, however, did not move.

Until the sudden roar of thunder rumbled over the sea.

Like an avalanche of boulders tumbling down a distant mountain, the thunder rolled over the waves and onto the shore, turning the heads of everyone but the mighty Drales. With the sound, the giants roared in response, and raised their shields to block the falling arrows. Before a second volley could be released, the Drales bellowed a cry that was equal parts fervour and warning, and for the first time that day, they ran.

Doran and his companions ran as well, though in an opposite direction. The king growled his eagerness as he sped for the gate. The smoke grew thicker, but he could not help but feel the tides had now turned. Boots thudded heavily as they raced down the walkway. Doran smiled, in spite of the scene before him. *These beasts will be driven from our walls yet.* Though he could not see through the rising smoke, it seemed that the majority of the monsters had left the gate to engage the Drales.

In true savage form, the creatures of Dreg ran directly through the archers and infantry of the Isrorian army, trampling supposed allies in their lust for blood. While many soldiers were able to avoid being crushed, others met a bloody death beneath clawed feet. Some Nylacci struck out against the Isrorians, knocking them to the side with swords and cudgels. The Isrorians did not know where to turn; some stood ready against the Drales while others turned to draw swords against the ferocity that approached from behind.

The Nylacci tore their way through the Isrorians, like hungry brudogs chasing hares through a cornfield. At the head of the columns, commanders could be seen screaming orders at the beasts, and also at the soldiers to break rank and allow the monsters through. In the pure chaos, the orders went unheard. Within minutes, the Nylacci had made their way through the black and silver force, leaving a path of crimson and broken bodies in their wake.

The crash of the Nylacci and Drale collision was rivalled only by the second rumble of thunder that shook the sky. Swords and cudgels and huge muscular bodies came together with an impact that sent blood and steel into the air. This impact, Doran noted, did not involve the usual clash of metal that accompanied such a battle. While the Nylacci used swords and axes, the Drales used no blade. As such, the sound of battle was comprised more of thuds and vicious slices, roars of rage and cries of anguish. The Isrorians suffered the worst initial losses, finding themselves trapped – save for those on the eastern flanks that were able to squeeze through the armies. Doran saw a sizable number of these soldiers fleeing the bedlam, some atop horses but most running on foot. One soldier missing an arm simply stood and screamed at everyone around him.

The Drales stood about a head taller than the Nylacci, though they did not have the girth of the enemy. While they also didn't have numbers to match the beasts, they ran into the fray without reservation, their long, pale bodies rippling with muscle that could be mistaken for marble. Doran watched, grimacing as the Drale men and women swung their cudgels with a speed that was staggering, their wooden shields held high. Indeed, the attack did more than stagger the Nylacci. The beasts that were unable to block the cudgels or were caught unaware suffered crushing blows. If a beast was felled with a strike to the head, there was no rising.

An arrow struck a wooden beam near Doran, and he crouched with a start, cursing his lack of caution. The main battle was between the colossals, but one would do well to realize that death sought its prey at every opportunity. Smoke filled his nostrils, and soon began to obscure his view. The sounds of the battle, however, supplemented his impeded vision.

The sound that bothered him more than the terrible cries on the field was the steady thumping of the battering ram. He spat out the foul taste of smoke and pitch, and squinting though watery eyes chanced a quick glance though the parapets. *Creation! These brutes are determined to have the gate.* Below him, the Nylacci continued to spread the burning pitch along the base of the wall. As the smoke grew ever thicker, the water that was thrown from above did little to assuage the blinding curtain that rose along the wall. Doran was momentarily able to make out at least three solid ladders on the burning gate. *Damnation!* He continued to run.

Weaving his way through the archers, he finally reached the gate. On the platform beside it, Kellert Sentero and his captains were ushering soldiers away from the giant doorway. Some were sent to the street below to reinforce the braces, while others continued the assault from above. Archers to the left and right of the gate continued to fire, and be fired upon in return, but the defence seemed to have little effect against the hundreds of Nylacci that attempted the breach.

More noxious than the plumes from the burning wood, he could now discern the sharp smell of burning hair. The king leaned through the stone bulwark again, and watched as a Nylac pounded his way up a ladder on the gate, its entire body aflame. A virtual fireball, the creature disappeared into the black smoke that clung to the reverberating gate. He turned and screamed at Kellert. "Top of the gate! Nylac!"

Doran drew his sword, and pushed past the archers to reach Kellert and the others. As he did so, the Nylac rolled over the top of the gate, a grotesque ball of growling flame. Its roar of challenge was ferocious, but was little defence against the swords and spears that immediately pierced its body. The creature fell with a thud to the cobbled street below, all the more hideous for its hairless, blackened body.

Kellert spun on the king. "Doran?! What in Dahnu's name are yo–"

"You're taking the brunt here. Quickly. Come with me."

Kellert grunted, then began to cough as the smoke

All Paths Taken

moved over them again. They moved down the walkway. Below them, the soldiers that Santor had sent from the Center Gate had arrived and were ascending the stairs.

Doran watched them take places along the wall. "We thought this migh–"

Screaming from all around them. Doran spun, watching in horror as two more Nylacci emerged from the smoke and flame atop the gate. Between them, they carried some type of container. Metal. Rectangular.

It appeared heavy.

"*Oh, you bastards,*" whispered Doran.

The two beasts upended the misshapen cauldron, and burning pitch of their own splashed over the walkway and onto the street below. Soldiers screamed in shock and pain. Wasting no time, the Nylacci unsheathed their swords and bounded down the stairs, killing several soldiers on their descent. Behind them, two more monsters rolled over the top of the gate, snarling.

"Fire!" Kellert screamed at the archers.

Arrows flew. A few were able to find the Nylacci, but did not stop them. In mere moments, the beasts were down amongst the soldiers, the archers hesitating with fear of hitting their comrades. Swords were drawn, but the Nylacci charged through them, mouths dripping with froth and fury. Two of the singed horrors attacked the gate's draw bar. The great wooden beam spanned twenty feet, slotted into four wrought iron brackets. Doran and Staid raced down the nearest staircase to assist in the defence. The Nylacci threw themselves under the beam and, with arrows protruding from various body parts and heedless of the burning pitch in which they stood, heaved upward against the bar as the ram outside crashed again and again.

More arrows were fired, and one of the beasts fell. As the other continued to push, another terrible splash of black death rained down, and through the smoke Nylacci poured over the gate. Arrows were fired in both directions, the street hissed with smoke and steam, and creatures once unheard of in the fair city of Orshos made their way down into the flagstone street. With Staid by his side, Doran attacked the descending beasts. Several jumped the staircase halfway down, eager to get at the draw bar. Then, the pitch on the street was sparked, and the entrance of Orshos turned to hell.

"Hold the gate!" screamed Kellert. But the draw bar had been loosened, and the battering ram was finally able to achieve its goal.

One snap, and then another. The crushing weight of the Nylacci finally broke the remaining slots that held the bar, and the gate gave way.

As the North Gate of Orshos crashed open, Doran watched helplessly as the streets of his city were flooded with bloodthirsty Nylacci and the bitter stench of death.

28

FOR WHAT IS SOWN

Blood. So much blood.

Sivino could scarcely believe that one person could shed as much so quickly. He was on his knees at Dels' side immediately, Leath with him.

"No," he said through clenched teeth. "Father. No!"

Around him, he could hear the sobs of his friends. Niamh attempted to stand, but could not. Lomin cursed beneath his breath, his hard eyes on Cehron. Drip stood motionless, paralyzed by the sight of Dels' condition. Dahlah moved to action, with Stellen close behind.

Ripping strips of cloth from the hem of her dress, she urged Sivino and Leath to move aside, and pulled Dels' Ryndarra garb away from his midsection. The wound was surprisingly small. Whatever the weapon was, thought Sivino, it seemed to have put something inside Dels. He glanced over at Cehron, who held the weapon still, then back at his father. Somewhere behind him, he could hear the moans of Idach Garron and, though quieter, the Shepherd also. *Daniel*, Niamh had called him. *His birth father.*

He was bleeding just as much as Dels, his pant leg soaked around his hip. Sivino turned back to his father. He remembered Niamh helping Lomin days before as he lay injured in the forest after battling the Nylac. In her weakened condition, he doubted she could be of any help to Dels. In truth, she looked very much near death herself.

Dahlah pressed the folded cloth against the wound, and called Torla to her side. The other young ones came as well, eager to help in the confusion and uncertainty. In moments, the blood had soaked through the cloth, and Dahlah had Torla tear away several more pieces. All the while, Dahlah spoke softly to Dels, imploring him to stay still. Dels smiled weakly in response, his eyes on Sivino and Leath.

Sivino tried to return the smile, but couldn't. He took Dels' hand, remembering how he'd marvelled at these hands as a child, as he'd held them on walks through the fields or the narrow dirt roads of Egim. They'd seemed huge; powerful hands calloused from years of hard work. And now, though the size was unchanged, Dels' hands trembled, his clammy fingers struggling to return the squeeze that Sivino gave them. Dels looked from one boy to the other and, with a gesture almost too subtle to notice, he gently shook his head.

"No," Sivino said firmly. "You're not going anywhere. We're going back to Egim, Father. There are fields to harvest." His voice was shaking now, and cracked with desperation. "There are fields to harvest!" he shouted. "You always told us, you reap what you sow!" Beside him, Dahlah stifled a sob as she continued to minister to the wound. Leath put a hand on Sivino's shoulder as the boy held his father's hand in both of his own. "You reap what you sow."

Dels nodded slightly, and smiled. "Perhaps… it's not so much what you sow, but how… well you care for what is sown." Dahlah looked from the wound to Dels' face as he continued. "Leath, I swore on the day your parents died that I would raise you as best I could." Dels grimaced as Dahlah pushed fresh cloth onto the one that was soaked through. "You've grown into a mighty oak of a man. I couldn't be prouder." Leath fought back tears, pushing Dels' sweaty hair away from his eyes.

"Sivino." Dels smiled, considering his words carefully. "Your mother carried you when she came to me. I fell for her instantly, and loved you before you were born." Sivino began to cry in earnest, his shoulders shaking silently. "Make no mistake, both of you – you are my harvest. I could have yielded no better."

The boys continued to kneel beside their father, as Stellen placed a strong hand on the shoulder of each. Torla stood between Tonnis and Kef. Off to the side, Drip paced back and forth, his face twisted in rage. He did not take his eyes off Cehron Cen Kohr, though the faerae showed no sign of noticing the hatred emanating from the trenoc. The Cernunnos moved past Idach, who sat on the ground nursing his bleeding arm. The king attempted to rise and engage the faerae, but Cehron hummed a little tune and made a gentle pushing gesture toward Idach. The king sat back down. The faerae then moved past the Shepherd, who lay on his side bleeding as he watched those who tended to Dels. It was Sivino, however, that the bleeding man watched most closely.

Cehron sat beside Niamh on the overturned boat. Lomin's face tightened, as did the arm he'd placed around Niamh's shoulder. Absently, Cehron picked at the flaking yellow paint.

"It didn't have to be this way," said Cehron. He didn't look at Niamh.

"No, it didn't." Barely a whisper.

"My point will be proven, Niamh. Your father will, *must*, put an end to the shifting and the meddling that the Faant have facilitated for too long."

"It's been this way for millennia. He will not change the ancient ways of *Fae* because of the actions of one mad faerae."

Cehron smiled. "Madness, Niamh, is what results from mixing worlds. Oil and water; swirling around each other, never becoming one, never–" Cehron was interrupted as Dels began to cough. His face was deathly pale as Dahlah's cloths continued to soak up his blood. "Look at these results, my dear," Cehron continued. "How fast he fades. All because of a weapon that has no place in his land. Oil and water."

Sivino stood quickly, and moved to the faerae. He didn't look at Cehron as he stood before Niamh. He wiped tears from his eyes, his face resolute. "Is there nothing you can do, Niamh?"

The faerae held his eyes for several moments before she spoke. "If I could have prevented any of this, I would have." She tried to stand, but failed. "Sivino, I know it pains you to hear me say that all things unfold as they are meant to, but it has always been so. Your father does not deserve this, truly. I am fading, Sivino. I wish there was more I could do."

Sivino looked from her to Lomin, who stood and pulled the boy to him with a strong arm. He held Sivino for a moment, before moving toward Dels and the others, fully aware that there was nothing he could do to reverse what had been done. As Sivino turned to follow him,

Cehron spoke quietly to the boy. "What about him?"

The Cernunnos inclined his head toward the Shepherd. Sivino, who had been doing everything in his power to avoid looking at the injured man, turned and looked down at him. His clothing was soaked in blood, and the man made no effort to stay the bleeding. He looked at the sky; strings of long, wet hair lay over his face like the slashes of a knife. He was as white as Dels, but showed none of the resolve the other man showed in fighting to stay alive.

"Have you forgotten the prophecy, boy? The blood of the Shepherd, on your blade. Does it not say the madness will end?" He studied a large yellow flake he'd picked from the boat, before dropping it and turning his gaze to Sivino.

Sivino turned to Niamh, who struggled to keep her eyes open. He waited for her to tell him what he should do, but no guidance was forthcoming. When he was finally instructed on how to proceed, it came from an unlikely source.

"Do it."

Sivino turned around, and looked at the man on the ground. Blood soaked the dirt. *My blood,* thought Sivino.

"Do it," the Shepherd repeated. He tried to maintain his stoic composure, but his breathing was rapid and shallow. "But... I need you to know... I was misled." Cehron scoffed quietly as he looked to the slow-moving waters of the lake. The Shepherd continued. "Told she was stolen from me. Told... they took her. I see the truth now. She did what she had to do." Sivino moved nearer the man. He could see that he was shivering. "Misled," he repeated. "But if I can... right any wrongs, I'll do so now. There have been wrongs, though I remember them little. Memory is mist. Blurry. Insubstantial." He turned his head then, and looked at his son. "She is dead? Truly?"

Sivino nodded.

"Then please, end this life, Sivino." He nodded at the sword in the boy's hand. "Perhaps..." He tried to smile, and in the gesture, Sivino saw a glimpse of the man that Rhenna must have fell in love with many years ago. "Perhaps all might be right once more. Perhaps I... might yet see her again..."

Sivino's hands shook. He looked around, looked for someone, anyone, to tell him what he should do. Niamh had withdrawn into herself, struggling with an internal battle that none present could fathom. Dels – his rock, the man to whom he'd turned for every major decision in his life – lay silent, his life slowly bleeding away.

None could tell him what to do. His legs felt weak, the world spinning. Could killing the Shepherd reverse what had been done to his father. He shook his head. *Father.* The concept of the word was forever altered. *Kill one father to save another?* The Shepherd – *Daniel* – should mean nothing to him. If anything, he deserved Sivino's loathing for the part he'd played in assisting with the Nylacci. *But that was the* Shepherd, *wasn't it? Not Daniel.* Sivino took a deep breath, trying to steel himself. He felt light-headed, and was about to sit down when he felt strong hands grab him by the shoulders and turn him around.

Leath's grip was rock solid. He shouldn't have been surprised. It had always been so – Sivino feeling weak, needing assistance while Leath, powerful and sure, took charge.

"I can't do it," Sivino muttered. He looked to the ground.

For several moments, Leath didn't speak. He watched

the boy; seemed to consider what to say. Finally, he put a hand on the younger boy's face, and lifted it to his own.

"Do you know what you are?" he asked quietly.

Sivino considered the question. *Spineless? Inept?* A plethora of answers came to mind; names that had been hurled at him through years of torment and inadequacy. *Weak? Useless?* Sivino shook his head, and began to lower his eyes again.

"I don't kn–"

Leath grabbed him by the chin, and lifted his face once more. "You're my *brother*, Sivino. *That's* what you are. All of this–" He swept his hands across the group, his eyes never leaving Sivino. "All of this means nothing. You are a *Spallic*. As am I. As is Father. Nothing changes."

Behind them, Cehron laughed. It was not malicious or mocking. It was, to Sivino's ear, full of incredulity, as though Cehron could not believe Leath's words, or the naivety from which they were voiced.

"Nothing changes?" The faerae smiled, folding his arms and shaking his head. "Oh, dear brother, if you only knew how *much* things change."

Leath bristled at the familial word Cehron used to address him, but said nothing as Cehron continued. "Consider how your life has changed in just a few days, boy. Gone are the sleepy days of your little hamlet. ...Well, gone is your *hamlet* for that matter, no?" A smirk, as he gave a quick incline of his head to indicate Daniel. "Consider how his life has changed in recent times." The faerae moved closer to the Egimian boys. "*All* must change. It's inevitable."

Sivino jerked away from Leath, and moved quickly toward Cehron Cen Kohr. Though the boy moved with purpose, the Cernunnos showed no sign of fear. Narrowed eyes and a tilt of his head indicated that he was intrigued by the boy's actions. Sivino stopped mere inches from the faerae, his mouth opening and a finger coming up to Cehron's face, but a voice to the side cut him off before he could speak.

"All must change," said Daniel. Sweat continued to run down his pale face, his breathing increasingly difficult. "Yes, all must change." He panted, struggling to continue. "But many things, Cehron, change *back*..." He smiled at the faerae. "Many things, given time, come full circle."

Cehron smirked. "My dear Shep—"

"Shut up." Daniel's words were quiet, gentle. "I beg you, please, just shut your mouth. For long years you've been one of the few voices I've heard. I would not waste my final breath on a conversation tainted with your dark arrogance."

Cehron opened his mouth to speak, but Daniel spoke to Sivino.

"You must do this now, boy." His head hung limp to the side, and he assessed the blood that soaked into the dirt beneath him. "I know little of prophecies, but," he gasped, and a shiver ran through his body. "But, I do know that my life is just about spent, and I'd have you see if together, we truly can end this madness." He put his head back, his heavy lids pulling him down into his final sleep. "Do this, Son. My blood must run upon your sword."

Sivino felt all eyes on him. For everything that he had seen, everything that he'd faced in these last few days, nothing had prepared him for the position in which he now stood. For his entire life he'd shied away from violence, mainly because both Leath and Drip had directed most of their aggression toward him. But also because his father – who himself had needed to be aggressive in his life as a warrior – had always told him that there was usually a better way. He turned quickly to Dels, and saw how he faded as Daniel did. Two lives, bleeding quietly into the dirt on either side of him as he stood unmoving.

Then, a quiet voice spoke to his side.

"I always thought you were incapable," said Drip. "Your entire life, I saw you as a weak shadow of the Spallics. But I was wrong." As the trenoc spoke, he stood reverently by Dels' side, watching his friend slip away. "I don't know what you'll do, Sivino, but I know now that you are capable of much." Drip crouched beside Dels, and took the man's hand in his own. Dels gasped, unable to speak, and Sivino saw that he'd have but one chance, and it must be now. He saw Cehron smile. The sword in his hand rose slightly, as if of its own will.

It happened quickly.

With three quick strides, Sivino was above the man named Daniel. The sword came up higher still, but as it did so, it seemed to grow heavier. It was as if the Faant, the creators of this mysterious sword, worked their power upon it still, pulling it toward the body of the man on the ground. Sivino instinctively resisted the force, but it was too strong and, as if pulled, he fell to his knees, the sword falling upon Daniel's already ruinous wound.

Instantly, Daniel gasped, and his hands flew to his burning abdomen. Some primal instinct must have told him to grasp the sword, to pull it from his body and relieve himself of its cold, sharp sting.

But his hands grasped nothing.

The sword, rather than impaling the dying man, lay flat upon his bloody midsection. Sivino cried out, his hands white-knuckled on the hilt. His body trembled with the strange, uncontrollable energy that coursed through him. His hands tingled, as if losing sensation. An unsettling feeling – *like a buzzing*, he'd later think – shot up through his arms, similar to the feeling of striking that odd bone at one's elbow, only significantly more intense. And then, as suddenly as he'd lost it, he realized that he had full control of the blade once more. Before him, Daniel continued to struggle for breath as he gasped and moaned from deep within his body. Sivino looked at the blade, now covered in his father's blood, and pulled it away.

He tossed the sword to his side, and as it struck the ground he watched in amazement as every speck of Daniel's blood ran from the gleaming metal. In a matter of moments, the surface of the sword was completely untarnished. He turned then to see the end of Daniel Byrne's suffering.

Indeed, it had ended. Daniel pushed himself up onto one elbow and reached down, pulling the crimson-stained shirt away from his stomach. No blood ran from the wound, which Sivino now saw had almost entirely healed.

Cehron looked from Daniel to Sivino and back again. "Most... *unexpected*," he said quietly.

Silence descended on the quay as Daniel slowly sat up, and gauging himself, cautiously stood.

"*Niamh?*" Cehron turned to her slowly. "Did you know that this would happen?"

The faerae turned her gaze slowly from Sivino and looked at Cehron. For several moments she looked at him, her face unreadable. Sivino watched them both. Niamh did not speak. The blade lay on the ground, its metal shining brilliantly on a backdrop of blood and dirt.

Did Niamh know this would happen? thought Sivino. As

he steadied himself on his feet, recovering from his misdirected attack on Daniel and his unexpected healing, he wondered if she had always–

He stopped. *Healing!*

"Father!" Sivino cried. If the sword had healed Daniel, there was no reason to think it couldn't do the same for his father! He spun, and scrambled to where he'd thrown the sword, scooping it up as he ran. *Dels did not have to die,* he told himself. *Dels* would *not die.* He was but a couple of strides from his father when he halted abruptly. His arms, which had held the sword aloft, gently lowered. His breathing slowed, and he felt a great sense of ease replace the panic he'd felt just a moment ago. He fought against the feeling. Thoughts of saving his father seemed to melt away under this sudden feeling, this euphoria that washed over his mind. *No, don't listen,* that steadfast part of his consciousness demanded. *Don't let him stop you! You're so close. Just a few more steps...*

But it was futile. Sivino dropped the sword, took a step backward, and then another until any thought of saving his father was but a formless mist. All he knew, all he wanted, was to lose himself in the voice that weaved its way through them all. He thought he heard another voice, Niamh's perhaps, rise in an effort to interject, but it was almost instantly silenced. She had not the strength to stand against this power.

There were few who could resist the song of Cehron Cen Kohr.

29

BREACH

As Orshos' northern gate splintered and fell beneath the Nylacci surge, so too did the last vestiges of hopes held by Orshos' defenders.

The monsters roared into the city, their grotesque cries now punctuated with deep, primal grunts, so excited were they for the taste of flesh. Those soldiers who'd been trying to brace the gate fell first. Some deep part of Doran – beyond the horror – felt a surge of pride as his kinsmen fought these snarling monsters with a bravery that was unsurpassed. Scores of soldiers raced to hold back the Nylacci, but the surge was relentless. *It will end here*, Doran thought. *With your back to a cliff on the edge of the sea, there can be no retreat.*

As he looked around, he saw Inlonia racing down the wooden steps to reach the street, her sword held ready. Kellert Sentero was only a step behind. Though he could not hear their voices, he knew that both were screaming for him to move back from the gate. Doran spun, shouting orders and gesturing for the soldiers on the wall to get down to street level. The Nylacci that entered the city had tasted the blood of Orshos. The fervour of the beasts was evident; wide eyes rolled with pleasure as the creatures sank their teeth into their victims, their blood-stained maws emitting sickening crunches and satisfied groans as they revelled in the suffering.

The realization that the city was breached spread through the Nylacci army and the cries of victory were sounded. So many now raced for the northern gate that they trampled their brethren to death to get to the humans within. Through the destroyed gate and the smoke, Doran caught a glimpse of the battle on the northern field. If he was not mistaken, the beasts were steadily beginning to overwhelm the Drales; the big northern race was slowly pushed back.

Goddess help us, he thought.

Within the city, the scene grew more horrific by the moment. Blood ran in the gutters. It filled the seams between the cobbled stone. It spilled from everyone, friend or foe, who fought below the gate. Doran grabbed up an abandoned bow and began to fire at the Nylacci before him. Behind the soldiers that were engaged in hand to hand combat with the nightmares, dozens of other soldiers were doing the same.

"You need to get off this street!" Kellert, now beside the king, roared at him above the din of battle. He took hold of the king's cloak, pushing him further back from the chaos.

"No!" Doran shouted back. "We need every able body! Every set of hands!"

"The realm needs its king alive!" Kellert cried.

"Enough, Kellert! There'll soon be no realm!" Doran fired another arrow. "My place is here! There's no oth–"

The arrow struck the king squarely in his left shoulder, spinning him around. His legs lost their strength and he fell hard to his knees. Everyone was screaming at once. Kellert went to his knees on one side of Doran, Inlonia on the other. Wyncor shrieked, fluttering around the queen as if imploring her to run. Staid moved behind the king to assess the injury.

"How bad?" Doran yelled to the trader, turning to see his face.

He saw Staid look at Inlonia, who leaned back to see the damage for herself.

"It can be removed," said Staid. "The arrow is unbroken. If we just–"

"Not here," the queen replied. Blood began to spread more quickly from the wound. "He needs a healer."

"Leave it in!" Doran growled. "I'll not leave this gate!"

Kellert began to protest, reaching for the king, but Doran shoved his hand away. Before any could stop him, he pushed himself to his feet. "I'm still king here," he said. He attempted to take a step, but his head grew light, and his vision quickly wavered. "I'll do… what must be done. It's what–"

Again, his legs failed him. Kellert quickly put himself beneath the king's good arm, noting how his face blanched. Staid put two steadying hands on Doran's midsection.

"You!" Inlonia called to the nearest soldier. The man ran over instantly. His hair, so blonde it was almost white, was streaked with blood, but he appeared uninjured. "Help him get the king away from here!"

As the soldier put gentle hands on the king, Kellert jerked his head to the left. "That doorway. Now!"

Doran made a feeble attempt to resist, but the injury had taken the fight out of him.

"Highness," Staid called to Inlonia. Doran watched as Staid moved toward the queen, still bent low as a precaution. "I beg you. Go with the king. See him to the inner streets where the healers wait. Take the arrows. Fire on any that get too near. Kellert and the soldier could surely use the protection, and we can't spare any more soldiers from the wall."

They looked at each other for a moment. Doran saw that it was merely an excuse to get the queen to safer ground, something Inlonia likely saw as well. She glanced over and Doran nodded to her.

"We have to go!" shouted Kellert, and started toward the doorway.

"I'll go," Inlonia shouted. "But I'm coming back. I intend to stand with my people." The wall shuddered as the Nylacci continued to pound against it, and Staid spun away from the queen. A soldier still on the walkway screamed a warning of ladders and Staid raced for the stairs.

As they moved through the stone archway, Doran could see Kellert's head twisting, obviously seeking out the safest route. He decided on a stone rampway that led up from the street and cut into the heart of Lower Orshos. Behind him, the roar of Nylacci suggested that they were advancing.

The group raced on, as fast as was possible with Doran's injury, and as they gained more height, Doran called them to a halt.

"There," he said.

He pointed to a wooden structure, a lookout of sorts. It was one of several that were built for the families of the fisherfolk of Lower Orshos. From these, the families could look out for their loved ones as they returned from the sea. *A widow's walk*, it was called. Doran grunted at the irony as he ascended – to the loud objections of his group – the half a dozen steps.

What he saw broke his heart.

Slowly, but surely as the ocean tide at sunset, the beasts of Dreg advanced. They moved into Lower Orshos, the blood of the Rentorrians wet upon their hairy maws. The defences were broken. In the fields beyond, he could see the Drales continuing to lose ground. Continuing to lose warriors.

The city would fall.

Doran whispered a silent plea for mercy – not for himself, but for his people – that death be quick when it arrived.

What arrived, however, was not what he expected.

A commotion arose amongst the Nylacci beyond the gate. Doran thought he could discern a collective growl from the beasts, as their savage cries took on a more apprehensive note. There was a shift in their ranks as their attention turned north. Those engaged with the Drales continued to fight, but the others seemed more concerned with something to the west of the big creatures of Ras.

It was then that Doran saw the rider.

Instantly his mind recalled Staid Dyrro's report, and the horseman that supposedly led the monsters. He'd shown no fear of the Nylacci, and in return, the beasts had seemed to show an uneasy deference to the rider. Doran felt his blood run cold.

"Doran!" Kellert yelled, but the king was transfixed.

Slowly, deliberately, the rider made his way to the field of battle. How long he'd been standing there, Doran couldn't know. Perhaps the slaughter was but a gruesome entertainment for the wretch, and now that he sensed it was near completion, he moved in to witness the blood-bath more closely. Behind the rider, high on the hill, the mists began to swirl. The trees wavered at their touch. On the field, the Nylacci were equally unsettled, as the mass of bodies shifted uneasily, many of them focused on the enigmatic rider.

A strange reaction, Doran thought, *if it was indeed their leader who approached.*

The rider showed no fear, even as the first section of Nylacci broke from the battle and began to advance on him. Even from a distance, Doran could discern that the Nylacci were bracing for an attack as they approached the rider! He noted that many of those battling the Drales in the field and at the gate were now moving as well.

"Now, Doran!" Kellert shouted, pulling his arm. "We have to go! The beasts are through! They're coming!"

Perhaps, Doran thought as he nodded to Kellert, *the cloaked figure was not in fact the man from the Erratics; the leader of the Nylacci.*

Perhaps he was someone else entirely.

As if to answer Doran's thought, the rider stopped his horse and pulled back his hood. A shock of dark, red hair fell around his shoulders, and he drew his sword.

30

NO TRUMPET WILL SOUND

Six hundred years, thought Obaeron, king of the Fae, *since last this weapon was drawn in battle.* And longer still, since he'd laid eyes on a creature of Dreg.

He'd been a boy when the beasts had been removed from this world. The Nylacci were a race that had evolved in a manner that the Faant themselves had not foreseen. These beasts, covering the field, revelling in the havoc they wreaked, were the very first race that the Faant saw fit to *shift*. Obaeron's own father had overseen the great shift, having been instructed by the Faant to initiate the movement, and in doing so, create a balance in several worlds that would not be attainable so long as the Nylacci were allowed to reign. It was a dark memory for all Fae. *How fitting*, Obaeron thought, *that Cehron Cen Kohr would choose the Nylacci in his attempt to force the hand of the king.*

The beasts gained momentum as they closed in on him, and still, no shadow of concern darkened his face. He wished it didn't have to be like this. He silently cursed Cehron for putting him in this position. As king, he'd been able to convince the Council that this action was necessary, but it stung nonetheless. All these centuries later, he still could not say whether shifting these creatures to Dreg had been right and justified. Never had he voiced this sentiment, for who was he to question the will of the Faant. But occasionally, sitting before a roaring fire late at night, he pondered the decision. Yes, the beasts had dominated and destroyed much of the world they'd inhabited. But given the inestimable lifespan of a world, and the worlds that lay over it in the complex juxtaposition of the multiverse, who was to say that these worlds which had borne the devastation of the Nylacci would not have eventually righted themselves; would not have found some way to even out the balance, and correct what had been destroyed.

For all things broken shall return to fullness, given enough time.

And here, on this Cahruian field that in many ways reflected the plains of his own adjacent world, he felt that it was incumbent upon him to right the wrong that one of his own had inflicted on this unsuspecting land.

He sighed, and turned his face to the mists above.

"Ar aghaidh…"

No sooner had the words of his forefathers been spoken than the mists were torn apart, and several dozen hyter sprites fell from the sky like incensed angels of death. Their shrieks obliterated the cries of the Nylacci, and everyone on the plains now looked skyward as the winged Fae dove into the fray. Ripping and dismembering as they went, they weaved through the battle, taking down as many of the hairy monsters as they could. Their lean, sinewy bodies appeared formed entirely of clenched muscle, save for the massive wings that spanned at least fifteen feet. A dozen or so hyters left the field and flew into the city. It took only moments, Obaeron saw, for the Rentorrians, Embarrians and Drales to realize that these horrific flying creatures were indeed allies. He watched as the enraged Nylacci and several of the takahtars – those insectile predators that Cehron must also have brought from Dreg – turned their attention skyward.

The shrieks of the hyter sprites then took on an eerie pitch, morphing into a howl that seemed to unsettle even the Drales. The mists that clung to the forest wall swirled and shimmered, and from its center, Obaeron watched as the creatures of Tir Na N'og burst forth.

The defenders of Orshos watched in disbelief as the Fae poured from the forest and spread across the field, racing toward and through the confused Nylacci. Some rode upon horses while others ran upon their own hoofed legs. Arrows were drawn and fired at a speed that the eye could barely perceive, swords flashed like lightning, and the elemental magic of some of the more powerful creatures threw back the Nylacci which attempted to resist the otherworldly creatures. Short stocky creatures, whose speed belied their size, headed straight toward the battle between the Nylacci and the Drales. Holding axes in both hands that were almost as long as themselves, these faeraes flew into the madness, bringing down the Nylacci and their beasts with ferocious speed and intensity. They fought intently, but no scream or cry of rage was heard as they battled the beasts of Dreg. This was a battle of necessity, and the Faer folk derived no pleasure in this taking of life. With an aim and precision as true as it was quick, almost every stroke felled a Nylac; the face of the assailants dispassionate as the earth was covered with fallen bodies.

While those wielding axes stood firm beside the Drales, their equestrian counterparts turned their focus to the overthrown gate to the city. With hyters flying in shrill circles above the city's entrance – and the soldiers within the wall fighting with renewed strength and hope – the Fae on horseback looked to tip the precarious scale. With the advantage of height, and long, gently curved swords that cut smoothly through the thick skin of the beasts, the riders soon separated the main mass of Nylacci from the besieged wall of Orshos.

Fear was now evident on the faces of the beasts. While still engaged in the fight, many could be seen looking around the field, assessing the enemy, looking for weak spots or possibly, an opportunity to escape the inevitable slaughter. White arrows now rained down from the north as the Fae continued to flow through the Mist Gate by the forest. Sporadic black arrows were fired in return, only to be sidestepped easily by the ancient race of Tir Na N'Og. All across the field, the Nylacci fell. Everywhere they turned, they found death.

Too much death, thought Obaeron.

The king of the Fae stood suddenly in the stirrups of his great steed. Towering over those who surrounded him, he turned and extended an open hand to the forest behind him. Though it appeared to the enemy that he was calling for more aid from the misty woodland, this was not his intention. Narrowing his eyes, he closed his extended hand, and with the other, sheathed his sword. A disturbance in the mist occurred, as though a breeze had issued from the trees. In moments, the breeze intensified, and the sudden wind made its way down across the plain. It grew in strength as it approached the battle, and, as if feeding on the blood of the field, it gusted with greater fury as it reached those who fought still. The mists of the forest disappeared, swept away by the wind that presently bent the trees at their tips. Stronger and stronger it grew, causing all on the field to steady themselves against its force. As the moments passed, the gusts became almost impossible to resist, and the fighting was stayed as every creature in the land bent themselves into the face of the gale. The Fae, for their part, disengaged and moved themselves back a few steps from the enemy. Overhead, the hyters revelled in the maelstrom.

Obaeron noted the separation of the opposing sides, and dropped his hand. In the sudden and eerie silence that followed the dying of the wind, he stood tall and bellowed aloud for the entire field to hear.

"Tarc ay ruarg!"

The Nylacci, steadying their feet in the absence of the wind, spun abruptly toward the king. It was not confusion or intimidation that caused them to heed Obaeron. It was the fact that the faerae had addressed them in their own tongue. Listen to me, he had ordered them. And the Nylacci had.

"Paths, like lives, are created and destroyed. Paths may be opened, though many lead to death." The king's firm voice rang over the crowd. It held no magic, no trickery. There was simply urgency and authority. *"These lands are not yours, any more than they are mine. Ancient powers far greater than I determined that you should leave this world, and I cannot reverse that decision. None shall. Yet, I would not see you wiped from this and all other worlds because of the deeds of one of my brethren. No pleasure is taken from spilling your blood. No trumpet will sound upon your defeat. Choose to remain, and your death is certain. Choose to leave, and you shall live to fight once more."* He turned, and cast a gaze on the distant for-

est. Below the branches of the trees, a mist rose from the ground, thickening steadily as he spoke. *"These people are not your enemy. The enemy is one of my own, and he will be reckoned with before the sun sets on this day. The great plan has been disturbed..."* His face was hard. *"But now, we shall set it right."* He turned, and gestured to the forest. *"Through the mists, you shall find your place. You shall find your home. Go now... or die without need."*

Across the field, growls of uncertainty rose from the Nylacci. Around them, the creatures of faerae stood ready, weapons held firm but in a manner not intended to threaten or provoke. Obaeron watched from his steed. He offered no more words, no further ultimatum. The beasts of Dreg knew their options, and Obaeron waited patiently, his face indifferent.

From the ranks closest to the Gate, a massive, severely bloodied Nylac stepped forth. He lurched toward Obaeron, as two other beasts fell in behind him. The faerae king silently considered whether there was indeed an ordered hierarchy in the mass of monsters. Nylacci parted as the blood-covered Dregian made his way to the king. When the beast at last reached the faerae, he stopped and held his gaze. Nearby faerae held their bowstrings taut, ready to release at a moment's notice, though Obaeron needed no assistance. The Nylac growled, and muttered a rough utterance to the king. Obaeron inclined his chin, considered the Nylac's words. A moment later, he spoke in the Nylac tongue. *"That will not be for me to decide."*

The Nylac grunted, and bared his teeth toward the king. Those nearest Obaeron would later debate whether the Nylac, in exposing those dark brown fangs, had actually smiled.

Most argued not.

The beast strode past the king, within arm's reach, and as though signalled, the creatures of Dreg began moving toward the forest. Fae, Drale and Humanfolk parted cautiously, never letting their guard down as the horrors filed by.

At their head, the bloody leader paused before the mist. Apprehensive, dirty fingers splayed at its sides, the beast raised its head and sniffed the air with its massive snout. As the smell of sulphur and rotting meat wafted from the mist, the Nylac turned and bared his fangs once more. Quickly, he stepped through the mist and was gone.

The others followed, lumbering through the mist into a world where they would roam once more through dark forests and ancient mountain ranges under a blackened sky.

Home.

Staid Dyrro walked among the dead.

He stepped carefully between the lifeless legs and limp arms of those who'd defended Orshos, and those who'd sought to destroy it. Around him, men and women who were able went from body to body, looking to aid fallen comrades and finish any enemy that still clung to life. The streets were strewn with bodies, and shouted orders and cries of agony rang through Lower Orshos. Healers, recognizable by their deep blue robes and white armbands, tended to the gravely wounded. Soldiers suffering lesser injuries were helped toward the makeshift infirmaries set up in buildings adjacent to the street.

Hearing cries from beyond the buildings of the main street, Staid ran down an alleyway beside a fish merchant's store. He found bodies there as well, both ally and enemy, though they were fewer. Quickly, he scanned the area and saw an Embarrian soldier lying on his side, his hand twitching in an effort to get Dyrro's attention.

The soldier was barely able to breath, let alone move. In addition to an ugly slash on his face and neck, both legs appeared to be badly broken. He opened his mouth, and spoke in a raspy voice that gurgled from his throat. *"Help."* Tears shone in his eyes. "You… must…"

"It's alright, friend," Staid whispered as he knelt by the bloody soldier. "Just breathe. The healers are near. Just breathe."

As Staid stood to sound a call for assistance, his wrist was grabbed and the soldier pulled him back to his knee. The soldier looked Staid squarely in the eye and shook his head. He then lifted a limp arm to point to the alleyway behind him, and spoke two words before he lost consciousness. "Help *her!*"

In the narrow alley, beside a dead Nylac and a dead soldier whose hair was so blonde it could have been white, the queen of Embarria lay on her back, a black arrow protruding from her blood-soaked thigh.

31

RIGHT EVERY WRONG

"The time I've lost in wooing, in watching and pursuing
The light that lies, in woman's eyes,
Has been my heart's undoing.

Though Wisdom oft has sought me, I scorn'd the lore she brought me,
My only books were woman's looks,
And folly's all they've taught me..."

The company followed, helpless. The voice of Cehron Cen Kohr created a longing in them, though what they longed for no longer reflected their desires of moments before. What they now sought was to lose themselves in the song, and indeed, they followed the path of enchanted lyric that pulled them deeper and deeper into an incomprehensible bliss.

There was a freedom, thought Sivino on some subconscious level, which was so welcomed after the agony of the day's events and the dreadful decisions he'd been forced to make. Gone were the worries that had plagued him. He saw Dels lying silently on the ground, unable to move, but there was a peace on his father's face that eclipsed the pain of his wound. Dahlah stood slowly, and moved toward Cehron. Behind her, Leath and Stellen did the same. There was a moment's hesitation in Drip, but he too soon fell under Cehron's sway.

> *"Her smile when Beauty granted, I hung with gaze enchanted,*
> *Like him the Sprite, whom maids by night*
> *Oft meet in glen that's haunted."*

Sivino saw Niamh slide to the ground beside the dory. Her hand grasped Lomin's, but despite her best effort she could not hold it, and her old friend pulled slowly away. Sivino could see the pain in her face, but could not understand what caused it. *Just listen to the song,* he thought as he looked away from her. *Let the warm notes soothe the aching that has all but crushed us these past days. Just listen to the song.* As did Torla, and beside her, the rest of his young friends. They let the melody settle upon them; let it lead them to Cehron, and the lake beside which he now stood. Daniel, who had spent years bending to the intricate will of the faerae, easily fell into step with the others. Even the gentle breeze seemed to fluctuate and swing round to enshroud them, the song a vortex that became the center of everything.

> *"Like him, too, Beauty won me, but while her eyes were on me,*
> *If once their ray was turn'd away,*
> *Oh! Winds could not outrun me."*

Idach was the first to go. As he made his way along the soft, faded planks of the quay, his eyes never left the water. The whirlpool seemed to undulate with Cehron's voice, dancing, its ebb and flow matching the pitch, its speed following the intensity with which he sang. The king of Isror moved to the edge of the planks, tilting his head as he attempted to see beyond the murky waters. On some level, he may have understood what lay beneath the surface, but his resolve meant little when pitted against the magic of Cehron Cen Kohr. Slowly, he stepped up to the edge of the quay, like a man standing on the precipice of a beautiful land.

The whirlpool had meandered slowly to the lake's edge and settled just below Idach, as if it too had been drawn in by the power of the Cernunnos. There was no hesitation on the part of the Isrorian king. His mind was not his own. There was no consideration of what he ought to do, no debating the best course of action. He closed his eyes, his smile almost greedy, and let himself fall head-long into the gaping mouth of the Path and the dark world beyond.

"And are those follies going? And is my proud heart growing
Too cold or wise, for brilliant eyes
Again to set it glowing?"

Before the splash subsided – the foamy disturbance itself was pulled into the overpowering Path, leaving the whirlpool smooth within seconds – Sivino reached the platform. The breeze from the water tossed his hair before his eyes. Behind him, the rough, solid heels of Daniel's boots clunked steadily as he too crossed the wooden planks, seeming to keep slow time with the words sung by the creature who'd misled him so terribly over the long, dark years.

Here it is, Sivino thought as he moved to the edge. *Freedom*. He smiled and stepped up onto the footing where once boats had been securely tied to the rusty cleat hitches. He looked upon the whirlpool like a man whose thirst had all but driven him insane. Tears of joy ran down his face. There was a peace in the slow-turning waters that brought an ecstasy to his heart, the hair on the nape of his neck rising as he imagined spinning along this Path, its warm waters wrapped around him like the arms of his mother when he was a boy. He let himself lean forward, his arms open, eager for the embrace.

> *"No, vain, alas! Th'endeavour, from bonds so sweet to sever;*
> *Poor Wisdom's chance, against a glance*
> *Is now as weak as ev–"*

Cehron's head was jerked to the side, his words cut off as a thin hand clapped over the faerae's mouth and pulled. On the quay, Sivino continued to fall, his momentum carrying him toward the water. In the moment he began to fall, Sivino came to himself and was keenly aware of two things; the water that rushed up toward him, and the hand that, in that instant, grabbed him by the wrist and yanked him backward. He crashed with Daniel onto the boardwalk.

Dazed, he twisted around in an effort to understand what was happening. His world spun. Cehron Cen Kohr stood a dozen paces from him with Tonnis wrapped tightly around his back. *Of course*, thought Sivino. *The blasted song would have no effect on Tonnis Fernika*. The two struggled as the others watched in horror and confusion. Cehron pulled at the boy's arms, which were locked around the faerae's head. Though the boy was scarcely a footlength shorter than the faerae, he clung to Cehron's back like a child, his legs wrapped around the faerae's chest.

Cehron growled through the fingers that covered his mouth, his hands pulling those of the deaf boy away. As they swayed back and forth, Daniel reached over and grabbed Sivino by his collar, pulling him close.

"The sword!" he hissed. *"Your father!"*

Sivino's eyes widened, and he was instantly on his feet. He ran for the sword, casting a sidelong glance at his father, who lay silent twenty feet away. Scooping the sword up, he made for Dels, as Ston, realizing what was happening, rushed toward Cehron and Tonnis. Stellen was right behind his son as Sivino ran in the opposite direction. Behind him, Sivino soon heard the Tros men join in the struggle, seeking to give Sivino a chance to save his father as they engaged the furious Cernunnos.

Following Sivino, Leath ran to his father, Dahlah and the others close behind. Sivino slid on his knees to Dels' side, pulling the injured man's bandages away from the wound. Part of his mind registered Ston shouting, and the faerae spitting curses at the men who fought him. Another shout. The crash of a body hitting the wooden platform. Then another.

"Hold on, Father," Sivino pleaded. He laid the sword quickly on Dels' wound, his knuckles white as he gripped the hilt. He squeezed his eyes shut, willing the magic to come forth, begging it to emerge and heal the wound as it had for Daniel.

"Sivino."

He refused to look up, to break his concentration. Silently, he waited for the familiar feeling, the slight numbness that had entered his fingers when he'd brought the sword down on Daniel.

"Sivino."

It has to come, he thought. *It will come. The magic that so recently worked for one must work for the other. Such power was not something that would expire so quickly. It would just take a little longer, perhaps. It would–*

"Sivino." This time his name was whispered. He didn't know how much time had passed, how long he'd knelt beside the man who'd taught him what it was to be a person of integrity. He opened his eyes. Leath was gripping his face, gently, with both hands. To the side, Dahlah and the others cried silently, Torla's face buried in her mother's shoulder. Sivino turned slowly and looked at the face of his father.

Dels' smile graced his face still. His head was tilted gently to one side, and his unblinking eyes were fixed on his youngest son. *You have a power within you,* he'd said to Sivino one summer evening as they'd stood in a field of swaying golden wheat. *A strength that you do not yet understand.* He'd smiled, a smile not unlike the one that hung now on his lifeless face. *Never doubt that such strength is there…*

Sivino held his gaze, and reaching out, laid a hand on Dels' cheek. Slowly, he moved his fingers to Dels' eyes and gently closed them. He felt Leath's hands grip his shoulders, and he let them hold down the rage and the pain as he forced himself to breathe.

"Go… Go walk with Mother," he said quietly, his hand again on his father's cheek. He closed his eyes. "Tell h–" His voice cracked. "Tell her that her sacrifice and yours will not be in vain. I'll find a way to make things right, Father. I'll right every wrong that I'm able. I *promise*." Tears fell from his eyes; fell on the proud face of his father. "And tell her… that her strength and yours will never die."

Such power was not something that would expire so quickly.

Sivino Spallic stood, raised his sword and turned to face the faerae.

32

THE SWORD OF A BOY

Tonnis, Ston and Stellen lay at Cehron's feet; alive, but incapacitated. None dared assist them as the faerae stood over their motionless bodies, his hands joined behind his back, head raised in challenge. A small trickle of blood ran from the corner of his twisted mouth. He raised a slow hand to wipe away the blood, and in doing so, pulled his lips into a malicious smile that masked the greater part of his anger. He turned toward Daniel.

"I cannot recall, my Shepherd, a day in the last sixteen years that's been quite as interesting."

Sivino was moving then. Pulling away from Leath's grip, he made for the faerae. He'd not taken three steps when the faerae swept a hand alongside himself, like a child lobbing a heavy stone into a stream. The gesture pulled dirt from the ground in a whirling gust, and struck Sivino square in the face.

Blinded, he fell backwards. He tried to open his eyes, tried to blink away the tiny grains, but the effort was agonizing. He felt Leath's hands support him again, and felt the tears come to assuage the dirt, the pain, and grief. He could hear the shuffling of feet, the whispers of some, the whimpers of others. Through it all, he felt the responsibility. They were here, all of them, because of him; because of a prophecy that had dragged him and those he loved across the lands. This was not something that he'd wanted or sought, and he'd forced none of them to remain with him. But the guilt remained, as it always did. It would continue to do so, Sivino realized, unless he did something to bring this to an end.

He blinked away most of the grains, and exhaled his uncertainty. With Leath's hand on his arm, he got to his feet and lifted his head, determined to show the faerae his resolve. He passed a hand over his face, wiping away the tears, and the faerae slowly came into focus. At first, Sivino thought the faerae's expression the result of his blurred vision, but as his sight cleared, there was little doubt that a shadow of fear stained the face of Cehron Cen Kohr.

"My… *king*," the faerae muttered, and the fear was replaced with a look of malice. The look was not directed at Sivino, but behind him. He turned, as did the others, to follow Cehron's gaze.

Sitting astride his horse in the open gateway of the great city wall, Obaeron, king of the Fae, surveyed the group before him.

"My dear, *old* king," Cehron continued. "I guess what they say is true; no sooner does one king depart than another rises to take his place." The faerae king dismounted, seeming to dismiss Cehron as he did so, though the Cernunnos continued to address him. "You missed poor Idach by mere moments. He's on his own path to glory as we speak."

Obaeron still did not respond. He walked to his daughter and knelt by her side as Lomin stepped back with a slight bow. The faerae placed a hand on Niamh's cheek, and her eyes opened a fraction. Her smile was weak, but present. She attempted to reach up to her father, but he took her hand in his own and lowered it again. He leaned in close, sharing words that Sivino could not hear. Lomin moved back further to give the pair privacy. Cehron waited until they had finished speaking and Obaeron had stood once more before he continued.

"Bear witness, Obaeron." His dark tone mocked the king. "See how the shifting has wilted your precious flower."

Obaeron's jaw was set, his face stoic. For a moment, Sivino could see a fury boiling beneath the composure; a heavy, roiling water that threatened to break the levee at any moment. But as quickly as the look had risen in Obaeron's eyes, it receded. Replacing it, an equally heavy disappointment, which slowly pulled his eyes shut.

"I have failed," Obaeron said quietly.

Cehron's mouth opened to speak, but closed just as quickly. His left eye narrowed a little. *He didn't expect that*, thought Sivino.

"Noble of you to admit so, my king. I would think–"

"I have failed *you*, Cehron."

A silence amongst the group. Behind the faerae, Stellen and the boys were slowly beginning to move. Daniel stood by the water. The others were still gathered near Dels, Sivino standing before them.

"Failed *me*?" A chuckle. "Oh, my king, by whose standards do you measure this failure? Your own? Let me assure you, I relinquish you of all responsibility over me. That is no longer your place."

"No longer my place? Would you so readily shift *me*?

Shift the authority of Elysium? I know my place, as you once knew yours. The problem, young Cernunnos, is that you grew too concerned with the place of *others*. In doing so, you were lost. I lost you. *This* is my failure."

Cehron's chin came forward, his head tilting as if to relieve a crick in his neck. His frustration was growing, Sivino could see. With the Egimians and their companions, he could spin his words, sing his tunes, and leisurely pick his nails as he played his game. Now, facing the king of the Fae, things were different. Cehron, Sivino knew, was vexed.

"I failed you, and I failed her." Obaeron turned his head to look at Niamh. "And you are right. She has wilted. Of her own accord, but wilted nonetheless. Yet–" He turned back to Cehron. "Is wilting not preferable to *rotting* from the inside? Yes, I failed you Cehron... but you *shamed* us all."

The ground shook as Cehron swung his arms wide apart, and then brought them forward to throw a staggering gust at the fisherman's shack behind the dory upon which Niamh leaned. The shanty exploded, raining splintered wood down toward Niamh and those around her. Obaeron reacted equally fast, using his magic to push the flying boards away as one swats a relentless mosquito. Sivino cringed as debris fell in front of him. A rusty shovel, its shaft broken, skidded to his feet. Instantly, he was taken back to a recent afternoon, just days ago, when Leath had broken the blade of his shovel. He'd been infuriated by a rock that he could not dislodge from the corner of the potato garden, and was absolutely livid when the metal blade split. Sivino had kept a safe distance until his father had arrived and reminded his eldest son of his philosophy on all things broken.

Sivino and the others watched the faeraes in silence; one regal, the other renegade. Cehron's eyes were narrow as he sought a weakness to exploit. Obaeron's stance was defensive, more so for his daughter than himself. Sivino wondered when, if ever, such an encounter between two of these otherworldly creatures had occurred. He cast a quick glance toward Dels. Dahlah continued to kneel beside him, holding his hand in both her own as she watched the faeraes. She was pale, her face worn and still. She seemed as broken as the man she held, resigned to the madness, ready to collapse. Torla's hands on her shoulders attempted to steady her.

Sivino heard a grunt, and spun back as Cehron brought forth his magic once more. Elemental, he'd called it. Drawing on the life force, the energy within everything. His right hand swung sideways, and the dory, along with the surrounding remains of the shack, were thrown at the base of the city wall. Obaeron threw out a hand, stopping Niamh from being carried along. Posts snapped, and then an entire section of wall groaned as Cehron swung his left hand in the opposite direction, attempting to pull the wall down from the top. Lomin swept Niamh from the ground and rushed her away, allowing Obaeron to push back on the wall. As the king did so, Cehron's right arm swept forward again, and dirt and debris flew directly at the king. Obaeron faltered momentarily. Sivino could see that the king was caught off guard by the power and ferocity that Cehron now exhibited. The younger faerae would be considered by his kind to be in his prime, and his mad resolve only seemed to lend him further strength.

Still pushing the wall, Obaeron tried to shield himself from the onslaught. He ducked, escaping the flying shovel by mere inches. Twisting his right arm again, Cehron pushed a gust toward Lomin and Niamh. The power of the magic was such that water was pulled from the lake behind him, a fine mist pulled along with the force that struck the pair. Sivino watched as they were thrust forward, Lomin spinning as he fell, attempting to absorb most of the impact with the ground. Straining with the effort, Obaeron stepped back far enough to allow the wall to come down without being crushed beneath. As he turned to check Niamh, his eyes momentarily caught those of Sivino. The king's eyes held a fear the Egimian could not dismiss. Sivino fought against despair as the king struggled to keep his feet. *Creation! He's the king of Elysium! If he can't end this madness, who could? Surely, he could resist the power of Ceh—*

Sivino froze.

Oh, Creation.

A cold wave of realization washed over him; that all too familiar pressure constricting his chest. He watched as Cehron pushed his magic against Obaeron, the shimmering lines of elemental power visible in the air. The king pushed back, his own magic now melding with that of the Cernunnos. The distance between them closed, barely a dozen paces now separated them.

"It's over, Cehron," the king said. "The Nylacci, the takahtar, they've been driven from this land. Those not killed have been sent back to Dreg! The Isrorians at Orshos have been defeated. For the love of Elysium, stop this!"

Cehron knew that he spoke truth – that he *must* speak truth – and was enraged.

"I *shall* prove my point, Obaeron! The Nylacci are but *one* hideous race of so many that I can summon to wreak havoc." He turned to Niamh, hissing. "I'll show you your folly!"

The lakeside air spun, churning as the two pushed against each other. Dirt, leaves and mist were sucked into the magic, drawn in by the power. The magic droned in the heavy air, and Sivino was reminded of warm, unsettled winds that preceded a lightning storm.

He saw what he had to do. He stepped closer to the faeraes, each of them pushing with all their might, their eyes intent on the other. Only when he was several paces away did he catch the Cernunnos' attention.

"Back, boy!" Cehron grunted, sparing him a moment's glance. "Your part in this is over!"

Sivino shook his head, the magic wind whipping his hair away from his face. He saw it all clearly now.

"Sivino! *Back away!*" Lomin's voice cut through the growing din, but Sivino did not heed him.

"The Shepherd!" Sivino bellowed at the Cernunnos. "True and dark!"

"One more step!" Cehron shouted. His dark eyes were fixed on the Egimian, who stood with his sword drawn but still out of striking distance. "Just. One. More," he grunted. "It'll be your last." The faerae grimaced as he renewed his push against Obaeron. Sivino could see the Cernunnos' power piercing the king's defence, pushing at Obaeron's face; rigid neck muscles fighting the force; tendons wrenched in agony. The king groaned.

Sivino pulled his eyes from the king and looked at his father. *Never doubt that such strength is there.* Sivino's teeth clenched. *In the shadow of loss.*

Cut through the power.

Sword of a boy.

He spun back toward Cehron, and the Cernunnos must have seen the undeniable resolve in his eyes. No doubt remained. Sivino Spallic had decided.

"Do it, then," Cehron growled. "You've decided your fate. Do it!" He kept his attack directed at Obaeron, but inclined his head toward Sivino in invitation. "Foolish child," he spat. "Come to me!"

"No, *Shepherd*." Sivino lifted his head as well, every bit the faerae's equal. "I would have you come to *me!*" With the speed and strength of a hardened warrior, Sivino Spallic swung his blade upward, slicing through the shimmering waves of power that were joined before him. The magic severed instantly, and both Cehron and Obaeron were thrust forward in the absence of the power. The king fell to the ground heavily.

Cehron fell toward Sivino, who spun lithely and, with a determined thrust, drove his sword deep into the midsection of the Cernunnos.

33

NO BEGINNING, NO END

The air was still.

Leaves and the feathers of lake fowl floated back to the ground. The faerae and the boy faced each other, unmoving. Cehron Cen Kohr's face contorted, changing with each passing moment. Confusion. Anger. Disbelief.

Sivino pulled back, withdrawing the sword from the abdomen of the Cernunnos. Cehron Cen Kohr gasped as it was removed. He looked down at his midsection, then back at the boy. His mouth worked into an unreadable smile. It seemed to mock Sivino, a condescension that was a fixture on the faerae's lips. He exhaled gently, a slight rattle coming from deep within.

"A *boy*," he muttered.

Cehron took a cautious step, and Sivino backed up further. Yet, there was no threat in the faerae's movement. He continued to look at his wound, at his hand that struggled to stay the flow. Deep maroon covered his hand, which he raised before him. It dripped from his fingers, seeming to mesmerize him.

"A boy, spilling my blood." His voice was low. He looked from his hand to the sword, and Sivino saw his eyes narrow. Sivino followed his gaze. He held the sword limply in his hand, its tip resting on the earth. From the blade, every drop of Fae blood had run to the ground, leaving the blade clean, glinting defiantly.

The faerae coughed a laugh, though the humour dissipated immediately. He struggled for his breath, and took a few more steps. Obaeron, having gotten to his feet, moved to kneel beside Niamh, whose head rested on Lomin's lap. The king gave the Cernunnos a warning look. Cehron shook his head.

"I am no threat, old king," he whispered. His feet shuffled, but all knew he was not above deception. "I... I am however–" He coughed again, and stopped walking. "...unsettled."

"You've been unsettled for far too long, Cehron." The king spoke gently, his voice held no anger. He held his daughter's hand, though Sivino noted that he kept one hand ready for any sign of further attack. Niamh's eyes were open just enough to watch her long ago friend ease himself to the ground. He sat, favouring his side, then slowly lay near Niamh's feet, his face to the sky.

Sivino recalled the old folktales told to him by his mother on stormy nights. He recalled the heroes, the great warriors who seemed to always release their hold on life with their heads in the lap of a lover, not unlike the way Niamh now rested on Lomin.

Cehron lay on the dirt. As he turned his face toward Niamh, he sighed. His dusty hair held stray leaves that no lover would remove. Niamh closed her eyes and spoke.

"A boy," she repeated Cehron's earlier words. "A boy destined to bring madness to an end, to bring things full circle, as it were." She took a deep breath, drawing strength from her father's grip. "It would *have* to be this boy, Cehron." She opened her eyes slowly, her intense stare directed at Sivino though she continued to speak to the faerae. "You were unsettled, Cehron, and subsequently, you unsettled everything you touched. Shifting those beasts. Misleading Daniel, shepherding him through ever-darkening valleys. Your rod and staff brought no comfort. Only pain, Cehron. Only pain."

Cehron looked beyond Niamh, his eyes on the distant sky that slowly faded to purple. What he was thinking, what past events and distant times he was seeing, Sivino knew, was beyond anyone but himself.

Obaeron held Niamh's hand in both his own now and urged her to rest, but she continued on. Her weak voice cracked as she spoke.

"I know only too well the feeling of being unsettled," she whispered. "The feeling of being broken." She looked at Cehron. "You killed the man who made me whole." Sivino could hear emotion creep into her voice. "You killed him, and in doing so, you destroyed me." She paused. Breathed. "But you did not *end* him." Her eyes and Cehron's locked. "He died never knowing that I carried his child." She watched the Cernunnos' eyes fall shut. "Yes, Cehron, his *child*. A boy, strong and proud. And in his veins, Oisin's blood coursed. In his blood, Oisin lived on. And on and on, generation after generation. For countless years, I have loved and protected the descendants of myself and Oisin, through every generation. I have protected them all... right down to the boy you see before you."

A breath escaped Sivino. His grip on the sword slackened, but rather than let it fall, he grasped it all the tighter.

Myriad thoughts and questions would flood his mind, but in that moment, he latched on to the one thought that was ultimately the most important; the answer he'd sought through all of this: *Why me?*

Now, he knew.

"Can you now see why he could stand against you, Cehron? Can you now see the source of his power, the reason he threw aside all fear? In his veins flows the magic of a faerae... and the strength of a warrior." She looked at Sivino, and though her smile was slight and fleeting, her eyes shone with a mother's love. "Be proud, Sivino," she whispered, as her eyes fell shut.

Beside her, the Cernunnos lay still.

The king of the Fae traced a hand down the side of his daughter's face.

Niamh continued to rest on Lomin, who whispered words to her that none but she and the king would ever hear. A slight breeze caught the end of her white gown. It was the only movement Sivino could see. They watched silently as Lomin continued to whisper. It might have been a prayer, Sivino thought, but he couldn't be sure.

Niamh might have been able to hear the words, but again, he couldn't be sure.

Obaeron stood, but didn't turn as another faerae emerged from the trees in the distance, and made his way across the field to the dockside. When he reached those gathered, he looked at Obaeron and Niamh for long moments before he spoke, obviously uncomfortable with what he was seeing.

"My king," the faerae said.

"Tryn," Obaeron nodded.

The faerae king turned his attention to the group. No

tears welled in his eyes. He simply looked older. Sivino wondered if the Fae were capable of shedding tears. There was so much he did not know about their kind.

About *his* kind.

Obaeron turned to Sivino and the others. "I know little of what fills the forests to the north. I cannot say if your path home is clear." He looked at his daughter. "It rarely is."

Sivino heard Torla sniffle beside him.

"The greater threat has been removed," Tryn said, "but that is not to say that all danger has left this land."

"Orshos is safe," the king said. "The Nylacci have been shifted, and the process of rebuilding will soon begin." He looked at Sivino. "I understand that your queen is in the city as well." Sivino felt relief seep into him. He nodded, letting a breath out slowly. Ston clapped Kef on the back, rubbing his shoulder. "Perhaps your best option is to go there, and seek her assistance," Obaeron continued. "There are boats that remain." He glanced in Niamh's direction before he spoke. "The surest paths are found on the water."

Several moments passed in silence. Sivino didn't move, only looked toward Dels, who lay still on the ground, his head resting on Dahlah's lap. Obaeron moved toward Sivino, his voice taking on a fatherly tone as he placed a hand on the boy's shoulder.

"Let us see to him. And then, we shall all of us move on." Obaeron looked to Tryn. "Morning Glory, my friend, if you can find some." Tryn nodded respectfully, and headed to the forest.

He returned in short time, carrying a length of vine that was easily twice his length. Obaeron, who had been kneeling beside Niamh, moved back to the group as Tryn returned. The king stopped beside Sivino and Leath, and reached out to accept the vine from his friend.

"Morning Glory," he said. He held the vine up to more closely inspect it, smelling it briefly. "Bindweed, others call it. If you would allow us, we would help prepare your father for the journey." He looked at Sivino. "Though the road may be long, we have the means of seeing that he is able to return to your homeland, free of the effects of death and time until he reaches his final place of rest."

"That–" But Sivino was uncertain how to continue. What Obaeron was suggesting was entirely foreign to him. Strange, in too many ways. But if the Fae had a method of preservation that would allow Dels to find his rest in the embrace of Egimian soil, then he would accept it, no matter how strange it seemed. It was, to be sure, what his father would have wanted. "That would be very kind."

Obaeron nodded, his face serious. "Tryn, one last favour, for your king."

Again, the faerae nodded and walked away.

Obaeron moved toward Dels as all gathered watched in silence. Reluctantly, Dahlah moved and let Dels' head rest on the earth. She fussed over his cloak, buttoning it neatly with her trembling hands. She smoothed out his clothing, and ran her fingers through his thick black hair, parting it from his face. For every adjustment she made, she found another that needed her attention. It was the mother in her. But no amount of maternal attention could undo what had been done. Sivino knew well that Dels' passing was also reopening the wounds that she'd suffered when her husband and her son had been stolen from her. It was not until Sivino placed a hand on hers that she ceased.

"He is ready," he whispered.

She stopped and nodded before slowly gaining her feet.

When she'd stepped aside, Obaeron knelt beside Dels. For a couple of moments, he looked at the Egimian, though his face was as unreadable as ever. Slowly, he took Dels' hands, and joined them across his chest.

"Wait," Leath said. "Please, just a moment." Sivino watched as the young man ran to a shack that had survived the recent encounter between Cehron and Obaeron, and threw the door open. He emerged almost instantly, holding the sword that had been taken from Dels by the Isrorian soldiers upon their arrival. He walked back toward his father, holding the sword with something akin to reverence. He knelt opposite Obaeron and laid the sword upon his father, bringing one of Dels' hands to the hilt, while placing the other on the blade about halfway down the sword's length. He beckoned Sivino closer, as he ran his thumb along the edge of the blade, drawing a thin line of blood. Leath looked again at Sivino, and nodded toward the blade, suggesting he do likewise. When he'd done so, Leath reached out and traced a crimson waterdrop on the hand with which Dels gripped the hilt. He turned back to Sivino, who did the same on the hand that rested on the blade.

And with that, the Ryndarran warrior was prepared for the Land of Ever.

The boys stepped back as Obaeron noted the custom silently. Following this, he placed the vine about Dels' neck, as a mother putting a scarf on her child to prevent a chill. Having adjusted it, he let its length run along each side of Dels' body. The tiny white flowers amongst the leaves swayed in the lake breeze.

Then, the king of the Fae placed a hand on Dels' cheek,

and closed his eyes. He quietly spoke words that Sivino was unable to hear, before opening his eyes and standing. He stepped back, and folded his hands before him.

"*Go n-éirí an bóthar leat,*" he said, and the vine began to move. There were several gasps from the group, and even Daniel moved closer to see what transpired, his arms wrapped about himself as if he too had a chill he couldn't dispel.

The bindweed vine crawled along the ground and, gentle as a lover's touch, wrapped itself around Dels' body. The two ends crossed each other upon his chest, before sliding underneath his back, only to emerge and do the same about his sword. Several more times they did this, until Dels was wrapped tightly in their embrace. When the wrapping was complete, the two ends met once more, and bonded together amongst the delicate white flowers.

"No beginning. No end," Obaeron said quietly as the leaves and flowers grew thicker still along the stem.

Leath took Sivino's hand.

Behind them, Tryn approached. He did so unceremoniously, carrying a long, wooden box. There was no mistaking what the box was, and it caught the company off guard. Dahlah's hand covered her mouth as Torla wrapped an arm around her mother's waist. Daniel rubbed his forehead, turning away slowly. Sivino steeled himself, and let the faerae approach.

Tryn carried the box, which was only slightly longer than Dels, with more ease than should have been possible. Sivino noted that it was made of rough wood, obviously collected nearby. He and the others had been so caught up in Obaeron's bindweed magic that they'd failed to notice the box's construction, though Sivino was certain that no hammering had taken place as it had been put together – its binding was of a different sort. Only when Tryn got closer did Sivino realize what the box had been made from.

Old boards. Flaking yellow paint.

Tryn looked at Dels' sons and gave them what might have passed for a smile.

"I met your father," he said to Sivino. "In Ras, not long ago. And your brother." He met Leath's eye before nodding in Stellen and Dahlah's direction. "And his friends. It seemed your father was the *charismatic* sort. A man of true honour." He laid the box beside Dels. "No man, to my knowledge – and my knowledge is vast – has ever been allowed to ascend the walls of Ras, and look upon the world from its summit. But the Drales saw fit to allow this of your father. Why they did this, I do not know. Perhaps they sensed that he was a man of integrity; a leader." He stood before Sivino, almost uncomfortably close. "He led his people on a very difficult journey, and he did it well." Tryn crouched, his elbows on his knees as he touched the boards of the old dory. "I am certain that Goddess Dahnu will ensure that this final journey befits a man of his character.

"As my king says, the surest paths are found on the water."

They boarded the boats, which had lain beneath rotting fishing nets and gear, but were watertight and in relatively good condition. Or, if they hadn't been, they were once the faeraes had seen to them in their unique way. Sivino watched silently from the quay as water lapped against the solid wood. The city stood empty, but would fill once more. The citizens would return, amidst the pain and destruction. Things would never be the same, Sivino thought, but time would flow on, like the certain waters of the Andel. Losses would be grieved for years to come. But in times such as these, Sivino thought, there was but a single option.

Rebuild.

He stood by the king, who watched as the group climbed into the faded fishing dories. Lomin had relinquished his hold on Niamh and allowed the king to take his daughter into his arms. Her head rested on his strong shoulder. A wisp of hair fell in front of her face. Sivino struggled to ask the question that currently pulled at his pounding heart.

"Is she—"

"She is going home," the king replied. He brushed the hair from her face with his right hand as his left arm supported her weight. She seemed so small now to Sivino, like a child. He recalled how powerful she had appeared when she'd faced Cehron in that first encounter by the river, and even when she'd stood up to the brudogs days later. He couldn't help but think of how his own strength and ability had grown as hers had faded. Walking the same path, they'd both reached this destination as very different people. He could only hope that she was satisfied with how things had ended. He then recalled the words of the king. *No beginning. No end.*

It gave a measure of comfort, though it was small indeed.

"I'm sorry," Sivino whispered. He didn't know what else to say.

Obaeron continued to watch the boats, his sombre face framed by his red hair.

"We make our decisions," the king said. "We live with the consequences. The Fae do everything of their own free will, and trust that their actions serve the greater purpose.

Though influenced by the Faant, Niamh's choices were her own." He paused. "It is in our blood, and will always be so. My blood. Niamh's blood. Yours. There is nothing for which to be sorry. Our decisions to intervene are just that; *our* decisions."

"I've never been good with decisions," Sivino said, rubbing his sword hilt.

"Few are," Obaeron replied. "The fear of making the wrong one can be paralyzing." He watched as Sivino's fingers slid down the sword's metal.

"Be wary of magic, Sivino Spallic," Obaeron said. "It is not something to be used frivolously."

Sivino stopped, and turned his face to the king, intent on his words.

"It may be, young one, that this was the only time that you'll ever use this sword in such a way. It is not a child's playtoy, not an instrument with which to be experimented, though I assume you know this. It holds power beyond reckoning, though it cannot bring back a life that has already slipped away." Sivino swallowed hard, but continued to listen. "It will only heal those who are virtuous, and will only heal those who are entirely doomed without its aid. If one can heal without its aid, the sword will be rendered useless. In such cases, attempts to use it could even have detrimental effects. So again, consider your decisions carefully." He nodded toward the water, the boats, and Daniel Byrne standing on the quay. "I trust you'll make the right ones.

"So, go now, Sivino Spallic. There is work yet to be done." He looked to the sky, and the fading light of day.

"I would see my daughter home."

Sivino began to speak, but the faerae king was already moving away. Having said all that needed to be said, Obaeron departed. He carried Niamh to the city gate, where a soft mist had begun to form. Sivino felt the desire to call out, to run to them and touch Niamh's face; to thank her for what she'd done. Instead, he let them go. He whispered thanks to the faerae, and watched as the king and his daughter disappeared into mist and magic under the shadow of an empty city.

Sivino walked toward the boats, where all but Daniel now sat waiting for him. The first dory held Dahlah, Kef, Torla and Tonnis, with the second holding Lomin, Stellen and Ston. In the final boat, Drip and Leath sat, with the enclosed body of Dels resting between them. Sivino stopped next to Daniel, and looked at him expectantly.

"I don't..." Daniel began, but couldn't find words. "I'm..."

"Come," Sivino gestured to the boat with Lomin and the Tros men. An uncomfortable silence fell over the water.

"I'm not sure–" Daniel began, but Sivino cut him off, his voice heavy with authority, but not unkind.

"Your part in this is not over," said Sivino. He gestured once more to the boat. "Come."

For a few moments, Daniel looked back at the city and the lands beyond; lands he'd traversed as a very different man. Then, opening his cloak, he unhooked his belt and removed it from his waist. Sivino looked at the belt, and saw the leather straps on the side that must have held the weapon that had afforded him his terrible power. Daniel dropped the belt on the boards. He turned back to Sivino and nodded. Assisted by Ston, he stepped into the boat.

Sivino took a breath, and was about to step into the boat, when he heard the neighing of a horse. Turning, he saw Tryn, who stood amongst several magnificent horses that he had gathered to himself.

"Where did they–" Sivino began.

"Horses of Ras," Leath said. "They were given to us for our journey south by Daurr, the Drale leader." His voice grew sombre. "Father promised they would be returned."

Tryn nodded to Leath. He rubbed the mane of the nearest mare. "I assure you that these beasts will soon graze the forest meadows in the shadow of the stone city." Again, Sivino thought that he could discern a smile on Tryn's mouth, but like Niamh's, it was a smile that held the slightest hint of sadness.

"There are few certainties in these worlds, but there's one you can hang your hat on…" He mounted the mare, and turned north, speaking over his shoulder. "The Fae will see all promises kept."

The company watched him ride away.

Sivino moved to the final boat, trying not to focus on the box that held his father. He felt unsteady as he stepped onto the bottom boards, and might have fallen had Drip not put out a strong hand and helped the boy into the stern of the rocking dory.

"Thank you, Drip," Sivino said, forcing a smile of gratitude. For a moment, he considered how uncomfortable Drip must be with the prospect of travelling by water. Yet the trenoc said nothing. He simply sat, took an oar in his hands, and looked at the boy. Sivino was shocked to see tears in the trenoc's eyes. It was only then that Sivino considered how deeply Dels' passing would affect the trenoc who'd spent most of his life by the side of that great man.

The trenoc seemed about to say something, but hesitated, unable to find words. A moment later, he reached out and awkwardly patted Sivino's shoulder.

"*Little warrior*," he said, low enough that only Sivino heard.

34

SIMILAR NOTIONS

Kellert Sentero was the first to see them.

For days, he and the residents of Orshos had worked steadily through a period of slow convalescence, wrapping their wounds, ridding themselves of the dark disease that had worked so hard to infect the great coastal city. Across the bloody fields, numerous pyres were tended. As the Nylacci carcasses were burned, the stench served as a constant reminder of the horrors that had been experienced. The infirmaries, full for the first day, were now beginning to release those who'd sufficiently healed. Many of these recent patients left the infirmaries and proceeded directly to the wall, wanting nothing more than to be part of the greater healing process.

Kellert, deep in conversation with a couple of carpenters, noticed the group walking up the beach. Ten figures moved across the sand. He excused himself from the men, and moved in the direction of the travellers. As he got closer, he could discern nine weary people, as well as a trenoc, trudging slowly though the sand. Four of them carried a casket.

"Creation," Kellert whispered, and began to run.

Having been fed sufficiently for the first time in recent memory, Sivino and his companions sat around the long table at the center of Doran Dunarrk's chamber, awaiting the king's arrival. After a cursory introduction on the beach, Kellert had recognized the members of the group as those Ennis Tinod'atu had recently discussed. He'd quickly called for horses and carts, and had the group escorted to the Keep with orders for them to be fed and made comfortable while he went to retrieve the king.

The group sat quietly, tired from their journey and uncomfortable in the stately surroundings. Sivino watched Daniel, standing alone by the unlit fireplace. He'd not wanted to come to the Keep, preferring to stay on the beach, but Sivino had insisted. Interactions with the man had been infrequent and awkward. The group had spent little time in conversation as they crossed the lake and subsequently made their way down the wide river. They slept fitfully both nights, and during the day had focused all their energies on reaching the city as quickly as possible, stopping only to answer nature's call and forage the small amount of food they were able to find.

And through it all, they grieved.

Dahlah busied herself with clearing the food and plates that remained, but realized quickly that she had no idea where she should take them. A servant entered the room, giving her a warm smile as he took the plates, nodding his thanks.

Lomin moved about the room quietly, studying the tapestries and making quiet comments about the paintings on the wall.

Drip sat on a stone bench by one of the windows, looking out over the city. He'd not eaten with the others, had simply shook his furry head when implored by Torla to at least have a few bites of bread.

The others sat around the table, grappling with fatigue and dark thoughts that refused to give them any peace.

After an indeterminable time, Sivino heard deep voices and heavy footsteps in the stone hallway outside. Though he'd never seen Doran Dunarrk, Sivino readily identified the king as he entered the room. As he moved through the stone archway, Sivino saw the severe look on the king's face fade, to be replaced almost immediately with one of gentle compassion. His left arm was in a sling, and Sivino could see that padding – likely bandages – filled the shoulder of his cloak. Directly behind Doran Dunarrk, three men followed; Kellert, whom they'd just met, a second, unfamiliar man, and behind the stranger, Ennis Tinod'atu.

"Ennis!" Sivino and his companions ran to him immediately, embracing him like a lost family member.

The big man smiled, welcoming the affection. Ruffling the hair of Kef, he greeted each of them. "Goddess, I tried to keep hope, but it wasn't easy. And here you are, alive and well."

"We were not all so fortunate," said Drip from the window. He sat facing them, leaning forward, his hands folded in front of him. It was an uncharacteristic stance for the trenoc, Sivino thought. It was more reminiscent of the way Dels would have sat.

As an uncomfortable silence fell over the group, Doran took the opportunity to ask them to sit. He waited as they did so, and then introduced his companions, Kellert Sentero, Ennis Tinod'atu, and Staid Dyrro. Lomin did the same for his company; just names, no context, no relationships. There would be time for that later.

"What of the queen?" asked Torla.

Shadows on the faces of the men. "She lives," Doran answered. "She was injured in the battle, struck down by a Nylac arrow and her own bravery. We came upon one of the monsters, and tucked ourselves in an alley for cover. When it was obvious that we'd be found, Inlonia and another soldier sacrificed themselves to save myself and Kellert. We tried to stop them, but she wouldn't listen to reason. They led the beast in the opposite direction; a foolhardy diversion." He shook his head. "Inlonia was struck by an arrow. The other soldier, Hoak, was lost – Dahnu give him peace – saving the queen when the beast reached them. The queen's wound was grave. She will recover, though the healing process will be slow." The king's eyes moved around the table, and Sivino could see that he was quietly studying them – Dahlah, whose mind seemed a thousand leagues away; Tonnis, who watched the king's face so intently; and Daniel, severe and troubled, distant even from those with whom he'd arrived.

"The faerae?" Ennis asked. "Niamh. Did she not make the journey with you?"

Sivino looked to Lomin, waiting for him to respond, but his old friend could do no more than smile painfully and wring his hands.

"Perhaps we should start at the beginning," said Sivino. His elbows rested on the edge of the table, a hand on his forehead. "Perhaps the whole story needs to be told."

He began with the discovery of the cow, on an evening that seemed a lifetime ago. He talked of the next morning, the fishing excursion on the Andel, and the dis-

covery of Lomin and the first beast. Leath, though he'd
already filled in his companions on the journey to Orshos,
described what had happened to the village of Egim, the
subsequent exile, and the journey to Ras.

Slowly, between all gathered, the story was painfully
recounted. Sivino led the narrative, with Leath, Lomin,
and Ennis adding details that filled in the gaps. The encounters, the battles, and the prophecy that ultimately led
to the final act played out on the shore of Lake Madimest. Sivino struggled as he spoke of the revelation of his
lineage, Daniel's complicated involvement, the wound
that Dels' had suffered, how Tonnis had broken Cehron's
enchantment, and the arrival of the faerae king. At this
point, the man named Staid interrupted, his head jerking
up suddenly.

"That was *you?*" He turned to Daniel. "At the Erratics... The hooded man, on the horse. Riding with the Nylacci!" He seemed almost prepared to draw a sword, but
he restrained himself, satisfied to use the sharp edge of his
words. "What kind of man *are* you? How could you watch
that, be part of that? The horror of those monsters!?"

All eyes were on Daniel, whose dark face was unaf-
fected by the words. He looked up at Staid, his voice barely a whisper.

"I was a monster myself," he said.

Staid seemed about to say more, but the king laid a
firm hand on his arm.

"The power of Cehron Cen Kohr was great," said
Sivino. "He twisted and tormented everyone unfortunate
enough to cross his path. Even the most virtuous could
not withstand his influence."

"And your father?" asked the king, though he surmised the man's fate.

"He has journeyed a little farther than us, to a place free of pain." Sivino's lips tightened. "As has Niamh."

Doran rose and leaned his solid fists on the table, his head bowed. When he lifted his face, Sivino saw that his eyes burned.

"This war has taken a toll on each and every one of us." He moved from his place at the head of the table, and began to circle the room. He laid a hand on Sivino's shoulder as he passed him. "And the faerae king was able to defeat this Cen Kohr?"

"No," Leath said quickly. "My brother was."

With quiet pride, Leath told of how Sivino had brought down the Cernunnos. Sivino listened as Leath spoke; uncomfortable, slightly embarrassed as Leath recounted the brave act.

They discussed with some difficulty how the faeraes had helped prepare Dels for the journey, and with that final act shared, the tale came to an end.

"And so..." Sivino sat back in his chair, folding his hands in his lap as he looked at the king. "...we came here."

"We're glad you did," Doran said. He looked around the room, at each of them in turn. "I pray that your path to healing begins on this shore."

At these words, Ston reached out and grabbed Sivino's arm. "Sivino! The queen! Your *sword*. Could you not heal–" But Sivino was already shaking his head.

"I thought on this, but Obaeron explained to me the nature of the sword's power. It will not heal a wound unless death is absolutely imminent, unless the victim is entirely doomed. To use it regardless could have terrible results." He paused a moment, and glanced at Daniel. "Obaeron also told me it will not save a life unless that life is truly virtuous." He watched as Daniel looked up, his face unreadable. Beneath the table, Sivino ran a finger along the cold metal of the sword. "The queen shall live. Without my help, she shall live. As is generally the case, the healing process cannot be hurried."

He stood then, and moved from the table to stand beside the trenoc. Drip looked up at him. Sivino noted how strange it was to meet the trenoc's eyes, and find them void of the contempt which had filled them for so many years. "Sometimes," Sivino continued as he looked out the window, "the healing process is painfully slow."

"But heal we shall," said Doran. "Our lands, our peoples will flourish once more. It's what we do." He glanced at the empty vase on the ancient mantle, and closed his eyes. "We do what we must. When we find ourselves broken, we rebuild…"

By the window, Sivino sat down beside the trenoc. He leaned forward, and folded his own hands in a likewise posture. Turning to Drip, he smiled. It was a smile full of strength; a strength that he had come by honestly. He raised an arm, and put it around the shoulders of the trenoc.

"We knew a man who held similar notions," said Sivino Spallic.

Beside him, the trenoc cried silently.

35

ALL THINGS BROKEN

The late afternoon sun slowly made its way toward the horizon, and the boats that returned from Solla gleamed on the water.

As the meeting in the king's chamber ended, Doran arranged for warm baths and comfortable rooms to be made ready for his guests. Sivino asked that they be allowed to visit the queen, but Ennis told them that it would be a couple of days before Inlonia could accept visitors. *The healers take no chances,* he noted. *Especially when the patient happens to be a queen.*

"And as she heals," Doran interjected, "I'd be most grateful if you agreed to stay with us also. I know you must be eager to return to your kin, but a few days of convalescence will only aid your journey. And by that time, the Drales will be preparing to return to Ras. I'd feel much better knowing you travelled in their company."

"Sorry?" Kef leaned forward in his chair. "Did you say *Drales*? They're still here?"

"Did you not see any on your ascent to the Keep?"

Kellert asked.

The boy shook his head.

"At least half their ranks remained after the final battle," Kellert said as he moved to the window. "They wanted to help in the process of rebuilding." He paused, and looked out over the city. "It was… most unexpected. Their leader told me that seeing the creatures of faerae come to our aid suggested that perhaps we were actually worth helping. Rest assured, they'll likely not return to dance with our ladies at next year's *Sea Harvest Festival*, but it's a small improvement in relations." He smiled and turned back to the company. "It gladdens us."

"Can we go see them?" Kef asked, turning from Kellert to his mother. Then he turned to Stellen. "Are they really as big as people say?"

"Twice as big," Stellen replied. "And half as pleasant. In truth, I don't think they'll suffer the gawking of a scrawny little Egimian." He gave Kef a playful shove.

Leath smiled. "And their tolerance of fools is minimal at best."

"Then it's settled," said Ston, standing. "Myself and my comrades will go see the great giants, and the fool can stay and draw up those hot baths." He patted Leath's shoulder as he walked past. "Extra lavender in mine, if it's not too much trouble."

Sivino heard Dahlah chuckle. A soft sound, but it did him more good than anything he'd heard these past several days.

"Speaking of lavender," Lomin pulled Ston behind him as Leath made a swat at the boy. "I'd take a walk in the Royal Garden with the young ones, if your Grace doesn't mind."

"By all means." Doran's smile couldn't hide the pain

in his eyes. "I regret, it's not as fair as it once was."

"Few things are," Lomin replied. He put an arm around Sivino's shoulder as he led the young ones to the door. "But in my humble experience, I've seen the hands of time do some absolutely magical things…"

The gardens were quiet and empty.

In the distance, Sivino could hear the sound of hammers and saw as the people of Orshos rebuilt the lower streets. The sounds, like the smoke that slowly wafted from the dying fires, faded as they reached the city summit, before disappearing entirely in the pale orange sky.

Dahlah, Stellen, Leath and Tonnis had accepted the king's invitation and gone to find some rest. Drip, regaining some of his usual, cantankerous composure, muttered that he'd go find some meaningful work to do. Trenocs, he noted, are slow to tire.

Daniel excused himself quietly, and said he wished to go to the beach to spend some time thinking things through. Sivino had watched him leave the room with the weight of the worlds on his shoulders.

In the garden, the sun's brilliant rays competed with the long shadows that stretched over everything. Lomin led the group through the lawns that desperately needed cutting, though the dishevelment seemed fitting for those who now traversed the grounds.

"You've learned things recently that bear explanation," he said as he looked out over the cliffs.

They stopped in the cool shade of the trees and faced each other. Sivino turned and regarded his friend with thoughtful eyes.

"Cehron," Sivino began, "He said that Niamh and you would have kept me in darkness. What *did* you know, Lomin?"

Lomin smiled, and gestured for the group to continue walking. He sighed as he walked with his hands behind his back, his eyes upon the sky.

"It was my plan to tell you everything when we returned to Egim... *if* we returned to Egim. I feared that Cehron Cen Kohr's comments might lead you to believe that I played some sinister role in keeping you from the truth. However, that is simply not the case.

"Niamh came to me many years ago, when I was a young man. While I'll not bore you with the details of my life, I *will* tell you that I was running, unable to find purpose, unable – as Cehron said – to control the magic which resided in me. One day, I found myself outside a little hamlet called Egim, and in the nearby forests I made a temporary shelter. Was it chance that led me to the little village?" He smiled. "That's for you to decide.

"Three days later, Niamh appeared. I was deep in the forest that day, the only place I would dare experiment with my power... as you would one day discover." There were small smiles and flushed cheeks as Lomin continued. "Niamh made a proposition. She said that she could teach me to tame my wild gift, to an extent, if I would do something for her in return. I was so overwhelmed with the possibility of gaining control over my magic that I agreed instantly. What she wanted from me, she stated, was a promise. She said that a child would be born in the town of Egim. She would not tell me exactly when, and she would not tell me who. Only a rough approximation. She told me the child was of her bloodline, and she asked that I use my magical skills to help her watch over and protect the child. Her visits could not be frequent of course, though she probably shifted to Embarria more than we will ever know. She said that it was better if I didn't know who the child was, that no one knew who it was. I asked her, *If I do not know who the child is, how can I protect him… or her?* She smiled at me and said, *I guess you'll have to protect them all.*

"And so I did. I couldn't understand why she wouldn't tell me the identity of the child. She merely stated that it was better this way; there would be fewer complications, and I would find out when the time was right.

"I kept my promise, and stayed in Egim far longer than I ever intended. I travelled only on rare occasions, for my thirst for knowledge could not be sated in our little town. And so, through the years, I protected you as best I could. I tried to keep my interference hidden, and in most cases I succeeded. I accepted the fact that I'd be viewed as the contrary, meddling old man." He grunted a laugh, and plucked a weed from the rosebush beside him. "It was an easy role to play.

"I kept my promise, and I became your keeper as well. I became fairly adept at barking at the lot of you." He looked at Sivino. "At the foolish, tiny young boy who'd wander much too far up the Andel, unaware of the dangers that lurk in the dusk."

His eyes met Torla's. "At an equally foolish girl, who saw her increasing skill with a bow as an opportunity to scare the hellfire out of her friends."

"Damn right," Ston muttered.

"And those," Lomin continued, "who fail to look before they leap." His mouth turned down as Kef nodded slowly. Sivino could see the pain equally on both faces as he recalled that morning. Kef, intent on impressing the crowd gathered at the Falls. Too young to jump from that height, too small to leap past those rocks at the base, but he jumped anyway. Despite Torla's shrieks, despite Lomin roaring at him as he ran toward them in the distance, Kef had jumped. Sivino could see him, sailing through the air, falling directly toward the smooth, water-worn rocks below. But at the last moment, his body had lurched forward as if struck by a gust of wind; not enough to clear the rock entirely, but enough to save his foolish ass. And then Lomin, diving into the water, that strange stick held tight in his hand.

Kef stared at Lomin. "Lomin," he said quietly. "You... I should have been *killed*."

"Had your leg not been broken so badly, I'd have beaten you on the spot," Lomin noted. "Understand, I don't tell you these things so that I might receive credit or praise. I tell you because I need you to understand..." He looked at Sivino as he spoke. "I was in the dark also."

Lomin Lailoken smiled, the crow's feet around his eyes deep in the dying sunlight. Torla moved forward, and wrapped her arms around her old friend.

"Thank you," she whispered. "For everything. We can never repay what you've done for us."

Lomin continued to smile and shook his head. "You've grown," he said. "You've grown and you've learned, and, despite my certainty that it wouldn't be the case, you've all survived." He tilted his head, grimacing as he stretched his tired neck. Then he looked at Sivino. "I'm not certain, but this may in fact mean that I've fulfilled my promise to Niamh." He pulled his cloak tighter around him as the evening air cooled. "You nuisances are on your own now," he said, shooting a glance at Ston. "I only hope I've helped teach you to choose the right path."

"You'd actually give up your meddling ways?" Ston asked. "Won't your life become dreadfully boring?"

"That, dear boy, is precisely the plan."

Sivino smiled, but it faded quickly as he looked out over the city. The sound of tools began to fade as the day came to a close. The time had come to rest, to rejuvenate for the work that lay ahead. Upon the sea, the sun began to set.

"I have to go see him," Sivino said suddenly. They all knew of whom he spoke.

"Yes," said Lomin. "That might be a good idea."

Sivino looked back at his friends, and nodded. "I'll see you in a bit."

"You know what else would be a good idea?" Sivino heard Kef say as he walked across the lawn toward the gate of the Keep. "Hitting the lower streets to see some *Drales…*"

"Actually," Ston replied. "I was thinking we might sneak past the healers. Have a little visit with our friend Inlonia. Seeing us is bound to do her good, right? What do you say, Lomin?"

Lomin put a tired arm around the shoulder of each boy as they walked away. "I would say," he answered with a sigh, "that my days of boredom are still a distant dream."

Sivino had almost reached the gate when he felt a hand on his shoulder.

He stopped, recognizing the hand instantly, and turned around to face Torla Rallo.

She let a few moments pass before she spoke. In years past, Sivino knew, this silence would have been decidedly awkward, but in this moment, for reasons he didn't fully understand, it felt right.

When Torla finally spoke, her eyes, which had been

narrowed in thought, softened immediately.

"I... I just wanted to... thank you again. For what you did in Nahcin and... for everything."

Sivino nodded.

"It... I can't really..." She stopped, and sighed silently. "It's hard to explain," she continued, her eyes on the ocean. "Since we found Tonnis, I've felt... I've kind of felt the need to stay close to him, to help him... and give him the love he needs."

Sivino nodded again, and smiled a little harder than felt natural. "I understand."

"No, I don't think you do..." Torla said, looking back at him. "I need you to know... I..." She stopped and looked away, pushing a wisp of hair behind her ear as a tear rose in her eye. She quickly wiped it away. Sivino could see the conflicting emotions, and searched for the words to give her comfort. As he opened his mouth to speak, she moved forward suddenly and embraced him. His arms gripped her instantly, and for just a moment, the madness of his life seemed to fade into nothingness. One of her slender hands reached down then and grasped his own, as her other went to his cheek. She leaned in beside his face and whispered in his ear.

And then she was gone, disappearing around the corner of the Keep to leave him before the open gate. He looked down, struggling with the meaning of the words she'd spoken, and the small acorn she'd left in his hand.

On the cliff's edge, high above the rugged beach, a swallow sang in a Whispering Leah that swayed gently in the evening breeze.

He walks toward the man whose eyes look beyond the vast ocean.

Aside from their recent arrival on Orshos' beach, he's never walked the shores of the ocean; this is new ground for him. He removes his thin boots to feel the embrace of the warm sand. He breathes deeply of the sea air as he walks, and as he closes his eyes, he searches within himself for the strength of his father, the courage of his mother as he navigates the uncertain path before him.

He has no idea what he will say when he reaches the man upon the rocks. He only knows that there are things that need to be said; thoughts, feelings which need to be expressed.

They may find that they have very little to say to each other. Yet, they may find that what needs to be shared could never fit into one short conversation on a beach below Orshos.

As he approaches the man sitting on the rocks, who himself is more conflicted than most could ever imagine, he feels sympathy. This man's life – torn apart, ravaged by a creature he'd never understand – might never be able to be pieced back together. But if he can help in some way, and in doing so, bring some peace to his own mind, then that is what he'll do.

He recalls the words of his father, kneeling beside him in the forest many years ago as the two placed a small ash branch back in the earth.

All things broken may be made whole again.

36

POWER ENOUGH

On the docks of the broken city of Nahcin, a great wooden door swung slowly open. Its rusted hinges moaned in the near silence, which was disturbed only by the scattering of leaves that rustled across the ground in the morning breeze.

Time seemed to stand still.

The leaves moved at the will of the wind, gathering in small piles where they accumulated against the side of a warehouse, or at the base of the monstrous wooden wall.

Or beside the body of the faerae.

The wind rose, just a little, as the morning waned. By midday, its movement through the sharp spaces of Nahcin created a soft, even whistle. It would not be considered musical to the trained ear, but it might be able to dupe a fool into believing that there was a song hidden within.

The hand of Cehron Cen Kohr rose slowly, so slowly, and removed a leaf that had stuck in the hair that fell over his face.

The faerae moaned, and the old rusted hinges fell

silent. He opened his eyes long enough to see a bird of some sort – a swallow, perhaps – sitting intently on a dock post.

He moaned once more, and let his eyes fall shut.

A flash, not unlike lightning.

Then another, but rather than a quick strike, the light fades more slowly this time.

It shimmers, and within the soft light, Cehron Cen Kohr sees a figure. At a subconscious level, the faerae struggles to make out the figure. It is a man, standing in a great stone archway. The walls around him are high, like those of a palace. They appear to be white marble, laced with black veins.

The light wavers. Then, it bursts again. Though it illuminates the man more fully, it is not the face that initially catches Cehron's attention.

Light catches on the rings upon the man's hand, reflecting brilliant rays in myriad directions.

Diamond.

Another flash, and light catches on the crown upon the man's head.

A king, but not one the faerae has ever met. The man's face roils with emotion. There is a look of anger. *Anger, and something else. Resentment? Betrayal?* The faerae cannot say. But under it all, Cehron sees, there is a look of sadness, of utter disappointment.

Whatever the cause, this man is most vexed.

A final flash of light. This time, the light is focused almost entirely on the weapon the man holds in his hand. He's holding a sword, almost greedily. His knuckles are white as he grips the sword.

A sword with a black pommel.

A sword with a… carving of some kind on the grip. He struggles to make out the-

This sword. He *knows* this sword.

The sharp, stabbing pain roars to life at his side, and he screams as the light fades to nothingness.

The Faant are silent once more.

He opened his eyes some time later. By the position of the sun, hours had passed. Yet, he thought, perhaps it's been days. One can never tell.

Wisps of memory moved in and out of his consciousness then. *A man. A crown.* His face sneered as recalls the next. *The sword.* Piece by piece, the fragments of vision returned to him, illuminating the message he'd been sent.

The man was obviously royalty. He'd stood in the archway of a great marble palace. He'd-

Cehron stopped. *White and black marble.*

The man had been *Jhoran*. The *king* of Jhora - *Erol Thoccien.*

And he'd held the boy's sword.

The faerae heard something then, a soft thudding in the distance.

Footsteps.

He sighed. Deciphering this blasted message would have to wait. What now approached would require his fullest attention.

With great effort, he turned his head to face the gate that opened into the city. The sound of footsteps grew closer, and in short moments, he could discern the shapes of bodies walking through the gate and toward him.

He realized only too well how pathetic he must look at the moment, how *vulnerable* he would appear. The thought sickened him. He lay broken, dying no doubt, and completely unable to defend himself. Whatever power he'd retained after the attack, he'd poured into the wound at his side - not enough to heal it, of course, but enough to keep death at bay for just a little longer.

The figures grew larger as they closed the space between them and the faerae. He could see them clearly now. They were big - tall and muscular. They wore the furs of a variety of wildlife around their broad shoulders, some hanging as low as the knee. From a distance one could certainly mistake them for Nylacci, though they were not quite of the same height. In the place of horns were locks of thick, matted hair which hung to the shoulder and blended with the pelts, which were fastened with metal links. Unruly beards, some containing bits of food or other debris, completed the shaggy profiles.

Their mean faces looked as though they'd never had a thought that didn't include pain or punishment.

And despite this, the pale face of Cehron Cen Kohr smiled as they stopped, standing over him, casting shadows that enveloped him completely.

The Kourg.

"Your timing," the faerae rasped through his toothy grin, "could not be better…"

The faerae had met with the Kourg for the first time just over a year prior, in the months leading up to the onset of the Three Realms war. He knew that the Kourgan desire to conquer was as strong as the feelings of superiority held by the Jhorans. He'd shared with the Kourg his horrific plan for the Three Realms – a plan that would effectively see them all weakened to a shadow of their former *glory*, if it could be called such. Kroven Stonebreaker, the leader of the Kourg, had scoffed at this, but he'd been intrigued nonetheless. The strength of Isror was in fact the only thing that kept the Kourg – whose population continued to grow in size and hunger – from a full-on invasion.

Cehron had seen this hunger in Kroven's eyes, and had assured him that no small amount of blood would be spilled when he initiated the war within the Realms. Although sharing the location of the ore deposits with Idach Garron had resulted in the desired conflict, he'd needed to shift the Nylacci to reap the full devastation required. And, he conceded, he *did* like to make a rather dramatic point, given the opportunity. Now, with so many dead or incapacitated by the yearlong war, the stage had finally been set.

Although, Cehron thought, he could have done without the piercing of a sword at the hands of that wretched lad.

He breathed slowly, carefully, as the shadows loomed over him.

"Idach Garron is gone," he said in little more than a whisper. "His forces are decimated. He lost many over the last year, and the recent battle at Orshos, I'm told, finished them off. They'll... not recover any time soon." One of the Kourg moved, and sunlight fell over the Cernunnos' face. He squinted – the light and the pain of speaking causing him equal discomfort. "The other armies are weakened terribly." He coughed, then took another breath. "The time has come."

"It would appear, faerae, that *your* time has come." A voice rumbled from several paces off. Kroven Stonebreaker faced away from the faerae, looking out onto the expanse of Lake Madimest, and beyond, where its rivers wound their way to the west.

Cehron smiled. It was a smile that covered his rage,

his frustration, and most importantly, his fear. But then, he was a master of deception, and was sure that his confident face would assure all gathered that he was still in full command.

Well, all but Kroven perhaps.

The big Kourg turned from the water and moved toward the faerae. He kicked aside bits of broken board, and stopped to scrutinize discarded weapons. Already, the little scouting force of Kourg that had arrived in Nahcin had begun plundering weapons and stores of goods. Cehron could see carts loaded down near the gate, bloody swords laid upon sacks of grain. The Kourg, Cehron knew, felt that if a thing could be taken, the only sensible course of action was, of course, to take it. And that is what they did. Beautiful or broken, if it was within grasp, it belonged to them.

And what, Cehron wondered, did that mean for him.

He was indeed broken, and surely the Kourg would see that in such condition, he would be of no use to them. But if he could be restored to his former strength, or something very close to it, then yes, he would prove to be very valuable indeed.

"I should remind you, Master Stonebreaker, that it is folly to so readily discount the power of the Fae."

Stonebreaker responded immediately. "And what power, Mischief Maker, do you think remains in that leaking husk of yours?"

Mischief Maker. Cehron smiled, and in truth, it was a testament to his power that he was able to reign in his fury and convert his snarling mouth into a harmless smile before anyone around him noticed. Oh, the lice-ridden brute would rue the day that he dared to mock the Fae. But now, right now, there was no time for discord or the breaking of partnerships, however tenuous they might be. He would take the slight and put it aside for safekeeping. For the faerae knew that with all the days granted him, a day would come where the slight would be fully addressed. But first, there were more pressing matters that needed to be addressed.

Namely, the bleeding hole the boy had left in his body.

"I've power enough, my Kourgan *friend*." The word was as foul on his tongue as it appeared to be to the big man to whom he spoke. "But, to be sure, there are places where I would find my convalescence hastened, you see. This–" He gestured painfully with a weak sweep of his arm, "–is not a place of healing. It is a morgue."

The Kourg leader surveyed the area around them. Flies buzzed in the stillness of the air, and his companions swatted at them with irritation. Cehron realized that this irritation was exacerbated by the fact that the group now stood idle on a dock, speaking with a dying faerae, while a world ripe for killing awaited them. He knew their patience would soon grow short.

"I've kept my word," the Cernunnos continued. "I've unleashed a war on the land that has reduced the forces of the realms terribly. I've created a condition that will see your bloody efforts reach levels of dominion you've only dreamed of."

"Yes… you've kept your word," Kroven acknowledged. "Scouts recently found the streets of Iskall to be emptier than we'd ever seen. Some have fled into the surrounding lands. But many–" he smiled, his yellow teeth gleaming, "–many remain. They will be dealt with in a short matter of time. The preparations are being made." Several of his companions smiled and grunted in a most disconcerting manner as Kroven turned to Cehron. "They will all die."

Cehron nodded.

"We'll take what resources we can from the capital and the other towns. Ronec is a pile of ash. And Crend, that dirty mining town, is in shambles. They must have abandoned the caves and turned all the miners to soldiers, for what good it did them." He smiled again. "And we may even find some new recruits. Some may come willingly. Some may not. For those that don't, we'll find ways for them to *serve*."

Kroven Stonebreaker scratched roughly at the back of his head. "My question to you, faerae, is what purpose do you now serve?"

Cehron closed his eyes, and considered how to respond. The race of Fae inspired no awe – and indeed no respect – with the Kourg. He was to them simply an individual – one who had served a purpose but was now a weak, bloody mess.

"It's a big world, Kroven." Cehron had lowered his voice. He spoke only to the leader now, a subtle message to the others that they were not worthy of his words. "It's a very big world... one of many, in fact." He coughed. "Perhaps... you'd be content to wreak your havoc on this tiny corner of the continent, but I ask you, have you ever imagined the scope of what's really out there? Are you truly content to crack the heads of weak young soldiers in ill-fitting uniforms? What conquest is that? I've seen places, Kroven, of which you could not dream. With the help of one such as I, your dominion could spread beyond these feeble realms." He paused, fully holding the other's attention now. "With my help, friend, even the mighty *Jhorans* could be brought to their knees..."

Cehron knew well that, despite the focus on the decimated realms, the conquest of the land of Jhora remained the ultimate objective to these fur-clad barbarians. It was the ancestors of Jhora that had driven the Kourg from their rich homeland in centuries past. And it was their descendants who continued to expand the Jhoran realm, and in doing so, expropriated the lands of the Kourgan people.

Cehron could see the hunger now in Kroven's dark eyes.

"The Jhoran walls are impenetrable," Kroven rumbled quietly. "Our small victories – the few that we've had – are mere border skirmishes. We take some satisfaction in an occasional kill, but it's small satisfaction." He looked down, his eyes hard upon Cehron's face. "I am a proud Kourg. But I am not stupid. I see no way to gain access to the cities of Jhora."

Of course you wouldn't, you bloody oaf, thought Cehron. However, he kept that thought to himself. "When restored to my former strength, Kroven, there are very few places to which I cannot gain access." Cehron's eyes narrowed as he studied the leader of the Kourg. "I'm sure you know the lore. I'm sure you appreciate your heritage. Those rich lands, all lost to you. Stolen from you!" He was sure the Kourg was about to growl. "I can help you regain land, Kroven… Sealed doors have a way of opening for me, you might say.

"I find paths where none exist."

The Kourg was silent for long moments. His eyes, narrow under his thick, dark eyebrows, were set to the west. He took a deep breath, seeming to have made up his mind, and turned to the faerae.

"And your word is good?" he asked, his eyes narrow. "Do I have your word, your *promise*, that this can be achieved?"

The Cernunnos smiled.

Having convinced the Kourg of his considerable usefulness, the faerae allowed himself a silent sigh of relief. He could now see new roads, new possibilities laid before him, but to achieve these goals, he would need to take an old path.

With rough hands, two of the Kourg lifted him from the ground. The Cernunnos struggled not to cry out in pain, but his grimace brought restrained smiles to the faces of the brutes that carried him.

Cehron gritted his teeth through the pain and the humiliation of being carried in such an undignified manner. The heavy footfalls echoed on the dock boards as the faerae was carried to the edge of the quay. Cehron hoped that he had made the right choice. But then, what choices remained? It was rare, …no, unheard of, for him to find himself in such a circumstance. But just this once he would bear the shame, for his subsequent victories would be all the sweeter.

When they reached the end of the dock, the faerae slowly turned his head and looked into the water. His vision was somewhat blurry given his deteriorating state, but after a few moments, he found what he sought.

"There," he whispered, inclining his head almost imperceptibly.

In the waters below him, a small, steady vortex turned. Slowly, so slowly it moved in concentric circles. It was weak, he could tell. Weak, like himself. But still alive. Still intact.

Cehron made eye contact with Kroven, and nodded.

"Remember your word, Small One," the brute muttered in return.

One final insult to close this chapter, the Cernunnos

thought as he was hefted from the dock's edge into the waters below.

The water embraced him, and almost instantly he felt himself touched by the magic of the path. Those beautiful, intangible threads that encircled him closed into tighter circles, holding his body for just a moment before they did their work, and pulled him along the Path's length, to a place where he might just find the salvation he needed.

Upon the Path, he finally allowed the sickening smile to twist into the snarl that had been pent up for far too long.

Cehron Cen Kohr shifted.

37

BLOOD OF THE BOND

Daniel Byrne.

Sivino said the name silently in his head. Over and over.

He walked toward the man, with no real idea of what he would say. They had spent some time together on the river as they made their way from Lake Madimest to the city of Orshos, but Sivino could not really say that they'd truly *talked*. With the death of Dels, and the entire horrible ordeal that had come at the hands of Cehron Cen Kohr, the little company had made the journey in a relative state of quiet shock. Conversations were stiff, and mainly of a practical nature. The difficult work of processing what had happened, and what was to happen next, had mainly been done by each individual in their own way. Of the entire company, none had been quieter than Daniel Byrne.

The Shepherd.

Even now, the name caused a pain within Sivino, a hurting in his head and heart. For so many years, Sivino had heard Dels refer to the townsfolk as 'the flock' – not that he considered himself their shepherd, far from it. Rather, Dels had seen the town as a cohesive group, a collection of mainly gentle souls who would band together in the face of adversity, as this instinctual banding would likely be their greatest protection against predators. Indeed, this had proven to be the case as Egim had fled the terrors that chased them, and worked to bring the town to safety. Leath had spoken of their father's leadership in their conversations since the reunion. Sivino was not surprised. His father was born to lead.

His father.

He looked up again, tearing his eyes from the sand and pebbles over which he now walked. Daniel Byrne. Dels himself had confirmed that Daniel was in fact the true father of Sivino. But really, what did true mean? He'd often heard that old expression tossed about, *Blood is thicker than water*. However, in a conversation with Lomin just a couple of months ago, he'd used the adage and was met with an unexpected scoff.

"Do you know that to be *truth*, Sivino?" the older man had asked. He'd been standing in a shady area beside his hut, finishing the cleaning of a recently snared hare with a sharp boning blade. He'd stopped what he was doing, rested both hands on the cutting table, and waited for the boy to answer.

"I… guess so," Sivino had replied. "It makes sense. The ties that bind family should in fact be the strongest ties, shouldn't they?"

Lomin had started to speak, but hesitated and considered his words. He had taken a slow breath, his eyes following the path of a crow that flew overhead. When he spoke again, his voice was quiet, his eyes on the knife in his hand.

"We get a lot of things wrong, lad. *People*, I mean. *Blood is thicker than water*. I've heard that phrase repeated more times than I can count in more places than you could imagine. Let me tell you something… well, a couple of things, maybe." He'd almost smiled, but not quite.

"The actual phrase," Lomin continued, "or more rightly, the precept, is not the one you just spoke. The correct wording is, *The blood of the bond is thicker than the water of the womb.*" He'd paused. "I know this to be true, Sivino. Throughout my life, I've formed bonds with those with whom I've not shared a familial relationship, but they have proven to be the most trusted and dear friends imaginable. And–" Here he'd paused again, and seemed to be unsure how to proceed. "Well, let's just say that family cannot always be trusted to have your best interests at heart." He'd likely seen confusion in Sivino's eyes, and he'd clarified. "You're lucky, Sivino. You have a good family. An honourable one. *My* family, however…" He scoffed. "They're complicated. They're not like you Spallics. Every family has its secrets, lad… and it's hardships." He'd smiled a little, having counselled Sivino on many occasions regarding the dynamics of his relationship with Leath. However, his face had turned serious again almost as quickly. "I may actually have to take a little trip soon, to see my own siblings." Sivino's brows had lifted, for it was rare indeed for the old wolf to travel these days. "I have matters to attend to. If what I hear is accurate, my older brother is not long for this world." Sivino had begun to question him, but Lomin had waved his questions off as he walked away. "Another time, Sivi. I won't go into it too deeply now. Just remember that bonds of blood may take forms that have little to do with family relations." He wiped his blade in his tattered robe, and then spit heavily on the cuff of his sleeve. "Blood is thicker than water?" It was a question that did not require an answer. Lomin scoffed once more, as he used the wet cuff to carefully rub the blade clean.

"So is saliva, my friend."

On the beach, Sivino's step faltered a little as he recalled Lomin's words. Torn with thoughts of his own tribulations, he now realized that in all the time since his reunion with Lomin following the wolf's trip west, he had not once asked about what had transpired in the distant coastal city. Lomin's brother had been deathly ill; he'd trekked across the realm to be by his side, to be with his sisters, and Sivino had not once inquired how things had turned out. Interestingly, Lomin had not spoken of the trip either.

He inhaled, breathing in time with the ocean; the waves brushed the shore before softly receding as the cool water repeated the act over and over. He was close enough now to see Daniel's face. The man's eyes were hard; narrowed as they looked out over the ocean. *Beyond it, likely*, thought Sivino. Daniel sat a distance from the water, where the sand gave way to pebbled rocks. When he saw Sivino approaching, he gave a start and sat up a little straighter. The hardness in his eyes softened a little, and Sivino saw all too easily the pain that filled this man. Pain was something that Sivino understood. *It's the second most plentiful thing in the world*, Rhenna had once told Sivino as they'd sat on the front step of their home. He'd been nine years old, and Whisper – a young foal to whom Sivino had grown quite attached – had inexplicably gotten sick and died. Through tears, Sivino had asked her what she thought was the most plentiful thing. *Love*, she'd replied.

Sivino sat beside Daniel. Uncharted territory, he thought. He watched as boats made their way to the docks, far off to their left. He could hear someone, presumably a captain, yelling orders on the closest vessel, directing the crew as they performed their tasks. In the silence, he wished someone would tell *him* what to do, how to proceed in this situation he now found himself navigating. He began to wonder what Dels would say to him, but the thought of his father, guiding him in how to relate to the man who had actually fathered him, was more painful than he could bear at the moment. Yet, it was in fact something that Dels would have done, despite the pain. Had he survived, Sivino had no doubt that Dels Spallic would have wanted him to establish where things stood with Daniel, however they stood. On that fateful day in Nahcin, it seemed that the Shepherd had, in some way, been put aside. *How*, Sivino could not say, but there seemed to be no malice whatsoever in the husk of a man that now sat beside him.

The silence continued, pierced only by the shriek of the gulls around them. One particularly bold gull landed before them. It tilted its head, likely assessing the possibility of being tossed some morsel of food. When it realized there was none forthcoming, it flew off.

Daniel watched it go, raising his head to the sky.

"I called her Rhen," he said.

Sivino said nothing, but turned to look at Daniel who squinted in the bright sunlight, his eyes still skyward.

"It was a little joke between us. I referred to her as my *wren*... the bird, you know?" There was pain in his eyes, along with the sun. He continued, "I thought it was sweet. It was because she sang so much. Only small, but a voice that could fill a forest. She pretended to take offence, being compared to a round, plump little creature, but I know she was happy to be my little songbird. My God, how she sang."

Sivino was jarred by the reference to the deity. *God*. Not Goddess. He wanted to question the man, but wanted more to hear what else he had to say. Daniel, it seemed, hadn't noticed Sivino's reaction.

"It was constant. Whatever time of day or night. Whatever she was doing. Out picking berries. Or washing the clothes. Or cooking."

"Gardening." The word was out of Sivino's mouth so suddenly that they both started a little. Daniel turned and looked at Sivino before taking a long breath. When he spoke, his voice was lower.

"Yes… I guess you would know even better than me. My…" He seemed to struggle for words. "My time with her was shorter than yours, but…" Sivino watched, and waited. "But how I loved her. With more heart than I knew I possessed." Sivino could tell that Daniel's emotions roiled. The man's soft smile quickly turned dark. "The creature, *Cehron*, convinced me that he could help me find her. That I could get her back." He shook his head slowly. "As time passed, things grew… hazy, I guess you'd say. My memory is unclear. I wandered in places I can no longer recall. I did his bidding. It was as if I had lost my own will, lost… myself. He twisted words just enough to keep me going, and at some point, I just began to follow his commands. Blindly. Without thought. Without feeling."

There was silence then as the conversation lulled, each of them obviously processing what had been said. After several minutes had passed, Daniel spoke.

"Cehron told me, some time ago, that he'd learned she had died. Didn't tell me how. He just kind of implied it was at the hands of those who'd taken her. Did she suff–" He stopped, and gave a quick shake of his head. "I'm sorry, Sivino. I shouldn't be asking you to re-live such painful memories, especially after losing your fa–" He stopped again. Closing his eyes, he sighed. "I'm… really bad at this, lad. Sorry."

Sivino watched the sun flicker on the ocean surface. It was so vast, the sea. He'd learned a bit from Lomin, who'd seen the sea many times, but actually sitting before it was almost overwhelming. He was, of course, no stranger to the feeling of insignificance, but here, there was a *smallness* that could not be described. One almost felt inconsequential.

He looked for the right words to say to Daniel. Did such words exist? Or were there only words that were *less* wrong, *less* awkward. He still didn't know what kind of connection, if any, he wanted with this man. It would require – as his mother had often said with a wry smile – a period of great reflection.

"My father," Sivino said suddenly, "believed that we cannot know what healing will take place until we let the healing begin. All we can do is create a situation where healing is possible." He paused, and turned to Daniel. "For you, and for me, there's a long road ahead. Whether those roads are separate or intertwined, only time can tell. However, to create that circumstance, to allow even some chance of healing, I think we should tread the same road, the same path, as it were. At least for a time."

Daniel nodded. Sivino couldn't tell if it was in agreement with what he had just said, or if it was simply that, *Yes, I hear what you're saying*, sort of nod. Maybe great reflection was a habit for Daniel as well. He thought of his mother. If Rhenna had loved this man – and Sivino assumed she had, as their bond had caused him to go to such great lengths to search for her – then he would try to give the man a chance. He realized that he wanted to know the man Daniel had been before meeting Cehron Cen Kohr.

"She died happy." Sivino spoke with a sad smile, thinking back on that day. Daniel turned to look at him fully. "When the time came, she knew. She was ready, as much as you can be ready, I suppose." Sivino reached out, and for the first time since healing Daniel's wound he touched the man, laying his hand on the other's shoulder. He hoped that, like the sword, his words could help with healing as well. Daniel flinched at the contact, but recovered quickly. Sivino dismissed the awkwardness, and kept his hand where it was.

"I want you to know," he said, "that when she passed from this world, she did so surrounded by love. Surrounded by song."

Sivino could see the tears brimming in Daniel's eyes. Moments later, he felt his own tears slip down his cheek.

The healing had begun.

38

WORLDS TO SEE

Death, it is said, does not come easy to a faerae.

On the shores of a lake as black as tar, Cehron Cen Kohr knelt before the king. It vexed him, greatly, to be kneeling, but he truly did not know if he'd be able to stand unsupported. He'd crawled from the putrid waters, on hands and knees, until he could move no more. And so he stayed where he was and with some effort took slow, even breaths as he attempted to steady his mind. No waves lapped the shore behind him. In addition to an appearance similar to pitch, it had a consistency that rivalled it as well. Though not as thick, there was a foulness to the murk that caused one such as him to cringe at the touch. Its presence on his clothing was… *indecorous*.

But really, what did he currently care for appearances? He was, at present, essentially lying prostrate before royalty. Granted, what was left of the king was but a blackened torso and half of his right leg.

Decorum, Cehron knew, *was no longer a concern of Idach Garron.*

The Cernunnos grunted a low chuckle, but it quickly turned into a bout of painful, uncontrollable coughing and he swayed. Leaning forward, he extended one arm to steady himself. Even the rock on which his hand rested had a feeling of wrongness to it. He would not allow himself to fall on his face, to lie fully on this shore of sticky shale, defeated and debased. He would not show weakness to the creature that stood before him. He had to prove that there was power still within, power enough to return from this shade of his former self. Power enough to exact vengeance on those who'd brought him to his knees in the first place. He stared down at the ground, willing himself to rise. *In just a moment,* he thought. *Just one more moment, and I'll be able t–*

A deep huffing sounded just before him, and the air filled with the smell of sulphur. The faerae lifted his head, acknowledging the creature with all the respect he could muster.

The dragon stood motionless. Its hard, black eyes held those of Cehron with a gaze from which the faerae dared not turn. It was regal in its posture, its back straight and sure. The hind legs were massive, supporting a body of what appeared to be the hardest muscle under the scaly, black exterior. Its front legs, though slightly smaller, seemed tense as they gripped the ground twenty paces from the faerae.

For the better part of an hour, the two creatures had faced each other on the craggy shoreline of Dreg. The dragon had not blinked, hadn't moved a muscle until Cehron had faltered slightly and needed to support himself with his arm. The snort had almost been a question, asking the faerae if he was ready to give up this struggle and allow himself to succumb to the fate of the former king of Isror.

Between the front feet of the dragon, the weapons that Idach Garron had carried sat in a sooty pile. A claw the length of Cehron's forearm rested on the king's crown.

Such creatures, it was said, liked their jewels.

Cehron implored himself to show strength, to get to his feet and engage this creature – well, not face to face, surely, but at least standing as tall as possible. The dragon, Cehron estimated, reached a height that must have been about twenty feet, and its full length was well over twice that measure.

Using every bit of strength that he could muster, the faerae pushed himself from the ground, and on legs that wobbled so terribly that it would have appeared comical in any other circumstance, he faced the dragon.

The dragon didn't move.

The creature could have been a statue; some grotesque creation erected on the Dregian coast to forewarn those who ventured onto the land. Indeed, in the absence of the snort, an unfortunate visitor to the horrid beach could have convinced themselves that this was the case. Those glassy black eyes had yet to blink.

As Cehron wavered, the dragon continued to regard him. It could, the faerae decided, be a test of sorts. How long could the little creature attempt to prove his resolve before he fell to the ground, rolling over and begging the monster for mercy? But what the dragon didn't realize, Cehron knew, was that he had resolve in spades, and would rot in place before he begged mercy or quarter of any kind.

More time passed. Cehron attempted to keep his mind clear, focused on his breathing and the gentle swaying of his body as he attempted to shift his weight back and forth, keeping the pressure off his left side as much as possible. *Had an hour passed? Surely not two*, he thought. Time was as still as the dragon.

Cehron wondered how much time remained for him.

Despite his efforts to focus his mind, his thoughts kept returning to the whelp of a boy and his companions. He used whatever mental fortitude was available to him to keep these thoughts at bay.

Especially those of Niamh.

Had he indeed witnessed her demise? As he lay on the quay in Nahcin, in a state very close to unconsciousness, he had heard snippets of the conversations. *She is going home*, he'd heard Obaeron say. *Niamh's choices were her own*. His mind could not reconcile with the idea that Niamh was no more. For so many years, his feelings toward her had been so intense, so complicated. Even in the throes of his attempts to find vengeance, his thoughts of Niamh were as raucous as a tiny dory set upon a stormy sea. He wondered if this storm would ever settle. Perhaps owing to the great stress he was under, his thoughts uncharacteristically gave way to what could have been, to the calm seas that might have waited had it not been for the intrusion of that blasted foreigner, forging a path where he most assuredly did not belong.

Oisin.

Cehron's lip curled at the thought of the human – a momentary sneer – and for a moment, he forgot the dragon before him. The dragon missed nothing though, and it likely noted the change in Cehron's disposition, the curl of his lip.

The dragon stepped forward, a growl slowly rolling from its throat.

The movement jerked Cehron back to the present moment. His physical state precluded any preparation beyond the sudden intake of a breath, but his mind instantly dismissed everything except the hulking body that slowly moved toward him.

The dragon stood before Cehron; above him really. The creature towered over the faerae, who now noticed tiny tendrils of smoke issuing from the beast's snout. Slowly, the creature lowered its great head until it was almost level with Cehron. The faerae could now see with great detail the incisors that protruded from each side of the dragon's mouth, each of them a length to rival its claws. They stood so closely together that Cehron could see the imperfections of the teeth – scores and chips marked teeth which had likely devoured countless victims over the years. He could see how skin and scale was pulled taut over the mandible, a powerful jaw that was likely capable of snapping fully grown trees without thought. And beyond all this, the eyes. Those eyes never left Cehron. They bore into him, imploring him to cave, to fall apart before the creature's might. A deeper rumble issued from the dragon's long neck. It was, Cehron thought, the sound of hunger. He could be devoured for this little transgression. And how fitting it was. Oisin had taken everything from him. And now, years later, fleeting thoughts of the man might cost the faerae his life. How he'd despised the fellow, with his warrior gait, walking through the forest, singing that song so out of tune that the birds had–

Song. It struck Cehron suddenly that he might not be as powerless as he feared. A song, a quiet little melody might be enough to influence the plans of the dragon. But he must be quick. The beast leaned ever closer, the smell of its breath – the sulphur, rot, and remains of a king – almost choking the faerae now. He began to hum, then mixed in the first words of an old ballad that–

The blast of air knocked Cehron back, and he fell roughly on his side with a cry of pain. Two quick steps and the dragon was above him. The eyes, still unyielding, seemed to have grown harder. This was not a creature to be trifled with, Cehron thought. It would not fall victim to tricks or treachery. The time for games was done.

"You win," the faerae gasped a short breath. "You win. I... am spent." His hand rested on his wounded side. "Have at me, and... be done with it. There's nowhere I can go." He smiled ruefully, and closed his eyes. "Of all the worlds I've seen... to end things in a place such as this." His voice was little more than a whisper. "I had imagined open fields and... grazing horses perhaps. A fo–" He struggled as racking pain gripped him. "A forest, filled with roaming deer, where eagles soar majestically overhead. And a young fox bounds about my feet. That... that is where I'd go, if only I were whole once more."

He stopped speaking. Waited.

Slowly, he opened his eyes and looked at the dragon.

The eyes of the dragon were on the lake.

Searching.

The faerae almost smiled. Truly, life was nothing but a grand, unending game. And he had no intention of losing.

He turned his head, the raw grimace on his face was by no means an act. He blinked, and then looked at the dragon.

"You know of the Paths?"

The dragon didn't move. It did, however, do something that caused Cehron to experience a rush of hope; a relief so intense it momentarily eased the pain of his wound.

The dragon blinked.

"I know… who you are, friend." Cehron knew his time was getting short. There was little to waste. "You are… of the first inhabitants of the world of Dreg. The first of the Dregians. The *Dragons*."

For a moment, Cehron thought the creature would snap its teeth around the faerae for even speaking the name. But the beast held. Its gaze was still locked on the lake, and the slightest movement that could be detected on the surface.

"A Path… brought you here long, long ago. I know the lore, friend. You once ruled the skies of Annwn." He took a slow breath, cognizant of the fact that he was overextending himself. "Of Annwn, and of… all the other worlds to which you were given access… by your master, the Lord of Death." At this, the dragon turned his head.

"Yes, I know of Arawn." Cehron closed his eyes. "I know of his battle with Obaeron, king of the Fae. I know of his defeat, and how those who served him most loyally were banished to the far reaches of all worlds. Believe me, friend, I know."

Cehron reached down slowly, not wanting to arouse suspicion with a sudden movement. Carefully, he pulled open his cloak, exposing the wound he'd suffered at the hands of the boy.

"This wound," he said, "I received quite… recently, while engaged in battle with none other than Obaeron himself."

A huff of black smoke issued from the dragon.

"With… my help, I could bring you to… the world in which this battle occurred. In this world, perhaps you'd find the vengeance you seek. Perhaps you'd right the wrongs done to yourself, and to the Lord of Death as well."

The dragon was motionless, regarding Cehron. The ragged breathing of the faerae was the only sound to be heard. After what seemed to be a dark eternity, the dragon blinked. And then, as the dark skies of Dreg turned darker still, the creature moved slowly forward, lowered its head and allowed its cold, emotionless tears to fall upon the searing wound of the faerae.

Cehron Cen Kohr gasped, and closed his eyes.

Slowly, he inhaled, and as he did so his perfect lips curled into a chilling smile. Quietly, he whispered to the massive black dragon that loomed above him as he opened his eyes once more.

"There are worlds to see, my friend. Worlds in which you could hold dominion." Cehron looked to the bleak black skies, devoid of life. "Worlds in which you might find your *kin.*"

There was no reaction. The dragon stood, silent. Motionless. The faerae wasn't sure how much time passed until, finally, the dragon stepped forward.

He stepped toward the lake, and the sludgy whirlpool that spun still on the dark surface.

The faerae smiled.

"You'll not regret this decision, my friend.

"*I promise...*"

39

ALL PATHS TAKEN

Days passed.

On a warm morning that hinted of rain, Sivino ascended the streets of Orshos. Slowly, the people of the city – and of both realms – continued the work of putting their lives back together. There were, of course, some wounds that were far deeper than others, some losses that would take substantially more time to process and accept, but most had fallen into some form of routine that promised a return to normalcy. *Or*, thought Sivino, *the closest one could come to what had once been normal.*

But it was time, as Doran had said, to rebuild. To heal.

Inlonia Talchol, Sivino had learned, was determined to get back on her feet quicker than any thought possible. Not that she'd done so yet. She had a dedicated team of healers surrounding her at all times, and when they were otherwise engaged, Ennis Tinod'atu and Staid Dyrro kept a vigil by her bedside. This, of course, irritated the queen immensely. Sivino and his friends had paid a visit to Inlonia the previous evening, and had been almost amused at the frustrated annoyance of the queen. When Ennis and Staid had refused to leave the queen's chamber as she received the company, Inlonia had sighed and told the young ones that she could scarcely scratch her left breast without *these two fools jumping to ensure I don't strain myself.*

Ennis shook his head and rolled his eyes as he set to making tea. Staid, Sivino noted, tried unsuccessfully to not turn every possible shade of crimson.

There's something there, Torla would later whisper to him as they'd left the room.

Indeed, Staid seemed to have assumed responsibility for the queen since her rescue. *Rescues,* Sivino corrected himself. First, from the forests to the north of Orshos, and then from the alleyway after she'd been stuck down by the Nylac. He seemed determined to prevent a third trial of fate. But it seemed more than that. Sivino could see it as readily as Torla, and everyone else.

There's something there.

Something. He himself seemed to understand *something,* for he was unable to keep thoughts of Torla from his mind these past few days. He thought on the acorn she'd given him. He'd not asked her about it, hadn't dared to, but pondering its meaning had consumed much of his time and energy.

He recalled the conversation, how Torla had discussed the need to stay close to Tonnis, to give him the love that he needed. Truly, had any suffered as greatly as Tonnis? Sivino shook his head as he recalled his own selfishness, his jealousy. He would learn that Torla had been doing what Torla did best – she was protecting Tonnis, as she protected them all. And then, the words that Torla had whispered to him, which had let him see things much more clearly.

There is hurt there. So much hurt, Torla had said. *But there is love too. He has a heart bigger than most of those I know, Sivino. You'll come to see this as well. And there's a place in his heart for me, but not in the way you think. When he's finally able to open his heart fully to another, it won't be me he lets in.* She'd paused for a moment. *You'd have a better chance than I. As would Kef. Or Ston. Maybe Moppy Harmino perhaps?* Torla had smiled. *I will, forever, be just his friend.*

You haven't lost me.

As Sivino reached the courtyard of the Keep, he looked about the bustling activity to find his friends. Preparations were being made. Reconstruction of the city was well in hand, and plans were being implemented to assist every corner of each of the realms. Groups comprising of both armed forces and common citizens had set out for Nahcin, Ronec and other settlements that had been devastated by the Nylacci and Isrorians. On the Sinking Sea, supplies were being shipped from the city of Salkor, and fresh Ryndarran forces came to relieve those that had been engaged in the conflict and its aftermath.

A horse-drawn cart had just arrived from the lower part of the city, laden with water-filled barrels and other foodstuffs. Sivino moved quickly to help the men and women unload the water and place it on the hand-drawn carts that would disperse it though the Keep.

"Thanks, Son," one of the men grunted as he slung a barrel. "Many hands, light work, and all of that."

Sivino forced a smile. Those words; how many times had his father uttered them on their homestead. He could see Dels now, kneeling as he pulled carrots, lending encouragement to the entire family as they reaped the crop. Himself and Leath, Drip, Rhenna, perhaps even Lumb on occasion, all surrounding Dels as he praised their work. *Reap what you sow.*

He continued to help until all the barrels had been unloaded, and gratefully accepted a waterskin from the nearest man.

"'Tis warm work today, lad."

Sivino nodded, and raised the skin to splash the water over his head, onto his face. As he wiped his eyes with the heel of his hand, he found Lomin and Leath approaching him. Leath watched appraisingly, one of his eyebrows raised slightly.

"In the water again?" He gripped Sivino on the shoulder. "Should've been a merrow."

Sivino grinned, and flicked water from the skin at Leath's face.

"Come now!" Lomin said with mock authority. "These poor steeds didn't bring water up those meandering streets just to have two fools splash it back on the stones." He put his hands on his hips, and looked to the upper levels of the Keep. When he looked back at Sivino, his face was more serious.

"We've had some conversations, Sivino. With Doran and Kellert, as well as Inlonia. Stellen and Dahlah... Daurr too. The Drales are making their preparations to return to Ras, and Daurr has said that those of us from Egim are welcome to join them on the journey. The day after tomorrow..." He smiled, and Sivino thought a thousand emotions could be read in that one small smile. There was sadness on the periphery of happiness. Determination that almost masked the uncertainty. Relief, tinged with hope. He looked at the horizon. "It's time to go home, Sivi."

Sivino's felt his breath catch. *Home.* He'd known that this day would come before too long, talks would turn to when and how they'd make their way back to the northeast. The rebuilding that was happening in Orshos would happen all over Rentorria and Embarria. Board by board, brick by brick, the land would be put back to right. He stopped then, suddenly, and thought of Dels. Not entirely back to right, he conceded. But, as right as could be achieved. *As right as possible.*

Things will never be perfect, his mother had once said. *If you are unhappy with anything less than perfect, you'll always be unhappy. Set your sights on perfection, aim high, certainly, but remember to find contentment in good. Perfection is not attainable, love. But there is wonder in good.*

Sivino smiled at Lomin. It was a genuine smile. "That's good," he said.

They were going home. Dels would return to Egim. He would find his place of rest next to the love of his life. He would, Sivino knew, find contentment in this. Lying side by side under a magnificent silver birch and the flowering branches of Whispering Leah, they could be at peace. Sivino could not pretend to understand the mysteries of the Land of Ever, but he truly believed, now more than ever, that there were worlds and ways of being that were well beyond anything he could have ever imagined. Perhaps, as Obaeron had said, there was no beginning, no end. Perhaps it was like the cycle of water that Lomin had tried to explain to them long ago; icy rivers ran from the mountains, and made their way around any and every obstacle they encountered. They divided, they reunited. They were taken in by larger bodies of water, or became tributaries that attempted to forge their own paths. But ultimately, they all had the same destination.

The sea.

Here, all became one until the cycle began anew, and the waters were set free to soar across the lands until the time came once more to accept the fall, to touch the earth and be guided by its embrace.

Upon this earth, the path was never certain. Only the destination.

All paths taken eventually lead home.

The horses were ready.

Surrounded by his friends and kin, Sivino held tight to the reins and hoped that the people were equally prepared.

They had gathered on the fields to the north of Orshos, under the shadow of the forest where not so long ago, Staid and the Rentorrian soldier Von had raced to save the queen of Embarria. Von had lost his life, as had so many others, but had done so valiantly and would be remembered for his sacrifice for the queen.

Inlonia, having recovered enough to almost be able to sit up unassisted, would return to Levebule when the healers – and Ennis and Staid – saw fit. A three-masted barque sat in the harbour and would – despite the queen's aversion to travel upon the sea – carry her safely home when the time was right.

Or as right as possible, Sivino thought.

To his left, the Egimians and Tonnis – who Sivino now considered an Egimian in both spirit and residency – waited impatiently. They were ready to go. They were eager to return to the village that, while stained and battered by the rage of the Nylacci, would never cease being home.

Doran had provided a beautiful cart – more akin to a small carriage, Sivino thought – to convey the body of

Dels Spallic to his homeland. Stellen and Dahlah took up positions on either side of Dels, while Leath rode the mare that would lead their father home.

Ahead of them, the Drales prepared to lead the march. It had been thought that the small contingent of soldiers would lead the march, but Daurr had had other ideas. *Excepting the Good Mother and the Just Father, we've never followed*, he'd said. *And we shall never follow.*

So severe had been Daurr's face that Doran seemed on the cusp of a chuckle. Sivino was grateful that he did not. Doran had looked to his commander, smiled, and said that they would take up the rear of the procession.

And near the end of the procession, off to the right, there was Daniel. In the conversation that Sivino had shared with the man the previous evening, he'd reiterated his thought that they should *tread the same road*, for some time at least. Daniel had nodded. He was, Sivino had seen, as broken as any of them. He was a man without a people, a man without a home, without a purpose. Sivino did not feel that it was his responsibility to *save* this man exactly, but...

But what, he wondered. *What was it he was supposed to do?* He'd agonized over this question for days now, trying to figure out what role he was to play in Daniel's life; in his recovery. In his future.

He realized that he had no answers to the questions he continued to ask himself. But perhaps, this too was right. He remembered that old chestnut of knowledge that Lomin had shared with them so long ago, something about judging wisdom not by the answers that are given, but by the questions that are asked. Sivino knew that he was far from wise, but he did presently have more questions than the Nucono had acorns.

Maybe that counted for something.

He reached up, and gently touched his left breast pocket, touching the acorn that he kept safely within.

He looked at the trees, and then the path that would lead them through the forest. So many questions.

He sighed, and then smiled to himself.

To his side, the trenoc grunted.

"That's the smile of one who's eager to be on his way," Drip muttered. He looked away from Sivino, his hard eyes on the forest. "But I'd remind you that the forest holds dangers still. There may be a scattered Nylacci about yet. Some may wander still, lost and hungry. I'd keep my wits about me if I was you, little warrior."

Kef looked at Ston, and rolled his eyes.

Torla nudged Tonnis, pointed covertly at Drip, then the forest, then put the fingertips of both hands to her mouth and shivered with great exaggeration.

Tonnis looked at the trees, shrugged and tried unsuccessfully to smile. He pointed to Drip, then tapped his temple a couple of times. *The trenoc is smart.*

Sivino continued to smile as he considered the moniker Drip had used to address him. He looked at the trenoc, whose eyes were darting every which way, until a great shout of command came from Daurr. He did not sound the Father's Call – there was no need.

They knew they were on the right path.

Moments later, Sivino realized that the Drales would not in fact lead the procession. The foul-mouthed, cantankerous trenoc suddenly burst ahead of the entire group, leapt toward the nearest branch and disappeared into the depths of the trees.

They were going home.

High above the forests of Rentorria, the midday sun broke through a cloud with all possible brilliance as the band of travellers disappeared into the trees. Its radiance was marred for only an instant as a great soaring mass flew before it. While the obstruction was not enough to blot out the light entirely, nor enough to be noticed by those deep beneath the canopy of the forest, the shadow it cast was distinct, and indeed, foreboding.

It moved east.

HERE ENDS BOOK TWO
OF
THE EGIMAN CHRONICLES

ACKNOWLEDGEMENTS

The writing process can be a solitary journey. Hours are spent alone, during which I have nothing but my thoughts and an endless supply of blank pages to keep me company. However, I've been fortunate enough to have a wonderful group of supporters who keep me buoyed when I'm in real danger of drowning in the sea of self-doubt. In truth, I could copy and paste my acknowledgements page from Book One and include it here, as it is still a comprehensive list of those who have done so much to help me through the years. I thank each and every one of you once again, and would like to add a couple of extra thanks this time around.

Thank you to the *Readers*; not just the readers of my work, but readers in general. One of the greatest rewards of writing is knowing that you have an opportunity to share elements of yourself with others. In a world where streaming and social media scrolling are the go-to pastimes of so many, I want to thank those who take up our stories and walk through our worlds alongside our characters; their journey would be pointless without you walking beside them.

Thank you to the *Encouragers*. It's one thing to sell a few copies of a novel. It's another thing entirely to be approached by those who've read it, who eagerly share their thoughts, and press you for details on the next project. For those of you who stop me in a grocery store to share a kind word, who show up at a book signing, or post a review to help get the book noticed, know that these seemingly small actions have immeasurable impacts.

Lastly, thank you to the *Creators*. I can let you in on a secret here – we are, each and every one of us, creators. Yes, some will create prose, paintings or poignant music, but every day, we *all* have an opportunity to create something remarkable. With a thoughtful gesture, we create joy. With genuine empathy, we create connection. With an encouraging word, we create hope. Thank you to all the creators in my life who continue to shape me into the person I strive to be. I'm happy to have you by my side on this journey.

Let's see where the path takes us.

GLOSSARY

Cen Kohr, Cehron (SEN-COOR, SEAR-un): An ancient faerae (see *Cernunnos*) from the world of Elysium. Once friend to the faerae Niamh and confidant to the faerae king Obaeron. In recent years, his behaviour has grown unpredictable and dangerous.

Cernunnos (KER-NOON-ous): The Cernunnos has the appearance of a human, though he possesses the antlers of a stag. A faerae with deep connections to nature, the Cernunnos will often appear in the company of animals.

Dahnu (DAH-new): Known as the *Flowing One*. Once a faerae, she was long ago elevated to the status of Goddess by the beings known as the Faant. Having been made a deity, it was the role of Dahnu, as a Goddess, to convey the messages of the Faant to the Fae, the first race trusted to hear and act upon the wishes of the Faant in order to protect and maintain balance between and within worlds. She has been known to take the form of a swallow.

Daurr (Dow-Er): The active leader of the Drales. Though he is their leader, he will defer to the authority of the Drale elders, as is the way of the Drale culture.

Drales: An enigmatic, reclusive race that lives in Ras, a city carved into the rock of the Cudgel Mountains. Much taller than humans, they possess pale skin and sharp, muscular features. Most Drales maintain a bald head.

They practice the polytheistic religion of Antrohkism, which holds divine two deities, the *Just Father* and the *Good Mother*.

Drip: A trenoc whose predecessors formed a partnership with the Spallic family in a previous generation. He lives on the Spallic property, and is generally considered a part of the family.

Dunarrk, Doran (Done-Ark, DOOR-An): The king of Rentorria

Dunarrk, Solstia (Done-Ark, SOLE-Stee-Ah): The queen of Rentorria

Dyrro, Staid (DIE-Ro, Stayed): Once a trader throughout the realms, he becomes a spy during the war, and comes to be seen as a valuable asset – and perhaps friend – to King Doran Dunarrk.

Faant (FAH-nt): Demiurges, or Beings responsible for the creation of the universe. Of incalculable age, the Faant is thought to be comprised of three distinct yet connected entities. They created the First world of Pange, and subsequently, all worlds that were created following its destruction. Their connection to each other and to all worlds of the multiverse remains intact, in no small measure due to the Paths, the *Fingers of the Faant*, which still maintain the connection between worlds known and unknown. Serving still as caretakers of these worlds, they relay their wishes and requests in the form of *visions*; messages relayed to Gods, Goddesses and Fae who might see their wishes made manifest.

Fae (FAY): The term given to the race of faerae, the *First Ones*, also known as the *First Children*. From this race, a select few are chosen to receive the wishes and requests of the creators, known collectively as the Faant, in order to influence and regulate the balance of life upon the worlds.

The Fae live primarily in the world of Elysium (known also as Avalon, Otherworld, and Tir Na N'Og). Many of their race have an inherent command of magic that allows them to exert a natural influence upon others, though the extent of the power wielded varies amongst the race. They are known to live exceedingly long lives, seeming immortal to other races. They are unable to tell a lie, but are known to mislead and create mischief when interacting with other races, quite often through the use of their song and music which can have an enchanting effect on any who listen.

First Ones, or First Children: See *Fae.*

Garron, Idach (GAH-Run, EYE-Dak): The king of Isror. He has formed a tenuous alliance with the faerae Cehron Cen Kohr after being told that there are mineral resources in the realm of Rentorria that Isror will need in order to thrive. For this reason, Idach leads an invasion of Rentorria.

Kourg (CORG): The inhabitants of the realm of Kourghutt, located to the south of Jhora. The Kourg are seen as brutes; tall and muscular, and generally clad in fur. In years past, they unsuccessfully attempted to seize the Rentorrian capital of Orshos in the *Battle of the Cliffs.*

Lailoken, Lomin (LIE-LOW-Kihn, LOW-min): A reclusive man of sixty years, who lives on the outskirts of Egim. Sometimes referred to as the *old wolf,* he is a friend of Sivino and his peers, and plays a protective role in their lives. He has a small command of magic.

Niamh (NEEV): The daughter of Obaeron, king of the Fae. She fell in love with the mortal man, Oisin, and brought him to Elysium. Once friend of Cehron Cen Kohr.

Nylacci (NYE-Lock-EE): A race of violent creatures who,

in an age long passed, roamed the world of Cahruia. They were removed from this world, banished to the world of Dreg, by the Fae, at the behest of the Faant.

Obaeron (O-BER-on): The king of the Fae. He has ruled Elysium, and influenced other worlds, for most of his three thousand years.

Oisin (O-SHEEN): Mortal man and former warrior who falls in love with the faerae Niamh and travels with her to the land of Elysium. Son of Sabd (Mother) and Finn (Father) MacComhal. Finn is the leader of the legendary Fenian warriors.

Paths: The Fingers of the Faant (See Faant). Powerful, ethereal passages that connect worlds, and places within worlds, created by the breaking of the First world, Pange. Travel upon these Paths (most commonly formed within bodies of water, Mist Gates, and Faerae Rings) may only be initiated by the Fae, though mortal beings are sometimes conveyed by faerae creatures when necessary.

Rallo, Kef (RAH-low, KEF): A young man of fourteen years, close friend of Sivino Spallic, and brother of Torla.

Rallo, Torla (RAH-low, TORE-la): A young woman of sixteen years, close friend of Sivino, and sister of Kef.

Ryndarra (Rin-DARR-ah): A militarized organization responsible for the maintenance of peace, law and order in the realm of Embarria. In times of war, the Ryndarra comprise the greater part Embarria's force, in addition to those recruited/conscripted.

Sentero, Kellert (SEN-Tear-O, KELL-urt): Friend and closest advisor to king Doran Dunarrk. He is also the head of the Rentorrian Council.

Shepherd: The enigmatic servant of the faerae Cehron Cen Kohr. The Shepherd appears to be human, but is said to possess a destructive power that is known only to himself and Cehron. This power allows him to lead the Ny-lacci on their destructive path.

Spallic, Dels (Spah-lick, DELS): A farmer and widower from the village of Egim. A former respected member of the Ryndarra. Father of Sivino and adoptive father of Leath. Respected as a leader in his village.

Spallic, Leath (Spah-lick, LEE-th): Eighteen-year-old nephew/adopted son of Dels Spallic, and cousin/step-brother of Sivino.

Spallic, Rhenna (Spah-lick, REN-Nah): The deceased mother of Sivino and partner of Dels Spallic. Rhenna died of the illness known only as the darkness. Her shifting, while necessary, may have sped up her deterioration.

Spallic, Sivino (Spah-lick, Suh-VEE-No): A young man of sixteen years, from the small farming village of Egim.

Stonebreaker, Kroven (CROW-ven): The leader of the Kourg.

Talchol, Inlonia (TAL-kole, In-LOW-NEE-a): The queen of Embarria.

Tinod'atu, Ennis (TIN-OH-Dah-Too, ENNIS): A childhood friend of Inlonia Talchol who is now her most trusted advisor and sometime protector. He will generally be found at the side of the queen.

Trenocs (Tren-OCKs): A race originally from the eastern realm of Jhora. Forty years ago, they were driven from the land following an edict of the Jhoran king meant to cleanse the lands of the trenoc presence. Short in stature, covered in fur, and foul-tempered, they are hard workers, and loyal to those who have earned their respect.

Tros, Ston (TROWEs, STONN): A young man of fifteen years, best friend of Sivino Spallic.

Tryn (Trinn): Faithful advisor to Obaeron, he also serves as the king's confidante and messenger.

ABOUT THE AUTHOR

David James Lynch is an award-winning author who has spent the last two decades working as an educator and school counsellor.

He grew up in the small town of Bellevue Beach, and currently lives in Paradise, Newfoundland and Labrador with his wife Tara, and their children, Norah and James.

His short fiction won both the 2022 and 2021 WritersNL Nightmare Writing Contests.

He has a habit of purchasing more books than he'll ever be able to read, believing a home always has room for one more bookcase.

His first novel, *All Things Broken*, was released in 2022.